科技英文導讀
Selective Readings in
Technology and Managemenet

李開偉 編著

全華圖書股份有限公司

科技英文選讀

Selective Readings in
Technology and Management

李開偉 編著

Preface

　　科技英文導讀自 2005 年出版以來，已邁入第 17 年，撰寫這本書的目的是希望能夠提供一本內容貼近當代科技發展與國內產業特色的英語教材。由於科技與產業的快速變遷，這本書也歷經多次改版，每次改版都新增若干單元與相關內容，以期讀者在學習英文字彙、語法的同時，也能增加新興科技知識的攝取。

　　新冠疫情是目前全球正在遭遇的最主要問題，新冠病毒的流行不僅對各國的製造、物流、觀光、商旅、教育等產業產生重大影響，也影響了我們每日生活作息。特斯拉的誕生也在全球電動汽車界產生了革命性的影響。此次修訂針對許多老師與讀者的反應來調整內容外，更新增 "COVID-19" 及 "Tesla" 兩個新單元，希望讀者能夠了解新冠疫情及特斯拉有關的英語字彙與基本知識，並有能力閱讀相關英文文件。

　　此次修訂後，全書共有 26 個單元。如果課程時數有限制，教師可依學生背景來選取適當的單元來授課；對學生來說，單元的閱讀自然是多多益善。

李開偉

2022 年 6 月

Content

COVID-19 Pandemic

Questions & Discussions

1. What are the common symptoms of COVID-19?
2. Discuss the advantages and disadvantages of the two types of COVID-19 tests mentioned in the text.

Vocabulary

1. pandemic [pæn`demik]
   流行病 (n)；流行的 (adj)

2. viral [`vaiərəl]
   病毒的 (adj)

3. pneumonia [nju:`məunjə]
   肺炎 (n)

4. conjunctivitis [kən͵dʒʌŋkti`vaitis]
   結膜炎 (n)

5. diarrhea [͵daiə`riə]
   腹瀉

6. nausea [`nɔ:ʃiə]
   噁心、作嘔 (n)

COVID-19 [1]pandemic is the disease caused by a new coronavirus called SARS-CoV-2. This new virus was known to the public on 31 December 2019, following a report of a cluster of cases of '[2]viral [3]pneumonia' in Wuhan, China.

The most common symptoms of COVID-19 include fever, dry cough, and fatigue. Other symptoms that are less common and may affect some people include:

• loss of taste or smell,
• nasal congestion,
• [4]conjunctivitis (also known as red eyes)
• sore throat,
• headache,
• muscle or joint pain,
• [5]diarrhea,
• different types of skin rash,
• chills or dizziness,
• [6]nausea or vomiting.

Symptoms of severe COVID-19 disease include shortness of breath, loss of appetite, confusion, persistent pain or pressure in the chest, and high temperature. Other less common symptoms include irritability, confusion, reduced consciousness, anxiety, depression, and sleep disorders. More severe and rare [7]neurological complications include strokes, brain inflammation, delirium and nerve damage.

People of all ages who experience fever and/or cough associated with difficulty breathing or shortness of breath, chest pain or pressure, or loss of speech or movement should seek medical care immediately. Among those who develop symptoms, about 80% recover from the disease without needing hospital treatment. About 15% become seriously ill and require oxygen and 5% become critically ill and need intensive care.

Complications leading to death may include respiratory failure, [8][a]acute respiratory distress syndrome (ARDS), [9]sepsis and [10]septic shock, [11]thromboembolism, and/or [b]multi-organ failure, including injury of the heart, liver or kidneys. People aged 60 years and over, and those with underlying medical problems such as high blood pressure, heart and lung problems, diabetes, obesity or cancer, are at higher risk of developing serious illness. However, anyone can get infected with COVID-19 and become seriously ill or die. Some people who had COVID-19, whether they have needed hospitalization or not, continue to experience symptoms, including fatigue, respiratory and neurological symptoms.

Viruses constantly change through [12]mutation and sometimes these mutations result in a new [13]variant of the virus. Some variants emerge and disappear while others persist. New variants will continue to emerge. Five SARS-CoV-2 variants have been designated as variants of concern by the WHO: the

Vocabulary

7. neurological [ˌnjuərəˈlɔdʒikəl]
   神經系統的 (adj)

8. acute [əˈkjuːt]
   急性的、劇烈的 (adj)

9. sepsis [ˈsepsis]
   敗血症 (n)

10. septic [ˈseptik]
    敗血症的、能使腐敗的 (adj)

11. thromboembolism [ˌθrɔmbəuˈembəlizəm]
    血栓性栓塞 (n)

12. mutation [mjuːˈteiʃən]
    突變 (n)

13. variant [ˈvɛəriənt]
    易變的 (adj)；變種 (n)

Terminology

a. acute respiratory distress syndrome
   急性呼吸窘迫症候群

b. multi-organ failure
   多重器官衰竭

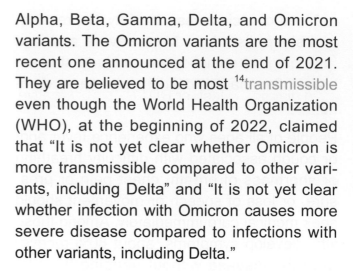

Alpha, Beta, Gamma, Delta, and Omicron variants. The Omicron variants are the most recent one announced at the end of 2021. They are believed to be most [14]transmissible even though the World Health Organization (WHO), at the beginning of 2022, claimed that "It is not yet clear whether Omicron is more transmissible compared to other variants, including Delta" and "It is not yet clear whether infection with Omicron causes more severe disease compared to infections with other variants, including Delta."

WHO is working with researchers and patient groups around the world to design and conduct studies on patients beyond the initial acute course of illness to understand the proportion of patients who have long term effects, how long they persist, and why they occur. These studies will be used to develop further guidance for patient care.

Stay safe by taking some simple [15]precautions, such as physical distancing, wearing a mask, especially when distancing cannot be maintained. Keeping rooms well ventilated, avoiding crowds and close contact, regularly cleaning your hands, and coughing into a bent elbow or tissue. Check local advice where you live and work.

In most situations, a [16]molecular test is used to detect SARS-CoV-2 and [c]confirm infection. [17][d]Polymerase chain reaction (PCR) is the most commonly used molecular test. Medical personnel may collect samples from your nose or throat with a [18]swab. Molecular tests detect virus in the sample by amplifying viral genetic material to detectable levels. For this reason, a molecular test is used to confirm an active infection, usually within a few days of

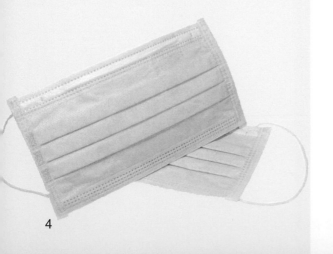

exposure and around the time that symptoms may begin.

Rapid [19]antigen test (sometimes known as a rapid diagnostic test, or RDT) is an alternative in screening people infected by COVID-19. It detects viral [20]proteins (known as antigens). In this test, samples are also collected from the nose or throat using a swab. This test is cheaper than PCR and will offer results more quickly, although they are normally less reliable. Rapid antigen tests perform best when there is more virus circulating in the community and when sampled from an individual during the time they are most infectious.

Both [21]isolation and [22]quarantine are implemented in preventing the spread of COVID-19. Quarantine is required for anyone who has contacted someone infected with the SARS-CoV-2 virus, whether the infected person has symptoms or not. Quarantine means that you remain separated from others because you have been exposed to the virus and you may be infected. Quarantine can be implemented in a designated facility or at home for a period of time (check the announcement of local government). Isolation is adopted for people with COVID-19 symptoms or who have tested positive for the virus. Being in isolation means being separated from other people, ideally in a medically facility where you can receive clinical care. If isolation in a medical facility is not possible and you are not in a high risk group of developing severe disease, isolation may also take place at home. If you are infected with or without symptoms, you should report to the local government and follow their instructions. You may need medical care if you do have symptoms.

Vocabulary

19. antigen [ˈæntɪdʒən]
抗原 (n)

20. protein [ˈprəutiːin]
蛋白質 (n)；(adj) 含蛋白質的

21. Isolation [ˌaɪsˈeʃən]
隔離、孤立 (n)

22. quarantine [ˈkwɔrənˌtin]
隔離、檢疫 (n)

5

23. immune [ɪˈmjun]
    免疫者 (n)；免疫的 (adj)
24. efficacy [ˈɛfəkəsɪ]
    效力、功效 (n)

Vaccines provide protection to people to against virus. They save millions of lives each year. Vaccines work by training and preparing the body's natural defenses, the [23]immune system, to recognize and fight against the viruses and bacteria they target. After vaccination, if the body is later exposed to those virus or germs, the body is immediately ready to destroy them, preventing illness.

There are several safe and effective vaccines that prevent people from getting seriously ill or dying from COVID-19. This is one part of managing COVID-19, in addition to the main preventive measures of staying at least 1 m away from others, covering a cough or sneeze in your elbow, frequently cleaning your hands, wearing a mask and avoiding poorly ventilated rooms or opening a window.

As of 15 November 2021, WHO has announced that the following vaccines against COVID-19 have met the necessary criteria for safety and [24]efficacy:

- AstraZeneca/Oxford
- Johnson and Johnson
- Moderna
- Pfizer/BionTech
- Sinopharm
- Sinovac
- COVAXIN

Take whatever vaccine is available to you first, even if you have already had COVID-19. It is important to get vaccinated as soon as possible once it's your turn and do not wait. Approved COVID-19 vaccines provide a high degree of protection against getting seriously ill and dying from the disease, although no vaccine is 100% protective.

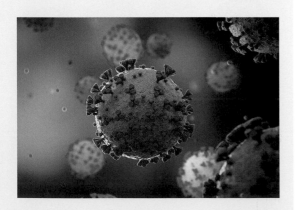

1. viral (adj) 病毒的;

   virus (n) 病毒; coronavirus (n) 冠狀病毒; virulent (adj) 劇毒的、致命的; virulence (n) 劇毒、毒性、惡意、狠毒

   (1) The viral load on this patient is too low and is undetectable.

   這個病人身上的病毒載量太低並無法偵測到。

   (2) COVID-19 is the disease caused by a new coronavirus.

   COVID-19是一種由新冠病毒引起的疾病。

   (3) Human immunodeficiency virus or HIV is an example of a virulent virus. It is the causative agent of AIDS.

   人類免疫缺陷病毒或 HIV 是劇毒病毒的一個例子,它是愛滋病的病原體。

   (4) Virulence is described as an ability of an organism to infect the host and cause a disease.

   毒性被描述為生物體感染宿主並引起疾病的能力。

2. infect (v) 傳染、感染 ⟷ disinfect (v) 消毒

   infection (n) 傳染、傳染病 ⟷ disinfection (n) 消毒

   infectious (adj) 有傳染力的   disinfectant (n)消毒劑;消毒的(adj)

   infective (adj) 感染的   anti-infective (adj) 抗感染的

   (1) Every employee entering the company must be disinfected first.

   每位進公司的員工都必須先消毒。

   (2) The flu virus infected almost the entire class.

   全班幾乎人人都染上了流行性感冒病毒。

   (3) The viral pneumonia is an infectious illness.

   病毒性肺炎是一種傳染性疾病。

   (4) Several staffs in the company suffered from a lung infection.

   公司中有多位職員肺部受到了感染。

   (5) The infection rate of the COVID-19 vaccine is less than 50% in this city.

   這個城市的COVID-19疫苗注射率低於50%。

(6) An infectious disease, also known as a transmissible disease or communicable disease, is an illness resulting from an infection.

傳染病，也稱為傳染性疾病或傳染病，是由傳染引起的疾病。

(7) Medicinal alcohol is the most commonly used disinfectant during the COVID-19 Pandemic.

藥用酒精是 COVID-19 大流行期間最常用的消毒劑。

3. short (adj) 短的、短缺的；(n) 短（文、片、物件）；
   shortage (n) 缺乏、缺口
   shortness (n) 缺乏

   (1) Face masks are again in short supply as Covid-19 cases surge.

   隨著 Covid-19 病例激增，口罩再次供不應求

   (2) It has been more than 18 months, the global semiconductor chip shortage that started last year is still plaguing various industries.

   18個多月過去了，從去年開始的全球半導體晶片短缺，此時依然像瘟疫般困擾著各個行業。

   (3) The total vaccine shortage in this country is 2.5 million doses.

   這個國家疫苗總共缺2.5萬劑。

   (4) Shortness of breath is one of the severe symptoms of COVID-19.

   呼吸急促（喘不過氣）是COVID-19的嚴重症狀之一。

4. ventilate (v) 通風
   ventilation (n) 通風
   ventilative (adj) 通風的
   ventilator (n) 風扇、抽風機、通風換氣設備、呼吸器

   (1) Cool breezes ventilated the house.

   涼風讓屋子裡通風。

   (2) Open the windows so as to have the room ventilated.

   把窗戶打開讓屋裡通風。

   (3) Ventilation is the process of replacing air to provide high indoor air quality.

   通風是換氣的過程，已提供高室內空氣品質。

(4) A ventilator is a machine that provides mechanical ventilation by moving breathable air into and out of the lungs, to deliver breaths to a patient who is physically unable to breathe, or breathing insufficiently.

呼吸機是一種通過將可呼吸的空氣移入和移出肺部來提供機械通氣的機器，以便為身體無法呼吸或呼吸不足的患者提供呼吸。

(5) The COVID-19 pandemic has led to shortages of essential goods and services including hand sanitizers, masks, beds in hospitals, and ventilators.

COVID-19 大流行導致必需品和服務短缺，包括洗手液、口罩、醫院病床和呼吸機。

5. vaccine (n) 疫苗；(adj) 疫苗的

vaccinate (v) 接種疫苗

vaccination (n) 接種疫苗

vaccinator (n) 注射疫苗的人員

(1) All children must be vaccinated against measles.

所有孩童都必須接種麻疹疫苗。

(2) Mary has symptoms of diarrhea, muscle pain, and fever after being vaccinated.

Mary打疫苗後有腹瀉、肌肉疼痛與發燒症狀。

(3) A vaccine is a substance used to stimulate the production of antibodies and provide immunity against one or several diseases.

疫苗是一種物質，用來刺激抗體的產生及提供免疫力，來對抗一種或多種疾病。

(4) People with underlying health conditions that weaken their immune systems or who have severe allergies to some vaccine components may not be able to get vaccinated with certain vaccines.

具有削弱免疫系統的潛在健康狀況或對某些疫苗成分嚴重過敏的人可能無法接種某些疫苗。

(5) Total number of vaccination doses may not equal to the total number of people vaccinated, depending on the specific dose regime (e.g. people receive multiple doses).

疫苗施打總劑量可能不等於已接種疫苗總人數，要視施打劑量的安排（例如有些人施打了多劑量）。

(6) COVID-19 vaccination is an ongoing immunization campaign against severe acute respiratory syndrome coronavirus, in response to the ongoing pandemic in the country.

COVID-19 疫苗接種是一項針對嚴重冠狀病毒急性呼吸症候群的持續免疫運動，以應對全國持續的大流行。

6. variable (adj) 可變的；(n) 變數；

variability (n) 變化性、可變性

various (adj) 不同的、各式各樣的；

variously (adv) 不同的、各式各樣的；

variety (n) 多樣化、變化、變種；

variant (n) 變種

(1) There are many variables affecting the willingness of local people to get vaccine injection.

影響本地人接種疫苗意願的變數很多。

(2) A simple measure of variability of the data is the range. It is the difference between the highest and lowest scores in a set.

數據變異性的一種簡單度量是全距，它是一組數據中最高與最低分數的差異。

(3) Many students were late to the class for various reasons.

許多學生因各種原因都上課遲到。

(4) Hospitals deal with diseases of every variety.

醫院診治各種各樣的疾病。

(5) Several new variants of the coronavirus have been found in many countries.

許多國家發現好幾種新冠病毒的新變種。

7. complicate (v) 使複雜化、使惡化、併發；

   (1) complicated (adj) 複雜的；complication (n) 複雜、混亂、困難，在醫學上是指併發症

      Calculus is a required course and is too complicated for many college students.

      微積分是必修課，它對許多大學生都太難了。

   (2) The design of this mechanism adds complications to maintenance workers.

      這個機構的設計給維修工人增添困難。

   (3) Diabetes could lead to complications on the eye, kidney, and the heart.

      糖尿病可能導致眼睛、腎臟和心臟的併發症。

   (4) Complications of COVID-19 leading to death include respiratory failure, acute respiratory distress syndrome, sepsis, and multi-organ failure.

      COVID-19 導致死亡的併發症包括呼吸衰竭、急性呼吸窘迫症候群、敗血症和多重器官衰竭。

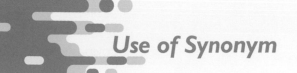

Use of Synonym

1. shortage（名詞：短缺）可用lack, deficiency, scarcity取代；lack一般當動詞使用，其餘兩者為名詞

   Many countries are in shortage of goods and materials to against COVID-19 including alcohol for disinfection, facial mask, and forehead thermometer.

   許多國家都缺乏對抗COVID-19的貨物與物資，包括消毒用酒精、口罩、及額溫槍。

   ⇒ Many countries are l_____king of goods and materials to against COVID-19 including alcohol for disinfection, facial mask, and forehead thermometer.

   ⇒ Many countries are in d_____ of goods and materials to against COVID-19 including alcohol for disinfection, facial mask, and forehead thermometer.

   ⇒ Many countries are in s_____ of goods and materials to against COVID-19 including alcohol for disinfection, facial mask, and forehead thermometer.

2. amplify (v)（放大、累加、強化）可視語意來用augment（擴增）, enlarge（放大）, magnify（放大）, boost（增加）, accumulate（累加）, intensify（強化）等字取代

   Molecular tests detect virus in the sample by amplifying viral genetic material to detectable levels.

   分子測試通過將病毒遺傳物質放大到可檢測水平來檢測樣本中的病毒。

   ⇒ Molecular tests detect virus in the sample by a_____ing viral genetic material to detectable levels.

   ⇒ Molecular tests detect virus in the sample by b_____ing viral genetic material to detectable levels.

   ⇒ Molecular tests detect virus in the sample by m_____ing viral genetic material to detectable levels.

   ⇒ Molecular tests detect virus in the sample by i_____ing viral genetic material to detectable levels.

3. recognize (v)（辨認、識別）可用identify（辨識）, find out（找出）取代

Vaccines work by training the body's immune system to recognize and fight against the viruses they target.

疫苗的工作原理是訓練身體的免疫系統識別和對抗它們所針對的病毒。

⇒ Vaccines work by training the body's immune system to i_____ and fight against the viruses they target.

⇒ Vaccines work by training the body's immune system to f_____out and fight against the viruses they target.

4. persist (v)（持續、存留）可用continue, last, endure

Contact your doctor if the symptoms persist for more than a few days.

如果症狀持續幾天，聯絡你的醫生。

⇒ Contact your doctor if the symptoms c_____or more than a few days.

⇒ Contact your doctor if the symptoms l_____for more than a few days.

⇒ Contact your doctor if the symptoms e_____for more than a few days.

5. severe（嚴重的、劇烈的）可用acute, serious 取代

Symptoms of severe COVID-19 disease include shortness of breath, loss of appetite, confusion, persistent pain in the chest, and high temperature.

嚴重 COVID-19 疾病的症狀包括呼吸急促、食慾不振、意識模糊、胸部持續疼痛和高溫。

⇒ Symptoms of a_____COVID-19 disease include shortness of breath, loss of appetite, confusion, persistent pain in the chest, and high temperature.

⇒ Symptoms of s_____COVID-19 disease include shortness of breath, loss of appetite, confusion, persistent pain in the chest, and high temperature.

SOCIAL
—— 2m ——
DISTANCING

(　　) 1. What is the difference between quarantine and isolation?

A. quarantine must take place in a medical facility;

B. quarantine is required for anyone who has contacted someone infected with the SARS-CoV-2 virus, whether the infected person has symptoms or not while isolation is adopted for people with COVID-19 symptoms or who have tested positive for the virus;

C. quarantine is not required if you don't have COVID-19 symptoms;

D. isolation cannot take place at home.

(　　) 2. Among those who develop COVID-19 symptoms, what is the percentage of those who need intensive medical care?

A. 5%

B. 20%

C. 50%

D. 80%

(　　) 3. What is the difference between a rapid antigen test and a PCR test?

A. The rapid antigen test is more reliable;

B. The rapid antigen test is cheaper than the PCR test;

C. The PCR tests perform best when there is more virus circulating in the community and when sampled from an individual during the time they are most infectious.

D. Both tests need blood testing.

(　　) 4. For the WHO certified COVID-19 vaccines, which one in the following is correct?

A. All of them can protect you from getting infected;

B. All of them provide a high degree of protection against getting seriously ill and dying from the disease.

C. You should wait until a vaccine can provide 100% protection to get vaccinated.

D. You may give yourself a shot to get vaccinated.

(   ) 5. About coronavirus variant, which one in the following is correct?

    A. Some variants emerge and disappear while others persist.

    B. There are only five variants found so far.

    C. The Omicron variants are the most recent one announced at the end of 2021.

    D. The Omicron variants could cause more severe disease compared to infections with Delta variants.

(   ) 6. Which one in the following is not one of the most common symptoms of COVID-19?

    A. fever

    B. dry cough

    C. fatigue

    D. brain inflammation

(   ) 7. Which one in the following is not one of the complications of COVID-19 which could lead to death?

    A. sore throat

    B. thromboembolism

    C. acute respiratory distress syndrome

    D. sepsis

(   ) 8. PCR is the abbreviate of

    A. Persistent Chain Reactor

    B. Polymerase Chain Reaction

    C. Polyester Chain Reaction

    D. Polyester Chain reactor

(   ) 9. For COVID-19, which one in the following is true?

    A. The WHO certified vaccines provide 100% protection against infection.

    B. Physical distancing may reduce the risk of getting infected.

    C. People who have had COVID-19 will never get infected again.

    D. Omicron is the most severe variants which lead to severe disease than all other variants.

(   ) 10. People have high risk of serious COVID-19 illness if they have
        A. headache,
        B. diarrhea,
        C. nausea,
        D. diabetes.

Tesla

Questions & Discussions

1. What is the unique marketing strategy of Tesla as compared with other traditional automobile manufacturers?
2. What are the most important features of Tesla cars?

Tesla Inc. is an electric vehicle and clean energy company based in California, USA. Tesla's products include electric cars, battery energy storage from home to [1]grid scale, solar products and related products and services. Founded in 2003 by Martin Eberhard and Marc Tarpenning, the company's name is a [2]tribute to inventor and electrical engineer Nikola Tesla. Elon Musk, who formerly served as chairman and is the current CEO, said that "the overarching purpose of Tesla is to help [3]expedite the move from a [a]mine-and-burn hydrocarbon economy towards a solar electric economy" and it would build a wide range of electric vehicles, including affordably priced family cars.

With the Model S, Tesla started to build an integrated computer hardware and software architecture at the center of its vehicles. Musk indicated that Tesla is a software company as much as it is a hardware company. Tesla provides online software upgrade to its cars.

This allows improvement of the functionality and performance of the cars already-sold for free. Tesla is the first automaker that sells cars directly to consumers. All others use independently owned dealerships. Musk believes existing dealerships have a [b]conflict of interest and will not promote electric cars from Tesla or any manufacturer, because they make more money servicing than selling cars, and electric cars have lower servicing costs. For this reason, Tesla's sell its vehicles online rather than through a conventional dealer network. The service strategy of Tesla is to service its vehicles through [4]proactive monitoring, remote diagnosis and repair, mobile technicians, and Tesla-owned service centers. Tesla's goal is not to make a profit on service.

Tesla's manufacturing strategy is to continuously improve the hardware of its cars, rather than waiting for announcement of a new model. Tesla's production strategy includes a high degree of [c]vertical integration which includes producing vehicle components as well as building [5]proprietary stations where customers can charge Tesla vehicles. Vertical integration is rare in the automotive industry, where companies typically [6]outsource 80% of components to suppliers, and focus on engine manufacturing and final assembly.

In 2014, Tesla [7]discreetly launched its charging network by providing chargers to hotels, restaurants, shopping centers and other full service stations to provide on-site vehicle charging at twice the power of a typical

Vocabulary

4. proactive [proˈæktɪv]
   主動的 (adj)

5. proprietary [prəˈpraɪəˌtɛrɪ]
   有產權的 (adj)；財產、產權 (n)

6. outsource [ˈaʊtsɔːs]
   外包 (v)

7. discreetly [dɪˈskritlɪ]
   慎重的 (adv)

Terminology

b. conflict of interest
   利益衝突

c. vertical integration
   垂直整合

8. cell [sɛl]
電池、細胞、小房間、小單位 (n)

9. feature [ˈfitʃɚ]
以...為特色、由...主演 (v) 特色、特徵 (n)

10. redundant [rɪˈdʌndənt]
多餘的 (adj)

11. intumescent [ˌɪntjuˈmɛsnt]
膨脹的、鼓起的 (adj)

12. trunk [trʌŋk]
後車（行李）廂、軀幹、樹幹、幹線 (n)

13. armor [ˈɑrmɚ]
提供防護 (v)；盔甲、防護裝置 (n)

14. counterpart [ˈkaʊntɚˌpɑrt]
對應的人（或物）(n)

15. source [sors]
從其他公司、國家購得零件、材料等 (v)；
來源 (n)

16. in-house [ˈɪnˌhaʊs]
不假外力、自行（設計、生產）(adj)(adv)

Terminology

d. free of charge
免費

e. armor plate
防護板

f. mass-produce
大量生產

home charging station. Destination chargers are installed [d]free of charge by Tesla-certified contractors. The locations must provide the electricity at no cost to their customers. All installed chargers are shown in the in-car navigation system. Unlike other automakers, Tesla does not use individual large battery [8]cells, but thousands of small, cylindrical, lithium-ion commodity cells like those used in consumer electronics. Tesla uses a version of these cells that is designed to be cheaper to manufacture and lighter than standard cells by removing some safety [9]features. According to Tesla, these features are [10]redundant because of the advanced thermal management system and an [11]intumescent chemical in the battery to prevent fires. Panasonic is Tesla's battery supplier. The batteries of Tesla cars are placed under the vehicle floor. This saves interior and [12]trunk space but increases the risk of battery damage by debris or impact. The Model S has 6.4 mm aluminum-alloy [13][e]armor plate. In 2020, Tesla announced a new design for their future batteries. This design will increase the range of Tesla Vehicles. It will also allow future electric vehicles prices to compete with their gas-powered [14]counterparts. Currently, Tesla [15]sources their batteries from Panasonic, however with the new design of the batteries Elon Musk has announced plans to manufacture the batteries [16]in-house. The new batteries are expected to be [f]mass-produced by 2023. They will be 56% cheaper and allow the cars to travel 54% more miles.

[g]Autopilot is an important feature of Tesla cars in addition to clean energy. Autopilot is designed to assist drivers with the most [17]burdensome parts of driving in order to make Tesla cars safer and more capable over time. Tesla states that current autopilot features require active driver supervision and do not make the vehicle [18]autonomous. Starting 2014, all Tesla cars are shipped with [19]sensors and software to support autopilot. Tesla upgraded its sensors and software in 2016 to support full [h]self-driving. The system includes eight cameras, twelve ultrasonic sensors, and forward-facing radar. Musk predicted that drivers would be able to sleep in their vehicle while it drives itself. In April 2019, Tesla announced that all of its cars will include Autopilot software as a standard feature moving forward. Full self-driving software is an extra cost option. On April 24, 2020, Tesla released a software update to its full self-driving capability. With this update, cars recognize and automatically stop at stop signs. The cars also automatically slow down and eventually stop at traffic lights until the driver has indicated that it is safe to proceed. Tesla acknowledges that the software is still in a [i]beta phase and far from being finished.

Vocabulary

17. burdensome [ˈbɝdnsəm]
    有負擔的、累人的 (adj)

18. autonomous [ɔˈtɑnəməs]
    獨立自主的 (adv)

19. sensor [ˈsɛnsɚ]
    感應器 (n)

Terminology

g. autopilot
   自動駕駛

h. self-driving
   自動駕駛

i. beta phase
   （產品開發的）第二階段

1. certify (v) 擔保、證明、認證

   certified (adj) 被證明的、有保證的、被認證的

   certificate (n) 證書、執照、憑證

   certification (n) 證明、保證、認證；指認證過程

   (1) Destination chargers are installed free of charge by Tesla-certified contractors.

   站點充電樁均由經特斯拉認證的承包商來免費安裝。

   (2) All the applicants must submit a certificate to prove they have passed the degree requirements.

   所有申請人都必須提交證書，以證明他們已通過學位要求。

   (3) All the research assistants must have a valid certificate of attending the scientific ethic class.

   所有的研究助理必須有一份參加學術倫理課程的證明（證書）。

   (4) Anyone classified as being physically handicapped must have certification from a hospital.

   任何一位被歸為殘障人士的人，必須要有醫院的證明（非證書）。

2. charge (n) 電荷、費用、指控、掌管

   charge (v) 充電、控訴、收費　　←→　　discharge (v) 放電、排放

   charger (n) 充電器

   (1) We're going to charge you fifty dollars.（此句中charge是動詞）

   我們要跟你收取50元的費用。

   (2) The charge of the service was fifty dollars.（此句中charge是名詞）

   服務的費用是50元。

   (3) My laptop needs to be charged.

   我的筆記本電腦需要（被）充電。

   (4) The murderer was charged with three degree murder.

   兇手被以三級謀殺罪起訴。

(5) Mike is in charge of this branch. (in charge of 是「掌管」之意)

Mike掌管這個分行。

(6) I need a charger to charge my battery.

我需要一個充電器來幫電池充電。

(7) The Taipei MRT company has decided to allow the passengers to charge their cell phones inside the MRT stations without charge.

臺北捷運公司決定允許旅客免費在捷運車站內幫手機充電。（第一個charge是充電，為動詞；句尾的charge是費用，為名詞）

3. sense (v) 感覺到、測到；(n) 感官、感覺、觀念

sensor (n) 感應器

sensory (adj) 感覺的、知覺的

sensation (n) 感覺、知覺

sensational (adj) 感覺的、知覺的、引起轟動的

sensationalise (v) 大肆渲染

sensationalism (n) 感官主義

(1) This worker has no sense of time.

這個工人沒有時間觀念。

(2) Mark has a good sense of humor.

Mark很有幽默感。

(3) All Tesla cars are shipped with sensors and software to support Autopilot.

所有的特斯拉汽車都安裝了感應器與軟體來支援自駕。

(4) The car will alarm when the sensors sense an object within a short distance.

當感應器感應到近距離內有物體時，汽車會警示。

(5) Sensation refers to the processing of senses by the sensory system of our body.

感覺功能是指我們身體的感覺系統對感覺之處理。

(6) The news that both Donald Trump and his wife tested positive for the coronavirus was sensational to the world.

川普與他妻子的新冠病毒檢測結果，都是陽性的消息，震驚全世界。

(7) Donald Trump has been sensationalized that China is to be blamed for the widespread coronavirus infections.

川普一直在廣泛喧染，新冠病毒感染的事應該怪中國。

4. deal (n) 交易、待遇、政策；經營、分配、處理(v)

dealer (n) 經銷商、業者

dealership 代理權；經銷權 (n)

(1) Mark is dealing with this case.

Mark正在處理這個案件。

(2) Tesla has just finalized a big deal with SolarCity.

Tesla剛剛與SolarCity談成一筆大交易。

(3) Mr. Chang is a dealer of used cars.

張先生是二手車經銷商。

(4) Our company owns the dealership of Toyota automobiles in this region.

我們公司擁有這個地區的豐田汽車經銷權。

5. acknowledge (v) 承認、告知、致謝

acknowledged (adj) 公認的、被承認的、被感謝的

acknowledgment (或acknowledgement) (n) 承認、確認、致謝 (n)

(1) Both Donald Trump and Joe Biden wave their hands to acknowledge the cheers of the crowd.

川普與拜登同時向大眾揮手，對大眾的歡呼表示感謝。

(2) We acknowledge her contribution in this study.

我們感謝她在這個研究裡的貢獻。

(3) The authors must acknowledge the financial support of their research funding on their study in the Acknowledgments.

作者必須在「致謝」中，感謝其研究計畫對其研究之經費贊助。

Fill in the blanks
using the words you have just learned in this lesson

With the Model S, Tesla started to build an integrated computer hardware and software architecture at the center of its vehicles. Musk indicated that Tesla is a software company as much as it is a hardware company. Tesla provides online software upgrade to its cars. This allows improvement of the functionality and performance of the cars already-sold for free. Tesla is the first _____（汽車製造廠）that sells cars directly to consumers. All others use independently owned _____s（經銷權）. Musk believes existing _____s（經銷權）have a _____（衝突）of _____（利益）and will not promote _____（電動）cars from Tesla or any manufacturer, because they make more money servicing than selling cars, and _____（電動）cars have lower servicing costs. For this reason, Tesla's sell its vehicles online rather than through a conventional _____（經銷商）network. The service strategy of Tesla is to service its vehicles through proactive monitoring, remote _____（診斷）and repair, mobile technicians, and Tesla-owned service centers. Tesla's goal is not to make a profit on service.

1. expedite (v) 加速，可用accelerate、speed up取代。

Musk give an order to expedite the research and development of the next generation automobile energy.

馬斯克下令加快下一代汽車能源的研發。

⇒ Musk give an order to a_____ the research and development of the next generation automobile energy.

⇒ Musk give an order to s_____ up the research and development of the next generation automobile energy.

2. feature (n) 特色、特徵，可用characteristics, attribute取代feature（以…為特色），為及物動詞，可用character取代；feature（發揮…特色），為不及物動詞。

(1) Touch screen operation is one of the major features of a tablet computer.

觸控螢幕操作是平板電腦的主要特徵之一。

⇒ Touch screen operation is one of the major c_____ of a tablet computer.

(2) Asus' Transformer followed, continuing the common trends towards multitouch and other natural user interface features.

華碩變形金剛隨後誕生，延續走向多點觸控與其他自然使用者介面的共同趨勢。

⇒ Asus' Transformer followed, continuing the common trends towards multi-touch and other natural user interface c_____.

(3) A tablet computer is featured by touch screen operation.

平板電腦是觸控螢幕操作來凸顯特質。

⇒ A tablet computer is c_____ by touch screen operation.

(4) Autopilot is one of the major features of Tesla cars.

自動駕駛是特斯拉汽車的主要特色之一。

⇒ Autopilot is one of the major c_____ of Tesla cars.

⇒ Autopilot is one of the major a_____ of Tesla cars.

3. discreetly (adv) 慎重的，將字尾的ly去掉則為形容詞；與carefully, prudently意思相同；反義字為indiscreetly不慎重的、草率的，carelessly, imprudently。

(1) Tesla discreetly launched its charging network by providing on-site chargers for vehicle charging at twice the power of a typical home charging station.

特斯拉謹慎地啟動了其充電網絡，為汽車提供現場充電器，其功率是普通家用充電站的兩倍。

⇒ Tesla p＿＿＿＿＿＿ launched its charging network by providing on-site chargers for vehicle charging at twice the power of a typical home charging station.

⇒ Tesla c＿＿＿＿＿＿ launched its charging network by providing on-site chargers for vehicle charging at twice the power of a typical home charging station.

(2) This company has shut down ten of its branches indiscreetly.

這家公司草率關閉十家分支機構。

⇒ This company has shut down ten of its branches imp＿＿＿＿＿＿.

⇒ This company has shut down ten of its branches c＿＿＿＿＿＿.

4. outsource (v) 外包，可用subcontract取代。

(1) Automobile companies typically outsource 80% of components to suppliers, and focus on engine manufacturing and final assembly.

汽車公司通常將80％的組件外包給供應商，並專注於引擎製造和最終（整車）組裝。

⇒ Automobile companies typically s＿＿＿＿＿＿ 80% of components to suppliers, and focus on engine manufacturing and final assembly.

(2) Personal computer manufacturers normally outsource the printed circuit boards and batteries to their local suppliers.

個人電腦製造商通常將印刷電路板與電池外包給當地的供應商。

⇒ Personal computer manufacturers normally s＿＿＿＿＿＿ the printed circuit boards and batteries to their local suppliers.

Choose the most appropriate one in the following questions

(   ) 1.   Tesla _____ launched the Destination Charging Location project.

      A. secret

      B. disrcreeted

      C. discreet

      D. discreetly

(   ) 2.   Tesla's sell its vehicles online rather than through a conventional _____ network.

      A. deal

      B. deals

      C. dealer

      D. dealership

(   ) 3.   These features are _____.

      A. redundant

      B. include

      C. discreetly

      D. dealer

(   ) 4.   Both Donald Trump and Joe Biden wave their hands to _____ the cheers of the crowd.

      A. acknowledge

      B. acknowledged

      C. acknowledgment

      D. knowledgement

(   ) 5.   The news that both Donald Trump and his wife tested positive for the coronavirus was _____ to the world.

      A. sense

      B. sensory

      C. sensation

      D. sensational

(　　) 6.　All Tesla cars are shipped with _____ and software to support Autopilot.

　　　　A. sense

　　　　B. sensors

　　　　C. sensations

　　　　D. sensory

(　　) 7.　Tesla uses a version of these cells without some safety _____.

　　　　A. beat

　　　　B. gestures

　　　　C. futures

　　　　D. features

(　　) 8.　The car will alarm when the sensors _____ an object within a short distance.

　　　　A. sense

　　　　B. sensors

　　　　C. sensations

　　　　D. sensory

(　　) 9.　Elon Musk has announced plans to manufacture the batteries _____.

　　　　A. at house

　　　　B. house

　　　　C. housely

　　　　D. in-house

(　　) 10. The current autopilot features require active driver supervision and do not make the vehicle _____.

　　　　A. automatic

　　　　B. automatically

　　　　C. autonomous

　　　　D. autonomously

(   ) 11. Mr. Chang is a used car _____.

        A. deal

        B. deals

        C. dealer

        D. dealership

(   ) 12. Destination chargers are installed free of charge by Tesla-_____ contractors.

        A. certify

        B. certified

        C. certification

        D. certificate

(   ) 13. "Expedite" means

        A. except

        B. speed up

        C. exception

        D. exclude

(   ) 14. This design will increase the range of Tesla Vehicles. In this sentence, "range" means

        A. size

        B. weight

        C. carrying capacity

        D. mileage

(   ) 15. Who is the founder(s) of Tesla Inc.?

        A. Nikola Tesla

        B. Elon Musk

        C. Martin Eberhard and Marc Tarpenning

        D. Nicolas Pippin

Tablets

Questions & Discussions

1. What are the differences between a tablet and a PC?

2. Do PC users replace their PCs with tablets? Why?

Vocabulary

1. tablet [ˈtæblɪt]
   藥片；古代用以書寫的木片、石板，碑；
   平板電腦 (n)

2. laptop [ˈlæptɑp]
   膝上型電腦（即筆記本電腦）(n)

3. hideable [haɪdˈebl]
   可隱藏地 (adj)

4. convertible [kənˈvɝtəbl]
   可轉換的 (adj)；敞篷跑車 (n)

5. swivel [ˈswɪvl]
   轉環、旋轉 (n)；旋轉、使旋轉 (v)

6. joint [dʒɔɪnt]
   接頭、接合處 (n)；聯合的、共同的 (adj)；
   接合 (v)

7. hybrid [ˈhaɪbrɪd]
   混種、混血兒 (n)；混合的 (adj)

8. detachable [dɪˈtætʃəbl]
   可分開的 (adj)

9. stand-alone [ˈstændəˌlon]
   獨立的、獨自存在的 (adj)

10. booklet [ˈbʊklɪt]
    手冊、小冊子 (n)

11. dual [ˈdjuəl]
    雙數 (n)；兩的、雙的 (adj)

Terminology

a. slide joint
   旋轉接頭

A [1]tablet computer, or simply tablet, is a one-piece mobile computer, primarily operated by touchscreen. When using a tablet, the user's finger essentially functions as the mouse and cursor, removing the need for traditional input devices necessary for a desktop or [2]laptop computer. An onscreen and [3]hideable virtual keyboard is integrated into the display for text input purposes. There are various tablet designs. [4]Convertible notebook computers have an integrated keyboard that can be hidden by a [5]swivel joint or [a]slide [6]joint, exposing only the screen for touch operation. [7]Hybrids have a [8]detachable keyboard so that the touchscreen can be used as a [9]stand-alone tablet. [10]Booklets include [11]dual-touchscreens, and can be used as a notebook by displaying a virtual keyboard in one of them. Available in a variety of sizes, even the smallest touchscreens are much larger than those of a smart phone or personal digital assistant.

Tablets [12]differ considerably from PCs in many ways, including user interface, operating system, processor, and applications. Another [13]crucial difference is that tablets are used primarily as inexpensive media consumption devices, so raw processing power is not as important as the content distribution platform. In many ways, tablets are similar to and often derived from the architecture of smartphones. Tablets have a higher [14]disruptive impact on PCs on the market than smartphones do. Smartphones and PCs are complementary, but tablets not as much. Tablets have dramatically changed user behaviors for PCs, not so much by [15]cannibalizing PC sales, but by causing PC users to shift usage to tablets rather than replacing older PCs.

The tablet computer and the associated special operating software is an example of pen computing technology, and thus the development of tablets has deep historical roots. Electrical devices with data input and output on a flat information display have existed as early as 1888 with the [16]telautograph. Some things similar to the contemporary tablets appeared in a number of works of science fiction in last century. The Calculator Pad described in the 1951 novel *Foundation* written by Isaac Asimov was an example. Alan Kay has published an article "A Personal Computer for children of all Ages" in 1972 where he proposed a touchscreen as a possible alternative means of input for the device and coined this device Dynabook. Star Trek, a popular TV series in the USA, featured tablet computers in the show and termed them "padds".

Vocabulary

17. usability [ˌjuzəˈbɪlətɪ]
    可用性 (n)

18. release [rɪˈlis]
    釋放、發表 (n)(v)

19. simplicity [sɪmˈplɪsətɪ]
    簡潔 (n)

20. shape [ʃep]
    形狀 (n)；使…成形、塑造 (v)

Terminology

b. media consumption
   媒體消費；看影片、上購物網站等行為

In 1999, Intel announced a touchscreen tablet computer and named WebPAD. This tablet was later re-branded it as the "Intel Web Tablet." During the 2000s, Microsoft attempted to define tablet computer concept as a mobile computer for field work in business. Their devices, however, failed to achieve widespread usage mainly due to price and [17]usability problems that made them unsuitable outside of their limited intended purposes. In 2010, Apple Inc. [18]released the iPad, a tablet with an emphasis on [b]media consumption. The shift in purpose, together with increased usability, battery life, [19]simplicity, lower weight and cost, and overall quality with respect to previous tablets, was perceived as defining a new class of consumer device. This tablet has [20]shaped the commercial market for tablets in the following year.

The most successful tablet computer is the iPad using the iOS operating system. Its [21]debut in 2010 popularized tablets into mainstream. Asus' Transformer Pad and others followed. They continue the common trends towards [c]multi-touch, natural user interface features, and flash memory solid-state storage drives. In addition, standard external USB and Bluetooth keyboards can also be used. Some of the tablets have 4/5G mobile [22]telephony capabilities.

As of March 2012, 31% of U.S. Internet users were reported to have a tablet, which was used mainly for viewing published content such as video and news. Among tablets available in the market in 2012, the top-selling device is the iPad with 100 million sold by mid October 2012 since it was released, followed by Amazon's Kindle Fire with 7 million, and Barnes & Noble's Nook with 5 million.

Vocabulary

21. debut [dɪˋbju]
    首次露面 (n)
22. telephony [təˋlɛfənɪ]
    電話通訊 (n)

Terminology

c. multi-touch
   多點觸控

Families of Vocabulary

1. appear (v) 出現

    disappear (v) 沒出現、消失

    appearance (n) 出現、外觀　　⟷　　disappearance (n) 失蹤、消失

    (1) All the tablets have similar appearance.

    　　所有的平板電腦都有類似外觀。

    (2) It is not a surprise that trackballs disappeared after their short appearance in the market.

    　　軌跡球在市場上短暫的出現後，再度消失不算意外。

2. complement (v) 補充

    complementary (adj) 互補的

    complementarily (adv) 互補的

    complement (n) 補充物

    Mouse and keyboard are complementary input devices.

    鍵盤與滑鼠是互補的輸入裝置。

3. use (v) 使用

    useful (adj) 有用的　　　　　⟷　　useless (adj) 無用的

    usefully (adv) 有用的

    usable (adj) 可用的　　　　　⟷　　unusable (adj) 不可用的

    usability (n) 可用性

    usefulness (n) 有用性

    (1) Usability testing is essential in the design and developing of a tablet.

    　　可用性測試在平板電腦上的設計與開發，是不可或缺的。

    (2) The usefulness of this device has been questioned in the market.

    　　這個裝置的可用性在市場上被質疑。

    (3) The human-computer interface of iPad is simple for most users.

    　　對於多數使用者而言，iPad的電腦介面很簡單。

    (4) The design was simplified by removing several unnecessary components.

    　　經由移除幾件不必要的零件，設計被簡化了。

4. differ (v)不同於

different (adj) 不同的

differently (adv) 不同的

difference (n) 差異

(1) Tablets differ from smart phones mainly in the size of the device.

Tablets are different from smart phones mainly in the size of the device.

平板不同於智慧型手機，主要在於裝置的尺寸。

(2) The main difference between tablets and smart phones is the size of the device.

平板與智慧型手機主要差別在於裝置的尺寸。

5. popularize (v) 使普及

popular (adj) 風行的、受歡迎的 ⟷ unpopular (adj) 不風行的、不受歡迎的

popularly (adv) 大眾化的、通俗的

popularity (n) 風行 ⟷ unpopularity (n) 不受歡迎

(1) The i-series products of Apple Inc. have become popular worldwide.

蘋果公司的i系列產品變得世界風行。

(2) The popularity of the i-series products of Apple Inc. has become a legend in industry.

蘋果公司i系列產品風靡一時，成為工業界的一個傳奇。

6. simplify (v) 簡化

simple (adj) 簡單的、輕易的

simply (adv) 簡單的、輕易的

simplified (adj) 被簡化的

simplification (n) 簡化

simplicity (n) 簡潔

(1) The i-series products of Apple Inc. are characterized by their simplicity in design.

蘋果公司的i系列產品之特色，為其設計之簡潔。

(2) The simplified process has save us a lot of time in inventory management.

簡化的過程，讓我們在庫存管理上，節省許多時間。

When using a _____（平板電腦）, the user's finger essentially functions as the mouse and _____（游標）, removing the need for traditional input devices necessary for a desktop or laptop computer. Available in a variety of sizes, even the smallest's touchscreens are much larger than those of a smart phone or personal digital assistant. _____s（平板電腦）differ considerably from PCs in many ways, including user interface, operating system, and applications. Another crucial difference is that _____s（平板電腦）are used primarily as _____（不貴的）media consumption devices, so raw processing power is not as important as the content distribution platform. _____s（平板電腦）have dramatically changed user behaviors for PCs, not so much by _____（侵蝕）PC sales. In 2010, Apple Inc. released the iPad, a _____（平板電腦）with an emphasis on media consumption. The shift in purpose, together with increased usability, _____（簡潔的）, lower weight and cost, and overall quality with respect to previous _____s（平板電腦）, was perceived as defining a new class of consumer device.

1. feature（特色）為名詞，可用characteristics取代；feature（以…為特色），為及物動詞，可用characterize取代；feature（發揮…特色），為不及物動詞。

(1) Touch screen operation is one of the major features of a tablet computer.

平板電腦的主要特徵之一為觸控螢幕操作。

⇒ Touch screen operation is one of the major c_____ of a tablet computer.

(2) Asus' Transformer followed, continuing the common trends towards multi-touch and other natural user interface features.

華碩變形金剛隨後誕生，延續走向多點觸控與其他自然使用者介面的共同趨勢。

⇒ Asus' Transformer followed, continuing the common trends towards multi-touch and other natural user interface c_____.

(3) A tablet computer is featured by touch screen operation.

平板電腦使用觸控螢幕操作來凸顯特質。

⇒ A tablet computer is c_____ by touch screen operation.

2. detachable（可分離的）可用separable或removable取代。

Hybrids have a detachable keyboard so that the touchscreen can be used as a stand-alone tablet.

混合型有一個可分離的鍵盤，如此觸控螢幕可做為獨立的平板電腦使用。

⇒ Hybrids have a s_____ keyboard so that the touchscreen can be used as a stand-alone tablet.

⇒ Hybrids have a r_____ keyboard so that the touchscreen can be used as a stand-alone tablet.

3. stand-alone（獨立的、自立的、個體的）可用independent（獨立的）或individual（個體的）取代。

Hybrids have a detachable keyboard so that the touchscreen can be used as a stand-alone tablet.

⇒ Hybrids have a detachable keyboard so that the touchscreen can be used as an i_____ tablet.

⇒ Hybrids have a detachable keyboard so that the touchscreen can be used as an i_____ tablet.

4. crucial（決定性的、重要的）可用vital、important、essential取代。

A crucial difference between a tablet and a laptop is that the former does not have a keyboard.

平板與膝上型電腦的一個重要差異是前者沒有鍵盤。

⇒ A v_____ difference between a tablet and a laptop is that the former does not have a keyboard.

⇒ An i_____ difference between a tablet and a laptop is that the former does not have a keyboard.

⇒ A e_____ difference between a tablet and a laptop is that the former does not have a keyboard.

5. debut（首次出現）可用first appearance或者是口語化的coming out取代。

Its debut in 2010 popularized tablets into mainstream.

它在2010年首次出現讓平板風行成為主流。

⇒ Its f_____ a_____ in 2010 popularized tablets into mainstream.

⇒ Its c_____ o_____ in 2010 popularized tablets into mainstream.

6. release 一般是釋放的意思，也可當作發表解釋，此時與announce（名詞為announcement）、introduce（名詞為introduction）同義。

(1) The ASUS has released the Transformer Book as both a laptop and a tablet.

華碩推出Transformer Book同時作為膝上型與平板電腦。

⇒ The ASUS has a_____ the Transformer Book as both a laptop and a tablet.

⇒ The ASUS has i_____ the Transformer Book as both a laptop and a tablet.

(2) Ten million iPads have been sold since this tablet was released in 2010.

自2010年這款平板上市以來，iPad已銷售了一千萬臺。

⇒ Ten million iPads have been sold since this tablet was a_____ in 2010.

⇒ Ten million iPads have been sold since this tablet was i_____ in 2010.

(3) The release of iPad has defined a new personal mobile device in the market.

iPad的上市在市場上定義了一種新的個人移動裝置。

⇒ The a_____ of iPad has defined a new personal mobile device in the market.

⇒ The i_____ of iPad has defined a new personal mobile device in the market.

7. shape作為動詞是塑造、塑型之意，可用sculpt（雕塑）、mold（製作模型）或model（製作模型）取代。

This tablet has shaped the commercial market for tablets in the following year.

這款平板在次年為平板的商業市場定型。

⇒ This tablet has s_____ the commercial market for tablets in the following year.

⇒ This tablet has m_____ the commercial market for tablets in the following year.

⇒ This tablet has m_____ the commercial market for tablets in the following year.

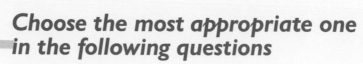

Choose the most appropriate one in the following questions

(   ) 1. Microsoft's tablet devices for field work in business failed to achieve widespread usage mainly due to what problems?

     A. touchscreen

     B. battery life

     C. internet

     D. price and internet

     E. price and usability

(   ) 2. Which ones in the following include dual-touchscreens, and can be used as a notebook computer by displaying a virtual keyboard in one of them?

     A. Booklets

     B. Convertibles

     C. SmartBooks

     D. Hybrids

     E. Touchpads

(   ) 3. Which ones in the following have a detachable keyboard so that the touchscreen can be used as a stand-alone tablet?

     A. Booklets

     B. Convertibles

     C. SmartBooks

     D. Hybrids

     E. Touchpads

(   ) 4. Which computers in the following have an integrated keyboard that can be hidden by a swivel joint or slide joint, exposing only the screen for touch operation?

     A. Booklet

     B. Convertible

     C. SmartBook

     D. Hybrid

     E. Touchpad

(　　) 5.　What are the main tablet usages of the U.S. Internet users?

    A. viewing published content

    B. playing games

    C. telecommunication

    D. paying e-bill

    E. text input

(　　) 6.　The crucial difference between tablets and PCs is that tablets are used primarily as inexpensive _____ devices.

    A. word processing

    B. graphing

    C. media consumption

    D. computation

    E. networking

(　　) 7.　Which one in the following is true?

    A. Ipad is the first commercially available tablet computer.

    B. The idea of tablet has appeared in science fiction novels in last century.

    C. Smartphones have a higher disruptive impact on PCs on the market than tablets do.

    D. Intel attempted to define tablet computer concept as a mobile computer for field work in business.

    E. In 1999, Intel announced a touchscreen tablet computer and named Dynabook.

(　　) 8.　The _____ of the i-series products of Apple Inc. has become a legend in industry.

    A. popular

    B. popularly

    C. popularize

    D. popularity

(　　) 9.　The i-series products of Apple Inc. are characterized by their _____ in design.

A. simplify

B. simplification

C. simplicity

D. simple

(　　) 10.　Mouse and keyboard are _____ input devices.

A. complement

B. complementary

C. complementarily

D. complemented

Touchscreens

Questions & Discussions

1. Discuss the differences between the two major touch screen technologies.
2. Give some examples of the kiosk you have seen in the local area and discuss how did you interact with them.

Vocabulary

1. console [kənˋsol]
   操控臺 (n)

2. gesture [ˋdʒɛstʃɚ]
   姿勢、手勢 (n)；做手勢 (v)

3. stylus [ˋstaɪləs]
   針筆、探針、唱針 (n)

4. kiosk [kɪˋɑsk]
   亭子、資訊臺 (n)

Terminology

a. personal digital assistant
   個人數位助理

b. satellite navigation device
   衛星導航裝置

Touchscreens are common in devices such as game [1]consoles, all-in-one computers, tablet computers, and smartphones. They also play a prominent role in digital appliances such as [a]personal digital assistants and [b]satellite navigation devices. A touchscreen is an electronic visual display that users input through simple or multi-touch [2]gestures by touching the screen with one or more fingers. Some touchscreens also detect objects such as a [3]stylus or ordinary or specially coated gloves. Users can use touchscreens to react to what is displayed and to control how it is displayed, for example to zoom the text size.

The popularity of smartphones, tablets, and many types of information appliances has driving the demand and acceptance of common touchscreens for portable and functional electronics. Touchscreens are popular in both medical and heavy industries, as well as in [4]kiosks such as museum displays or room automation. In those industries and locations, keyboards and mouse systems normally do not allow a suitably intuitive, rapid, or accurate interaction between users and content of the display.

Historically, touchscreen sensors and their accompanying controller-based [5]firmware have been made available by a wide array of system integrators, and not by display, chip, or motherboard manufacturers. Display manufacturers and chip manufacturers worldwide have acknowledged the trend toward acceptance of touchscreens as a highly desirable user interface component and have begun to integrate touchscreens into the fundamental design of their products.

[6]Resistive and [7]capacitive touches are the two major touchscreen technologies. A resistive touchscreen panel is comprised of two thin, [8]transparent electrically-resistive layers. These layers are separated by a thin space. The two layers face each other with a thin [9]gap between. The top screen, or the one that is touched, has a coating on the underside surface. Just beneath it is a similar resistive layer on top of its substrate. A voltage is applied to one layer, and sensed by the other. When an object, such as a fingertip or stylus tip, presses down on the outer surface, the two layers touch to become connected at that point. The panel then behaves as a pair of voltage dividers, one axis at a time. By rapidly switching between each layer, the position of a pressure on the screen can be read.

Resistive touch is used in public locations such as restaurants, factories and hospitals due to its high resistance to liquids and [10]contaminants. A major benefit of this technology

Vocabulary

5. firmware [ˈfɝmˌwɛr]
   韌體 (n)

6. resistive [rɪˈzɪstɪv]
   電阻的、有阻力的 (adj)

7. capacitive [kəˈpæsətɪv]
   電容的 (adj)

8. transparent [trænsˈpɛrənt]
   透明的 (adj)

9. gap [gæp]
   縫隙、缺口 (n)；使裂開 (v)

10. contaminant [kənˈtæmənənt]
    污染物 (n)

is its low cost. Additionally, as only sufficient pressure is necessary for the touch to be sensed, they may be used with gloves on, or by using anything rigid as a finger/stylus substitute. The disadvantages of this technology include the need to press down and a risk of damage by sharp objects. Due to having additional reflections from the extra layer of material placed over the screen, resistive touchscreens also have poorer contrast.

A capacitive touchscreen panel consists of an [11]insulator such as glass, coated with a transparent conductor. As human body is an electrical conductor, touching the surface of the screen results in a [12]distortion of the screen's [c]electrostatic field, measurable as a change in capacitance. Unlike a resistive touchscreen, one cannot use a capacitive touchscreen through most types of electrically insulating material, such as gloves. This disadvantage affects usability in consumer electronics, such as touch tablets and capacitive smartphones in cold weather. It, however, can be overcome with a special capacitive stylus, or a special-application glove with an [13]embroidered patch of conductive thread passing through it and contacting the user's fingertip.

Vocabulary

14. house [haus]
    房子 (n)；儲藏、包含 (v)
15. pushbutton [ˈpuʃˌbʌtn]
    按鍵 (n)

Knowledge Plus

History

An electronic kiosk, or alternatively computer kiosk or interactive kiosk, [14]houses a computer terminal that often employs custom kiosk software designed for special functions. Computerized kiosks may store data locally, or retrieve it from a computer network. Some computer kiosks provide a free, informational public service, while others serve a commercial purpose. Touchscreens and [15]pushbuttons are typical input devices for interactive computer kiosk. Touchscreen kiosks are commercially used as industrial appliances to reduce lines, eliminating paper, improving efficiency and service. Their uses are unlimited from refrigerators to airports, train stations, health clubs, movie theaters and libraries.

Families of Vocabulary

1. accept (v) 接受

   acceptable (adj) 可接受的 ⟷ unacceptable (adj) 不可接受的

   acceptability (n) 可接受性

   acceptance (n) 接受

   (1) The acceptability of this touchscreen design has been reviewed by external experts.

   這個觸控螢幕設計的可接受性，經歷了外部專家的審查。

   (2) Touchscreen designs are widely accepted in wearable devices.

   觸控螢幕設計廣泛被穿戴式裝置接受。

   (3) Small touchscreens are unacceptable for older adults.

   小型觸控螢幕對老人來說，是不可接受的。

   (4) In assembling touchscreens, defective electronic components are not acceptable.

   In assembling touchscreens, defective electronic components are unacceptable.

   組裝觸控螢幕時，無法接受有缺陷的電子零件。

2. compute (v) 計算

   computable (adj) 可計算的

   computably (adv) 可計算的

   computer (n) 電腦

   computation (n) 計算

   (1) This device encompasses a computer to compute the walking speed of the user automatically.

   這個裝置內含一個電腦，來自動計算使用者的走路速度。

   (2) The computation of the walking speed of the user is not complicated.

   使用者的走路速度計算不複雜。

3. capacitive (adj) 電容的

  capacitance (n) 電容

  capacitor (n) 電容器

  Capacitive touchscreen will not work when the user is wearing gloves.

  使用者戴手套時無法用電容式的觸控螢幕。

4. resist (v) 抵抗、阻止

  resistible (adj) 可抵抗的　　　⟷　　irresistible (adj) 不可抵抗的

  resistive (adj) 抵抗的、電阻的

  resistivity (n) 抵抗性、電阻性

  resistance (n) 抵抗力、電阻

  resistor (n) 電阻器

  (1) Resistive touchscreen is normally used in public locations due to its high resistance to liquids and contaminants.

     由於對於液體與污染物的高抵抗力，電阻式觸控螢幕常用於公共場所。

  (2) The popularity of touchscreens is irresistible.

     觸控螢幕的風行是無法抵抗的。

  (3) The price of this new wearable device is irresistible to the younger generation.

     這個新的穿戴式裝置價格，對於年輕世代來說是無法抗拒的。

  (4) Resistive touchscreens have poor color contrast and are not commonly used in smart phones.

     電阻式的觸控螢幕有較差之色彩對比，比較不常用在智慧型手機上。

  (5) There are more than 50 resistors in this printed circuit board.

     這個印刷電路板上有超過50個電阻。

Use of Synonym

1. drive（驅動）可用compel（強制、使…不得不）、push（推動）、propel（推動）取代。

The popularity of information appliances has driving the demand of touchscreens.

資訊家電的風行，促進了觸控螢幕的需求。

⇒ The popularity of information appliances has c_____ the demand of touch-screens.

⇒ The popularity of information appliances has p_____ the demand of touchscreens.

⇒ The popularity of information appliances has p_____ the demand of common touchscreens.

2. gap（縫隙）為名詞時，可用break（破損）、crack（裂縫）、split（分隔、裂縫）取代。

The two layers face each other with a thin gap between.

兩層對接期間並有一細微的隙縫。

⇒ The two layers face each other with a thin b_____ between.

⇒ The two layers face each other with a thin c_____ between.

⇒ The two layers face each other with a thin s_____ between.

3. coating（塗層）可用covering（覆蓋物）、spreading（塗佈層）取代。

The top screen, or the one that is touched, has a coating on the under-side surface.

上面的螢幕，或者被觸摸的那一面，在下方有一塗層。

⇒ The top screen, or the one that is touched, has a c_____ on the under-side surface.

⇒ The top screen, or the one that is touched, has a s_____ on the under-side surface.

4. behave（扮演、發揮功能）可用act（表現）、perform（發揮功能）、work（發揮功能）取代。

The panel then behaves as a pair of voltage dividers, one axis at a time.

板子接著扮演一對電壓分配者的角色，每次一個軸向。

⇒ The panel then a_____ as a pair of voltage dividers, one axis at a time.

⇒ The panel then p_____ as a pair of voltage dividers, one axis at a time.

⇒ The panel then w_____ as a pair of voltage dividers, one axis at a time.

5. distortion（扭曲、變形、失真）可用contortion（扭曲）、deformation（扭曲）取代。

As human body is an electrical conductor, touching the surface of the screen results in a distortion of the screen's electrostatic field, measurable as a change in capacitance.

由於人體是帶電的導體，碰觸螢幕的表面造成螢幕靜電場的變形，這可由電容改變量得。

⇒ As human body is an electrical conductor, touching the surface of the screen results in a c_____ of the screen's electrostatic field, measurable as a change in capacitance.

⇒ As human body is an electrical conductor, touching the surface of the screen results in a d_____ of the screen's electrostatic field, measurable as a change in capacitance.

6. house（儲藏、容納、包含）為動詞時，可用accommodate（能容納）、contain（包含）、lodge（提供空間存放）取代。

An interactive kiosk houses a computer terminal that often employs custom kiosk software designed for special functions.

一個互動資訊臺容納一個通常為特殊功能設計之客製資訊臺軟體之電腦終端機。

⇒ An interactive kiosk a_____ a computer terminal that often employs custom kiosk software designed for special functions.

⇒ An interactive kiosk c_____ a computer terminal that often employs custom kiosk software designed for special functions.

⇒ An interactive kiosk l_____ a computer terminal that often employs custom kiosk software designed for special functions.

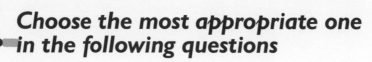
(   ) 1.   A stylus is a _____.

      A. knife

      B. style

      C. drill

      D. eraser

      E. pen

(   ) 2.   Resistive touch is used in public locations due to its high resistance to liquids and _____.

      A. dust

      B. heat

      C. humidity

      D. contaminants

(   ) 3.   An electronic kiosk is _____.

      A. a facility houses a computer terminal

      B. computer software

      C. electronic framework

      D. a telephony facility

      E. a ticket booth

(   ) 4.   For resistive touch, which one in the following is true?

      A. It allows single touch.

      B. It allows multi-touch.

      C. It allows the using of a stylus.

      D. It may be operated when wearing an electrically insulating glove.

      E. All of above is true.

(   ) 5.   For resistive touch, which one in the following is true?

      A. It is low cost.

      B. One cannot use when wearing an electrically insulating glove.

      C. One cannot use a stylus.

      D. It is resistive to sharp objects.

      E. All of above is true.

(   ) 6.   For capacitive touch, which one in the following is true?

      A. It is low cost.

      B. One cannot use when wearing an electrically insulating glove.

      C. One cannot use a stylus.

      D. It is resistive to sharp objects.

      E. Have poorer contrast.

(   ) 7.   For capacitive touch, which one in the following is true?

      A. Must be touched by conductive material.

      B. Must be touched by an electrically insulating stylus.

      C. One can use when wearing an electrically insulating glove.

      D. It is pressure sensitive.

      E. It is commonly used in public locations.

(   ) 8.   What is the reason why resistive touchscreens have poorer contrast?

      A. Having additional pressure from the extra layer of material placed over the screen.

      B. Having additional voltage from the extra layer of material placed over the screen.

      C. Having additional reflections from the extra layer of material placed over the screen.

      D. Having additional current from the extra layer of material placed over the screen.

      E. Having additional polarization from the extra layer of material placed over the screen.

(   ) 9. When using a capacitive smartphone in cold weather, the touchscreen will not work unless _____.

A. the user wears an ordinary glove

B. the user uses a stylus with insulating material

C. the user wears a special-application glove with an embroidered patch of conductive thread passing through it and contacting the user's fingertip

D. the user pushes hard

E. the user wears a rubber glove

(   ) 10. The popularity of smartphones has driving the demand and _____ of common touchscreens for portable and functional electronics.

A. accept

B. acceptable

C. acceptance

D. acceptability

Unmanned Aerial Vehicle

Questions & Discussions

1. What are the typical functional categories of UAVs?
2. Which company is the leading consumer UAV supplier in the world?

Vocabulary

1. unmanned [ʌnˋmænd]
   無人的 (adj)

2. drone [dron]
   雄蜂、嗡嗡聲 (n)；嗡嗡叫 (v)

3. aerial [ɛrɪəl]
   航空的 (adj)

4. autonomously [ɔˋtɑnəməslɪ]
   獨立自主的 (adv)

5. lethal [liθəl]
   致命的 (adj)

6. payload [ˋpelod]
   裝載量 (n)

7. resemblance [rɪˋzɛmbləns]
   相似處 (n)

An [1]unmanned aerial vehicle (UAV), commonly known as a [2]drone, or by several other names, is an aircraft without a human pilot aboard. A UAV is defined as a "powered, [3]aerial vehicle that does not carry a human operator, uses aerodynamic forces to provide vehicle lift, can fly [4]autonomously or be piloted remotely, can be expendable or recoverable, and can carry a [5]lethal or nonlethal [6]payload". Therefore, missiles are not considered UAVs because the vehicle itself is a weapon that is not reused, though it is also unmanned and in some cases remotely guided.

Multiple terms are used for unmanned aerial vehicles, which generally refer to the same concept. The term drone, more widely used by the public, was coined in reference to the [7]resemblance of dumb-looking navigation and loud-and-regular motor sounds of old military unmanned aircraft to the male bee. The term has encountered strong opposition from aviation professionals and government regulators. The term unmanned aircraft system (UAS) was adopted by the United States

Department of Defense (DoD), the United States Federal Aviation Administration (FAA), and the European aviation authorities. This term emphasizes the importance of elements other than the aircraft. It includes elements such as ground control stations, data links and other support equipment. Similar terms are being used such as an unmanned-aircraft vehicle system (UAVS), remotely piloted aerial vehicle (RPAV), remotely piloted aircraft system (RPAS), and so on.

The earliest attempt at a powered UAV was in 1916. Advances followed during and after World War I. with the maturing and miniaturization of applicable technologies in the 1980s and 1990s, interest in UAVs grew within the higher [8]echelons of the U.S. military. In the 1990s, the U.S. DoD gave a contract to AAI Corporation along with Israeli company Malat. The U.S. Navy bought the AAI Pioneer UAV that AAI and Malat developed jointly. Many of these UAVs served in the 1991 Gulf War. UAVs demonstrated the possibility of cheaper, more capable fighting [9]machines, [10]deployable without risk to aircrews. Initial generations primarily involved [11]surveillance aircraft, but some carried [12]armaments, such as the General Atomics MQ-1 Predator, that launched AGM-114 Hellfireair-to-ground missiles.

UAVs are often preferred for missions that are too dull, dirty or dangerous for humans. They originated mostly in military applications, although their use is expanding in commercial, scientific, recreational and other applications, such as [13]policing and surveillance, aerial

Vocabulary

8. echelon [ˈɛʃələn]
   梯次編隊、階層 (n)

9. Mach [mɑk]
   馬赫（速度的單位：音速的倍數）(n)

10. deploy [dɪˈplɔɪ]
    部署、展開 (n)(v)；
    deployable 可部署的 (adj)

11. surveillance [sɚˈveləns]
    監視 (n)

12. armament [ˈɑrməmənt]
    武器、軍事力量 (n)

13. police [pəˈlis]
    警察 (n)；保衛、監視 (v)

14. decoy [dɪˋkɔɪ]
誘餌 (n)；引誘、誘騙 (v)

15. gunnery [ˋgʌnərɪ]
炮術；射擊 (n)

16. reconnaissance [rɪˋkɑnəsəns]
偵察 (n)

17. logistics [loˋdʒɪstɪks]
運籌學、後勤 (n)

18. tactical [ˋtæktɪk!]
戰術的 (adj)

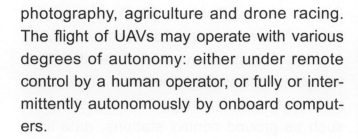

photography, agriculture and drone racing. The flight of UAVs may operate with various degrees of autonomy: either under remote control by a human operator, or fully or intermittently autonomously by onboard computers.

UAVs typically fall into one of six functional categories:

- Target and [14]decoy—providing ground and aerial [15]gunnery a target that simulates an enemy aircraft or missile
- [16]Reconnaissance—providing battlefield intelligence
- Combat—providing attack capability for high-risk missions
- [17]Logistics—delivering cargo
- Research and development—improve UAV technologies
- Civil and commercial UAVs—agriculture, aerial photography, data collection

The U.S. Military UAV tier system is used by military planners to designate the various individual aircraft elements in an overall usage plan.Vehicles can be categorized in terms of range/altitude. The following classifications have been adopted:

- Hand-held 2,000 ft (600 m) altitude, about 2 km range
- Close 5,000 ft (1,500 m) altitude, up to 10 km range
- NATO type 10,000 ft (3,000 m) altitude, up to 50 km range
- [18]Tactical 18,000 ft (5,500 m) altitude, about 160 km range

- MALE (medium altitude, long endurance) up to 30,000 ft (9,000 m) and range over 200 km
- High-Altitude Long Endurance (high altitude, long endurance - HALE) over 30,000 ft (9,100 m) and indefinite range
- Supersonic (Mach 1–5) or [19]hypersonic (Mach 5+) 50,000 ft (15,200 m) or [20]suborbital altitude, range over 200 km
- Low earth orbit (Mach 25+)
- Lunar Earth-Moon transfer

Other categories include:

- [21]Hobbyist UAVs - which can be further divided into:
  * Read-to-fly (RTF)/Commercial-off-the-shelf (COTS)
  * Bind-and-fly (BNF) - that require minimum knowledge to fly the platform
  * Almost-ready-to-fly (ARF)/Do-it-yourself (DIY) - that require significant knowledge to get in the air.
- Midsize military and commercial drones
- Large military-specific drones
- [22]Stealth combat drones

Classifications according to aircraft weight are quite simpler:

- Micro Air Vehicle (MAV) - the smallest UAVs that has a weight of less than 1g.
- Miniature UAV - approximately less than 25 kg.
- Heavier UAVs– have a weight of more than 25 kg.

Vocabulary

19. hypersonic [haɪpəˈsɑnɪk]
    超高音速的（5 到 10 倍音速的）(adj)

20. suborbital [sʌbˈɔrbɪtl]
    次軌道的（地球）(adj)

21. Hobbyist [ˈhɑbɪɪst]
    愛好者、玩家 (n)

22. stealth [stɛlθ]
    秘密行動、鬼鬼祟祟的動作 (n)

History

Shenzhen DJI Sciences and Technologies Ltd was founded in 2006 by Frank Wang. Frank enrolled in the Hong Kong University of Science and Technology in 2003. He built the first prototypes of DJI's projects in his dorm room, selling the flight control components to universities and Chinese electric companies. Using the proceeds, he founded DJI in Shenzhen in 2006. The company struggled at first, with a high degree of churn among employees that has been attributed to Wang's abrasive personality and his perfectionist expectations on his employees. In 2013, DJI released the first model of the Phantom drone, an entry-level drone which was significantly more user-friendly than any other drone on the market at the time. In 2015, DJI eclipsed the success of the Phantom with the release of the Phantom 3, whose even greater popularity was probably due to the introducing of a built in live-streaming camera. In addition to the Phantom, DJI is selling drones of the Inspire, Mavic, Matrice, and Spark series. The Mavic series drones have a foldable design that allow drones to be transported more easily. The Mavic Air is marketed as a smartphone-sized drone that can fit in a jacket pocket. DJI is now the largest consumer drone supplier in the world. DJI products are widely used by U.S. military, police, and fire departments. In January 2020, the United States Department of the Interior announced that it would be grounding around 800 DJI drones which had been using for wildlife conservation and infrastructure monitoring purposes. As of March 2020, DJI holds nearly 77% of the US market share for consumer drones, with no other company holding more than 4%.

1. aircraft (n) 飛機、航空器

   airborne (adj) 空運的、空降的、空中傳播的

   airfare (n) 飛機票價

   airtight (adj) 密閉的、不透氣的

   (1) Unmanned aircrafts are widely used in commercial aerial photography.

   無人飛行器廣泛地被用在商業的航空攝影上。

   (2) Airborne particles can also be changed in size and shape by coagulation with each other.

   空飄顆粒的大小與形狀也可能經由與其他粒子凝結而改變。

   (3) The travel agency has stopped the airfare quote service temporarily due to the heavy fluctuation of the market.

   由於市場的巨幅波動,旅行社已停止機票的報價服務。

   (4) The airfare is not included in the price.

   價格不含機票。

   (5) Airtight containers are been used for drug storage.

   密閉性的容器被使用於藥品儲存。

2. aerial (adj) 航空的、飛機的 (n)天線

   aero- 空氣的

   aerosol (n) 空氣中的懸浮物、噴霧、氣溶膠

   aerospace 航天空間(地球大氣層外空間)、航空工業

   (1) Unmanned aerial vehicles are widely used in national park surveillance.

   無人機已廣泛地用於國家公園的監控。

   (2) The generation of aerosols in polluted atmospheres has been investigated in several experiments.

   受污染大氣中之懸浮物已在多項實驗中被調查。

   (3) Aerospace manufacturing is a high-technology industry that produces aircraft, guided missiles, space vehicles, aircraft engines, propulsion units, and related parts.

   航太製造業是生產飛機、導向飛彈、天空載具、飛機引擎、推動單元、及相關零組件的高科技產業。

3. autonomy (n) 自主、自治;自治團體

   autonomous (adj) 自主的、自治的、獨立的

   autonomously (adv) 自主地、自治地、獨立地

   (1) In space flight, autonomy can also refer to manned missions that are operating without control by ground controllers.

   在太空飛行,自主是指不經由地面控制站控制之載人任務。

   (2) Autonomy is a property of the relation between two agents. In the case of robotics, it is the relations between the designer and the autonomous robot.

   自主是兩方關係的一種特性,在機器人的情況就是設計師與自主機器人間的關係。

   (3) A UAV may fly autonomously.

   一具UVA可以自主地飛行。

4. recreate (v) 消遣、(獲得)娛樂、再創造

   recreation (n) 娛樂

   recreational (adj) 娛樂的

   (1) One of the management innovations of this company is that all the employees may be recreated in the gymnasium in the flexible hours.

   這家公司的管理創新,是所有員工都可在彈性時間到健身房獲得消遣。

   (2) The design team has recreated a new prototype of the next generation smart phone.

   設計團隊再創造一個新世代智慧型手機的原型。

   (3) The recreational UAVs are becoming more and more popular in commercial market.

   休閒用無人機在商業市場愈來愈受到歡迎。

5. ground (n)地面、基礎、理由；ground (v) 停飛（飛機），擱淺（船舶）

(1) There is no ground for his complaints.

他沒有理由抱怨。

(2) Their ship was grounded.

他們的船擱淺了。

(3) The drones must be landed on a flat ground.

無人機必須降落在平坦的地面上。

(4) The United States Department of the Interior announced that it would be grounding around 800 DJI drones which had been using for wildlife conservation and infrastructure monitoring purposes.

美國內政部宣布，將停飛約800架用於野生動植物保護和基礎設施監測目的的DJI無人機。

(5) In March 2019, the Boeing 737 MAX passenger airliner was grounded worldwide after 346 people died in two crashes.

2019年3月，波音737 MAX客機在兩次墜機事故中造成346人死亡後，在全球範圍內停飛。

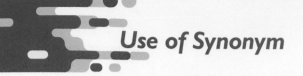

Use of Synonym

1. pilot 當名詞是飛行員或領航員（navigator），當形容詞是實驗的（experimental）、引導的（preliminary, guided或directed），當動詞是引導的、帶領的（direct或lead）。

   (1) This experiment is simply a pilot study of the project.

   這個實驗只是計畫裡的一個先導研究。

   ⇒ This experiment is simply a p_____ study of the project.

   (2) There is no human pilot in a UAV.

   UAV上沒有飛行員。

   (3) We need a pilot to pilot the ship into the harbor.

   需要一名引水人來引導船隻入港。

   ⇒ We need a n_____ to pilot the ship into the harbor.

2. reconnaissance (n) 偵查的意思，可用investigation, inspection, survey代替。

   Initially, UAVs are primarily used in reconnaissance missions in the battlefield.

   最初，UAV主要被使用在戰場偵查任務。

   ⇒ Initially, UAVs are primarily used in i_____ missions in the battlefield.

   ⇒ Initially, UAVs are primarily used in i_____ missions in the battlefield.

   ⇒ Initially, UAVs are primarily used in s_____ missions in the battlefield.

3. dull (adj) 單調的、乏味的（與boring, tedious, monotonous同義）；模糊不清的、灰暗的（與dingy同義）。

   UAVs are often preferred for missions that are too dull, dirty or dangerous for humans.

   ⇒ UAVs are often preferred for missions that are too b_____, dirty or dangerous for humans.

   ⇒ UAVs are often preferred for missions that are too m_____, dirty or dangerous for humans.

   ⇒ UAVs are often preferred for missions that are too t_____, dirty or dangerous for humans.

Choose the most appropriate one in the following questions

(   ) 1. A UAV can carry a lethal payload. Lethal payload in this sentence means _____.

A. weapons or bombs

B. chemicals

C. cargos

D. soldiers

(   ) 2. A UAV can fly autonomously or be _____ remotely.

A. pilot

B. piloted

C. piloting

D. pilots

(   ) 3. A stealth combat drone is a UAV for _____.

A. commercial photographing service

B. military defensing action

C. landscape surveillance

D. agricultural spraying

(   ) 4. The term dronewas coined in reference to the resemblance of old military unmanned aircraft to _____.

A. male hummingbird

B. malefly

C. male butterfly

D. male bee

(   ) 5. Missiles are not considered UAVs because the vehicle itself is a weapon that is not _____.

A. reused

B. deployable

C. expandable

D. recreational

(   )   6.   Some UAVs are used as a target which provides ground and aerial gun-nery a target that simulates _____.

     A. a commercial carrier

     B. an enemy aircraft or missile

     C. a racing aircraft

     D. a flying video camera

(   )   7.   Indefinite range for a UAV means a UAV may fly _____.

     A. a short range

     B. no more than 5 km

     C. no more than 10 km

     D. very long range

(   )   8.   A miniature UAV is one that is _____.

     A. less than 1 g

     B. less than 1 kg

     C. less than 10 kg

     D. less than 25 kg

(   )   9.   A micro air vehicle (MAV) is a UAV that has a weight _____.

     A. more than 1 kg

     B. less than 1g

     C. less than 1 kg

     D. less than 1 lbs

(   )   10.   Amazon Prime Air is a future service that will deliver packages up to five pounds in 30 minutes or less using small _____.

     A. boats

     B. cars

     C. drones

     D. miniature

Accelerometer & Gyroscope

Questions & Discussions

1. What is an accelerometer? What functions does it provide in a game controller?
2. What is the main difference between an accelerometer and a gyroscope?

Vocabulary

1. gyroscope [ˈdʒaɪrəˌskop]
   陀螺儀或迴轉儀 (n)

2. accelerometer [ækˌsɛləˈramɪtɚ]
   加速度計 (n)

3. inertial [ɪnˈɝʃəl]
   慣性的 (adj)

4. axis [ˈæksɪs]
   軸 (n)；複數為 axes

5. orientation [ˌorɪɛnˈteʃən]
   定位、方位 (n)

6. coordinate [koˈɔrdnet]
   座標 (n)

7. portrait [ˈportret]
   肖像畫 (n)。肖像畫都是以直式呈現，因此 portrait mode 為直式模式

8. landscape [ˈlændˌskep]
   山水畫、風景畫；風景 (n)。風景畫都是以橫式呈現，因此 landscape mode 為橫式模式

9. micromachined [ˈmaɪkroˌməˈʃind]
   精密加工的 (adj)

Accelerometers and [1]gyroscopes are devices widely used in contemporary portable electronic devices such as smartphones and tablet computers. An [2]accelerometer is a device that measures the acceleration of an object. Acceleration is quantified in the unit meters per second per second (m/s^2), or popularly in terms of g-force (g). Highly sensitive accelerometers are components of [3]inertial navigation systems for aircraft and missiles. Single and multi-[4]axis models of accelerometer are available to detect magnitude and direction of acceleration, and can be used to sense [5]orientation, [6]coordinate acceleration, vibration, and shock. Electronic devices use accelerometers to align the screen depending on the direction the device is held, for example switching between [7]portrait and [8]landscape modes. [9]Micromachined accelerometers are increasingly present in video game controllers, to detect the position of the device or provide for game input.

A free-fall sensor is an accelerometer used to detect if a system has been dropped and is falling. It provides safety measures such as parking the head of a hard disk to prevent a head crash and resulting data loss upon [10]impact. This device is included in many common computer and consumer electronic products. It is also used in some [a]data loggers to monitor handling operations for shipping containers. The length of time in free fall is used to calculate the height of drop and to estimate the shock to the package.

A gyroscope is a mechanical device comprised of a [11]rotor and two or more [12]gimbals. The rotor is installed to spin about one axis and this axis is mounted on an inner gimbal. The inner gimbal is spinning about another axis which is mounted on an outer gimbal, or the gyroscope frame. The outer gimbal or the gyroscope frame is mounted so as to pivot about an axis in its own plane determined by the support. The rotor simultaneously spins about one axis and is capable of oscillating about the two other axes, thus, it is free to turn in any direction about the fixed point.

In the 1860s, the advent of electric motors made it possible for developing [13]gyrocompasses. The first functional gyrocompass was [14]patented in 1904. In early 20th century, [15]inventors attempted to use gyroscopes as the basis for early navigational systems. Similar principles were later employed in the development of inertial guidance systems

Vocabulary

16. miniaturize [ˈmɪnɪətʃəˌraɪz]
使小型化 (v)

17. midget [ˈmɪdʒɪt]
侏儒、最小個體 (n)；極小的 (adj)

18. compass [ˈkʌmpəs]
羅盤、指南針 (n)

19. lone [lon]
單獨的 (adj)

20. robust [rəˈbʌst]
強健的 (adj)

Terminology

b. direction- and motion-sensing
方向與運動（位移）感應

for ballistic missiles. During World War II, the gyroscope became the prime component for aircraft. After the war, the race to [16]miniaturize gyroscopes for guided missiles and weapons navigation systems resulted in the development and manufacturing of [17]midget gyroscopes.

In addition to being used in [18]compasses, gyroscopes have been introduced into consumer electronics. Since the gyroscope allows the calculation of orientation and rotation, designers have incorporated them into modern technology. The integration of the gyroscope allows for more accurate recognition of movement within a 3D space than the previous [19]lone accelerometer. Gyroscopes in consumer electronics are frequently combined with accelerometers for more [20]robust [b]direction- and motion-sensing. Examples of smartphone using gyroscopes include the hTC® One series, Samsung® Galaxy series, and iPhone series. Nintendo® has integrated a gyroscope into the Wii Remote controller. The 3DS also uses a gyroscope to detect movement of the player when turning.

1. miniaturize (v) 使小型化

    miniaturization (n) 小型化、微型化

    miniature (n) 縮圖、縮樣、小型物件

    miniature (adj) 小型的、微型的

    (1) Miniaturized accelerometers are increasingly adopted in video game controllers to detect the position of the device.

    小型化的加速度計頻繁被用在電動遊戲控制器上，來偵測裝置位置。

    (2) Miniaturization is important in the design of mobile devices.

    小型化對移動裝置設計是很重要的。

    (3) Miniature rotors are used in gyroscopes so as to sense the rotation of the devices.

    微型轉子被用在陀螺儀裡面，來感應裝置的旋轉。

    (4) Miniaturization of electronic components make it possible to design miniature electronic devices.

    電子零件的微型化，使得設計微型電子裝置變為可能。

2. estimate (v) 估計、預估、估價

    estimated (adj) 被估計的、被預估的

    estimative (adj) 估計的

    estimation (n) 估計、預估、估價

    estimator (n) 估價者、鑑價者

    (1) The marketing division estimates that the annual demand of this device will be more than 50 million.

    市場行銷部門預估這個裝置的年需求將超過五千萬台。

    (2) The estimated annual demand of this device is more than 50 million.

    An estimation of the annual demand of this device is more than 50 million.

    這個裝置的預估年需求超過五千萬台。

3. rotate (v) 旋轉、輪調

    rotation (n) 旋轉、輪調

    rotational (adj) 旋轉、輪流的

(1) When you rotate your smart phone, the image will be changed from a portrait to a landscape one.

當你旋轉手機時，影像會從直式變為橫式。

(2) A gyroscope is a used to detect the rotation of the device.

陀螺儀是用來偵測裝置的旋轉。

(3) Job rotation is implemented every six months for all the first line workers.

所有第一線工人每六個月要進行一次工作輪調。

4. machine (n) 機械
   mechanics (n) 力學
   mechanical (adj) 機械的
   mechanist (n) 機械技師
   mechanism (n) 機構、機制
   mechanize (v) 機械化
   mechanization (n) 機械化

(1) The mechanist is studying the mechanics of the structure of this device.

機械技師在研究這個裝置結構的力學（行為）。

(2) The mechanical engineering division has recruited a mechanism engineer to handle the mechanization of the system.

機械工程部門招募了一名機構工程師，來負責系統的機械化工作。

(3) A local garage is recruiting more mechanists.

本地一家修車廠在招募更多的機械技師。

(4) Jason and ten other mechanical engineers are working on the research and design of the mechanism of this new product.

Jason與其他十名機械工程師在做新產品的機構研發與設計。

(5) Lubrication is required for all the rotational mechanism so as to reduce the friction.

所有旋轉的機構都需要潤滑來減少摩擦。

(6) Mechanization is the most commonly adopted approach to reduce the need of manpower on worksite.

機械化是最常用來減少工作現場人力需求的方式。

1. impact（衝擊）有兩種解釋，第一種衝擊是影響的意思，採用這個解釋時可用influence取代；第二種衝擊是物體衝撞的動作，用這個解釋時可用crash、collision替代。

   (1) This theory has great impact on the developing of contemporary bio-chemistry.

   這個理論對於當代的生物化學發展有很大衝擊（影響）。

   ⇒ This theory has great i＿＿＿＿＿＿ on the developing of contemporary biochemistry.

   (2) How does the impact of an automobile on a barricade affect the safety of the driver is an important research issue.

   一輛汽車撞擊障礙物會如何影響駕駛的安全是個重要的研究議題。

   ⇒ How does the c＿＿＿＿＿＿ of an automobile on a barricade affect the safety of the driver is an important research issue.

   ⇒ How does the c＿＿＿＿＿＿ of an automobile on a barricade affect the safety of the driver is an important research issue.

   (3) It provides safety measures such as parking the head of a hard disk to prevent a head crash and resulting data loss upon impact.

   它提供了諸如硬碟讀寫頭停駐以避免撞擊時，讀寫頭損毀而造成資料損失這方面的安全度量。

   ⇒ It provides safety measures such as parking the head of a hard disk to prevent a head crash and resulting data loss upon c＿＿＿＿＿＿.

   ★此句中已用了crash，若之後又用這個字感覺會有點彆腳。

2. pivot（以……為中心而旋轉）為動詞時，與spin同義；turn（轉），包括轉彎、旋轉等均可使用。

   (1) The outer gimbal is mounted so as to pivot about an axis in its own plane.

   外部的平衡環，是安裝來對其本身平面上的一個軸來旋轉。

   ⇒ The outer gimbal is mounted so as to s＿＿＿＿＿＿ about an axis in its own plane.

   (2) It is free to turn in any direction about the fixed point.

   它可對任何固定點在任何方向旋轉。

   ⇒ It is free to s＿＿＿＿＿＿ in any direction about the fixed point.

3. attempt（嘗試）可用try取代。

Inventors attempted to use gyroscopes as the basis for early navigational systems.

發明家嘗試使用陀螺儀作為早期導航系統的基礎。

⇒ Inventors t_____ to use gyroscopes as the basis for early navigational systems.

4. miniaturize（使物體變得更小）可用make...... smaller取代，此為較通俗的說法。

The race to miniaturize gyroscopes for guided missiles and weapons navigation systems resulted in the development and manufacturing of midget gyroscopes.

將用在導向飛彈與武器導航系統上的陀螺儀做得更小的競賽導致了微型陀螺儀的開發與製造。

⇒ The race to m_____ gyroscopes s_____ for guided missiles and weapons navigation systems resulted in the development and manufacturing of midget gyroscopes.

Choose the most appropriate one in the following questions

(   ) 1. An accelerometer is a device to measure _____.

    A. acceleration

    B. velocity

    C. force

    D. gravity

    E. rotation

(   ) 2. Acceleration is quantified in the unit _____.

    A. meters per second

    B. miles per hour

    C. in terms of g-force

    D. degree per second

(   ) 3. A gyroscope is a device to sense _____.

    A. acceleration

    B. velocity

    C. force

    D. gravity

    E. rotation

(   ) 4. A free-fall sensor is _____.

    A. a gyroscope

    B. an accelerometer

    C. a compass

    D. a radiator

    E. a gimbal

(   ) 5. The 3DS uses a gyroscope to _____.

    A. measure the velocity

    B. monitor the acceleration

    C. detect movement of the player when turning

    D. sense the force feedback

(   ) 6. Electronic devices use accelerometers to align the screen depending on the _____ the device is held.

    A. direction

    B. velocity

    C. pattern

    D. acceleration

(   ) 7. After the war, the race to _____ gyroscopes for guided missiles and weapon navigation systems resulted in the development of midget gyroscopes.

    A. miniature

    B. miniaturize

    C. miniaturized

    D. miniaturization

(   ) 8. _____ accelerometers are increasingly present in video game controllers to detect the position of the device.

    A. Mechanization

    B. Micromachined

    C. Micromechanism

    D. Mechanist

(   ) 9. _____ mode is commonly used when people are watching videos on a smart phone.

    A. portrait

    B. landscape

    C. free-fall

    D. inertial

(   ) 10. The length of time in free fall is used to calculate the height of drop and to estimate the _____ to the package.

    A. robust

    B. axis

    C. midget

    D. shock

Knowledge Management

Questions & Discussions

1. What is the definition of knowledge management?
2. Discuss the types of knowledge.

1. signify [ˈsɪgnə,faɪ]
   象徵、預示 (v)

2. strategically [strəˈtidʒɪklɪ]
   策略性地 (adv)

3. competence [ˈkampətəns]
   資格、能力、財產 (n)

4. asset [ˈæsɛt]
   資產 (n)

5. expertise [ɛkspəˈtiz]
   專業技術 (n)

6. revalidate [rɪˈvælə,det]
   再確認 (v)

7. tacit [ˈtæsɪt]
   無言的、緘默的 (adj)

8. explicit [ɪkˈsplɪsɪt]
   明確的 (adj)

The emergence of the knowledge economy [1]signifies that organizations' know-how is becoming more important than the sources of traditional economy. Moreover, knowledge is now regarded as the most [2]strategically important resource and learning the most strategically important [3]competence for business sectors. Thus, knowledge [4]assets must be managed carefully, systematically and with [5]expertise to guarantee company survival.

Knowledge management is defined as the process of persistently managing knowledge of all kinds to meet existing and emerging needs, to ascertain and utilize existing and acquired knowledge assets and to develop new opportunity. It may also be defined as the identification, optimization and active management of intellectual assets to create value, increase productivity and achieve and maintain competitive advantage. Knowledge management involves the sharing of knowledge and some processes. In 2002, Tiwana has identified these processes as find, create new, package and assemble, apply, reuse and [6]revalidate knowledge.

There are two types of knowledge: [7a]tacit knowledge and [8b]explicit knowledge. Tacit knowledge is highly personal, developed from experience, and hard to document. It is, therefore, difficult to communi-cate and [c]share. Explicit knowledge, on the other hand, is formal and systematic. Most of ex-plicit knowledge may be documented. All the knowledge published in books, manuals or on a web-site is explicit knowledge. This knowl-edge is easy to communicate and share. The traditional education and training program has been focused on the communication of the existing explicit knowledge or introduc-ing "what we know, we know." Sharing and management of tacit knowledge or "what we know, we do not know" is, on the other hand, extremely inadequate.

Many large companies have established a point of responsibility for knowledge manage-ment within the organization, and have made resources [9]accessible in terms of budget, staff, and IT [10]infra-structure. Whether those resources are adequate or not is difficult to evaluate. Different companies have different needs and different priorities; hence, [11]blan-ket proposals on knowledge management expenses are impractical. An organization needs to develop an implementation plan that covers both the short- and long-term needs.

Vocabulary

9. accessible [æk'sɛsəbl̩, ək⁻]
   可取得的 (adj)
10. infra [ˈɪnfrə]
    基礎的、基層的 (adj)
11. blanket [ˈblæŋkɪt]
    總括的、包裹的 (adj)

Terminology

c. share
   分享、分擔；也可為一股（股票的基本單位）

Source:

1. Carrillo, P., Robinson, H., Al-Ghassani, A., Anumba, B. (2004), Knowledge management in UK construction: strategies, resources and barriers, Project Management Journal, 35(1), 46-56.
2. Nonaka, I. (1991), The knowledge creating company, Harvard Business Review, Nov-Dec, 96-104.
3. Quintas, P., Lefrere, P., Jones, G. (1997), Knowledge management: A strategic agenda, Long Range Planning, 30(3), 385-391.
4. Tiwana, A.(2002), The knowledge management toolkit (2ⁿᵈ ed), Upper Saddle River, NJ: Prentice Hall.
5. Webb, S. P. (1998), Knowledge management: Linchpin of change, London, The Association of Information Management.

Families of Vocabulary

1. document (v) 提供文件
   documentary (adj) 文件的
   documentarily (adv) 文件的
   document (n) 文件
   documentation (n) 文件化

   (1) The documentation of the manufacturing process is very important in management.
       製造過程的文件化對管理是很重要的。

   (2) The manufacturing process must be documented.
       製造過程必須被製做成文件。

2. know (v) 知道
   knowledge (n) 知識
   This paper has expanded our knowledge on the characteristics of this composite material.
   這篇論文擴增了我們在這種複合材料特性方面的知識。

3. identify (v) 指出、識別
   identified (adj) 被識出的 ⟷ unidentified (adj) 未被識出的
   identifiable (adj) 可被識出的 ⟷ unidentifiable (adj) 不可被識出的
   identical (adj) 相同的
   identically (adv) 相同的
   identification (n) 識別（常用ID代表縮寫）
   identity (n) 身分、本體

   (1) The scientists could not identify the elements in this recipe.
       科學家們無法指出這個配方裡的元素。

   (2) The elements in this recipe are unidentifiable.
       這個配方裡的元素是無法被識出的。

   (3) Please show me your ID.
       請拿出你的身分證明。

   (4) The two recipes are identical.
       這兩種配方是相同的。

4. implement (v) 執行

implemented (adj) 被執行的

implementation (n) 執行

(1) The new regulations will be implemented.

新的規則將會被實施。

(2) The implementation of these regulations will be evaluated.

這些新規則的實施將會被評估。

5. manage (v) 管理

managed (adj) 被管理的

manageable (adj) 可管理的   ⟷   unmanageable (adj) 不可管理的

manageability (n) 可管理性

management (n) 管理

manager (n) 管理者

(1) Managers are hired to manage the operation of the business.

經理們被雇用來管理商業的營運。

(2) The external reviewer found that the management of this organization is awful. The operation seems to be unmanageable.

外部審查專家發現這個機構的管理很糟糕，它的營運似乎是無法管理的。

6. produce (v) 生產

producible (adj) 可生產的   ⟷   unproducible (adj) 不可生產的

productive (adj) 有生產力的   ⟷   unproductive (adj) 沒有生產力的

product (n) 產品

productivity (n) 生產力

(1) This division is very productive.

這個部門非常有生產力。

(2) The productivity of this division is very high.

這個部門的生產力非常高。

(3) Such a design is not producible.

像這樣的設計是無法被生產的。

7. strategy (n) 策略

strategical (adj) 策略的

strategically (adv) 策略的

(1) Strategy management is the responsibility of the top management.

策略管理是管理高層的責任。

(2) The company has acquired all the patents from another company strategically.

這家公司策略性的獲取另一家公司之全部專利。

1. persistently（持續的）可用 continuously, constantly, uninterruptedly 取代。

Knowledge management is defined as the process of persistently managing knowledge of all kinds to meet existing and emerging needs.

知識管理被定義為持續管理各種知識，以滿足現存與突然產生之需求過程。

⇒ Knowledge management is defined as the process of <u>c</u>_____ managing knowledge of all kinds to meet existing and emerging needs.

⇒ Knowledge management is defined as the process of <u>c</u>_____ managing knowledge of all kinds to meet existing and emerging needs.

⇒ Knowledge management is defined as the process of <u>u</u>_____ managing knowledge of all kinds to meet existing and emerging needs.

2. ascertain（確定、發現）可用 find out, discover 取代。

Knowledge management is defined as the process of persistently managing knowledge of all kinds to ascertain and utilize existing and acquired knowledge assets.

知識管理定義為持續管理各種知識，並確認與利用現有與新取得的知識資產之過程。

⇒ Knowledge management is defined as the process of persistently managing knowledge of all kinds to <u>f</u>_____ and utilize existing and acquired knowledge assets.

⇒ Knowledge management is defined as the process of persistently managing knowledge of all kinds to <u>d</u>_____ and utilize existing and acquired knowledge assets.

3. traditional（傳統的）可用 conventional 取代。

The traditional education and training program has been focused on the communication of the existing explicit knowledge.

傳統的教育訓練課程規劃，都專注於現存顯性知識的傳播上。

⇒ The <u>c</u>_____ education and training program has been focused on the communication of the existing explicit knowledge.

4. focus（集中）可用concentrate, center 取代。

The traditional education and training program has been focused on the communication of the existing explicit knowledge.

傳統的教育訓練課程規劃都專注於現存顯性知識的傳播上。

⇒ The traditional education and training program has been c_____ on the communication of the existing explicit knowledge.

⇒ The traditional education and training program has been c_____ on the communication of the existing explicit knowledge.

5. regard（認為、視為）可用 consider, esteem 取代。

Knowledge is regarded as the most strategically important resource and learning the most strategically important competence for business sectors.

知識被視為策略上最重要的資源，而學習則是企業策略上最重要的競爭力。

⇒ Knowledge is c_____ the most strategically important resource and learning the most strategically important competence for business sectors.

⇒ Knowledge is e_____ the most strategically important resource and learning the most strategically important competence for business sectors.

6. accessible（可擷取的、可取用的）可用 available, obtainable, reachable 取代。

Many large companies have made resources accessible in terms of budget, staff, and IT infra-structure.

許多大公司都以預算、人力、及資訊技術等方式提供可供擷取的資源。

⇒ Many large companies have made resources a_____ in terms of budget, staff, and IT infra-structure.

⇒ Many large companies have made resources o_____ in terms of budget, staff, and IT infra-structure.

⇒ Many large companies have made resources r_____ in terms of budget, staff, and IT infra-structure.

7. adequate（足夠的、恰當的）可用enough, sufficient 取代。

Whether those resources are adequate or not is difficult to evaluate.

這些資源是否足夠是很難評估。

⇒ Whether those resources are e_____ or not is difficult to evaluate.

⇒ Whether those resources are s_____ or not is difficult to evaluate.

(   )   1.   Tiwana pointed out that knowledge management involves some processes in the followings except _____.

      A. find new knowledge

      B. package knowledge

      C. apply knowledge

      D. revalidate knowledge

      E. patent knowledge

(   )   2.   Which one is not the difference between tacit and explicit knowledge?

      A. The former is highly personal while the latter is not.

      B. The former is developed from experience while the latter is not.

      C. The former is hard to document while the latter is not.

      D. The former is difficult to communicate and share.

      E. The training program of the former is easy to administer.

(   )   3.   Which term is not one of the resources that many large companies have made accessible in knowledge management?

      A. budget

      B. staff

      C. subcontracting

      D. IT infra-structure

(   )   4.   Which one in the followings may be a synonym of explicit knowledge?

      A. What we know, we know.

      B. What we know, we do not know.

      C. What we do not know, we know.

      D. What we do not know, we do not know.

(   )   5.   Which one in the followings is not regarded as explicit knowledge?

      A. knowledge in books

      B. procedures in manuals

      C. information on a web-site

      D. methods on a handout

      E. someone's experience

(   ) 6. Sharing and management of tacit knowledge is, on the other hand, extremely _____.

    A. unadequate

    B. inadequate

    C. imadequate

    D. disadequate

    E. iladequate

(   ) 7. Inadequate means _____.

    A. inappropriate

    B. impossible

    C. not enough

    D. not proper

    E. enough

(   ) 8. Knowledge _____ must be managed carefully, systematically and
with expertise.

    A. assets

    B. business

    C. product

    D. systems

    E. validation

(   ) 9. Tacit knowledge is _____.

    A. easy to teach

    B. easy to share

    C. easy to communicate

    D. easy to document

    E. highly personal

(   ) 10. Blanket proposals on knowledge management are _____.

    A. impossible

    B. impractical

    C. inconvenient

    D. independent

What are Trademarks?

Questions & Discussions

1. What is the difference between a trademark and a service mark?
2. What are the advantages of owning a registered trademark?

Vocabulary

1. servicemark [ˈsɝvɪsˌmɑrk]
   服務標章 (n)

2. confusingly [kənˈfjuzɪŋlɪ]
   混淆的 (adv)

3. trademark [ˈtredˌmɑrk]
   商品標章 (n)

4. designation [ˌdɛzɪgˈneʃən]
   名稱 (n)

5. federal [ˈfɛdərəl]
   聯邦的 (adj)

Terminology

a. United States Patent and Trademark Office
   (USPTO) 美國專利與商標事務局

A trademark is a word, name, symbol or device which is used in trade with goods to indicate the source of the goods and to distinguish them from the goods of others. A [1]servicemark is the same as the trademark except that it identifies and distinguishes the source of a service rather than a product. The term "mark" is commonly used to refer to both trademarks and servicemarks.

Trademark rights may be used to prevent others from using a [2]confusingly similar mark, but not to prevent others from producing the same goods or from selling the same goods or services under a clearly different mark. [3]Trademarks which are used in interstates or foreign commerce may be registered with the [a]United States Patent and Trademark Office (USPTO).

Any time people claim rights in a mark, they may use the **"TM"** (trademark) or **"SM"** (servicemark) [4]designation to alert the public to their claim, regardless of whether they have filed an application with the USPTO. However, they may use the [5]federal registration symbol "®" only after the USPTO actually registers a mark, and not while an application is [6]pending. Also, they may use the registration symbol with the mark only on or in connection with the goods and/or services listed in the federal trademark registration.

Owning a federal mark registration provides a number of advantages such as:

- a notice to the public of the [7]registrant's claim of ownership of the mark;

- a legal [8]presumption of the registrant's ownership of the mark and the registrant's [9]exclusive right to use the mark nationwide on or in connection with the goods and/or services listed in the registration;

- the ability to bring an action concerning the mark in federal court;

- the use of US registration as a basis to obtain registration in foreign countries; and

- the ability to file the US registration with the [b]US Customs Service to prevent importation of [10][c]infringing foreign goods.

The United States Patent and Trademark Office reviews trademark applications for federal registration and determines whether an application meets the requirements for federal registration. USPTO does not determine whether one has the right to use a mark. People may use any mark adopted to identify the source of their goods and/or services even without a registration. Once a registration issues, it is up to the owner of a mark to [11]enforce his/her rights in the mark based on ownership of a federal registration.

Source:
United States Patent and Trademark Office.

Vocabulary

6. pending [ˈpɛndɪŋ]
懸而未決的、審理中的 (adj)

7. registrant [ˈrɛdʒɪstrənt]
註冊者 (n)

8. presumption [prɪˈzʌmpʃən]
推定 (n)

9. exclusive [ɪkˈsklusɪv]
特有的、排他的 (adj)

10. infringe [ɪnˈfrɪndʒ]
侵害 (v)

11. enforce [ɪnˈfɔrs, ˈfors]
強制執行 (v)

Terminology

b. US Customs Service
美國海關

c. infringing foreign goods
侵權外國商品

Families of Vocabulary

1. apply (v) 申請、應用

   applied (adj) 已申請的、被應用的

   applicable (adj) 可應用的

   applicably (adv) 可應用的

   applicability (n) 可應用性

   application (n) 申請、應用

   applicant (n) 申請者

   appliance (n) 用品、裝置

   (1) This technology has been applied in manufacturing laptop computers.

   這個技術曾被應用在製造膝上型電腦（即筆電）。

   (2) This technology is not applicable.

   這個技術是不太可應用的。

   (3) The applicability of this technology is low.

   這個技術的可應用性很低。

2. confuse (v) 使困惑

   confused (adj) 困惑的

   confusedly (adv) 困惑地

   confusing (adj) 令人困惑的

   confusingly (adv) 令人困惑的

   confusion (n) 困惑、混亂

   The scientists are confused with the outcomes of this experiment.

   科學家們對這個實驗的結果感到困惑。

3. own (v) 擁有

   owner (n) 擁有人

   ownership (n) 擁有、擁有權

4. prevent (v) 防止

preventive (adj) 預防性的

preventable (adj) 可預防的　　⟷　　unpreventable (adj) 不可預防的

prevention (n) 防止

(1) Preventive medicine is one of the focuses of this school.

這個學校的重點之一是預防性醫學。

(2) Such a disaster is preventable.

像這樣的災難是可預防的。

(3) We need to prevent the occurrence of such a disaster.

我們必須預防像這樣的災難發生。

(4) Prevention of such a disaster is important.

像這樣的災難預防是很重要的。

5. register (v) 註冊

registered (adj) 已註冊的

registrable (adj) 可登記的、可註冊的

registrant (n) 註冊者

registration (n) 註冊

(1) The mark of iPad has been registered by others many years ago.

iPad的標章很多年前就被別人註冊了。

(2) All the authors must pay registration fee before the due date so as to attend the conference.

所有作者都必須在期限前支付註冊費，以參加這個會議。

(3) All the registrants will receive a ticket to attend the banquet on the evening.

所有註冊者都會收到一張票，以參加晚宴。

1. source（來源）可用 origin 取代，本文中的 source 是指製造商或供應商，因此也可用 manufacturer 或 supplier 取代。

A trademark is a word, name, symbol or device which is used to indicate the source of the goods and to distinguish them from the goods of others.

商品標章是在商品交易時，用來指明貨物來源以便與其他貨品有所區分的字、名稱、符號或圖案。

⇒ A trademark is a word, name, symbol or device which is used to indicate the o_____ of the goods and to distinguish them from the goods of others.

⇒ A trademark is a word, name, symbol or device which is used to indicate the m_____ of the goods and to distinguish them from the goods of others.

⇒ A trademark is a word, name, symbol or device which is used to indicate the s_____ of the goods and to distinguish them from the goods of others.

2. distinguish（區分）可用 characterize, differentiate, discriminate 取代。

A company needs to register a trademark so as to distinguish its goods from those of other companies.

一家公司必須註冊一個商標，來區分它的貨品與其他公司的（貨品）。

⇒ A company needs to register a trademark so as to c_____ its goods from those of other companies.

⇒ A company needs to register a trademark so as to d_____ its goods from those of other companies.

⇒ A company needs to register a trademark so as to d_____ its goods from those of other companies.

3. goods（商品）可用commodity, merchandise取代。

They may use the registration symbol with the mark only on or in connection with the goods and/or services listed in the federal trademark registration.

他們僅能在聯邦商標註冊列舉之商品與服務有關處使用註冊符號與標章。

⇒ They may use the registration symbol with the mark only on or in connection with the c_____ and/or services listed in the federal trademark registration.

⇒ They may use the registration symbol with the mark only on or in connection with the m_____ and/or services listed in the federal trademark registration.

4. advantage（好處）可用 benefit 取代。

Owning a federal mark registration provides a number of advantages.

擁有聯邦註冊標章有許多好處。

⇒ Owning a federal mark registration provides a number of b_____.

Choose the most appropriate one in the following questions

(   ) 1.   Which agency will accept trademark registration?

         A. United States Patent and Trademark Office

         B. Copyright Office of the Library of Congress

         C. Department of Commerce

         D. Governmental Documentation Bureau

         E. Media Administration Bureau

(   ) 2.   A trademark right owner may enforce his/her right in the following affairs except:

         A. prevent others from producing the same goods under a clearly different mark.

         B. prevent others from selling the same services under his/her mark.

         C. prevent others from producing the same goods under his/her mark.

         D. prevent others from selling the same goods under his/her mark.

         E. determine whether one has the right to use the mark.

(   ) 3.   The symbol "®" may be used only after the trademark has been _____.

         A. filed in Copyright Office of the Library of Congress

         B. filed in the United States Patent and Trademark Office

         C. adopted by the manufacturer

         D. registered in Copyright Office of the Library of Congress

         E. registered in the United States Patent and Trademark Office

(   ) 4.   The symbol "TM" may be used _____.

         A. only after the trademark has been filed in the USPTO

         B. only after the trademark has been filed in the Library of Congress

         C. only after the trademark has been registered in the USPTO

         D. only after the trademark has been registered in the Library of Congress

         E. regardless of whether they have filed an application with the USPTO

(   ) 5. Which one in the followings is correct?

A. People may use any mark to identify the source of their goods even the mark has been registered by others.

B. People may use any mark to identify the source of their goods so long as the mark has not been registered by others.

C. People may not use a mark to identify the source of their goods without the registration with USPTO.

D. People may not use a mark to identify the source of their service without filing with USPTO.

E. People may use any mark to identify the source of their goods.

(   ) 6. The owner of a trademark has the ability to file registration with the US Customs Service to prevent importation of _____ foreign goods.

A. refreging

B. infringed

C. infringing

D. refriged

E. infragament

(   ) 7. Which agency has the ability to file the US registration with the US Customs Service to prevent importation of infringing foreign goods?

A. US Costal Guard

B. US Navy

C. US Custom Service

D. US Postal Service

(   ) 8. The USPTO does not _____.

A. determine who has the right to use a trademark

B. accept application for a trademark

C. review trademark applications

D. open on Monday

(   ) 9. In this article, "good" means _____.

        A. business

        B. nice

        C. fine

        D. appropriate

        E. merchandises

(   ) 10. Which one in the following is not one of the benefits a trademark owner has in the USA?

        A. The ability to bring an action concerning the mark in federal court.

        B. A notice to the public of the registrant's claim of ownership of the mark.

        C. The ability to file the US registration with the US Customs Service to prevent importation of infringing foreign goods.

        D. The ability to arrest the people who use their own trademark.

What is Copyright?

Questions & Discussions

1. Under what conditions do you need to obtain permission from the owner of copyrighted work?
2. Are data protected by copyright law?

Vocabulary

1. copyright [ˈkɑpɪˌraɪt]
   著作權 (n)；宣告著作權 (v)

2. authorship [ˈɔθɚˌʃɪp]
   著作具名 (n)

3. literary [ˈlɪtəˌrɛrɪ]
   文藝的 (adj)

4. unpublished [ʌnˈpʌblɪʃt]
   未出版的 (adj)

5. act [ækt]
   法案 (n)

6. phonorecord [ˈfonoˌrəkəd]
   聲音記錄；唱片 (n)

Terminology

a. copyrighted work
   受著作權保護之作品

b. derivative works
   衍生作品，例如小說與電影的續集

[1]Copyright is a form of protection provided to the author of original works of [2]authorship including [3]literary, dramatic, musical, artistic, and certain intellectual works, both published and [4]unpublished. The US 1976 Copyright [5]Act generally gives the owner of copyright the exclusive right to reproduce the [a]copyrighted work, to prepare [b]derivative works, to distribute copies or [6]phonorecords of the copyrighted work, to perform the copyrighted work publicly, or to display the copyrighted work publicly. Copyrights in the USA are registered by the Copyright Office of the Library of Congress and may be claimed using "Copyright © year" on the work.

The copyright protects the form of expression rather than the subject matter of the writing. For example, a description of a machine could be copyrighted, but this would only prevent others from copying the description; it would not prevent others from writing a description of their own or from making and using the machine. Data itself can not be copyrighted either, only the format in which it is published. A table containing specific data could be copyrighted, but this would not prevent others from describing those data using a figure.

If one is interested in writing something based on others' works, it is his/her responsibility to obtain all necessary permissions for copyrighted material. Permission must be obtained from the original copyright holder, usually the [7]publisher. Some publishers may require that he/she obtains the original author's permission as a courtesy. If the permission request is denied, the author has three options: (1) significantly alter or redraw the material so that permission is no longer required, (2) find suitable substitute material, or (3) remove the material from his/her work.

Once permission is approved, the author should put [c]source lines (or credit lines) in the manuscript as required by the copyright holder. Insert the source lines where appropriate: beneath a table, following figure [8]captions, etc. Figures and tables do not have source lines are assumed to be original work and must be verified as such.

Using copyrighted works needs permission, including:

- any [9]passage from a play, poem, or song
- any [10]quote of 50 words or more from a [11]periodical
- any quote totaling 400 words or more from a book
- any table, diagram, figure or illustration

Vocabulary

7. publisher [ˈpʌblɪʃɚ]
   出版商 (n)

8. caption [ˈkæpʃən]
   標題 (n)；加上標題 (v)

9. passage [ˈpæsɪdʒ]
   段落 (n)

10. quote [kwot]
    引用 (n)(v)

11. periodical [ˌpɪrɪˈɑdɪkl̩]
    期刊、雜誌或定期出版之刊物 (n)

Terminology

c. source lines
   （資料）來源標示

Vocabulary

12. sponsorship [ˈspɑnsəˌʃɪp]
    贊助 (n)

Terminology

d. government-sponsored
   政府贊（補）助的

Many government materials falls within the public domain, i.e., they are not copyright protected. However, many [d]government-sponsored organizations copyright their own publications, and even though they have government [12]sponsorship, copyright permission must be obtained.

Source:

1. United States Patent and Trademark Office.
2. Permission Guidelines for Authors, UK Ergonomics Society.

1. publish (v) 出版

　　publishable (adj) 可出版的　　⟷　　unpublishable (adj) 不可出版的

　　published (adj) 已出版的　　⟷　　unpublished (adj) 未出版的

　　publication (n) 出版、出版品

　　publisher (n) 出版商、發行人

　(1) You need to find a publisher to publish a book.

　　　你必須找個出版商來出版書籍。

　(2) This article has been published five years ago.

　　　這篇文章五年前就出版了。

　(3) The editor has decided that this article is unpublishable.

　　　The editor has decided that publication of this article is unlikely.

　　　主編決定這篇文章是不可出版的。

2. include (v) 包括　　　　⟷　　exclude (v) 排除（include的反義字）

　　including (prep) 包括　　⟷　　excluding (prep) 不包括

　　included (adj) 被包括的　　⟷　　excludable (adj) 可排除的

　　includable (adj) 可包括在內的　⟷　　excluded (adj) 被排除的

　　inclusive (adj) 已包括的　　⟷　　exclusive (adj) 排他的、獨特的

　　inclusion (n) 包括　　　　⟷　　exclusion (n) 排除

　(1) Tips are not included in the fees.

　　　費用裡不包含小費。

　(2) The members of this club have exclusive right to use the facility in this park.

　　　這個俱樂部的會員擁有特別權利，來使用園內的設施。

3. permit (v) 允許

permissible (adj) 可允許的

permissibility (n) 可允許性、允許

permissive (adj) 許可的、寬容的

permitted (adj) 被許可的

permit (n) 許可、執照

permission (n) 允許

(1) Selling alcohol in this town isn't permissible.

在本鎮賣酒是不被允許的。

(2) You need a permit to sell alcohol in this town.

在本鎮，你要有執照才能賣酒。

4. sponsor (v) 贊助、發起

sponsored (adj) 被贊助的

sponsor (n) 贊助者、發起人

sponsorship (n) 贊助

(1) This program is sponsored by ASUS Inc.

本節目是由華碩公司贊助。

(2) ASUS Inc. is the sponsor of this program.

華碩公司是本節目的贊助者。

(3) This program was successful due to the sponsorship of ASUS Inc.

這個活動因為華碩公司的贊助而辦得很成功。

1. publicly（公開的）可用 in public, openly 取代。

The US 1976 Copyright Act generally gives the owner the exclusive right to display the copyrighted work publicly.

美國1976年的著作權法案，提供擁有人獨特之權利來公開展示受著作權保護的作品。

⇒ The US 1976 Copyright Act generally gives the owner the exclusive right to display the copyrighted work i_____ p_____.

⇒ The US 1976 Copyright Act generally gives the owner the exclusive right to display the copyrighted work o_____.

2. subject（主題）可用 topic 取代。

The copyright protects the form of expression rather than the subject matter of the writing.

著作權保護的是表達型式，而不是寫作的主題事物。

⇒ The copyright protects the form of expression rather than the t_____ matter of the writing.

3. description（描述）可用 depiction 取代。

It would not prevent others from writing a description of their own or from making and using the machine.

它不能防止他人來寫他們自己的敘述、製造與使用機器。

⇒ It would not prevent others from writing a d_____ of their own or from making and using the machine.

4. courtesy（禮貌）可用 politeness, civility 取代。

Some publishers may require that he/she obtains the original author's permission as a courtesy.

有些出版商可能會要求他得到原始作者的許可，以示禮貌。

⇒ Some publishers may require that he/she obtains the original author's permission as a p_____.

⇒ Some publishers may require that he/she obtains the original author's permission as a c_____.

5. form（型式）可用 kind, type 取代。

Copyright is a form of protection provided to the author of original works.

著作權是一種提供給原創性作品作者的保護。

⇒ Copyright is a k＿＿＿＿＿＿ of protection provided to the author of original works.

⇒ Copyright is a t＿＿＿＿＿＿ of protection provided to the author of original works.

6. prevent（防止）可用 preclude, prohibit 取代。

A copyright does not prevent others from writing a description of their own.

著作權不能防止他人寫作他們自己的描述。

⇒ A copyright does not p＿＿＿＿＿＿ others from writing a description of their own.

⇒ A copyright does not p＿＿＿＿＿＿ others from writing a description of their own.

(   )   1.   Which exclusive right of the owner of copyright was not included in the 1976 Copyright Act?

     A. reproduce the copyrighted work

     B. prepare derivative works

     C. distribute copies or phono-records of the copyrighted work

     D. perform the copyrighted work publicly

     E. prevent others from writing their own work

(   )   2.   Which agency will accept copyright registration?

     A. United States Patent and Trademark Office

     B. Copyright Office of the Library of Congress

     C. Department of Commerce

     D. Governmental Documentation Bureau

     E. Media Administration Bureau

(   )   3.   What can an author do if his/her permission request is not granted?

     A. significantly revise the material so that permission is no longer required

     B. ignore the rejection

     C. send the request again

     D. do nothing

(   )   4.   What is a source line?

     A. It is a line on the cover of a book.

     B. It is a line to claim copyright.

     C. It is a line to identify the source of the adopted material.

     D. It is a line to indicate the publisher.

     E. It is a line to mark the title of the publication.

(   )   5.   Under which condition does an author need permission to use materials from copyrighted work of others?

     A. drawing his/her own figure

     B. describing the same situation using his/her own wording

     C. using a table from other's

     D. making a table from other's data in the text

     E. using his/her own picture

(　　) 6. Under which condition does an author need permission to use materials from copyrighted work of others?

   A. a quote of 25 words from a book

   B. a quote of 25 words from a periodical

   C. a quote of 65 words from a book

   D. a quote of 450 words in total from a book

   E. rewriting an illustration from a book

(　　) 7. Which one in the following is correct?

   A. data itself can be copyrighted

   B. data itself cannot be copyrighted

   C. a table cannot be copyrighted

   D. a figure cannot be copyrighted

(　　) 8. Copyrights in the USA may be claimed using _____ on the work.

   A. "Copy © year"

   B. "Copyright ® year"

   C. "Copy ® year"

   D. "Copyright © date"

   E. "Copyright © year"

(　　) 9. Copyright is a form of protection provided to original works of _____, both published and unpublished.

   A. author

   B. authorship

   C. co-author

   D. corresponding author

(　　) 10. Figures and tables do not have source lines are assumed to be original and must be _____ as such.

   A. verify

   B. verifies

   C. verified

   D. verification

Patents in the USA

Questions & Discussions

1. How long will be a patent valid in the USA?
2. How long will a provisional patent expire?

Vocabulary

1. patent [ˈpætn̩t]
   專利、專利權 (n)

2. territories [ˈtɛrəˌtorɪ]
   領土、國土 (n)

3. possession [pəˈzɛʃən]
   領地、殖民地 (n)

4. enforce [ɪnˈfɔrs]
   執行 (v)

Terminology

a. intellectual property right
   智慧財產權

A [1]patent is a type of [a]intellectual property right. It gives the patent holder the right, for a limited time, to exclude others from making, using, offering to sell, selling, or importing into the United States the subject matter that is within the scope of protection granted by the patent. The term of a new patent is 20 years from the date on which the application for the patent was filed in the United States, or in special case, from the date an earlier related application was filed, subject to the payment of maintenance fees. US patent grants are effective only within the US [2]territories, and US [3]possessions.

The United States Patent and Trademark Office (USPTO) is the government agency responsible for examining patent applications and issuing patents. To get a US patent, an application must be filed in the USPTO. The USPTO determines whether a patent should be granted in a particular case. However, it is up to the patent holder to [4]enforce his or her own rights if the USPTO does grant a patent.

There are various types of patents – utility, design, and plant. There are also two types of utility and plant applications – [5]provisional and non-provisional. Each year the USPTO receives approximately 300,000 patent applications. Most of these are for non-provisional utility patents.

Utility patents may be granted to anyone who invents or discovers any new and useful process, machine, article of manufacture, or compositions of matters, or any new useful improvement [6]thereof. Design patents may be granted to anyone who invents a new, original, and [7]ornamental design for an article of manufacture. A utility patent protects the way an article is used and works while a design patent protects the way an article looks. Both design and utility patents may be obtained on an article if [8]invention resides both in its utility and ornamental appearance. While utility and design patents afford [9]legally separate protection, the utility and ornamentality of an article are not easily separable. Articles of manufacture may possess both functional and ornamental characteristics. Plant patents may be granted to anyone who invents or discovers and [10]asexually reproduces any distinct and new variety of plant.

A provisional application for patent allows filing without a formal patent claim, [11]oath or [12]declaration, or any information disclosure statement. A provisional application for patent has a [13]pendency lasting 12 months from the date the provisional application is filed. The

Vocabulary

5. provisional [prəˈvɪʒən!]
   臨時的 (adj)

6. thereof [ðɛrˈɑv]
   關於……的、它的 (adv)

7. ornamental [ˌɔrnəˈmɛnt!]
   裝飾的 (adj)

8. invention [ɪnˈvɛnʃən]
   發明 (n)

9. legal [ˈligl̩]
   法律的 (adj)

10. asexually [eˈsɛkʃuəlɪ]
    無性的 (adv)

11. oath [oθ]
    宣誓 (n)

12. declaration [ˌdɛkləˈreʃən]
    宣告、申報 (n)

13. pendency [ˈpɛndənsɪ]
    未定、懸置期 (n)

14. benefit [ˈbɛnəfɪt]
    受益於 (v); 利益、益處 (n)

15. attorney [əˈtɜnɪ] 律師、代理人 (n)

16. agent [ˈedʒənt]
    代理人、仲介 (n)

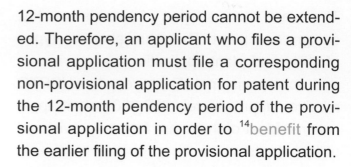

12-month pendency period cannot be extended. Therefore, an applicant who files a provisional application must file a corresponding non-provisional application for patent during the 12-month pendency period of the provisional application in order to [14]benefit from the earlier filing of the provisional application.

A provisional application automatically becomes abandoned when its pendency expires 12 months after the provisional application filing date by operation of law. Independent inventors should fully understand that a provisional application will not mature into a granted patent without further submissions by the inventor. Some invention promotion firms misuse the provisional application process leaving the inventor with no patent.

A patent application is a complex legal document, best prepared by one trained to prepare such documents. Thus, anyone who wishes to file a patent application may need to consult with a registered patent [15]attorney or [16]agent.

Knowledge Plus

History

There is evidence that something like a patent was used among ancient Greek and Roman cities. The inventor of a new recipe was granted an exclusive right to make the food for one year. In 1474, the Republic of Venice in Italy issued an order by which new and inventive devices, once put into practice, had to be communicated to the Republic so as to obtain the right to prevent others from using them. In 1623, England declared that patents could only be granted for "projects of new invention." During 1702 to 1714, the lawyers of the English Court developed the requirement that a written description of the invention must be submitted. These developments provided the basis for modern English and United States patent law. In the United Sates, several states adopted their own patent systems during the colonial period (1778-1789). In 1790, the Congress adopted the first Patent Act. The first patent was issued under this Act on July 31, 1790.

Source:

United States Patent and Trademark Office.

1. invent (v) 發明

   invented (adj) 被發明的

   inventible (adj) 可發明的

   inventive (adj) 發明的

   inventively (adv) 有創造力地

   inventiveness (n) 有創造力

   invention (n) 發明

   inventor (n) 發明人

   Many inventors participate in this invention exhibition.

   許多發明家參與這個發明展。

2. legalize (v) 使合法

   legal (adj) 法律的、合法的

   legally (adv) 法律的、合法的

   illegal (adj) 非法的   ⟷ illegally (adv) 非法的

   legalization (n) 合法化

   (1) One may legally use these materials for non-commercial purposes.

     人可以在非商業用途合法使用這些材料。

   (2) People are looking for the legalization of abortion.

     人們在追求墮胎的合法化。

   (3) It is illegal to gamble in this country.

     在這個國家賭博是不合法的。

   (4) Gambling will be legalized in Mazu.

     在馬祖，賭博將會被合法化。

3. maintain (v) 維護

maintainable (adj) 可維護的

maintainability (n) 可修護性

maintenance (n) 維護

(1) The maintainability of this machine is poor.

這臺機器的可維修性很差。

(2) You are responsible for the maintenance of this machine.

你負責這臺機器的維修。

4. sex (n) 性別、性

sexual (adj) 性的　　　⟷　　asexual (adj) 無性的

sexually (adv) 性的　　　⟷　　asexually (adv) 無性的

(1) Sex discrimination in the workplace is illegal.

職場性別歧視是違法的。

(2) Sexual harassment in the workplace is prohibited.

職場性騷擾是禁止的。

5. evidence (n) 證據

evident (adj) 明顯的

evidently (adv) 明顯的

evidential (adj) 證據的、可做為證據的

(1) He was punished for giving false evidence.

他因作偽證而受到懲罰。

(2) There is no evidence that this company has violated the law.

沒有證據顯示這家公司違法。

(3) It is evident that this company has violated the law.

Evidently, this company has violated the law.

很明顯的，這家公司已違法。

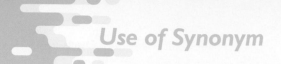

1. exclude（排除）可用 prohibit（禁止）, eliminate（消除）取代。

It gives the patent holder the right to exclude others from making, using, offering to sell, or selling the subject matter that is within the scope of protection granted by the patent.

它提供專利所有人權力，來排除他人來製造、使用、提供銷售、或銷售專利核准保護範圍內之主要事物的權利。

⇒ It gives the patent holder the right to p_____ others from making, using, offering to sell, or selling the subject matter that is within the scope of protection granted by the patent.

⇒ It gives the patent holder the right to e_____ others from making, using, offering to sell, or selling the subject matter that is within the scope of protection granted by the patent.

2. grant（允許、授與）可用 approve, permit 取代。

This company has granted one of its customers the right to sell its products in Thailand.

這家公司授權它的客戶之一在泰國銷售其產品的權利。

⇒ This company has a_____ one of its customers the right to sell its products in Thailand.

⇒ This company has p_____ one of its customers the right to sell its products in Thailand.

3. agency（機構）可用 organization 取代。

The United States Patent and Trademark Office is the government agency responsible for examining patent applications and issuing patents.

美國專利與商標事務局是負責審查專利申請與核發專利的政府機構。

⇒ The United States Patent and Trademark Office is the government o_____ responsible for examining patent applications and issuing patents.

4. formal（正式的）可用 official 取代。

A provisional application for patent allows filing without a formal patent claim.

臨時性的專利允許，沒有正式專利宣告的專利申請。

⇒ A provisional application for patent allows filing without an o_____ patent claim.

5. fully（完全的）可用 completely, thoroughly 取代。

Independent inventors should fully understand that a provisional application will not mature into a granted patent without further submissions by the inventor.

獨立的發明者應該完全了解臨時性申請在發明人未進一步提交申請下，不會自動獲得專利的核准。

⇒ Independent inventors should c_____ understand that a provisional application will not mature into a granted patent without further submissions by the inventor.

⇒ Independent inventors should t_____ understand that a provisional application will not mature into a granted patent without further submissions by the inventor.

6. consult（諮詢）可用 discuss, deliberate, talk 取代。

Anyone who wishes to file a patent application may need to consult with a registered patent attorney or agent.

任何希望提出專利申請的人，可能需要向註冊的專利律師或代理人諮詢。

⇒ Anyone who wishes to file a patent application may need to d_____ with a registered patent attorney or agent.

⇒ Anyone who wishes to file a patent application may need to d_____ with a registered patent attorney or agent.

⇒ Anyone who wishes to file a patent application may need to t_____ to a registered patent attorney or agent.

(   ) 1. How long will a patent be valid in the United States?

      A. 20 years

      B. 30 years

      C. 40 years

      D. 50 years

(   ) 2. A new patent will be valid subject to the following conditions except which one?

      A. it's been approved by USPTO

      B. payment of maintenance fees

      C. not more than 20 years

      D. effective only within the US territories, and US possessions

      E. it's been issued by the US Congress

(   ) 3. Which government agency is responsible for examining patent applications and issuing patents?

      A. The United States Patent and Trademark Office

      B. Copyright Office

      C. Department of Commerce

      D. Intellectual Property Administration

      E. US Customer Service

(   ) 4. Which one is not one of the types of US patents?

      A. utility

      B. design

      C. plant

      D. innovation

(   ) 5.   What is the difference between utility patent and design patent?

A. The former is temporary while the latter is permanent.

B. The former is good for 12 months while the latter is good for 20 years.

C. The former protects the way an article is used and works while the latter protects the way an article looks.

D. The former may be granted to anyone who invents a new ornamental design for an article while the latter may be granted to anyone who discovers any distinct new variety of plant.

E. The former protects the way an article looks while the latter protects the way an article is used and works.

(   ) 6.   What is the difference between provisional patent and non-provisional patent?

A. The former is temporary while the latter is permanent.

B. The former is good for 12 months while the latter is good for 20 years.

C. The former protects the way an article is used and works while the latter protects the way an article looks.

D. The former may be granted to anyone who invents a new ornamental design for an article while the latter many be granted to anyone who discovers any distinct new variety of plant.

E. The former protects the way an article looks while the latter protects the way an article is used and works.

(   ) 7.   The _____ of a new recipe was granted an exclusive right to make the food for one year.

A. organizer

B. governor

C. officer

D. attorney

E. inventor

(　　) 8. In the United States, several states _____ their own patent systems during the colonial period.

A. established

B. applied

C. adopted

D. adapted

(　　) 9. A patent gives the patent _____ the right to exclude others from making, using, offering to sell, selling, or importing into the United States the subject matter that is within the scope of protection granted by the patent.

A. holder

B. applicant

C. attorney

D. lawyer

(　　) 10. Anyone who wishes to _____ a patent application may need to consult with a registered patent attorney or agent.

A. requesting

B. combination

C. asking

D. application

E. file

(　　) 11. Each year the USPTO receives approximately 300,000 patent applications. Most of these are for _____.

A. provisional design patent

B. provisional utility patent

C. non-provisional design patent

D. non-provisional utility patents

E. non-provisional plant patents

(   ) 12. US patent grants are effective only within the US territories, and

        _____.

        A. Hong Kong

        B. US possessions

        C. South America

        D. UK, E. Europe

(   ) 13. Articles of manufacture may possess both _____ and ornamental

        characteristics.

        A. conditional

        B. transparent

        C. functional

        D. operation

Filing a Design Patent

Questions & Discussions

1. How can the applicant for a design patent present the surface ornamentation of his or her design?
2. What is a claim in a design patent application?

Vocabulary

1. ornamental [ˌɔrnəˈmɛntḷ]
   裝飾的、外觀的 (adj)

2. manifest [ˈmænəˌfɛst]
   顯現 (v)；分明的 (adj)

3. configuration [kənˌfɪgjəˈreʃən]
   構造、形態 (n)

4. ornamentation [ˌɔrnəmɛnˈteʃən]
   裝飾、外觀 (n)

5. definite [ˈdɛfənɪt]
   明確的 (adj)

A design consists of the visual [1]ornamental characteristics embodied in, or applied to, an article of manufacture. Since a design is [2]manifested in appearance, the subject matter of a design patent application may relate to the [3]configuration or shape of an article, to the surface [4]ornamentation applied to an article, or to the combination of configuration and surface ornamentation. A design for surface ornamentation is inseparable from the article to which it is applied and cannot exist alone. It must be a [5]definite pattern of surface ornamentation, applied to an article of manufacture.

An ornamental design may be embodied in an entire article or only a portion of an article, or may be ornamentation applied to an article. If a design is just surface ornamentation, it must be shown applied to an article in the drawings, and the article must be shown in broken lines, as it forms no part of the claimed design.

A design patent application may only have a single claim. Designs that are independent

Vocabulary

6. article [ˈɑrtɪk!]
   物品、物件、文章 (n)

7. vase [ves]
   花瓶 (n)

8. embodiment [ɪmˈbɑdɪmənt]
   具體化 (n)

9. consistent [kənˈsɪstənt]
   一致的 (adj)

10. terminology [,tɝməˈnɑlədʒɪ]
    術語、專業用語 (n)

and distinct must be filed in separate applications since they cannot be supported by a single claim. Designs are independent if there is no apparent relationship between two or more [6]articles. For example, a pair of eye-glasses and a door handle are independent articles and must be claimed in separate applications. Designs are considered distinct if they have different shape and appearances even though they are related articles. For example, two [7]vases having different surface ornamentation creating distinct appearances must be claimed in separate applications. However, vases with only minimal configuration differences may be considered a single design concept and both [8]embodiments may be included in a single application.

The claim in each patent application defines the design which applicant wishes to patent, in term of the article in which it is embodied or applied. The claim must be in formal terms to "The ornamental design for (the article which embodies the design or to which it is applied) as shown." The description of the article in the claim should be [9]consistent in [10]terminology with the title of the invention.

Source:

Patent Application Guidelines, the United States Patent and Trademark Office.

1. describe (v) 描述

   descriptive (adj) 描述的

   descriptively (adv) 描述的

   description (n) 描述

   (1) Descriptive statistics are used to describe the characteristics of the samples.

   描述性統計學被用來描述樣本的特徵。

   (2) Could you provide a drawing to describe your design?

   你能否提供一個圖樣來描述你的設計？

2. ornament (v) 裝飾

   ornament (n) 裝飾品

   ornamental (adj) 裝飾的

   ornamentality (n) 裝飾性

   (1) An ornamental attachment has been added to make the design looks better.

   這個設計加了一個裝飾性配件，來讓它看起來好些。

   (2) The ornamentality and function of a design may be inseparable.

   一個設計的裝飾性與功能，可能是無法分開的。

3. separate (v) 分開

   separable (adj) 可分的 ⟷ inseparable (adj) 不可分的

   separability (n) 可分離性

   separation (n) 分開

   (1) This design includes several separable components.

   這個設計包含多個可分離的元件。

   (2) It is difficult to separate the raw materials from this product.

   要把這個產品的原料分開，是很困難的。

4. vision (n) 視力、視覺

visible (adj) 可見的

visibility (n) 可見度

visual (adj) 視覺的

visually (adv) 視覺的

visualize (v) 視覺化

visualized (adj) 視覺化的

visualization (n) 視覺化

(1) The visibility of road conditions is very poor.

路況的能見度很差。

(2) The workers need to inspect the final products visually.

工人需要以視覺檢驗最終產品。

(3) Normally, a designer may visualize his / her design by making drawings.

通常設計師可以經由繪圖來將其設計視覺化。

(4) Visualization is important for designers to communicate with others.

視覺化對於設計師與他人溝通是很重要的。

(5) The visual information is displayed via an overhead colored monitor.

視覺的資訊是經由一個頭部上方的彩色監視器呈現。

1. inseparable（無法分開的）可用 indivisible, undividable 取代。

   A design for surface ornamentation is inseparable from the article to which it is applied and cannot exist alone.

   一件表面裝飾設計是無法與其應用之物件分開的，因此無法獨立存在。

   ⇒ A design for surface ornamentation is i_____ from the article to which it is applied and cannot exist alone.

   ⇒ A design for surface ornamentation is u_____ from the article to which it is applied and cannot exist alone.

2. definite（明確的）可用 explicit, unambiguous 取代。

   It must be a definite pattern of surface ornamentation, applied to an article of manufacture.

   它必須為應用到製造物件之一明確的表面裝飾型式。

   ⇒ It must be an e_____ pattern of surface ornamentation, applied to an article of manufacture.

   ⇒ It must be an u_____ pattern of surface ornamentation, applied to an article of manufacture.

3. drawing（圖樣）可用 sketch, draft, diagram 取代。

   If a design is just surface ornamentation, it must be shown applied to an article in the drawings.

   如果一個設計只是表面裝飾，它必須在圖面上顯示應用於一個物件上。

   ⇒ If a design is just surface ornamentation, it must be shown applied to an article in the s_____.

   ⇒ If a design is just surface ornamentation, it must be shown applied to an article in the d_____.

   ⇒ If a design is just surface ornamentation, it must be shown applied to an article in the d_____.

4. apparent（明顯的）可用obvious, evident 取代。

Designs are independent if there is no apparent relationship between two or more articles.

如果沒有明顯兩個或多個物件之間的關係，設計是獨立的。

⇒ Designs are independent if there is no o_____ relationship between two or more articles.

⇒ Designs are independent if there is no e_____ relationship between two or more articles.

5. distinct（個別的）可用 individual 取代。

Designs are considered distinct if they have different shape and appearances even though they are related articles.

即使是相關的物品，如果它們有不同的形狀與外觀，則設計可視為個別的。

⇒ Designs are considered i_____ if they have different shape and appearances even though they are related articles.

6. ornamentation（裝飾）可用decoration 取代。

Two vases having different surface ornamentation creating distinct appearances must be claimed in separate applications.

兩個不同表面裝飾的花瓶產生明顯不同的外觀，必須在分開申請案中宣告。

⇒ Two vases having different surface d_____ creating distinct appearances must be claimed in separate applications.

7. include（包括、併入）可用 incorporate 取代。

Vases with only minimal configuration differences may be considered a single design concept and both embodiments may be included in a single application.

僅有微小形態差異的花瓶可視為單一設計概念，兩者式樣可包含於同一申請中。

⇒ Vases with only minimal configuration differences may be considered a single design concept and both embodiments may be i_____ in a single application.

( ) 1. The subject matter of a design patent application may relate to several items except _____.

A. the configuration or shape of an article

B. the surface ornamentation applied to an article

C. the combination of configuration and surface ornamentation

D. the materials used in the article

( ) 2. Which one is correct concerning the claim(s) in design patent application?

A. A design patent application may have several claims.

B. A design patent application may only have a single claim.

C. If a design is just surface ornamentation, it may not have a claim.

D. Independent and distinct designs may be filed in a single claim.

E. If an ornamental design is embodied in an article then the whole article may be claimed.

( ) 3. If a design is just surface ornamentation, it must be shown applied to an article in the drawings, and the article must be shown in _____.

A. broken lines

B. solid lines

C. shade

D. grey

E. lines with arrow heads

( ) 4. Which one in the following is true?

A. A pair of eyeglasses and a door handle may be claimed in a single application.

B. Related articles may be claimed in a single application even if they have different shape and appearances.

C. An ornamental design may only be embodied in an entire article not in a portion of an article.

D. The description of the article in the claim should be consistent in terminology with the title of the invention.

(   ) 5. The _____ claim in each patent application defines the design which
         applicant wishes to patent.
         A. claim
         B. verification
         C. drawing
         D. oath
         E. declaration

(   ) 6. A design for surface ornamentation is _____ from the article and
         cannot exist alone.
         A. separate
         B. separated
         C. separation
         D. inseparable
         E. inseparation

(   ) 7. A design consists of the visual ornamental characteristics _____ in,
         or applied to an article of manufacture.
         A. body
         B. bodied
         C. embody
         D. embodies
         E. embodied

(   ) 8. Designs are independent if there is no _____ relationship between
         two or more articles.
         A. appendix
         B. append
         C. apparent
         D. apparance

(　　) 9. Designs are considered _____ if they have different shape and appearances even though they are related articles.

A. disorder

B. distinguish

C. dissect

D. distinct

(　　) 10. The _____ in each patent application defines the design which the applicant wishes to patent.

A. claim

B. oath

C. drawing

D. terminology

Non-Provisional Utility Patent Application

Questions & Discussions

1. What must be included in a non-provisional utility patent application?
2. What is the difference between an oath and a declaration?

Vocabulary

1. specification [ˌspɛsəfəˈkeʃən]
   規格、設計說明書 (n)

2. claim [klem]
   宣告、聲明 (n)

3. oath [oθ]
   宣誓 (n)

4. declaration [ˌdɛkləˈreʃən]
   宣言、申報 (n)

5. prescribe [prɪˈskraɪb]
   規定 (v)

6. concise [kənˈsaɪs]
   簡明的 (adj)

7. wording [ˈwɝdɪŋ]
   用字、措辭 (n)

A non-provisional utility patent application must include a ¹specification, a ²claim or claims, drawings when necessary, an ³oath or ⁴declaration, and the ⁵prescribed filing fee.

The specification is a written description of the invention and of the manner and process of making and using the same. The specification must be in such full, clear, ⁶concise, and exact terms as to enable any person skilled in the art or science to which the pertains to make and use the same.

The claim or claims must particularly point out and distinctly claim the subject matter which you regard as the invention. The claims define the scope of the protection of the patent. Whether a patent will be granted is determined, in large measure, by the choice of ⁷wording of the claims. A non-provisional application for a utility patent must contain at least one claim. The claim or claims section must begin on a separate sheet. If there are several sheets, they should be numbered consecutively in Arabic numerals, with the least restrictive claim presented as claim number 1.

A patent application is required to contain drawings if drawings are necessary for the understanding of the subject matter sought to be patented. The drawings must show every feature of the invention as specified in the claims. Omission of drawings may cause an application to be considered [8]incomplete.

The oath or declaration must be signed by all the actual inventors. An oath may be administered by any person within the United States, or by a diplomatic or consular officer of a foreign country, who is authorized by the United States to administered oaths. A declaration does not require any [9]witness or person to administer or [10]verify its signing. Thus, use of a declaration is preferable.

Source:

Patent Application Guidelines, the United States Patent and Trademark Office.

8. incomplete [ˌɪnkəmˈplit]
   不完整的 (adj)

9. witness [ˈwɪtnɪs]
   見証人 (n)

10. verify [ˈvɛrəfaɪ]
    驗證 (v)

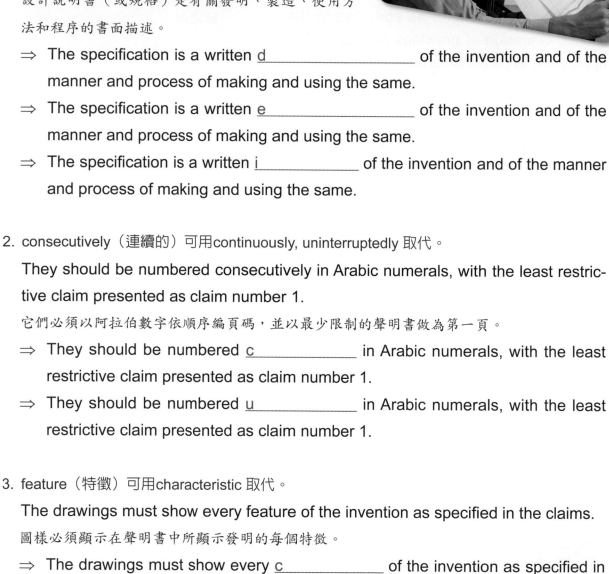

1. description（敘述、說明）可用 depiction, explanation, illustration 取代。

    The specification is a written description of the invention and of the manner and process of making and using the same.

    設計說明書（或規格）是有關發明、製造、使用方法和程序的書面描述。

    ⇒ The specification is a written d_____ of the invention and of the manner and process of making and using the same.

    ⇒ The specification is a written e_____ of the invention and of the manner and process of making and using the same.

    ⇒ The specification is a written i_____ of the invention and of the manner and process of making and using the same.

2. consecutively（連續的）可用continuously, uninterruptedly 取代。

    They should be numbered consecutively in Arabic numerals, with the least restrictive claim presented as claim number 1.

    它們必須以阿拉伯數字依順序編頁碼，並以最少限制的聲明書做為第一頁。

    ⇒ They should be numbered c_____ in Arabic numerals, with the least restrictive claim presented as claim number 1.

    ⇒ They should be numbered u_____ in Arabic numerals, with the least restrictive claim presented as claim number 1.

3. feature（特徵）可用characteristic 取代。

    The drawings must show every feature of the invention as specified in the claims.

    圖樣必須顯示在聲明書中所顯示發明的每個特徵。

    ⇒ The drawings must show every c_____ of the invention as specified in the claims.

4. contain（包含）可用 be comprise of , be consist of, include 取代。

A non-provisional application for a utility patent must contain at least one claim.

非臨時性實用專利申請必須包括至少一份聲明書。

⇒ A non-provisional application for a utility patent must be c_____ of at least one claim.

⇒ A non-provisional application for a utility patent must be c_____ of at least one claim.

⇒ A non-provisional application for a utility patent must i_____ at least one claim.

5. omission（省略、忽略）可用negligence, oversight 取代。

Omission of drawings may cause an application to be considered incomplete.

若未附上圖樣可能會導致申請被視為不完整。

⇒ N_____ of drawings may cause an application to be considered incomplete.

⇒ O_____ of drawings may cause an application to be considered incomplete.

6. verify（證明、證實）可用 confirm, prove, substantiate 取代。

A declaration does not require any witness or person to administer or verify its signing.

申報不需要人員當證人或證明其簽署。

⇒ A declaration does not require any witness or person to administer or c_____ its signing.

⇒ A declaration does not require any witness or person to administer or p_____ its signing.

⇒ A declaration does not require any witness or person to administer or s_____ its signing.

Choose the most appropriate one in the following questions

(　　) 1. A non-provisional utility patent application must include the following items except _____.

　　A. a specification

　　B. a claim or claims

　　C. an oath or declaration

　　D. filing fee

　　E. a prototype

(　　) 2. Which part of the non-provisional utility patent submission defines the scope of the protection of the patent?

　　A. a specification

　　B. a claim or claims

　　C. an oath or declaration

　　D. filing fee

　　E. a prototype

(　　) 3. Which statement in the followings is correct?

　　A. A non-provisional application for a utility patent must contain at least one claim.

　　B. Drawings are not required in patent application.

　　C. It is up to the inventor whether to submit with a written description of the invention.

　　D. Wording of the claims are not critical in determining whether a patent will be granted.

　　E. A declaration define the scope of the protection of the patent.

(　　) 4. Which one is true concerning an oath in the patent application?

　　A. does not require any witness

　　B. define the scope of the protection of the patent

　　C. is a written description of the invention

　　D. may be administered by any person within the United States

　　E. may be administered by any consular officer of a foreign country

(　) 5. A declaration does not require any _____ or person to administer or verify its signing.

A. witness

B. warning

C. announcing

D. inquiry

(　) 6. A non-provisional utility application must _____.

A. have no claim

B. have at least one claim

C. have more than one claim

D. have many claim

(　) 7. The drawings must show every feature of the invention as _____ in the claims.

A. specify

B. specified

C. specification

D. special

(　) 8. Omission of drawings may cause an application to be considered _____ .

A. inconsistent

B. inconvenient

C. inconsidered

D. incomplete

Flexible Manufacturing in the USA

Questions & Discussions

1. What are the benefits of implementing flexible manufacturing?
2. Flexible manufacturing is most suitable for what type of company?

Vocabulary

1. era [ɪrə]
   時代、世代 (n)

2. implementation [ɪmpləmɛnˋteʃən]
   導入、實施 (n)

3. competition [ˌkɑmpəˋtɪʃən]
   競爭 (n)

4. ever-increasing [ˋɛvɚ ɪnˋkrisɪŋ]
   一直增加的 (adj)

5. manufacturer [ˌmænjəˋfæktʃərɚ]
   製造商 (n)

6. productivity [ˌprodʌkˋtɪvətɪ]
   生產力 (n)

7. affordability [əˌfordəˋbɪlətɪ]
   可負擔性 (n)

The industry in the USA is, now, standing at the entrance of a new [1]era in manufacturing – an era that began with the [2]implementation of solid automation. With foreign [3]competition an [4]ever-increasing threat to the American [5]manufacturers, flexible manufacturing is becoming a significant part in the American approach to achieve competitiveness in manufacturing. Automation technology is moving out of the laboratory and into the workplace just when the industry needs it most.

Transfer lines that were adopted to cut the labor hours required to make a product are being substituted with systems with more flexibility. Flexible manufacturing provides better [6]productivity and product [7]affordability, yet it retains the advantage of enhanced quality. Flexible manufacturing not only offers greater production efficiency but also enables users to adapt to changes in product promptly. Furthermore, flexible manufacturing compensates for a decrease in the manufacturing

[8]professionals available in the US manufacturers.

Flexible manufacturing is particularly suitable to companies with complex manufacturing and small [9]lot sizes requirements. Aerospace industry is a good example. For industries with mass production such as automobile and [a]household appliance, capital investments must be re-examined when the lot size is small. A properly designed, automated flexible manufacturing system not only supports economical production of small lot sizes but also facilitates the transition from one production line to another.

Source:

Roch, A. F. Fr., Flexible Machining in an Integrated System, in Design and Analysis of Integrated Manufacturing Systems, National Academy of Engineering, 1988, pp34.

Vocabulary

8. professional [prəˈfɛʃənl̩, -ˌʃnəl]
专业人士 (n)

9. lot [lɑt]
批 (n)；lot size 批量、每一批的量

Terminology

a. household appliance
家電設備

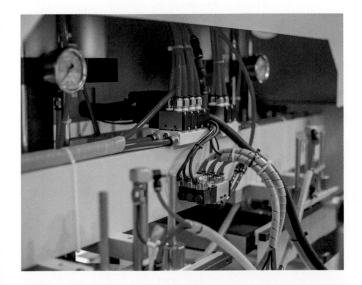

Families of Vocabulary

1. afford (v) 買⋯、負擔

   affordable (adj) 可負擔的   ⟷   unaffordable (adj) 負擔不起的

   affordability (n) 可負擔性

   (1) Most people in this country cannot afford to buy an iPhone.

   這個國家大部分人都買不起iPhone。

   (2) An iPhone is not affordable for most people in this country.

   這個國家大部分人都負擔不起iPhone。

   (3) The iPhone has poor affordability in this country.

   iPhone在這個國家的可負擔性很低。

2. compensate (v) 補償

   compensative (adj) 償還的

   compensation (n) 補償

   compensator (n) 補償者、補償物

   The dealer compensated the buyers by giving a discount on the price.

   經銷商提供價格折扣來補償購買者。

3. compete (v) 競爭

   competitive (adj) 競爭的

   competitively (adv) 競爭的

   competitiveness (n) 競爭力

   competitor (n) 競爭者

   competition (n) 競爭、競賽

   (1) The ASUS Inc. has strong competitiveness in portable electronic devices market.

   華碩公司在可攜式電子裝置市場有很強的競爭力。

   (2) The portable electronic devices of ASUS Inc. are very competitive in the market.

   華碩公司的可攜式電子裝置在市場上很有競爭力。

   (3) There are many competitors in Asian market.

   在亞洲市場有許多競爭者。

4. manufacture (v) 製造

manufactured (adj) 被製造的

manufacturing (n) 製造業、製造部

manufacturer (n) 製造者

(1) These products are manufactured by two different manufacturers in Asia.

這些產品是由亞洲兩家不同製造商所製造。

(2) Most of the iPhones are manufactured by Foxconn Inc.

大部分的iPhone都是由富士康公司所製造。

(3) Foxconn Inc. is one of the major manufacturers of iPhone.

富士康公司是iPhone的主要製造商之一。

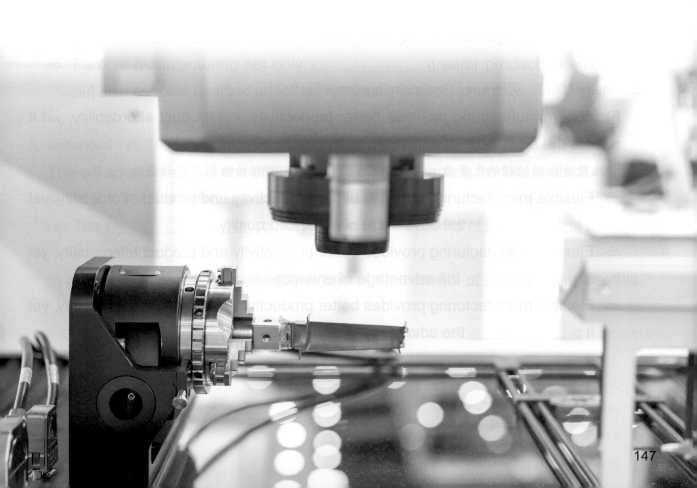

6. transition（轉移、轉換）可用 changeover, shifting, switching 取代。

A properly designed manufacturing system not only supports economical production of small lot sizes but also facilitates the transition from one production line to another.

一個設計適當的製造系統，不僅可以支援小批量的經濟化生產，也能加速由一條生產線轉換到另一條生產線的轉換。

⇒ A properly designed manufacturing system not only supports economical production of small lot sizes but also facilitates the c_____ from one production line to another.

⇒ A properly designed manufacturing system not only supports economical production of small lot sizes but also facilitates the s_____ from one production line to another.

⇒ A properly designed manufacturing system not only supports economical production of small lot sizes but also facilitates the s_____ from one production line to another.

Choose the most appropriate one in the following questions

(   ) 1. Which one is not the advantage of flexible manufacturing?

    A. provide better productivity

    B. provide better product affordability

    C. retain the enhanced quality

    D. offer greater production efficiency

    E. provide better customer satisfaction

(   ) 2. Which one in the followings is not related to flexible manufacturing?

    A. transfer line

    B. automation technology

    C. economical lot size production

    D. elimination of stockout

(   ) 3. Flexible manufacturing is particularly suitable to what kind of companies?

    A. companies with complex manufacturing and small lot sizes requirements

    B. companies with mass production

    C. companies have strong manufacturing division

    D. companies need many manufacturing professionals

    E. companies with strong design division

(   ) 4. Flexible manufacturing is particularly suitable to which kind of companies?

    A. household appliance

    B. IC manufacturer

    C. automobile manufacturer

    D. aircraft manufacturer

    E. PC manufacturer

(   ) 5. Flexible manufacturing provides better _____ and product affordability, yet it retains the advantage of enhanced quality.

    A. producible

    B. producibility

    C. productive

    D. productivity

    E. production

(   ) 6. Flexible manufacturing is becoming a significant part in the America _____ to achieve competitiveness.

    A. industrialization

    B. commercial

    C. territory

    D. method

    E. approach

(   ) 7. Flexible manufacturing provides better _____ and product affordability.

    A. produce

    B. productive

    C. productivity

    D. production

(   ) 8. Affordability means _____.

    A. the ability to buy a product

    B. the intention to buy a product

    C. the desire to buy a product

    D. the willingness to buy a product

(   ) 9. The company has _____ a flexible manufacturing system.

    A. implement

    B. implemented

    C. implementation

    D. implemental

(   ) 10. What is lot size?

    A. the size of a parking lot

    B. the size for each manufacturing order

    C. the size of a manufacturing facility

    D. the size of the product

Taguchi's Ideas about Quality

Questions & Discussions

1. Quality is related to the loss to the public. How does the loss occur to both a customer and a manufacturer?

2. What are the three stages in the design of a product or process in Taguchi's Ideas.

Vocabulary

1. minimal [ˈmɪnəməl]
   最小的 (adj)

2. parameter [pəˈræmətə]
   參數 (n)

3. tolerance [ˈtɑlərəns]
   公差 (n)

Terminology

a. life cycle
   生命週期

Products have characteristics that describe their performance relative to customer requirements or expectation. The quality of a product is measured based on these characteristics. Quality is related to the loss to the public caused by a product during its [a]life cycle. A high quality product will have a [1]minimal loss as it goes through this life cycle. The loss to the public is composed of the loss incurred by both the customer and manufacturer. The loss to a customer can take many ways, but it is generally a loss of product function or properties. If a product does not perform as expected, the customer experiences some loss. The loss to a manufacturer occurs when expensive materials, components, or processes are used unnecessarily. Taguchi established a loss function to recognize the customer's request to have products that are more consistent and a manufacturer's desire to make a low-cost product.

Taguchi considers the design of a product or process as a three-stage project: system design, [2]parameter design, and [3]tolerance design. System design is the stage when new concepts, ideas, methods, etc., are created to provide new or refined products to customers. Parameter design is used to improve quality without controlling or eliminating the cause of [4]variation, to make the product [5]robust against noise factors. The parameter design stage is essential to improving the [6]uniformity of a product and can be done at no cost or even at a savings. This means that certain parameters of a product or a process design are set to make the performance less sensitive to causes of variation.

Tolerance design is employed when the efforts of parameter design have not proved adequate in reducing variation. The tolerance design improves quality at a minimal cost. Quality is improved by [7]tightening tolerances on product or process parameters to reduce the performance variation. This is done only after parameter design. Typically, when a problem is encountered in product development, a designer may enter directly to tolerance design; when tolerances are tightened, variation will be reduced and quality improved. However, tightening tolerances may be expensive and completely unnecessary if parameter design were used first. One serious mistake a designer can make is to adopt expensive materials, components, or processes for a product when low-cost items may be used if a parameter design approach is applied.

Vocabulary

4. variation [ˌvɛrɪˈeʃən]
   變異 (n)

5. robust [roˈbʌst]
   強固的 (adj)

6. uniformity [ˌjunəˈfɔrmətɪ]
   均一性 (n)

7. tighten [ˈtaɪtn̩]
   緊縮 (v)

Genichi Taguchi

Genichi Taguchi (田口玄一) is a Japanese professor in engineering statistics. He received his doctorate from the Kyushu University in 1962. Starting 1950s, Dr. Taguchi has developed methods for applying statistics to improve the quality of manufactured products. His methods have been controversial among some conventional Western statistians but others have accepted his concepts as valid extensions to the body of knowledge. He has made seminal and valuable methodological innovations in statistics and engineering. His ideas of loss to society; techniques for investigating variation in experiments, and parameter and tolerance design have been massively influential in improving quality in manufacturing worldwide. The methods he has developed are called *Taguchi methods*.

註：doctorate (n) 博士學位；controversial (adj) 有爭議的；seminal (adj) 有發展性的

Source:

Ross, P.J., Taguchi Techniques for quality engineering, 2nd ed., McGraw Hill, 1996.

Families of Vocabulary

1. adequate (adj) 足夠的   ⟵⟶   inadequate (adj) 不夠的

   adequately (adv) 足夠的

   adequacy (n) 足夠

   The efforts in controlling the quality of this product are inadequate.

   控制這個產品品質的努力，是不夠的。

2. expense (n) 費用

   expensive (adj) 昂貴的   ⟵⟶   inexpensive (adj) 不貴的

   expensively (adv) 昂貴的

   expendable (adj) 可消耗的   ⟵⟶   unexpendable (adj) 不可消耗的

   expenditure (n) 消費

   All the employees may claim the travel expenses for business travels approved by the managers.

   所有員工都可以申請經由經理核准的出差旅費。

3. uniform (adj) 一致的

   uniformed (adj) 穿著制服的

   uniform (n) 制服

   uniformity (n) 一致性

   (1) All the workers are required to wear uniforms in this factory.

   　　這個工廠所有的工人都要穿制服。

   (2) All the uniformed workers belong to this division.

   　　所有穿著制服的工人都屬於這個部門。

4. variate (n) 改變

   variable (adj) 可變的

   variable (n) 變數

   variation (n) 變化、變異

   variability (n) 可變性

   The variation of product quality must be controlled.

   產品品質的變異必須被控制。

Use of Synonym

1. consider（把…當作或認為）常可用 treat, regard 等字取代。

   Taguchi considers the design of a product or process as a three-stage project.

   田口把一個產品或製程的設計，當成一個三階段的計畫。

   ⇒ Taguchi t_____ the design of a product or process as a three-stage project.

   ⇒ Taguchi r_____ the design of a product or process as a three-stage project.

2. employ（使用）常可用 use, adopt 取代。

   Tolerance design is employed when the efforts of parameter design have not proved adequate in reducing variation.

   公差設計是在參數設計的努力在縮減變異上，未被證實是足夠的才採用。

   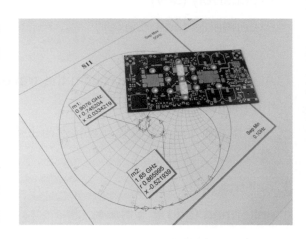

   ⇒ Tolerance design is a_____ when the efforts of parameter design have not proved adequate in reducing variation.

   ⇒ Tolerance design is u_____ when the efforts of parameter design have not proved adequate in reducing variation.

3. stage（階段）常可用 phase 取代。

   System design is the stage when new concepts or methods are created to provide new products to customers.

   系統設計是當新概念或方法被創造來提供新產品給消費者時的階段。

   ⇒ System design is the p_____ when new concepts or methods are created to provide new products to customers.

4. project（計畫）常可用 assignment, program 取代。

The company has started a new project to establish a quality management system.

公司啟動了一個新的計畫，來建立一個品質管理系統。

⇒ The company has started a new <u>a</u>_____ to establish a quality management system.

⇒ The company has started a new <u>p</u>_____ to establish a quality management system.

5. uniformity（均一性）可用 consistency, homogeneity 取代。

The parameter design stage is essential to improving the uniformity of a product.

參數設計階段對於改善產品的均一性是很重要的。

⇒ The parameter design stage is essential to improving the <u>c</u>_____ of a product.

⇒ The parameter design stage is essential to improving the <u>h</u>_____ of a product.

Choose the most appropriate one in the following questions

(   ) 1.   When will loss to a manufacturer occur?

        A. The products do not function as expected.

        B. Customers don't like the product.

        C. The users experience some loss.

        D. The products fail to meet international standards.

        E. Expensive materials, compo nents, or processes are used unne-cessarily.

(   ) 2.   What did Taguchi do to measure the loss to the public?

        A. tightening tolerances on product or process parameters

        B. establishing a loss function

        C. proposing a three-stage project

        D. establishing parameter design approach

        E. employing tolerance design for measurement

(   ) 3.   What can be done to improve the quality of a product?

        A. establishing parameter design approach

        B. determining appropriate design parameter

        C. establishing a loss function

        D. establishing parameter design approach

        E. tightening tolerances on product or process parameters

(   ) 4.   When should we employ tolerance design in the three-stage project?

        A. efforts of parameter design have not proved adequate

        B. before a parameter design stage

        C. right after system design stage

        D. when we need to improve the uniformity of a product

        E. when a product does not perform as expected

(   ) 5. What is the serious mistake a designer can make in improving the quality of a product?

A. employing tolerance design too early

B. neglecting the importance of a loss function

C. using expensive materials, components, or processes for a product when low-cost items may be adopted

D. skipping parameter design stage

E. failing to eliminate the cause of variation

(   ) 6. Which design is used to improve quality without controlling or eliminating the cause of variation, to make the product robust against noise factors?

A. parameter design

B. tolerance design

C. quality design

D. specification design

E. system design

(   ) 7. Which design is the stage when new concepts, ideas, methods, etc., are created to provide new or refined products to customers?

A. parameter design

B. tolerance design

C. quality design

D. specification design

E. system design

(   ) 8. If a product does not perform as expected, the customer _____ some loss.

A. experiencing

B. experiences

C. experienced

D. had experienced

(　　) 9. The loss to the public is composed of the loss _____ by the customer and manufacturer.

A. incurred

B. incur

C. incurring

D. incurred

(　　) 10. This means that certain parameters of a product are set to make the performance less sensitive to causes of _____.

A. variate

B. variance

C. variable

D. variation

CAD/CAM/CAE

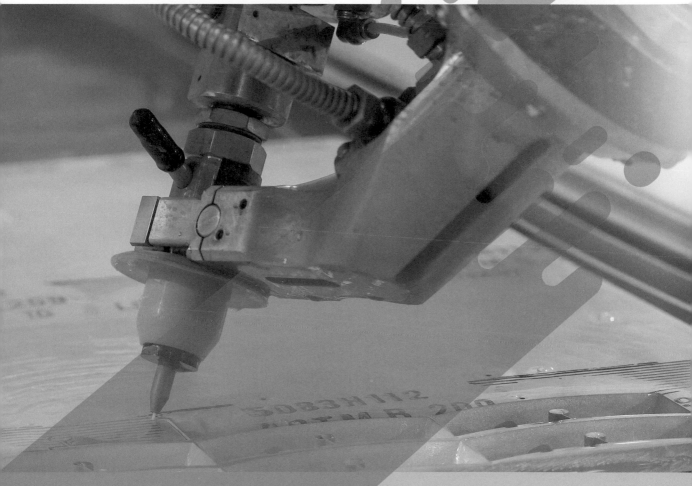

Questions & Discussions

1. What is the most fundamental role of CAD?
2. What is CNC?

1. manipulate [məˈnɪpjəˌlet]
   處理 (v)
2. customize [ˈkʌstəmˌɑɪz]
   訂製 (v)

Terminology

a. computer-aided-design (CAD)
   電腦輔助設計
b. tolerance analysis
   公差分析
c. finite-element modeling
   建立有限元素模型

With the remarkable advances in computing power and wider availability of software tools for design and production, engineers are now using CAD/CAM/CAE systems for every day tasks, not just for demonstrations.

[a]Computer-aided-design (CAD) is the technology concerned with the use of computers to support the construction, alteration, analysis, and optimization of a design. Any computer program that embodies computer graphics and application program facilitating engineering functions in the design process is categorized as CAD software. In other words, CAD tools can vary from geometric tools for [1]manipulating shapes at one side, to [2]customized application programs, such as those for analysis and optimization, at the other side. Between these two sides, typical tools currently existing include [b]tolerance analysis, [c]finite-element modeling, and visualization of

the analysis results, etc. Because the [d]geometric design is vital to all the [3]subsequent activities in the product developing stages, the most fundamental role of CAD is to define and delineate the geometry of design for mechanical parts, architecture structures, [e]electronic circuits, building layouts, and so on.

[f]Computer-aided-manufacturing (CAM) is the technology related to the use of computers to plan, manage, [4]supervise, and control of manufacturing operations via [g]computer interface with all the production resources. One of the most mature areas of CAM is computer numerical control or CNC. CNC is the technique of using programmed commands to control a machine tool that grinds, cuts, drills, punches, bends, or turns raw stock into a [h]finished part. Another noteworthy CAM function is the programming of robots. Robots may perform individual task such as [5]welding, assembling, or carrying parts in the machine shop. They may also operate in a [6]workcell layout, selecting and positioning tools and work pieces for CNC machines.

[i]Computer-aided-engineering (CAE) is the technology involves using computer systems to analyze CAD geometry. Designers are, then, allowed to [7]simulate and study the performance of various designs. This enables [8]refinement and optimization of the design of a product. CAE tools are obtainable for many

Vocabulary

9. kinematics [ˌkɪnəˈmætɪks]
   運動學 (n)

10. linkage [ˈlɪŋkɪdʒ]
    連接、聯繫、連鎖 (n)

11. displacement [dɪsˈplesmənt]
    位移 (n)

12. mechanism [ˈmɛkəˌnɪzəm]
    機構 (n)

analyses. [9]Kinematics programs used to determine motion paths and [10]linkage velocities in a structure is an example. Large-[11]displacement dynamic analysis programs have been used to determine loads and displacements in complex [12]mechanisms such as automobiles. Logic-timing software, simulating the operation of complex electronic circuits, is also a CAE tool example.

Source:

Lee, Kunwoo (1999), Principles of CAD/CAM/CAE systems, Addison-Wiley.

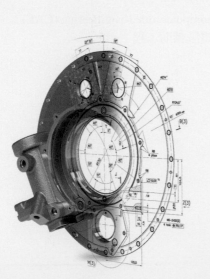

1. fine (adj) 精細的

   refine (v) 提煉、使精細

   refined (adj) 被加工的

   refinement (n) 提煉、加工、改良品

   (1) A process has been developed to refine the rare metals from the minerals.

   一個製程被開發來提煉礦物質中的稀有金屬。

   (2) Refinement of the rare metals from raw minerals are complicated.

   從原料礦物中提煉稀有金屬很複雜。

2. geometry (n) 幾何學

   geometric (adj) 幾何的

   geometrician (n) 幾何學家

   (1) All the designers must be good at geometry.

   所有設計師都要精通於幾何學。

   (2) Geometric design is the fundamental of all designs.

   幾何設計是所有設計的基礎。

3. manipulate (v) 處理、操作

   manipulative (adj) 操作的

   manipulation (n) 處理、操作

   All the parts will be manipulated using this robot.

   所有零件都將會使用這臺機器人處理。

4. simulate (v) 模擬

   simulative (adj) 假裝的

   simulation (n) 模擬

   simulator (n) 模擬器

   (1) A simulator was adopted to simulate the manufacturing process of this vehicle.

   一具模擬器被用來模擬這個載具的製造過程。

   (2) The simulation was performed by activating a computer software.

   模擬是經由驅動一個電腦軟體來執行的。

5. supervise (v) 監督

supervisory (adj) 督導的

supervisor (n) 督導者

supervision (n) 督導、管理

(1) The operation of this unit is supervised by the vice president directly.

這個單位的營運由副總裁直接督導。

(2) The vice president is the supervisor of this unit.

副總裁是這個單位的督導者。

1. vital（重要的）常可用 important, essential, crucial 等字取代。

Geometric design is vital to all the subsequent activities in the product developing stages.

幾何設計對產品開發階段中，所有後續的活動都很重要。

⇒ Geometric design is i_____ to all the subsequent activities in the product developing stages.

⇒ Geometric design is e_____ to all the subsequent activities in the product developing stages.

⇒ Geometric design is c_____ to all the subsequent activities in the product developing stages.

2. subsequent（後續的）可用 following 或 succeeding 取代。

There are many subsequent activities after the final design has been approved.

最終設計被核准後，還有許多後續的活動。

⇒ There are many f_____ activities after the final design has been approved.

⇒ There are many s_____ activities after the final design has been approved.

3. concerned with（與…有關的）；常可用 related to 或 involve 取代。

Computer-aided-design (CAD) is the technology concerned with the use of computers to support the construction, alteration, analysis, and optimization of a design.

電腦輔助設計 (CAD) 是用電腦來支援設計的建構、修改、分析和最佳化的技術。

⇒ Computer-aided-design (CAD) is the technology r_____ to the use of computers to support the construction, alteration, analysis, and optimization of a design.

⇒ Computer-aided-design (CAD) is the technology i_____ using computers to support the construction, alteration, analysis, and optimization of a design.

4. available（可用的、可取得的）可以 accessible 或 obtainable 取代。

CAE tools are available for many analyses.

現有許多可供分析的CAE工具。

⇒ CAE tools are a_____ for many analyses.

⇒ CAE tools are o_____ for many analyses.

5. refinement（精製、改良）可用enhancement, improvement 取代。

This enables refinement and optimization of the design of a product.

這使得一個產品設計的修改與最佳化變得可行。

⇒ This enables e_____ and optimization of the design of a product.

⇒ This enables i_____ and optimization of the design of a product.

6. allowed（被允許）可用 permitted 或 may 取代。

Designers are allowed to simulate and study the performance of various designs.

設計師被允許來模擬與研究不同設計的表現。

⇒ Designers are p_____ to simulate and study the performance of various designs.

⇒ Designers m_____ simulate and study the performance of various designs.

Choose the most appropriate one in the following questions

(   )   1.   Engineers are now using CAD/CAM/CAE systems for every day tasks because of the _____.

     A. remarkable advances in computing power and wider availability of software tools for design and production

     B. requirement from the customers

     C. pressure from the market

     D. company policies

(   )   2.   What is the most fundamental role of CAD in a design process?

     A. to define and delineate the geometry of design

     B. to determine the parameter of the design

     C. to optimize the design

     D. to analyze the design

     E. to simulate the design

(   )   3.   Which one in the followings may be regarded as a CAD tool?

     A. CNC

     B. robotics

     C. geometric manipulating tool

     D. kinematics program

     E. logic-timing software

(   )   4.   Programming of robots is a part of the function of _____.

     A. CAD

     B. CAM

     C. CNC

     D. CAE

     E. product design

(   )   5.   Which one in the followings is not directly related to product design?

     A. CAD

     B. CAM

     C. CAE

     D. tolerance analysis

     E. visualization

(　　) 6. Designers are allowed to simulate and study the performance of various designs using _____.

A. CAD tools

B. finite-element modeling

C. CNC

D. robotics

E. CAE tools

(　　) 7. Customize means _____.

A. regroup the customers according to their age

B. contact the customers periodically

C. classify the customers base on their income

D. manufacturing base on the need of each customer

(　　) 8. CAD tools include the _____ of the analysis results.

A. visual

B. vision, visualize

C. visualized

D. visualization

E. visualizational

(　　) 9. Robots may _____ individual task such as welding.

A. performing

B. perform

C. performance

D. performances

(　　) 10. This enables refinement and _____ of the design of a product.

A. optimize

B. optimal

C. optimize

D. optimized

E. optimization

Simulation of a Manufacturing/ Warehousing System

Questions & Discussions

1. What is a palletizer?
2. What are the two common types of conveyors?

Vocabulary

1. hierarchical [haɪəˋrɑrkɪkl̩]
   層級的 (adj)

2. discrete [dɪˋskrit]
   離散的 (adj)

3. event [ɪˋvɛnt]
   事件 (n)

4. eventual [ɪˋvɛntʃuəl]
   最終的 (adj)

5. tier [tɪr]
   層、等級 (n)；層層排列 (v)

6. conveyor [kənˋveɚ]
   輸送帶 (n)

7. photocell [ˋfotəsɛl]
   光電感應器 (n)；常用於自動系統偵側
   人或物

Terminology

a. R. J. Reynolds
   美國一家煙草公司

b. laser scanner
   雷射掃瞄器

[a]R. J. Reynolds had built a new manufacturing and warehouse facility containing many computers for controlling product flow. The capacity and potential bottlenecks of the warehouse were of concern to management since it involved a [1]hierarchical control system using ten computers. A combined [2]discrete [3]event-continuous simulation model of this facility was developed.

Basically, the warehouse receives boxes of finished goods from manufacturing and sorts them by brand before they are stored in a high-density storage area for [4]eventual shipment to local customers or distribution warehouses. The boxes are first received from the manufacturing floor and pass a [b]laser scanner to determine on which [5]tier the product is to be collected. Boxes then travel on two long [6]conveyors to an input scanner that determines a lane for the box. The box is then tracked by [7]photocells until it arrives at its assigned lane.

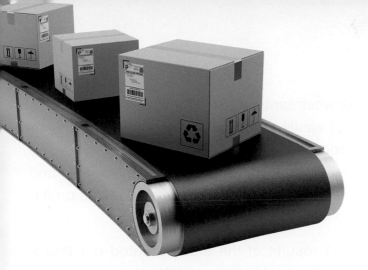

When an adequate number of boxes have been accumulated in a lane, the lane is ready for automatic [8]palletizing. An output belt and a verification scanner are used to [9]verify correct product codes and to build box trains. The box train is routed to a [10]contingency [11]diverter where trains from different tiers can be combined to an identical [12]palletizer in case of a palletizer failure. All boxes that were not properly verified at the output scanner are [13]diverted to a manual palletizing area. The verified boxes are then sent to the palletizer where they are automatically [14]palletized in a [15]brand-dependent pattern. Controllable logic and conveyor belts between the contingency diverter and the palletizers ensure space between boxes in several areas where box count is important. They also ensure the proper merging of box trains when operating in the contingency mode.

An interesting aspect of this simulation involved the modeling of the two common types of conveyors. The [c]roller conveyors are occasionally turned on and off because box spacing is not too important. Thus, loading and unloading of boxes can be modeled as discrete events. [d]Belt conveyors, however, are frequently turned on and off due to

Vocabulary

8. pallet [ˈpælɪt]
   棧板 (n)；在倉儲或運輸時，用來承載裝箱貨物的木製或塑膠墊板

9. verify [ˈvɛəfɑɪ]
   證實、查核 (v)

10. contingency [kənˈtɪndʒənsɪ]
    意外事故、意外狀況 (n)

11. diverter [daɪˈvɝtɚ]
    分流器 / 分向器 (n)

12. palletizer [ˈpælɪtaɪzɚ]
    棧板堆疊機 (n)

13. divert [daɪˈvɝt]
    分流、轉向 (v)

14. palletized [ˈpælɪtaɪz]
    把貨物疊到棧板上 (v)

15. brand-dependent [brændɪˈpɛndənt]
    視品牌而定的 (adj)

Terminology

c. roller conveyor
   滾筒式輸送帶

d. belt conveyor
   皮帶式輸送帶

Vocabulary

16. photocell [ˈfotəˌsɛl]
    光電開關 (n)

17. algorithm [ˈælgəˌrɪðəm]
    演算法 (n)

18. surge [sɜˈdʒ]
    突增 (n)(v)

Terminology

e. state variable
   狀態變數

f. contingency situation
   意外狀況

g. equipment down time
   設備停機時間

h. load leveling
   負載平衡

downstream conditions and box travel time is not easily controlled. These conveyors were modeled using [e]state variables where the belt position is treated as a state variable and pointers are used to identify the boxes on the belt.

The results of the study pointed out that a maximum utilization of 87% was achievable from the palletizers due to conveyor operations. The decrease to be expected in utilization due to down time of specific pieces of equipment was also estimated. By adding "zone clear" [16]photocells and changing the location of another photocell, an increase in the maximum utilization was achieved. The outcomes of the study were implemented. The predicted improvement in system performance was recorded for the [f]contingency situations involving [g]equipment down time. The simulation model has been expanded and has been used to assess various [17]algorithms for [18]surge controlled interleaving, zoning-based turnover, and [h]load leveling. Impressive improvements in system operations have been recorded by employing the simulation model.

Source:

Pritsker A.A.B. (1986), Introduction to simulation and SLAM II, Systems Publishing Co.

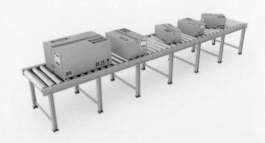

1. achieve (v) 達到

   achieved (adj) 達成的、獲得的

   achievable (adj) 可達到的 ⟵⟶ unachievable (adj) 不可達到的

   achievably (adv) 可達到的

   achievement (n) 成就

   (1) The goal was achieved earlier than expected.

   這個目標的達成，比大家期望的時間要早。

   (2) All the departments must establish at least one goal which is achievable for the year.

   所有部門必須建立至少一個當年可以達到的目標。

   (3) The achievements of this department have great contribution to the company.

   這個部門的成就對公司有很了不起之貢獻。

2. involve (v) 牽涉

   involved (adj) 牽涉到的 ⟵⟶ involvement (n) 牽涉

   (1) All the engineering staffs are involved in the research & design of this product.

   所有工程人員都涉入這個產品的研發。

   (2) The research & design of this product involve integration of system software and incorporation of advanced materials.

   這個產品的研發牽涉到系統軟體整合與先進材料之引入。

3. palletize (v) 把貨物疊到棧板上

   pallet (n) 棧板

   palletizer (n) 棧板堆疊器

   palletization (n) 棧板化

   (1) This marine company found that their pallets are inadequate to handle the cargos of this order.

   這家海運公司發現他們的棧板，不足以處理這張訂單的貨物。

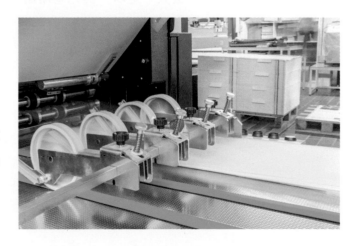

(2) Palletization is important to maximize the amount of cargos shipped in a container ship.

棧板化對於貨櫃船運送貨物量最大化是很重要的。

(3) The food industry has commonly adopted automatic palletization systems in their final packing operations.

食品工業在其最終包裝作業，常用自動化棧板堆疊系統。

4. utilize (v) 利用

utilization (n) 利用

utility (n) 效用、公用事業

All the materials are utilized in manufacturing the final products.

所有材料都被用在製造這個終端產品上。

5. verify (v) 證實、查核

verified (adj) 經查核的

verifiable (adj) 可查核的　　　⟶　　unverifiable (adj) 不可查核的

verification (n) 證實、查核

The number of pallet passing this check point is verified by a photocell.

The verification of the number of pallet passing this check point is performed by using a photocell.

通過這個檢核點的棧板數，是以一具光電開關來核實的。

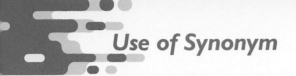

Use of Synonym

1. collect（收集）有時可用 accumulate
   （累積）取代。

   The boxes are first received from the
   manufacturing floor and pass a laser
   scanner to determine on which tier the
   product is to be collected.

   最初由製造樓層接收箱子，並通過一臺雷
   射掃瞄器來決定此產品要集中到哪一級。

   ⇒ The boxes are first received from the manufacturing floor and pass a laser
   scanner to determine on which tier the product is to be a_____.

2. occasionally（偶爾的、有時的）可用 infrequently, rarely, once in a while 取代。

   The roller conveyors are occasionally turned on and off.

   滾筒式輸送帶偶爾開啟與關閉。

   ⇒ The roller conveyors are i_____ turned on and off.

   ⇒ The roller conveyors are r_____ turned on and off.

   ⇒ The roller conveyors are turned on and off o_____.

3. combine（結合）可用 merge 及 joint 等字取代。

   The box train is routed to a contingency diverter where trains from both tiers can
   be combined to a single palletizer in the event of a palletizer failure.

   這一列裝箱子的載台被導引至一個應急用的轉向器，此轉向器可在某個棧板堆疊機故障時，
   將不同等級產品合併到同一棧板堆疊器上來處理。

   ⇒ The box train is routed to a contingency diverter where trains from both tiers
   can be j_____ to a single palletizer in the event of a palletizer failure.

   ⇒ The box train is routed to a contingency diverter where trains from both tiers
   can be m_____ to a single palletizer in the event of a palletizer failure.

4. adequate（足夠的）可用 sufficient 或 enough 取代。

   When an adequate number of boxes have been accumulated in a lane, the boxes
   are loaded on a pallet automatically.

   當一條線上足夠數量的箱子被收集後，箱子會自動被裝載在棧板上。

⇒ When a s_____ number of boxes have been accumulated in a lane, the boxes are loaded on a pallet automatically.

⇒ When an e_____ number of boxes have been accumulated in a lane, the boxes are loaded on a pallet automatically.

5. verification（證實、查核）可用 confirmation（確認）取代；同理 verify 可用 confirm 或 ensure 取代。

An output belt and a verification scanner are used to verify correct product codes and to build box trains.

一條輸出皮帶與一具驗證掃瞄器被用來驗證正確的產品編碼和建構箱子載台。

⇒ An output belt and a c_____ scanner are used to c_____ correct product codes and to build box trains.

⇒ An output belt and a verification scanner are used to e_____ correct product codes and to build box trains.

6. expand（擴充）可用 extend 取代。

The simulation model has been expanded and has been used to assess various algorithms.

這個模擬模型曾被擴充並被用來評估不同演算法。

⇒ The simulation model has been e_____ and has been used to assess various algorithms.

7. impressive（令人印象深刻的）可用spectacular（驚人的）或remarkable（非凡的）取代。

Impressive improvements in system operations have been recorded by employing the simulation model.

經由使用這個模擬模型，令人印象深刻的系統營運改善曾被記錄下來。

⇒ S_____ improvements in system operations have been recorded by employing the simulation model.

⇒ R_____ improvements in system operations have been recorded by employing the simulation model.

(   ) 1. What kind of simulation model was discussed in this lesson?

       A. a discrete event model

       B. a continuous event model

       C. a combined discrete & continuous event model

       D. a linear model

       E. a non-linear model

(   ) 2. The management concerned about the capacity and potential bottle-necks of the warehouse because _____.

       A. the system involved a hierarchical control system using ten comput-ers

       B. the system involved a semiautomated control system

       C. the palletizers have never been used

       D. the photocells have never been used

       E. the two-conveyor system has never been used

(   ) 3. Photocells are used to _____.

       A. monitor the utilization of the palletizers

       B. track the boxes until they arrive at their assigned lane

       C. track the movement of the belt conveyor

       D. monitor the travel time of the boxes

       E. monitor the failure of the palletizers

(   ) 4. Where are the boxes not properly verified at the output scanner diverted to?

       A. an automatic palletizing area

       B. a box-train area

       C. a contingency diverter

       D. a manual palletizing area

       E. a verification scanner

(   ) 5. The roller conveyors are turned on and off infrequently because _____.

       A. there are not many boxes being handled

       B. the box trains are slow

       C. box spacing is not too important

       D. the travel time of the boxes is not important

       E. the conveyors runs too fast

(   ) 6. The loading and unloading of the boxes on the roller conveyors are modeled as _____.

      A. state variable

      B. qualitative variable

      C. continuous events

      D. discrete events

      E. discrete-continuous events

(   ) 7. The verified boxes are sent to the palletizer where they are automatically palletized according to their _____.

      A. brand

      B. weight

      C. size

      D. travel time

      E. state variable

(   ) 8. The movement of the belt conveyors was modeled using _____.

      A. state variables

      B. qualitative variables

      C. continuous events

      D. discrete events

(   ) 9. Palletizer is a _____.

      A. organization

      B. manager

      C. department

      D. machine

      E. person

(   ) 10. Conveyer is a type of _____.

      A. material handling facility

      B. passenger transport facility

      C. safety alarming system

      D. security monitoring system

Development of E-commerce in Manufacturing Operations

Questions & Discussions

1. There are three broad aspects of organizational relationships between trading associates. What are they?
2. What are B2B and B2C?

Vocabulary

1. extraordinary [ɪkˋstrɔrdɪˌnɛrɪ]
   驚人的 (adj)
2. stakeholder [ˋstækˌholdɚ]
   賭金保管人利益相關者 (n)

Terminology

a. material requirement planning (MRP)
   物料需求計畫

b. enterprise resource planning (ERP)
   企業資源規劃

c. competitive advantage
   競爭優勢

New technologies such as World Wide Web (WWW), broadband, and wireless have brought [1]extraordinary economic and strategic changes in global business in recent years. They have extended the scope of commerce. In manufacturing operations, the role of these various electronic commerce (e-commerce) technologies has been speeding.

Manufacturing operations cannot function without its large business community and the relevant [2]stakeholders. Systems such as [a]materials requirement planning (MRP), [b]enterprise resource planning (ERP), product and process design systems, product document and data management are commonly used in manufacturing sectors. The extension and integration of such internally focused manufacturing systems has stepped forward significantly because of e-commerce technologies. For a company, it is no longer an issue of acquiring [c]competitive advantage in these areas but now a matter of just maintaining a business survival.

The continued advancement and maturation of e-commerce in manufacturing has emerged in industry, yet academics have been slow to investigate and assist industry to improve understanding and knowledge of this critical linkage. The concept of [3]virtual and [4]agile enterprises made clear the importance of the various e-commerce tools in management. Yet, the research in understanding and further advancing these has not flourished [5]accordingly.

Internet-based electronic marketplaces are becoming more com-mon in international competition and economy. E-commerce can take place among businesses (B2B) or between businesses and consumers (B2C), but the internet also covers a greater variety of potential commercial activities and information exchanges and chances in a virtual market. Three broad aspects of organizational relationships between trading associates have been identified including [6]transactional, information-sharing, and collaborative relationships. These relationships suggest that transactional-oriented markets are to a lesser degree relying on [d]supply chain management (SCM) principles than collaborative-oriented markets.

In 2000, the total investment in business-to-business (B2B) infrastructure exceeded $200 billion. Even with the eruption of the technology bubble, there is still continued growth in these technologies. E-commence technologies have become embedded in organizational functions, policy, and practice.

Vocabulary

7. leverage ['lɛvərɪdʒ]
   槓桿、損捍操作 (n)

8. tradeoff ['tredɔf]
   妥協 (n)

9. indispensable [,ɪndɪ'spɛnsəbl]
   不可或缺的 (adj)

Terminology

e. competitive advantage
   競爭優勢

The [7]leverage of power of the B2B market-place in a supply chain depends on sellers and buyers [e]competitive advantage. The internet has helped to resolve these [8]tradeoffs between buyers and sellers, and allowed integration necessary between every associate in the supply chain. Web-based technologies are now [9]indispensable for supply chain forecasting, planning, scheduling and implementation. The greater the integrated information flow between customers and suppliers, the easier it becomes to balance supply and demand across the entire network.

Source:

Editorial (2004), E-commerce enabled manufacturing operations: issues and analysis, Information Systems Journal, 14, 87-91.

1. dispense (v) 免掉、分發

    dispensed (adj) 免除的

    dispensable (adj) 可免除的　　　　　⟷　　indispensable (adj) 不可或缺的

    In e-commerce, the reorder cost may be dispensable.

    在電子商務，再訂成本或許可以免除。

2. emerge (v) 出現

    emerged (adj) 突然出現的

    emergent (adj) 突現地、緊急的

    emergence (n) 突現

    emergency (n) 緊急事故

    The emergence of both B2B and B2C e-commerce has changed global business model.

    B2B和B2C電子商務的湧現，改變全球商業模式。

3. organize (v) 組織

    organizable (adj) 可以組織起來的

    organized (adj) 有組織的　　　　　⟷　　unorganized (adj) 沒有組織的

    organizational (adj) 組織的

    organization (n) 組織

    organizer (n) 組織者

    (1) Dr. Li is one of the organizers of this international conference.
        李博士是這個國際研討會的組織者之一。

    (2) The company will organize people from different divisions for this project.
        公司為了這個計劃將會組織不同部門的人。

    (3) The presentation of this project seemed to be unorganized.
        這個計畫的簡報似乎缺乏組織。

4. practice (v) 練習

    practicable (adj) 能實行的

    practicably (adv) 能實行的

    practical (adj) 實務的、實習的、實際的　　　⟷　　impractical (adj) 不實際的

(   ) 10. _____-oriented markets rely on supply chain management more than other types of market.

     A. Collaboration

     B. Collaborative

     C. Collaborate

     D. Collaborated

Digitization in Telecommunications

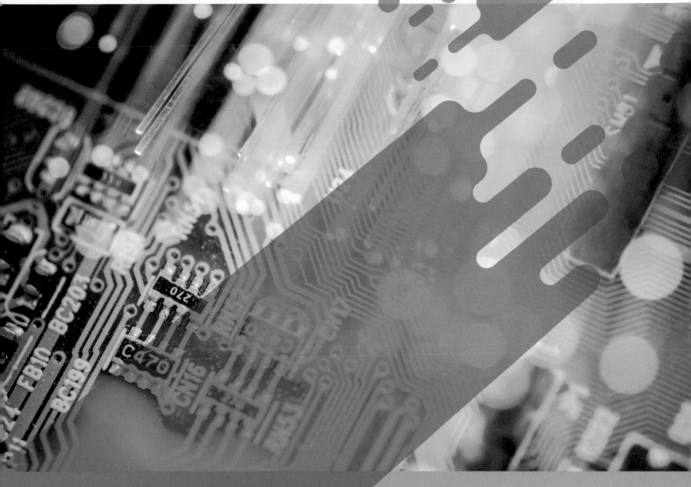

Questions & Discussions

1. What is VLSI?
2. In telecommunication fields, what technological innovations have been made?

Vocabulary

1. digitization [ˈdɪdʒə,taɪzeʃən]
   數位化 (n)

2. digital [ˈdɪdʒɪtl̩]
   數位的 (adj)

3. analog [ˈænəlɔg]
   類比 (n)

4. innovation [,ɪnəˈveʃən]
   創新 (n)

5. optic [ˈɑptɪk]
   光學的 (v)

6. lag [læg]
   落後 (n)

Terminology

a. VLSI circuit
   超大型積體電路

b. optic fiber communication
   光纖通訊

c. mobile radio communication
   移動無線通訊

[1]Digitization is a technical trend in telecommunications and in fields such as [2]digital audio systems (compact disk) and digital control of machines. A digital approach enjoys higher accuracy and stability of the system over an [3]analog system. Driving forces for digitization are [a]VLSI (very large-scale integrated) circuits and computers, which make it possible to implement circuits required for the digitization of systems.

In telecommunication fields, technological [4]innovations have been made on data and digital speech transmission on switched telephone networks, digital microwave communications, and digital [5][b]optic fiber communications. Digitization in [c]mobile radio communications has [6]lagged behind as compared to those developments. However, explosive activity in recent research and development of digital mobile communications seems to recover the delay in the digitization progress. This enhancement is further spurred by

[7]novel applications of digital mobile communications such as personal communication services, mobile computing, and mobile multimedia.

Some digital technologies can be applied in common to any field. However, others are not directly applicable because of [8]discrepancies in the requirements of a specific technical field. For mobile communications, robustness against fast fading, spectrum efficiency, power efficiency, and [9]compactness and low price of equipment are essential. Digital [10]modulation/[11]demodulation is the critical technology to fulfill these requirements for mobile communications.

Source:

Akaiwa, Yoshihiko (1997), Introduction to Digital Mobile Communication, John Wiley & Sons, Inc.

Vocabulary

7. novel [nɑˋvɛl]
   新的 (adj)

8. discrepancies [dɪˋskrɛpənsɪ]
   差異 (n)

9. compactness [kəmˋpæktnɪs]
   緊密、堅實、小巧 (n)

10. modulation [ˌmædəˋleʃən]
    調變（電子）(n)

11. demodulation [diˋmɑdʒəˌleʃən]
    解調變（電子）(n)

In telecommunication fields, technological innovations have been made on data and _____（數位的）speech transmission on switched telephone networks, _____（數位的）microwave communications, and _____（數位的）_____（光纖）communications. _____（數位化）in mobile radio communications has lagged behind as compared to those developments. However, explosive activity in recent research and development of _____（數位的）_____（移動的）communications seems to recover the delay in the _____（數位化）progress. This enhancement is further spurred by novel applications of _____（數位的）_____（移動的）communications such as personal communication services, _____（移動的）computing, and _____（移動的）multimedia.

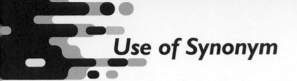

Use of Synonym

1. drive（驅動）可用 push 代替。

   Driving forces for digitization are VLSI (very large-scale integrated circuits) and computers.

   數位化的驅動力是超大型積體電路與電腦。

   ⇒ P_____ forces for digitization are VLSI (very large-scale integrated circuits) and computers.

2. novel（新的）可用 innovative, new, 或 original 取代。

   Many novel applications of digital mobile communications have been reported recently.

   許多數位移動通訊的新應用最近被報導出來。

   ⇒ Many i_____ applications of digital mobile communications have been reported recently.

   ⇒ Many n_____ applications of digital mobile communications have been reported recently.

   ⇒ Many o_____ applications of digital mobile communications have been reported recently.

3. spur（刺激、驅動）可用 advanced, impel, propel 或 stimulate 取代。

   This enhancement is further spurred by novel applications of digital mobile communications.

   這項擴充進一步被數位移動通訊的新應用向前驅動。

   ⇒ This enhancement is further a_____ by novel applications of digital mobile communications.

   ⇒ This enhancement is further i_____ by novel applications of digital mobile communications.

   ⇒ This enhancement is further p_____ by novel applications of digital mobile communications.

   ⇒ This enhancement is further s_____ by novel applications of digital mobile communications.

4. field（領域、範疇）可用 area, domain, province 取代。

Some digital technologies can be applied in common to any field.

有些數位技術可以共通的被應用到任何領域。

⇒ Some digital technologies can be applied in common to any a_____.

⇒ Some digital technologies can be applied in common to any d_____.

⇒ Some digital technologies can be applied in common to any p_____.

5. fade 可解釋為逐漸變弱或變淡，此處可用 weaken 取代。

Robustness against fast fading is essential for mobile communications.

強韌以對抗訊號快速衰退對移動通訊很重要。

⇒ Robustness against fast w_____ is essential for mobile communications.

6. fulfill（滿足、實現）可用 achieve, realize 取代。

Digital modulation/demodulation is the critical technology to fulfill these requirements for mobile communications.

數位的調變／解調是滿足這些移動通訊需求的關鍵技術。

⇒ Digital modulation/demodulation is the critical technology to a_____ these requirements for mobile communications.

⇒ Digital modulation/demodulation is the critical technology to r_____ these requirements for mobile communications.

Choose the most appropriate one in the following questions

( ) 1. What are the driving forces for digitization?

A. VLSI circuits and computers

B. microchips and automation

C. computers and network technologies

D. microchips and network technologies

E. automation and network technologies

( ) 2. What are the advantages of a digital system over an analog one?

A. the former cost less

B. the former is faster

C. the former has higher accuracy and stability

D. the former is easier to implement

E. the former has no advantage over the latter

( ) 3. Which one in the followings is essential to mobile communications?

A. robustness against fast fading

B. spectrum efficiency

C. power efficiency

D. compactness

E. low price of equipment

F. all the above items

( ) 4. Which one in the followings is true?

A. Development of digital speech transmission on switched telephone networks was lagged behind digital mobile radio communication.

B. Development of digital data transmission on switched telephone networks was lagged behind digital mobile radio communication.

C. Development of digital microwave communications was lagged behind digital mobile radio communication.

D. Development of optic fiber communications was lagged behind digital mobile radio communication.

E. Development of mobile radio communications was lagged behind optic fiber communications.

(   ) 5. In telecommunication fields, technological _____ have been made on data and digital speech transmission on switched telephone networks.

A. innovations

B. innovate

C. innovative

D. innovatively

E. innovated

(   ) 6. Many _____ applications of digital mobile communications have been reported recently.

A. notebook

B. noble

C. notary

D. novel

(   ) 7. Some digital technologies are not _____ to many fields.

A. apply

B. application

C. applying

D. applicable

(   ) 8. Some digital technologies can be applied in _____ to any field.

A. common

B. compound

C. condense

D. commute

(   ) 9. _____ against fast fading is essential for mobile communication.

A. Robustness

B. Robust

C. Robot

D. Robotic

(   ) 10. Digitization in mobile radio communications has _____ behind as compared to those developments.

A. legged

B. lagged

C. lag

D. lago

Origin of Integrated Circuit

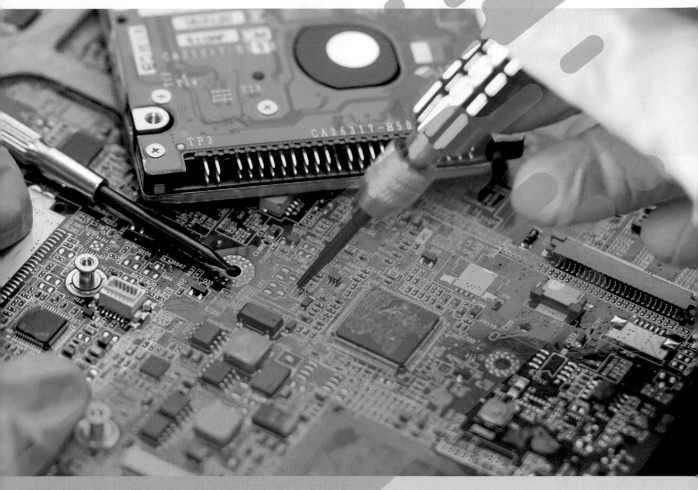

Questions & Discussions

1. The semiconductor industry is divided into two sectors. What are they?
2. What is Moore's law?

1. amplify (v) 放大

   amplified (adj) 被放大的

   amplification (n) 放大、強化

   amplifier (n) 放大器

   An amplifier is an electronic device used to amplify the electric current.

   放大器是用來放大電流的電子元件。

2. fabricate (v) 製作

   fabricative (adj) 製造的

   fabrication (n) 製造

   Fabrication of microchip required capital investment.

   微晶片製造需要資本投資。

3. perform (v) 執行、表演

   performer (n) 執行者、表演者

   performance (n) 表現

   The performance of the electronic device is tested via a complicated process.

   電子元件的性能，是經由一個複雜過程來測試的。

4. predict (v) 預測

   predicted (adj) 預測的（值）

   predictable (adj) 可預測的　　　⟷　　unpredictable (adj) 不可預測的

   predictability (n) 可預測性

   predictive (adj) 預測性的

   prediction (n) 預測

   (1) The performance of this new design is highly predictable.

   　　這個新設計的效能能夠高度地被預測。

   (2) The predictability of this new design is high.

   　　這個新設計的可預測性很高。

_____（固態技術）_____（元件）are manufactured in four stages. They are material preparation, crystal growth and _____（晶圓）preparation, _____（晶圓）_____（製作）, and _____（封裝）.

_____（元件）or _____（積體電路）are actually formed in the _____（晶圓）in stage three, or the _____（晶圓）_____（製作）stage. Up to several thousand identical circuits are formed on each _____（晶圓）, although 200 to 300 are common. Each area on a _____（晶圓）occupied by a discrete or _____（積體電路）is called a _____（晶片）. The _____（晶圓）_____（製作）process is also called fab, or microchip fabrication.

Choose the most appropriate one in the following questions

(   ) 1. Which device serves to limit current flow?

    A. capacitor

    B. resistor

    C. transistor

    D. diodes

    E. vacuum tube

(   ) 2. Which device stores charge in a circuit?

    A. capacitor

    B. resistor

    C. transistor

    D. diodes

    E. vacuum tube

(   ) 3. Which device is an improvement of vacuum tube?

    A. capacitor

    B. resistor

    C. transistor

    D. diodes

    E. chip

(   ) 4. Which device can not be made using solid-state technology?

    A. capacitor

    B. resistor

    C. transistor

    D. diodes

    E. vacuum tube

(   ) 5. Before 1959, the semiconductor industry produced individual tran-sis-tors, diodes, resistors, and capacitors, known as _____.

    A. discrete devices

    B. integrated circuit

    C. chips

    D. microchip fabrication

    E. individual devices

(　　) 6. On which year was the first solid-state transistor announced?

    A. 1930

    B. 1945

    C. 1947

    D. 1959

    E. 1964

(　　) 7. On which year was the first integrated circuit designed?

    A. 1930

    B. 1945

    C. 1947

    D. 1959

    E. 1964

(　　) 8. Who designed the first integrated circuit?

    A. Jack Kilby

    B. Gordon Moore

    C. Tom Schardt

    D. Jerry Macy

    E. Tim Klock

(　　) 9. What is Moor's law about?

    A. Discrete devices will be replaced by integrated circuit.

    B. Discrete devices account for 20 to 30 percent of the dollar volume of all semiconductor devices sold.

    C. Germanium may be used as natural resistor.

    D. predicted that integrated circuit density would double every year

    E. development of electronic industry

(　　) 10. Germanium is a type of _____.

    A. element

    B. technology

    C. manufacturing process

    D. methodology

Fabrication of Integrated Circuit

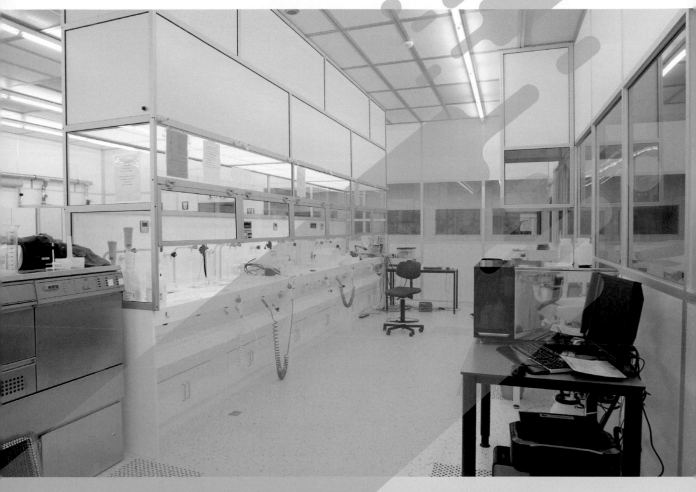

Questions & Discussions

1. Describe the four stages in IC fabrication.
2. What is spin coating? What is the objective of coating in IC fabrication?

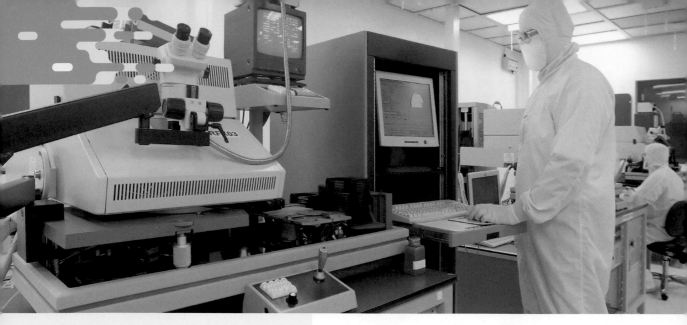

Vocabulary

1. imaging [ˈɪmɪdʒɪŋ]
   成像 (n)

2. deposition [ˌdɛpəˈzɪʃən]
   沉澱 (n)

3. etching [ˈɛtʃɪŋ]
   蝕刻 (n)

4. mask [mɑsk]
   光罩 (n)；遮光 (v)

5. silica [ˈsɪlɪkə]
   矽土、氧化矽 (n)

6. silicon [ˈsɪlɪkən]
   矽 (n)

7. agatize [ˈægəˌtaɪz]
   使成瑪瑙狀 (v)

8. furnace [ˈfɜnəs]
   加熱爐 (n)

9. purified [ˈpjʊrəˌfaɪd]
   純化的 (adj)

10. polycrystalline [ˌpɑlɪˈkrɪstəlɪn]
    多晶體的 (adj)

11. ingot [ˈɪŋgət]
    晶柱 (n)

12. crucible [ˈkrusəbl̩]
    坩鍋 (n)

The fabrication of ICs involves many complicated steps. These steps can be grouped into four stages of processes: (1) starting material, (2) [1]imaging, (3) [2]deposition and growth, and (4) [3]etching and [4]masking operations. The result of these stages is the transformation of raw [5]silica into many individual ICs, each containing up to several million circuits.

The first step in producing a [6]silicon wafer is purifying raw silica, which is mined from beach sand or taken in chunks from [7]agatized rock deposits. The raw silica is heated in a high-temperature [8]furnace. The result is the separation and removal of impurities, leaving a chemically [9]purified [10]polycrystalline silicon material. A single crystal [11]ingot is pulled in a machine containing a [12]crucible based on this purified raw material.

The ingot is grown by placing a single-crystal seed on the end of a shaft and rotating it slowly through and away from ᵃmolten silicon. The melting and refreezing of the silicon at the seed interface allows crystal formation to take place exactly following the crystal structure of the seed. Highly automated computer-controlled ᵇcrystal pullers are used to produce high quality ingots.

The ingots, produced by the crystal pullers, are sliced into wafers with diamond slicing saws. Sliced wafer are then ¹³lapped to remove the damage and irregularities caused by slicing. Mechanical lapping is performed in controlled ᶜlapping machines. The final step in producing high-quality surfaces for imaging is chemical etching of the silicon. This produces a surface of optical quality by simultaneously removing ¹⁴debris from the lapping operation and leveling the silicon surface, leaving a silicon "mirror".

¹⁵Spin ¹⁶coating is a technique for applying ¹⁷photoresist to wafers. The resist is applied onto the surfaces of the wafers, which are then accelerated on the spinning ¹⁸coater to provide a thin uniform film across the wafer surface. Coating is always performed in a highly controlled ᵈclean-room environment. The wafers are coated in automatic cassette-loaded systems with predetermined the coating parameters. The objective of coating is to provide a uniform and defect-free layer of a photo or ¹⁹electron-sensitive masking material.

Vocabulary

13. lap [læp]
    研磨 (v)

14. debris [ˋdebri]
    殘渣、顆粒 (n)

15. spin [spɪn]
    旋轉 (n)(v)

16. coating [kotɪŋ]
    塗層 (n)

17. photoresist [fotorɪˋzɪst]
    光阻 (n)

18. coater [kotə]
    塗佈機 (n)

19. electron [ɪˋlɛktran]
    電子 (n)

Terminology

a. molten silicon
   熔化的矽

b. crystal puller
   拉晶長晶機

c. lapping machine
   研磨機

d. clean room
   無塵室

Wet- and dry-etching techniques are commonly used in the imaging process. Etching is employed to remove the semiconductor layer as required. The etching control parameters are time, uniformity, temperature, and concentration of the [20]etch species (liquid or gas).

The oxidation of silicon is the most critical process in the deposition and growth stage. The [21]oxidation of silicon results in the formation of a highly stable and useful material, [e]silicon dioxide (SiO_2). Silicon dioxide is used as the surface for imaging operations. Silicon dioxide is formed in either an oxygen or steam atmosphere. This atmosphere is provided by an [f]oxidation tube (also called diffusion tube or oxide furnace).

Ion [22]implantation is also an important process which places impurity, or [23]doping, ions in semiconductor layers at various depths and with accurate control of dopant ion concentration. The [g]ion implanter functions by providing an ion source in which collisions of electrons and atoms result in many ions. The ions required for doping are selected out by a magnet and routed to an acceleration tube that goes directly onto the area on the wafer where the doping is desired.

Vocabulary

24. chromium [ˈkromɪəm]
（金屬）鉻 (n)

Terminology

h. Photomask
光罩

Production of [h]photomasks is required in IC fabrication. The photomask etching application is diversified into several different etch materials and their respective etches. Hard-surface masks are primarily glass-based masks with a coating of some metal or oxide. [24]Chromium is the predominant hard-surface photomask coating material. It provides advantages of high resolution, durability, and ease of fabrication. Positive resist is used to image and mask the etching of the chromium. Chromium can be shiny, black, or anti-reflective. Chromium mask etching results in very high quality masks for advanced VLSI and conventional IC fabrication.

Source:

Elliott, D.J. (1989), Integrated Circuit Fabrication Technology, 2nd ed, McGraw-Hill International.

Vocabulary

25. foundry [ˈfaʊndrɪ]
鑄造廠；鑄造 (n)

26. commercialize [kəˈmɝʃəˌlaɪz]
商業化 (v)

27. lithography [lɪˈθɑgrəfɪ]
平版印刷術 (n)

Terminology

i. nanometer
奈米

j. fabless
無廠的

History

Taiwan Semiconductor Manufacturing Company (TSMC) is a Taiwanese multinational semiconductor manufacturing company. It is one of Taiwan's largest companies, the world's most valuable semiconductor company, and the world's largest dedicated independent semiconductor [25]foundry, with its headquarters and main operations located in the Science Park in Hsinchu, Taiwan. TSMC has a global capacity of about 13 million 12 in equivalent wafers per year as of 2020, and makes chips for customers with process nodes from 2 micron to 7 nanometers. TSMC is the first foundry to provide 7 nanometer production capabilities and the first to [26]commercialize extreme ultraviolet [27]lithography technology in high volume. Founded in Taiwan in 1987 by Morris Chang, TSMC was the world's first dedicated semiconductor foundry and has long been the leading company in its field. Since 1994, TSMC has had a compound annual growth rate of 17.4% in revenue. Most of the leading fabless semiconductor companies such as Advanced Micro Devices (AMD) and Qualcomm are customers of TSMC. Some integrated device manufacturers that have their own fabrication facilities like Intel and Texas Instruments outsource some of their production to TSMC. The company has been increasing and upgrading its manufacturing capacity. In 2011, the company planned to increase research and development expenditures by almost 39% in an effort to fend off growing competition and to expand capacity by 30% to meet strong market demand. Apple has become TSMC's most important customer. TSMC's N7+ is the first commercially available extreme [28]ultraviolet lithographic process in the semiconductor industry. It uses ultraviolet patterning and enables more acute circuits to be implemented on the silicon. Compared with the previous technology node, N7+ offers a 15-20% higher transistor density and 10% reduction in [k]power consumption. The volume increase TSMC managed from the N7 was the fastest ever to meet the demands of the market, faster than 10 nm and 16nm. The N5 [29]iteration doubles transistor density and improves performance by an additional 15%.

Vocabulary

28. ultraviolet [ˌʌltrəˈvaɪəlɪt]
紫外線的 (adj)；紫外線 (n)
29. iteration [ˌɪtəˈreʃən]
迭代、重複 (n)

Terminology

k. power consumption
電力損耗

1. deposit (v) 沉澱、儲存

   deposit (n) 沉澱、沉澱物、存款、押金

   deposition (n) 沉澱

   Deposition is a physical process that solid particles in a solution deposit on the bottom of the container after a period of time.

   沉澱是一種物理過程，此過程溶劑中的固體顆粒，經過一段時間會沉至容器底部。

2. image (v) 想像

   imaginable (adj) 可想像的 ⟷ unimaginable (adj) 無法想像的

   imaginary (adj) 想像的

   imagination (n) 想像

   imagine (n) 影像

   imaging (n) 成像

   (1) Several chemicals are used in the imaging process.

   多種化學品用在成像製程。

   (2) It was once unimaginable that a microchip could store a huge amount of data.

   一片微晶片可以儲存大量數據，曾經是難以想像的。

   (3) Raw silica must be purified before single crystal ingots may be produced.

   原始的矽土必須先純化，之後才能生產單晶柱。

   (4) A high-temperature furnace is used for purification purpose.

   一個高溫爐被用來達到純化的目的。

   (5) The quality of the chip been produced is dependent on the purity of the raw silicon material.

   生產出來的晶片品質，要仰賴原始矽材料的純度。

3. pure (adj) 純的   ⟷   impure (adj) 不純的

   purity (n) 純潔   ⟷   impurity (n) 不純物、雜質

   purely (adv) 純的

   purify (v) 純化

   purified (adj) 純化的

   purifier (n) 純化劑

   purification (n) 純化

(1) The impurities on the chips must be removed.

晶片上的雜質必須被移除。

(2) The purified chemicals are stored in a cylinder.

純化的化學品被儲存在一個鋼瓶裡。

(3) The purification process involves removal of impurities on the wafers.

純化過程牽涉到移除晶片上的雜質。

4. oxidize (v) 氧化

   oxide (n) 氧化物

   dioxide (n) 二氧化物（「di」是二的意思）

   oxidant (n) 氧化劑

   oxidation (n) 氧化

   carbon dioxide 二氧化碳

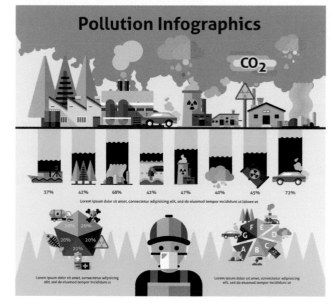

(1) Several oxidants are used to facilitate the chemical reactions in this process.

多種氧化劑被用來促進這個程序的化學反應。

(2) There is a sensor to detect the content of carbon dioxide in this room.

有一個感應器來偵測這個房間裡的二氧化碳含量。

(3) The oxidation of silicon is processed within an oxidation tube.

矽的氧化是在一個氧化管內進行的。

221

5. regular (adj) 規則的

   regularly (adv) 規則的

   irregular (adj) 不規則的   ⟷   irregularly (adv) 不規則的

   irregularity (n) 不規律（性）   ⟷   regularity (n) 規律（性）

   (1) The irregular surface of this part may be treated by a lapping operation.

   這個零件表面的不規則可經由一個研磨操作來處理。

   (2) An irregular job rotation system has been adopted in this chip manufacturing factory.

   這家晶片製造廠採用了一套不規則的輪班系統。

   (3) A new technique has been developed to reduce the irregularity of wafer surface in chip manufacturing.

   一個新技術被開發出來，以降低晶片製造中晶圓表面的不規則性。

6. fabless (adj) 無製造廠的

   fabric (n) 織物，織品，布料；構造，結構；組織

   fabricate (v) 製造

   fabrication (n) 製造

   fabricative (adj) 製造的

   (1) This fabless IC company has outsourcing its wafer fabrication to TSMC.

   這家無製造廠的IC公司，將其晶圓製作外包給了TSMC。

   (2) These clothes are made of imported fabrics.

   這些衣服用進口布料製成。

   (3) The whole social fabric was threatened with disintegration.

   整個社會結構受有瓦解的威脅。

7. commerce (n) 商業

commercial (adj) 商業的；(n) 商業廣告

commercially (adv) 商業的

commercialize (v) 商業化

commercialized (adj) 商業化的

(1) There are many commercial banks in Taipei.

台北有許多商業銀行。

(2) YouTube videos are embedded with too many commercials.

YouTube影片被植入了太多商業廣告。

(3) Facebook is becoming commercialized.

Facebook逐漸變得商業化。

(4) TSMC is the first foundry to commercialize extreme ultraviolet lithography technology.

台積電是第一家將極紫外光刻技術商業化的鑄造廠。

The _____（氧化）of _____（矽）is the most critical process in the deposition and growth stage. The _____（氧化）of _____（矽）results in the formation of a highly stable and useful material, _____ _____（二氧化矽）(SiO$_2$). _____ _____（二氧化矽）is used as the surface for imaging operations. It is formed in either an oxygen or steam atmosphere. This atmosphere is provided by an _____（氧化）tube. _____（離子植入）is also an important process which places impurity, or doping, _____s（離子）in semiconductor layers at various depths and with accurate control of dopant ion concentration. The _____（離子植入機）functions by providing an _____（離子）source in which collisions of _____s（電子）and _____s（原子）result in many _____s（離子）. The _____s（離子）required for doping are selected out by a magnet and routed to an acceleration tube that goes directly onto the area on the _____（晶圓）where the doping is desired.

1. separation（分離）可用 division, partition 取代。

The separation and removal of impurities of the raw silica is performed in a high-temperature furnace.

原料矽不純物的分離與移除是在一個高溫爐內進行的。

⇒ The d_____ and removal of impurities of the raw silica is performed in a high-temperature furnace.

⇒ The p_____ and removal of impurities of the raw silica is performed in a high-temperature furnace.

2. simultaneously（同時的）可用 at the same time, concurrently 取代。

This produces a surface of optical quality by removing debris from the lapping operation and leveling the silicon surface simultaneously.

經由同時移除自研磨作業來的殘渣與矽表面拉平，可產生一個具光學品質的表面。

⇒ This produces a surface of optical quality by removing debris from the lapping operation and leveling the silicon surface a_____.

⇒ This produces a surface of optical quality by removing debris from the lapping operation and leveling the silicon surface c_____.

3. debris（殘渣或顆粒）可用 wreckage, fragment, remains 取代。

By removing debris from the lapping operation and leveling the silicon surface simultaneously, the process produces a shiny surface on the wafer.

經由同時移除自研磨作業來的殘渣與矽表面拉平，這個製程在晶圓上產生一個光亮的表面。

⇒ By removing w_____ from the lapping operation and leveling the silicon surface simultaneously, the process produces a shiny surface on the wafer.

⇒ By removing f_____ from the lapping operation and leveling the silicon surface simultaneously, the process produces a shiny surface on the wafer.

⇒ By removing r_____ from the lapping operation and leveling the silicon surface simultaneously, the process produces a shiny surface on the wafer.

4. conventional（傳統的）可用 traditional, typical, customary 取代。

Chromium mask etching results in very high quality masks for advanced VLSI and conventional IC fabrication.

鉻光罩蝕刻可以產生非常高品質的光罩，使用於高階超大型積體電路與傳統積體電路的製作。

⇒ Chromium mask etching results in very high quality masks for advanced VLSI and t_____ IC fabrication.

⇒ Chromium mask etching results in very high quality masks for advanced VLSI and t_____ IC fabrication.

⇒ Chromium mask etching results in very high quality masks for advanced VLSI and c_____ IC fabrication.

5. objective（目的）可用 purpose, aim 取代。

The objective of coating is to provide a uniform and defect-free layer of a photo or electron-sensitive masking material.

塗料的目的是要提供一層均勻、無暇疵並且對光或電子敏感的光罩材料。

⇒ The p_____ of coating is to provide a uniform and defect-free layer of a photo or electron-sensitive masking material.

⇒ The a_____ of coating is to provide a uniform and defect-free layer of a photo or electron-sensitive masking material.

6. predominant（主要的、具支配地位的）可用 principal, superior（優越的）取代。

Chromium is the predominant hard-surface photomask coating material.

鉻是主要的硬表面光罩塗層材料。

⇒ Chromium is the p_____ hard-surface photomask coating material.

⇒ Chromium is the s_____ hard-surface photomask coating material.

(　) 1. What is the first step in producing a silicon wafer?

A. purifying raw silica

B. crystal ingot pulling

C. spin coating

D. silicon dioxide forming

E. doping

(　) 2. What is a crystal ingot?

A. It is a pie-shaped silicon solid.

B. It is a column-shaped silicon crystal.

C. It is molten silicon.

D. It is an agatized rock deposited.

E. It is a chemically purified polycrystalline silicon material.

(　) 3. What tools are used in slicing the ingots into wafers?

A. laser cutting machines

B. water streams

C. diamond slicing saws

D. spin coating machines

E. oxidation tube

(　) 4. What is the objective of photoresist coating?

A. to purify the silica

B. to remove the semiconductor layer as required

C. to level the silicon surface

D. to produce an anti-reflective surface

E. to provide a uniform and defect-free layer of a photo or electron-sensitive masking material

(　) 5. What is the objective of etching?

A. to purify the silica

B. to remove the semiconductor layer as required

C. to level the silicon surface

D. to produce an anti-reflective surface

E. to provide a uniform and defect-free layer of a photo or electron-sensitive masking material

(　　) 6. The oxidation of silicon is the most critical processes in _____.

    A. starting material

    B. imaging

    C. deposition and growth

    D. etching and masking operations

    E. purify silica

(　　) 7. What is an ion implanter?

    A. a machine containing diamond saws

    B. a machine containing a crucible

    C. a machine containing a diffusion tube

    D. a machine which places impurity ions in semiconductor layers

    E. a machine containing an ingot

(　　) 8. Which one in the followings is not one of the advantages of using chromium as the photomask coating material?

    A. high resolution

    B. durability

    C. ease of fabrication

    D. anti-reflective

(　　) 9. Sliced wafer are then lapped to remove the _____ caused by slicing.

    A. regular

    B. regularly

    C. irregular

    D. irregularities

(　　) 10. The _____ of silicon results in the formation of a highly stable and useful material.

    A. oxide

    B. oxidization

    C. oxided

    D. dioxide

Killers of Semiconductors

Questions & Discussions

1. There are four types of killers of semiconductor devices. What are they?
2. How do unwanted chemicals interfere with wafer processing?

1. vulnerable [ˈvʌlnərəbl̩]
   易受損的 (adj)

2. contamination [kənˌtæməˈneʃən]
   汙染 (n)

3. micron [ˈmaɪkran]
   微米 (n)

Terminology

a. rule of thumb
   經驗法則

Semiconductor devices are [1]vulnerable to many kinds of [2]contamination, including particles, metallic ions, chemicals, and bacteria. The sensitivity is mainly due to the small sizes of the devices and the thinness of deposited layers on the wafer. The dimensions of the devices are in the range of [3]micron (micrometer or μm). One micron is equal to 10^{-6} meters. Another way to image the size of a micron is that the diameter of a human hair is about 100 μm. The small physical dimension of the devices makes them very vulnerable to particles in the air, coming from the workers, or generated by the equipment. As the device size and films become smaller, the allowable particle size in the air must be controlled to a much smaller dimension.

A [a]rule of thumb is that the particle size must be smaller than one-tenth the minimum designed size. A 0.3 μm device is vulnerable to 0.03 μm diameter particles. Particles in a critical area of a chip damage its function and result in so-called killer defects. On any wafer there are particles. Some of the particles, located in less sensitive areas, are harmless. Current [b]state-of-the-art processing seeks to control the number of particles on a 200-mm wafer to no more than 10 particles, 0.3 μm in size.

Semiconductor devices are fabricated through our ability to create the two [4]conductivity types in wafers, control the [5]resistivity through doping, and create Negative-Positive junctions in the devices. These three properties are achieved by introducing specific [6]dopants into the crystal. Unfortunately, a small amount of certain [c]electrical [7]contaminants may deteriorate the electrical characteristics, performance, and reliability of the devices in the wafer. The contaminants causing these problems are known as mobile [8]ionic contaminants (MICs).

MICs are atoms of metals in the semiconducting materials in ionic form. These ions are highly mobile in semiconductor materials. This mobility enables movement of the metallic ions inside the device, even after passing electrical testing and packaging, and results in failure of the device. Unfortunately, the metals that cause these problems in silicon devices are present in most chemicals. On a wafer, MIC contamination must be less than 10^{10} atoms per square centimeter. [9]Sodium is the most common mobile ionic contaminant in most untreated chemicals. Control of sodium is, therefore, a primary task in silicon processing.

Vocabulary

4. conductivity [ˌkɑndʌkˈtɪvətɪ]
導電性 (n)

5. resistivity [ˌrizɪsˈtɪvətɪ]
電阻（係數）(n)

6. dopants [ˈdopənt]
摻雜劑 (n)

7. contaminant [kənˈtæmənənt]
汙染物 (n)

8. ionic [aɪˈɑnɪk]
離子的 (adj)

9. sodium [ˈsodɪəm]
鈉 (n)

Terminology

b. state-of-the-art
最新技術的

c. electrical
電的、帶電的與 electronic（電子的）不同，不可混用

A small amount of electrical contaminants may deteriorate the electrical performance of the electronic devices.
其中，
electrical contaminants 是指帶電的汙染物
electrical performance 是指電力機能
electronic devices 則指電子元件

10. contaminated [kən'tæmə,netɪd]
    被汙染的 (adj)

11. etching ['ɛtʃɪŋ]
    蝕刻 (n)

12. compound ['kɑmpaʊnd]
    混合物、化合物 (n)

13. chlorine ['klorin]
    氯 (n)

The third major contaminant in semiconductor process is unwanted chemicals. Process chemicals and process water can be [10]contaminated with unwanted trace chemicals that interfere with the wafer processing. They may result in unwanted surface [11]etching, create [12]compounds that cannot be removed from the devices, or cause non-uniform processes. [13]Chlorine is such a contaminant and is rigorously controlled in process chemicals.

Semiconductor may also be contaminated by bacteria. Bacteria are organisms that grow in water systems and on surfaces not cleaned regularly. Bacteria on a device act as particulate contamination and may contribute unwanted metallic ions to the chip surface.

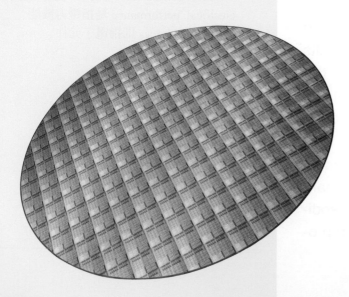

1. contaminate (v) 汙染

   contaminated (adj) 被汙染的

   contaminative (adj) 汙染的

   contamination (n) 汙染

   contaminant (n) 汙染物

   (1) The solvent discharged by this factory has contaminated the water in the river.

   這家工廠排放的溶劑汙染了河裡的水。

   (2) Environmental contamination problems are serious in this country.

   這個國家的環境汙染問題很嚴重。

   (3) Chlorine is one of the commonly used process chemicals which becomes an unwanted contaminant on the surface of wafers.

   氯是一種常用的製程化學藥品，它後來會變成晶圓表面上不要的汙染物。

2. conduct (v) 導電、傳導

   conductive (adj) 傳導的

   conductively (adv) 傳導的

   conductivity (n) 導電性

   conductance (n) 傳導

   conductor (n) 導體

   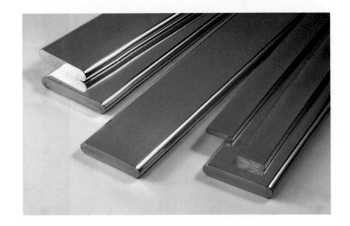

   (1) Copper has good conductivity.

   銅有很好的導電性。

   (2) Copper is a good conductor.

   銅是很好的導體。

3. fortune (n) 財富、幸運

   fortunate (adj) 好運的   ⟷   unfortunate (adj) 不幸的

   fortunately (adv) 好運的   ⟷   unfortunately (adv) 不幸的

   It was unfortunate that several contaminants were found on the semi-products.

   Unfortunately, several contaminants were found on the semi-products.

   很不幸地，半成品上發現多種汙染物。

4. treat (v) 處理

retreat (v) 撤退、退避

treated (adj) 被處理的　　　　⟷　　untreated (adj) 未被處裡的

treatment (n) 處理

(1) Discharge of untreated waste water into the public drainage is prohibited.

排放未被處裡的廢水到公共排水系統，是被禁止的。

(2) Treatments of waste water are required for all companies in the Science Park.

廢水處理是科學園區裡所有公司都必須做的。

5. want (v) 要

wanted (adj) 被通緝的；被徵求的　　⟷　　unwanted (adj) 不想要的

Unwanted chemicals may interfere the manufacturing process of wafer and must be removed.

不要的化學品會干擾晶片製程，必須移除。

6. vulnerable (adj) 易受損的

vulnerably (adv) 易受損的

vulnerability (n) 易受損、弱點

(1) All the IC chips are vulnerable before they are packing.

封裝前所有的IC晶片都是易受損的。

(2) Packing is required to reduce the vulnerability of chips before shipping to the customers.

封裝是必須的，以減少晶片在送交客戶前的易損性。

Semiconductor devices are very _____（易受損的）to many kinds of _____（汙染）, including _____s（固體顆粒）, metallic _____s（離子）, chemicals, and _____（細菌）. The sensitivity is mainly due to the small sizes of the devices and the thinness of deposited layers on the _____（晶圓）. The dimensions of the devices are in the range of _____（微米）(µm). One _____（微米）is equal to 10-6 meter. Another way to image the size of a _____（微米）is that the diameter of a human hair is about 100 µm. The small physical dimension of the devices makes them very _____（易受損的）to _____s（固體顆粒）in the air, coming from the workers, or generated by the equipment. As the device size and films become smaller, the allowable _____（固體顆粒）size in the air must be controlled to a much smaller dimension.

1. junction（連接）可用 joint, connection, intersection 取代。

Semiconductor devices are fabricated through our ability to create Negative-Positive junctions in the devices.

半導體元件的製造，是經由我們在元件上建立陰極－陽極接面的能力所達成。

⇒ Semiconductor devices are fabricated through our ability to create Negative-Positive j_____ in the devices.

⇒ Semiconductor devices are fabricated through our ability to create Negative-Positive c_____ in the devices.

⇒ Semiconductor devices are fabricated through our ability to create Negative-Positive i_____ in the devices.

2. dimension 當做「尺寸」或「尺度」解釋時可用 scale 取代。

The dimensions of the devices are in the range of micron (micrometer or μm).

元件的尺寸在數個微米之間（微米或μm）。

⇒ The s_____ of the devices are in the range of micron (micrometer or μm).

3. primary（主要的）可用 major, main 取代。

Control of sodium is, therefore, a primary task in silicon processing.

因此，在矽製程中鈉的控制是一件主要工作。

⇒ Control of sodium is, therefore, a m_____ task in silicon processing.

⇒ Control of sodium is, therefore, a m_____ task in silicon processing.

4. introduce 當做引入、摻入時可用 dope 取代。

These three properties are achieved by introducing specific dopants into the crystal.

這三種性質的獲得是經由在晶體中摻入特定之摻雜劑。

⇒ These three properties are achieved by d_____ specific dopants into the crystal.

5. create（創造、產生）可用generate, produce取代。

They may create compounds that cannot be removed from the devices.

它們可產生無法由元件移除的化合物。

⇒ They may g_____ compounds that cannot be removed from the devices.

⇒ They may p_____ compounds that cannot be removed from the devices.

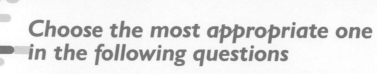

(   ) 1. Semiconductor devices are not vulnerable to _____.

      A. particles

      B. metallic ions

      C. humidity

      D. chemicals

      E. bacteria

(   ) 2. What are the scales of common semiconductor devices?

      A. centimeters

      B. microns

      C. millimeters

      D. nanometers

      E. gigameters

(   ) 3. How big should the particles in a semiconductor manufacturing environment be controlled?

      A. smaller than one-third the minimum designed device size

      B. smaller than one-tenth the minimum designed device size

      C. not more than 0.03μm in diameter

      D. not more than 0.3μm in diameter

      E. not more than 10-6 meter

(   ) 4. The bases for fabricating semicon-ductor devices include the followings of our abilities except _____.

      A. applying nanotechnology

      B. creating the two conductivity types in wafers

      C. controlling the resistivity through doping

      D. creating Negative-Positive junctions in the devices

(   ) 5. Which one is the most common mobile ionic contaminant in most untreated chemicals?

      A. germanium

      B. chlorine

      C. sodium

      D. silicon

      E. lithium

(   )   6.   How can we control the resistivity in chip fabrication?

     A. introducing germanium

     B. introducing silicon

     C. introducing dopants

     D. introducing MICs

     E. introducing bacterial

(   )   7.   MICs are detrimental to semiconductors because _____.

     A. they are highly mobile

     B. they may result in unwanted surface etching

     C. they may create compounds that cannot be removed

     D. they may cause non-uniform processes

     E. they are too small

(   )   8.   Which one is the most common unwanted chemical in chip fabrication?

     A. germanium

     B. chlorine

     C. sodium

     D. silicon

     E. lithium

(   )   9.   _____, the metals that cause these problems in silicon devices are present in most chemicals.

     A. Often

     B. Unfortunately

     C. Fortune

     D. Fortunate

(   )   10. These ions are highly _____ in semiconductor materials.

     A. movement

     B. automatic

     C. automobile

     D. mobile

240

TFT-LCD Displays

Questions & Discussions

1. What are liquid crystals?
2. A defective LCD pixel may be found as either a "lit" or a "dead" pixel. Which type is more common? Can we fix them?

Vocabulary

1. botanist [ˈbɑtṇɪst]
   植物學家 (n)

2. coin [kɔɪn]
   創造 (v)

3. physicist [ˈfɪzəsɪst]
   物理學家 (n)

4. transparent [trænsˈpɛrənt]
   透明的 (adj)

5. alignment [əˈlaɪnmənt]
   排列 (n)

Liquid crystals were first discovered in 19th century by an Austrian [1]botanist, Friedrich Reinitzer. The term "liquid crystal" was [2]coined later by Otto Lehmann, a German [3]physicist.

Liquid crystals are almost [4]transparent substances, exhibiting the properties of both solid and liquid. Light passing through liquid crystals follows the [5]alignment of the molecules that make them up. This is a property of solid substance. Scientist, in the 1960s, found that charging liquid crystals with electricity changed their molecular alignment, and consequently the way light passed through them.

Since its introduction in 1971 as a display medium, liquid crystal displays (LCDs) have been used in many consumer electronics, including miniature televisions, digital and video cameras and monitors. Today, the LCD is believed to be the most likely one to replace the CRT display. The LCD technology has been advanced remarkably since its origin, to the spot where today's products no longer [6]resemble the [7]clumsy, monochrome monitors of old.

Many firms have adopted [a]Thin Film Transistor (TFT) technology to improve color screens. In a TFT screen, a matrix of transistors (or active matrix) is connected to the LCD panel. One transistor corresponds to each color (RGB) of each pixel. These transistors drive the pixels, eliminating the problems of [8]ghosting and slow response speed that [9]afflict non-TFT LCDs. The result is the screen response times of 25 ms, [10]contrast ratios in the range of 200:1 to 400:1 and brightness values between 200 and 250 cd/m^2 ([b]candela per square meter).

Vocabulary

6. resemble [rɪˈzɛmbl̩]
   類似、比擬 (v)

7. clumsy [ˈklʌmzɪ]
   笨拙的 (adj)

8. ghosting [ˈgostɪŋ]
   鬼影 (n)

9. afflict [əˈflɪkt]
   困擾、折磨 (v)

10. contrast [ˈkɑntræst]
    對比 (n)

11. voltage [ˈvoltɪdʒ]
    電壓 (n)

12. passive [ˈpæsɪv]
    被動的 (adj)

13. polarize [ˈpoləˌraɪz]
    極化 (v)

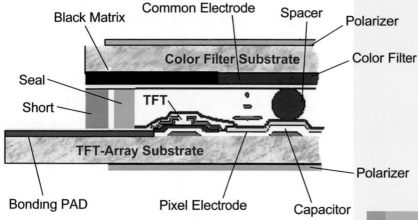

The liquid crystal elements of each pixel are arranged in such a way that in the state with no [11]voltage applied, the light coming through the [12]passive filter is [13]polarized so as to pass through the screen. When a voltage is ap-

Terminology

a. Thin Film Transistor (TFT)
   薄膜電晶體

b. candela per square meter
   平方米燭光

14. polarization [ˌpolərəˈzeʃən]
    極化 (n)

15. pixel [ˈpɪksəl]
    像素、光點 (n)

16. resolution [ˌrɛzəˈljuʃən]
    解析度 (n)

17. matrix [ˈmetrɪks]
    矩陣、陣列 (n)

18. impurities [ɪmˈpjʊrətɪ]
    雜質 (n)

19. dysfunction [dɪsˈfʌŋkʃən]
    功能不良 (n)(v)

20. disable [dɪsˈebḷ]
    使失能 (v)

Terminology

c. in proportion to
   ...與...成比例

plied across the liquid crystal elements, they twist by up to ninety degrees [c]in proportion to the voltage to alter their [14]polarization and thereby blocking the light's path. The transistors control the degree of twist and hence the intensity of the red, green and blue elements of each [15]pixel forming the image on the display.

TFT screens can be made much thinner than non-TFT screens, making them lighter. Huge amount of transistors are needed on each TFT screen. A screen with a [16]resolution of 1024x768 needs 2,359,296 (1024×768×3) transistors. Each transistor has to be perfect. The complete [17]matrix of transistors is produced on a single silicon wafer. The whole wafer must be discarded if more than a certain number of [18]impurities are found on it. The impurities may result in problematic transistors and hence defective pixels on the display.

A defective LCD pixel may be found as either a "lit" or a "dead" pixel. A lit pixel appears as one randomly-placed red, blue and/or green pixel element on a black background. A "dead" or "missing" pixel, on the other hand, appears as a black dot on white background. A lit pixel is more common. It is caused by the [19]dysfunction of a transistor which results in a permanently "turned-on" pixel. Unfortunately, fixing such a transistor is impossible after assembly. It is possible to [20]disable a problematic transistor using a laser. This, however, creates a black dot which would appear on a white or colored background.

Permanently turned on pixels are fairly common in LCD manufacturing. Based on user feedback and manufacturing cost data, LCD manufacturers have established limits for acceptable number of defective pixels on a given panel. The aim in establishing these limits is to maintain reasonable product pricing while minimizing user [21]dissatisfaction causing by the defective pixels. For example, a 1024×768 resolution panel contains a total of 2,359,296 pixels. A 10 defective pixels would have a [d]pixel defect rate of (10/2,359,296)×100% = 0.0004%.

Vocabulary

21. dissatisfaction [dɪssætɪsˈfækʃən]
不滿意 (n)

Terminology

d. pixel defect rate
光點故障率

1. botany (n) 植物學

   botanic (adj) 植物學的

   botanist (n) 植物學家

   Several famous botanists have jointed this conference and made speeches.

   多位知名的植物學家參加這個會議，並發表演說。

2. intense (adj) 強烈的

   intensive (adj) 密集的、加強的

   intensively (adv) 密集的、加強的

   intensity (n) 強度

   The intensity of the light may be measured using a light meter.

   光線的強度可用一個光表來量。

3. pole (n) 極地

   polar (adj) （南／北）極的

   polarize (v) 使極化

   polarization (n) 極化

   Polarization is the process that ions with positive and negative charge shift to two extremes.

   極化是帶正、負電荷的離子移動到兩個極端之過程。

4. satisfy (v) 使滿足　　　　　⟷　　dissatisfy (v) 使不滿意

   satisfied (adj) 滿足的

   satisfactory (adj) 滿意的　　　　⟷　　dissatisfactory (adj) 不滿意的

   satisfaction (n) 滿意　　　　　⟷　　dissatisfaction (n) 不滿意

   (1) User satisfactions are important for the success of this new design.

   　　使用者的滿意，對於這個新設計的成功很重要。

   (2) All the iPhone users are satisfied with this smart phone.

   　　所有iPhone使用者都對這個智慧型手機很滿意。

   (3) This smart phone is satisfactory to most users.

   　　這個智慧型手機對大部分使用者而言，是令人滿意的。

   (4) Many people are dissatisfied with this new design.

   　　許多人對這個新設計不滿意。

LCD displays use _____（液晶）, an almost _____（透明的）substance, to control the passage of light. The basic structure of a TFT-LCD panel may be thought of as two glass substrates sandwiching a layer of _____（液晶）. The front glass substrate is fitted with a color filter, while the back glass substrate has transistors fabricated on it. When _____（電壓）is applied to the transistors, the _____（液晶）elements twist to change their _____（極化）, allowing light to pass through to form a pixel. A light source is located at the back of the panel and is called a backlight unit. There is a _____（被動式）filter in the front glass substrate to control the color on each pixel. Combinations of pixels in different colors form the image on the panel.

1. origin（起源）可用 inception, beginning 取代。

   The LCD technology has been advanced remarkably since its origin.

   LCD技術自其誕生以來已有很快速的進展。

   ⇒ The LCD technology has been advanced remarkably since its i_____.

   ⇒ The LCD technology has been advanced remarkably since its b_____.

2. afflict（困擾）可用 bother, trouble 取代。

   These transistors drive the pixels, eliminating the problems of ghosting and slow response speed that afflict non-TFT LCDs.

   這些電晶體驅動光點消除困擾non-TFT LCD的鬼影與慢反應速度問題。

   ⇒ These transistors drive the pixels, eliminating the problems of ghosting and slow response speed that b_____ non-TFT LCDs.

   ⇒ These transistors drive the pixels, eliminating the problems of ghosting and slow response speed that t_____ non-TFT LCDs.

3. clumsy（笨拙的、彆腳的）可用 awkward 取代。

   The computer monitors used in 1970s were clumsy.

   1970年代使用的電腦螢幕很笨拙。

   ⇒ The computer monitors used in 1970s were a_____.

4. discard（拋棄）可用 throw away, abandon 取代。

   The whole wafer must be discarded if more than a certain number of impurities are found on it.

   如果晶圓上發現超過一定數量的不純物，則整個晶圓必須拋棄。

   ⇒ The whole wafer must be t_____ if more than a certain number of impurities are found on it.

   ⇒ The whole wafer must be a_____ if more than a certain number of impurities are found on it.

5. fairly（相當的）可用 quite, very 取代。

Permanently turned on pixels are fairly common in LCD manufacturing.

永久開啟之光點在LCD製造上是很常見的。

⇒ Permanently turned on pixels are q_____ common in LCD manufacturing.

⇒ Permanently turned on pixels are v_____ common in LCD manufacturing.

6. establish（建立）可用 set up 取代。

LCD manufacturers have established limits for acceptable number of defective pixels on a given panel.

LCD製造商已設定一塊面板上可接受瑕疵光點數目之限度。

⇒ LCD manufacturers have s_____ limits for acceptable number of defective pixels on a given panel.

(   ) 1. Which one in the followings is correct?

     A. Liquid crystal is liquid.

     B. Liquid crystal is solid.

     C. Liquid crystal was discovered by Otto Lehmann.

     D. Liquid crystal was named by Friedrich Reinitzer.

     E. Liquid crystal was discovered in 20th century.

(   ) 2. Which one was one of the major problems of the non-TFT LCD display?

     A. not bright enough

     B. not efficient enough

     C. ghosting

     D. clumsy

     E. too expensive

(   ) 3. Defective LCD pixels may be found because of _____.

     A. dysfunction of the liquid crystal

     B. high voltage in the liquid crystal

     C. polarization of the passive filter

     D. problematic transistors

     E. failure of liquid crystal elements to twist

(   ) 4. The degree of the liquid crystal elements twist is determined by

     _____.

     A. voltage

     B. number of transistor

     C. number of passive filter

     D. number of defective transistor

     E. number of impurity

(   ) 5. Which one in the followings is incorrect?

     A. Lit pixels are more common than the dead pixels.

     B. A lit pixel is a permanently turned-on pixel.

     C. A lit pixel can be fixed easily.

     D. A lit pixel may be killed using a laser.

     E. A lit pixel is the result of transistor dysfunction.

(   ) 6. It is caused by the _____ of a transistor which results in a permanently "turned-on" pixel.

A. functioning

B. foundation

C. dysfunction

D. foundamental

(   ) 7. It is possible to _____ a problematic transistor using a laser.

A. mobile

B. imable

C. inable

D. disable

(   ) 8. The whole wafer must be _____ if more than a certain number of
impurities are found on it.

A. discarded

B. card

C. carded

D. discare

(   ) 9. The complete matrix of transistors is produced on a single _____ wafer.

A. silicon

B. carbon dioxide

C. carbon

D. silica

(   ) 10. The aim in establishing these limits is to maintain reasonable product
_____ while minimizing user di ssatisfaction causing by the defective
pixels.

A. order

B. demanding

C. defects

D. pricing

LED and OLED Displays

Questions & Discussions

1. There are two types of light-emitting material used in LEDs. What are they?

2. A large number of research groups around the world have been engaged in OLED research. Before 2010, what were the two main weaknesses of OLED?

Vocabulary

1. compound [kɑmˋpaʊnd, kəmˉ]
   混合物、化合物 (n)

2. mount [maʊnt]
   架在…之上 (v)

3. encase [ɪnˋkes]
   裝入… (v)

4. epoxy [ɛpˋæksɪ]
   環氧樹脂 (n)；環氧的 (adj)

Terminology

a. light-emitting diodes (LEDs)
   發光二極體

[a]Light-emitting diodes (LEDs) are commonly used in indicator lights and numeric displays on consumer electronic products. The basic LED is a solid-state device that contains a chemical [1]compound that radiates light when an electric current passes through it. It consists of a semiconductor diode chip [2]mounted in the reflector cup of a lead frame that is connected to electrical wires then [3]encased in an [4]epoxy lens. LEDs emit light when energy levels shift in the semiconductor diode. The color of the light depends upon the energy levels and the type of semiconductor material used in the LED chip.

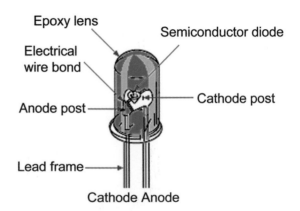

254

When the first LEDs became commercially available in 1960s, the semiconductor was made from a combination of three elements: [5]gallium, [6]arsenic and [7]phosphorus (GaAsP). They produced a red light. Other materials were studied and a combination which produced green light was discovered in the mid 1970s. In the late 1980s, a blue-producing compound was reported but the resulting LEDs were not very bright. The manufacturers of LEDs, then, used a process known as [8]epitaxy in which [9]crystalline layers of different semiconductor material are grown on top of one another. The epitaxial crystal growth processes resulted in the use of new compounds which enables the development of a bright blue LED.

LEDs are highly efficient because most of the lights they produced are within the visible [10]spectrum. However, until relatively recently, low light output and a lack of color options have severely limited their use. LEDs have extremely fast switching times. With the announcement of bright blue LEDs, it became possible to produce matrices of red, green and blue LED [11]clusters for use as large scale displays.

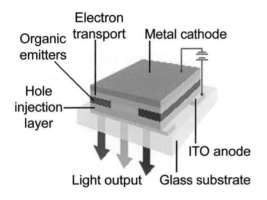

Organic emitters

Electron transport

Metal cathode

Hole injection layer

Light output

Glass substrate

ITO anode

Vocabulary

5. gallium [ˈgælɪəm]
   鎵 (n)

6. arsenic [ɑrˈsɛnɪk]
   砷 (n)；砷的 (adj)

7. phosphorus [ˈfɑsfərəs]
   磷的、亞磷的 (adj)

8. epitaxy [ˈɛpɪˌtæksɪ]
   外延、增生、磊晶 (n)

9. crystalline [ˈkrɪstl̩ɪn, ⁻ˌaɪn]
   水晶的 (adj)

10. spectrum [ˈspɛktrəm]
    頻譜 (n)

11. cluster [ˈklʌstɚ]
    一叢、一束、一團 (n)

Vocabulary

12. inorganic [ˌɪnɔrˈɡænɪk]
    無機的 (adj)

13. anode [ˈænod]
    陽極 (n)

14. substrate [ˈsʌbstret]
    基板 (n)

Terminology

b. emissive layer
   發光層

c. passive-matrix
   被動陣列

d. active-matrix
   主動矩陣

There are two types of light emitting material used in LEDs: [12]inorganic and organic materials. The conventional LEDs used inorganic materials. For those used organic materials are known as OLEDs. The basic OLED cell structure consists of a stack of thin organic layers sandwiched between a transparent [13]anode and a metallic cathode. When a voltage is applied to the cell, the injected positive and negative charges recombine in the [b]emissive layer to produce light. The structure of the organic layers and the choice of anode and cathode are designed to maximize the light output from the OLED.

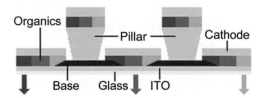

An OLED display may be driven by either a [c]passive-matrix or an active-matrix. To drive a passive-matrix OLED display, electrical current is passed through selected pixels by applying a voltage to the corresponding rows and columns from the drivers attached. An external controller circuit provides the necessary input power and video data signal.

In contrast to the passive-matrix OLED display, an [d]active-matrix OLED has a [14]substrate which comprises at least two transistors for every pixel. These transistors are connected to perpendicular anode and cathode lines. They can "hold" any active pixels in the "on" state until the next scan period.

Because of their additional parts requirement, active matrix displays are more complex to make, though they offer brighter images than their less costly passive matrix [15]counterparts.

A large number of research groups around the world have engaged in OLED research. Much of their efforts are directed towards solving the two main [e]Achilles heels of OLED: poor efficiency and short lifetime. However, it is expected that these problems will be overcome and that full-color OLED-based displays will replace TFT-LCDs as the market dominant display technology by around 2010.

OLEDs are classified according to the size of molecules of the light emitting materials as [f]Light-Emitting [16]Polymers (LEPs) and [g]Small Molecule Organic Light Emitting Diodes (SMOLEDs). The former uses relatively large molecules and the latter uses relatively small ones. Both generate light when an electric current is applied to a thin film section. Research results indicated that significant effort is required to improve SMOLED performance. By contrast, very high efficiency LEPs are achievable without much effort.

Vocabulary

15. counterpart [ˈkaʊntɚˌpɑrt]
    對應部分 (n)

16. polymer [ˈpɑlɪmɚ]
    聚合體 (n)

Terminology

e. Achilles heels
   罩門或弱點（阿基里斯是木馬屠城記中古希臘勇士，他的弱點就在腳後跟上）

f. Light-Emitting Polymers (LEPs)
   發光聚合體

g. Small Molecule Organic Light Emitting Diodes (SMOLEDs)
   小分子有機發光二極體

There are two types driving methods used in OLED displays: _____ （被動陣列）(PM) and _____ （主動陣列）(AM) driving. AMOLEDs use TFT with a capacitor to store data signals in order to control the brightness level. The manufacturing procedure for PMOLEDs is relatively simple and is less costly. However, PMOLEDs have the limitations of size (not more than 5 in) and low resolution. Large scale OLED displays with higher resolution can only be manufactured using _____ （主動陣列）driving. _____ （主動陣列）driving pixels can maintain their brightness after data line scanning. Pixels using _____ （被動陣列）driving, on the other hand, _____ （發射）light only when they are scanned. Therefore, active matrix driving results in longer lifetime, higher efficiency and higher resolution. Essentially, TFT-OLED with _____ （主動陣列）driving is suitable for display application of high resolution.

1. radiate（發射）可用 emit, give off, generate 取代。

The solid-state device contains a chemical compound that radiates light when an electric current passes through it.

這個固態元件包含一個當電流通過時，可以發光的化合物。

⇒ The solid-state device contains a chemical compound that e_____ light when an electric current passes through it.

⇒ The solid-state device contains a chemical compound that g_____ light when an electric current passes through it.

⇒ The solid-state device contains a chemical compound that g_____ light when an electric current passes through it.

2. limit（限制）可用 restrict, confine 取代。

Low light output and a lack of color options have severely limited their use.

低光輸出與缺乏顏色的選擇，嚴重限制了他們的用途。

⇒ Low light output and a lack of color options have severely r_____ limited their use.

⇒ Low light output and a lack of color options have severely c_____ limited their use.

3. announcement（公布）可用 declaration, proclamation 取代。

With the announcement of bright blue LEDs, it became possible to produce large scale LED displays.

在藍光LED問世後，生產大尺寸LED顯示器變為可能。

⇒ With the d_____ of bright blue LEDs, it became possible to produce large scale LED displays.

⇒ With the p_____ of bright blue LEDs, it became possible to produce large scale LED displays.

4. external（外部的）可用 exterior 取代。

An external controller circuit provides the necessary input power and video data signal.

一個外部控制電路提供必要的輸入電源與影像數據訊號。

⇒ An e＿＿＿＿＿＿＿ controller circuit provides the necessary input power and video data signal.

5. overcome（克服）可用 vanquish 取代。

It is expected that these problems will be overcome in the near future.

可以期望的是，這些問題在不久的未來將可被克服。

⇒ It is expected that these problems will be v＿＿＿＿＿＿＿ in the near future.

6. classify（分類、分級）可用 categorize 取代。

OLEDs are classified as Light-Emitting Polymers and Small Molecule Organic Light Emitting Diodes.

OLED可分為發光聚合體與小分子有機發光二極體。

⇒ OLEDs are c＿＿＿＿＿＿＿ as Light-Emitting Polymers and Small Molecule Organic Light Emitting Diodes.

(   )   1.   In addition to energy levels, which one in the followings determines the color of the light of an LED display?

     A. type of semiconductor material used in the LED chip

     B. type of matrix of the driving transistors

     C. type of light emitting material

     D. type of encased lens

     E. size of molecules of the light emitting materials

(   )   2.   In what years was the first LEDs became commercially available?

     A. 1940s

     B. 1950s

     C. 1960s

     D. 1970s

     E. 1980s

(   )   3.   In addition to arsenic and phosphorus, which element had been used in the semiconductors of first generation LEDs?

     A. liquid crystal

     B. gallium

     C. lead

     D. copper

     E. silicon

(   )   4.   What is epitaxy?

     A. a semiconducting material

     B. an organic material

     C. a plastic material

     D. a crystal growth process

     E. a synonym of epoxy

(   )   5.   Development of the bright blue LED became possible after _____.

     A. 1960s

     B. 1970s

     C. epoxy was discovered

     D. GaAsP was discovered

     E. epitaxy was used

(   )   6.   In addition to low light output, which one in the followings had been severely limited the use of LEDs?

A. lack of color options

B. slow switching time

C. lack of efficiency

D. too expensive

E. short lifetime

(   )   7.   What might a driver be in a passive- matrix OLED display?

A. a motor

B. a hand tool

C. a electric current

D. a material

E. a electronic devices

(   )   8.   Which one in the following is correct?

A. Active matrix display is more costly to make than passive one.

B. Passive-matrix OLED has a substrate comprising at least two transistors for every pixel.

C. Making passive-matrix display is more complicated as compared to that of the active one.

D. Active-matrix OLED needs an external controller circuit.

E. Active-matrix OLED needs drivers to apply voltage to the rresponding rows and columns.

(   )   9.   The "Achilles heels" means _____.

A. big

B. major

C. weakness

D. advantage

(   )   10.   LEDs are highly efficient because most of the lights they produced are within the _____ spectrum.

A. visible

B. visibility

C. visibly

D. visual

Virtual Reality

Questions & Discussions

1. Due to the technical limitations, which two types of senses can be duplicated almost flawlessly in VR technology?

2. Have you ever used a VR device? Discuss your experience of using it.

Vocabulary

1. stereoscopic [ˌstɛrɪəˈskɑpɪk]
   立體的 (adj)

2. artifact [ˈɑrtɪˌfækt]
   人工製品；人造品 (n)

3. treadmill [ˈtrɛdˌmɪl]
   跑步機 (n)

4. scenario [sɪˈnɛrɪo]
   情節、情境 (n)

Terminology

a. multi-modal
   多種型式的

b. wired glove
   線控手套

c. omni-directional
   全方位的

d. high-fidelity
   高傳眞

Virtual reality (VR) is a scientific discipline which allows users to interact with computer-generated environments. Most virtual reality environments are visual experiences. They are displayed either on a computer screen or through special [1]stereoscopic displays. Some simulations include additional sensory information such as sound through speakers or headphones. More sophisticated systems now provide tactile interaction, generally known as force feedback as commonly used in medical and gaming purposes. Users can interact with a virtual environment or a virtual [2]artifact (VA) by using either standard input devices, such as a mouse, or [a]multi-modal devices such as a [b]wired glove and a [c]omni-directional [3]treadmill. The virtual environment generated can be similar to the real world, for example, simulation of [4]scenarios for pilot or combat training. Or it can differ significantly from reality, as those in VR games. Due to the restrictions in technologies, it is currently very difficult to construct a [d]high-fidelity virtual reality environment. However, those restrictions will be removed in the long run as processor, imaging and data communication technologies become more powerful and cost-effective.

The inception of the term virtual reality is uncertain. The concept of virtual reality was popularized in mass media by television network. The earliest example of virtual reality on television is, perhaps, the Doctor Who serial. This story introduced a dreamlike computer-generated virtual environment. The most famous television series using the ideas of virtual reality is probably Star Trek. This film featured the [5]holodeck, a virtual reality facility on starships that allowed its crew members to recreate and experience any environment they liked. The VR research boom of the 1990s was motivated partially by the book Virtual Reality by Howard Rheingold. The book attempted to [6]demystify the [7]heretofore [8]niche area, making it more accessible to less technical researchers and [9]enthusiasts.

It is unclear exactly where the future of virtual reality is headed. In the short run, the images displayed via the [e]head mounted display (HMD) will soon reach a point of near realism. The [10]aural aspect will advance to a new realm of three-dimensional sound. This refers to the addition of sound channels both above and below the operator. The virtual reality application of this future technology will probably be presented over headphones.

Vocabulary

5. holo [ˈhɑlə]
   表示「完全」(pref)

6. demystify [diˈmɪstɪfaɪ]
   除去…中的神祕 (v)

7. heretofore [ˌhɪrtəˈfor]
   直到此時，在這以前 (adv)

8. niche [nɪtʃ]
   合適的 (adj) 利基 (n)

9. enthusiast [ɪnˈθjuzɪˌæst]
   狂熱者 (n)

10. aural [ˈɔrəl]
    聽覺的 (adj)

Terminology

e. head mounted display (HMD)
   頭帶顯示器

Vocabulary

11. therapeutic [,θɛrə'pjutɪk]
    治療的；治療學的；有療效的 (adj)

12. therapy ['θɛrəpɪ]
    治療，療法 (n)

13. phobia ['fobɪə]
    恐懼症 (n)

14. traumatic [trɔ'mætɪk]
    外傷的創傷的 (adj)；外傷藥 (n)

15. veteran ['vɛtərən]
    退役軍人 (n)

16. simulacrum [,sɪmjə'lekrəm]
    幻影；假象 (n)

17. limbic ['lɪmbɪk]
    邊的 (adj)

18. desensitization [di,sɛnətə'zeʃən]
    使…變得不敏感，脫敏療法 (n)

19. flawlessly ['flɔlɪslɪ]
    無瑕疵的 (adv)

Terminology

f. counterintuitive
   與直覺相反地

The primary use of VR in a [11]therapeutic role is its application to various forms of exposure [12]therapy, ranging from the treatment of [13]phobias to newer approaches to treating post [14]traumatic stress disorder (PTSD) in [15]veterans. A very basic VR simulation with simple sight and sound designs has been shown to be invaluable in the healing of phobias as a step between basic exposure therapy such as the use of [16]simulacra and true exposure. A recent research project is being conducted by the US Navy to use a much more complex simulation to immerse veterans suffering from PTSD in virtual environments of urban combat settings. While this sounds [f]counterintuitive, exposure therapy should have limited benefits for people with PTSD. A reasonable explanation is believed to be the result of psychological changes either to the [17]limbic system in particular or a change in stress response. Much as in the treatment of phobias, exposure to the subject of the trauma or fear seems to lead to [18]desensitization and a significant reduction in symptoms.

Due to the technical limitations, sight and sound are the only two senses that can be duplicated almost [19]flawlessly today. There are, however, endeavors made to duplicate smell. For example, research projects have been initiated aiming at treating the PTSD by exposing the veterans to virtual combat scenarios with different smells. The previous discussions illustrate the point that the future of VR is very much linked to therapeutic, training, and engineering demands. For this reason, duplicating a full sensory environment

beyond the basic tactile, sight, sound, and smell feedback is unlikely to be a goal in the industry. It's worth mentioning that simulating smells, while it can be done very realistically, requires costly research and design to make each [20]odor. The machine itself is expensive and specialized, using customized [21]capsules made for it. Thus far, basic and very strong smells such as burning rubber, [22]cordite, and [g]gasoline fumes have been made.

In order to generate other senses of touch and taste, the brain must be manipulated directly. This would push virtual reality into the [23]realm of a [24]vivid dream. Although no technology of this kind has been developed so far, Sony has taken the first step. In 2005, Sony announced that they had filed for and had received a patent for the idea of the [25]non-invasive beaming of different frequencies and patterns of ultrasonic waves directly into the brain to reconstruct all five senses. This is possible as have been shown by other investigators. Yet, Sony has not conducted any such tests and claims that it is only an idea.

Source:
Wikipedia, the free encyclopedia.

Vocabulary

20. odor [ˈodə]
    氣味 (n)

21. capsule [ˈkæps!]
    小容器、膠囊 (n)

22. cordite [ˈkɔrdaɪt]
    無煙火藥 (n)

23. realm [rɛlm]
    領域、範圍 (n)

24. vivid [ˈvɪvɪd]
    鮮明的、生動的 (adj)

25. non-invasive [nɑn,ɪnˈvesɪv]
    非侵入性的 (adj)

Terminology

g. gasoline fume
   （汽）油氣

Knowledge Plus

History

virtual reality (VR) is defined as the use of a computer-generated 3D, virtual, environment that one can navigate and possibly interact with, resulting in real-time simulation of one or more of the user's senses. In early 2016, VR [26]headsets became commercially available from hTC (Vive), Facebook (Oculus), and others. These products have different age instructions and limitations for users, e.g. 12+ or 14+. The [27]literature has shown that children, compared to adults, may respond [28]cognitively and behaviorally to immersive VR in ways that differ from adults. VR places users directly into the media content, potentially making the experience very vivid and real for children. The literature on VR user behavior or its effect on children indicates a [h]code of ethical conduct involving underage users are especially needed, given the availability of VR [29]porn and violent content.

Related research on violence in video games indicates that exposure to ¹media violence may affect attitudes and behavior. Early studies suggest that physiological [30]arousal and aggressive thoughts, but not [31]hostile feelings, are higher for [32]participants than for observers of the virtual reality game. Experiencing VR by children may further involve simultaneously holding the idea of the virtual world in mind while experiencing the physical world. Excessive usage of ʲimmersive technology that has very salient sensory features may compromise children's ability to maintain the rules of the physical world, particularly when wearing a VR headset that blocks out the location of objects in the physical world. Immersive VR can provide users with ᵏmultisensory experiences that replicate reality or create scenarios that are impossible or dangerous in the physical world.

Vocabulary

30. arousal [əˈraʊzl]
    喚起、覺醒、激勵 (n)

31. hostile [ˈhɑstɪl]
    有敵意的、不友善的 (adj)

32. participant [pɑrˈtɪsəpənt]
    參與者 (n)

Terminology

i. media violence
   媒體暴力

j. immersive technology
   沉浸式技術

k. multisensory experience
   多重感官經驗

Families of Vocabulary

1. real (adj) 真的、現實的、實際的、實在的

　　←→　　unreal (adj) 不真的、不現實的、不實際的、不實在的

realistic (adj) 現實的、注重實際的、逼真的

　　←→　　unrealistic (adj) 不現實的、不實際的、不逼真的

reality (n) 真實、現實

realism (n) 真實性, 現實性, 寫實主義　　　　　←→　　unrealism (n) = lack of realism

(1) His dream has become a reality.

　　他的夢想已成為現實。

(2) His proposal is unrealistic.

　　他的提案不實際。

(3) In a virtual reality environment, the virtual objects look real.

　　在虛擬現實的環境中，許多虛擬的東西看起來都像真的。

(4) Please be realistic in making this plan.

　　製訂這個計畫時，請實際一點。

2. order (v) 命令、指揮、訂購、點菜　　　　←→　　disorder (v) 使混亂、使失調

order (n) 命令、次序、整齊　　　　　　　←→　　disorder (n) 混亂、失調、疾病

(1) I have ordered some pizzas.

　　我訂了一些披薩。

(2) The officer has ordered his soldiers to cease fire.

　　軍官命令他的士兵停火。

(3) Musculoskeletal disorders are common among construction workers.

　　肌肉骨骼疾病在建築工人中很普遍。

3. immerse (v)

immersive (adj) 沈浸式的，身歷其境的 (adj)

immersion (n) 沈浸、浸沒

(1) Many linguists uphold that an immersive environment is most conducive to learning a new language.

許多語言學家認為，一個身歷其境的環境最有利於學習語言。

(2) The player has immersed himself totally in the scenarios of the game.

玩家將自己完全沉浸在遊戲場景中。

(3) Immersion of the player in the video game indicates the success of the design of the game.

玩家在視頻遊戲中的沉浸，指出了遊戲設計之成功。

4. expose (v) 使暴露

exposure (n) 暴露、揭露

exposition (n) 說明、展覽會

expositor (n) 講解者

expository (adj) 說明的

(1) Related research on violence in video games indicates that exposure to media violence may affect attitudes and behavior.

有關視頻遊戲中暴力的相關研究指出，暴露於媒體暴力可能會影響態度和行為。

(2) Many adolescents are exposing to media violence when playing video games.

許多青少年在玩視頻遊戲時，暴露於媒體暴力之下。

(3) The expositor has demonstrated that adolescents may be exposed to media violence when playing video games.

解說者說明，青少年在玩視頻遊戲時，可能會暴露於媒體暴力中。

A _____ glove（線控手套）is a glove-like input device for _____ （虛擬實境）environments. Various sensor technologies are used to capture physical data such as flexion of fingers. Often a motion tracker, such as a magnetic device or inertial tracking device, is attached to capture the global position/rotation data of the glove. These movements are then interpreted by the software that accompanies the glove, so any one movement can mean any number of things. Expensive high-end _____ gloves（線控手套）can also provide _____ （觸覺的）feedback, which is a _____ （模擬）of the sense of touch. This allows a _____ glove（線控手套）to also be used as an output device. An alternative to _____ gloves（線控手套）is to use a camera and computer vision to track the 3D pose and trajectory of the hand, at the cost of _____ （觸覺的）feedback.

Use of Synonym

1. tactile（觸覺的）可用haptic 取代。

More sophisticated virtual reality systems now provide tactile feedback.

更精良的虛擬實境系統現在可提供觸覺回饋。

⇒ More sophisticated virtual reality systems now provide h_____ feedback.

2. dub（命名）可用 coin 或name取代。

"Artificial reality," a related term dubbed by Myron Krueger, has been in use since the 1970s.

一個由Myron Krueger命名的相關名稱「人工實境」自1970年代以來就被使用。

⇒ "Artificial reality," a related term c_____ by Myron Krueger, has been in use since the 1970s.

⇒ "Artificial reality," a related term n_____ by Myron Krueger, has been in use since the 1970s.

3. present（呈現）可用 display 取代。

The virtual reality application of this future technology will probably be presented over headphones.

這個未來技術在虛擬實境的應用，大致應該在頭戴耳機上呈現。

⇒ The virtual reality application of this future technology will probably be d_____ over headphones.

4. illustrate（說明）可用 explain, demonstrate 取代。

The previous discussions illustrate the point that the future of VR is very much linked to therapeutic, training, and engineering demands.

前面的討論說明了未來虛擬實境的發展將與醫療、訓練與工程需求有關的論點。

⇒ The previous discussions e_____ the point that the future of VR is very much linked to therapeutic, training, and engineering demands.

⇒ The previous discussions d_____ the point that the future of VR is very much linked to therapeutic, training, and engineering demands.

5. duplicate（複製）可用copy, replicate, reproduce 取代。

For this reason, duplicating a full sensory environment beyond the basic tactile feedback, sight, sound, and smell is unlikely.

因為這個原因，超越基本觸覺、影像、聲音與嗅覺回饋之完整感覺環境之複製是不大可能的。

⇒ For this reason, c_____ a full sensory environment beyond the basic tactile feedback, sight, sound, and smell is unlikely.

⇒ For this reason, r_____ a full sensory environment beyond the basic tactile feedback, sight, sound, and smell is unlikely.

⇒ For this reason, r_____ a full sensory environment beyond the basic tactile feedback, sight, sound, and smell is unlikely.

6. conduct (v) 進行、執行，可用 perform, carry out 取代；conduct (n) 行為、品行、舉動。

Sony has not conducted any such tests and claims that it is only an idea.

Sony並沒有進行任何那樣的測試，並宣稱它只是一個構想。

⇒ Sony has not p_____ any such tests and claims that it is only an idea.

⇒ Sony has not c_____ any such tests and claims that it is only an idea.

7. costly（昂貴的）可用expensive 取代。

It's worth mention that simulating smells requires costly research and design to make each odor.

值得一提的是，模擬氣味需要昂貴的研究與設計來做出每一種味道。

⇒ It's worth mention that simulating smells requires e_____ research and design to make each odor.

8. multi（多的）放在形容詞的字首 = multiple + 後面的形容詞縮寫

例如 multisensory 多重感官的；multipurpose 多功能的；multilayer 多層的

multisensory = multiple sensory 的縮寫；multisensory experiences 寫成 multiple sensory experiences 冗長不順，可寫成 experiences of multiple sensory 較為通順

(1) Immersive VR can provide users with multisensory experiences that replicate reality or create scenarios that are impossible or dangerous in the physical world.

沉浸式VR可以為用戶提供多重感官體驗，這些體驗可以複製現實或創建在真實世界中，不可能或危險的場景。

⇒ Immersive VR can provide users with experiences of m_____ sensory that replicate reality or create scenarios that are impossible or dangerous in the physical world.

(2) This is a multipurpose headset.

這是件多功能耳機（或頭具）

⇒ This headset is a m_____ purpose one.

(3) This shop provides multilayer cakes.

這家店提供多層蛋糕

⇒ This shop provides cakes with m_____ layer.

( ) 1. To construct a high-fidelity virtual reality environment will become possible when _____.

A. processor, imaging and data communication technologies become more powerful and cost-effective

B. more television series adopt the ideas of virtual reality

C. more research are initiated in duplicating different odors

D. devices such as a wired glove and a omni-directional treadmill are used in a virtual environment

E. Sony conducts non-invasive test on human brain

( ) 2. Which television series adopted the ideas of presenting a virtual reality facility on starships that allowed its crew members to recreate and experience any environment they liked?

A. Doctor Who

B. Inspector Gagit

C. Dear Lucy

D. Star Trek

E. Clone Empire

( ) 3. The so-called post traumatic stress disorder (PTSD) normally occurs in _____.

A. veterans

B. nurses

C. post persons

D. factory workers

E. truck drivers

( ) 4. A phobia is _____.

A. a trauma disorder on low back

B. a trauma disorder on shoulder

C. a trauma disorder due to over stressed of the body

D. a mental illness with the main symptoms of having excessive, unreasonable desire to avoid the feared subject

E. a mental illness with the main symptoms of having excessive, unreasonable desire to avoid darkness

(　　) 5. Exposing the subject who suffers PTSD to a simulated combat environment has the advantage of _____.

    A. reducing his physical workload

    B. increasing of his battle skill

    C. desensitization

    D. minimizing his risk of injury

    E. receiving more experience of the combat environment

(　　) 6. Due to the technical limitations, which are the two senses that can be
duplicated almost flawlessly today?

    A. tactile and smell

    B. visual and auditory

    C. tactile and visual

    D. auditory and smell

    E. visual and smell

(　　) 7. Which company has announced that they had received a patent for the
idea of the non-invasive beaming of different frequencies and patterns
of ultrasonic waves directly into the brain to reconstruct all five senses?

    A. Sony

    B. Hitachi

    C. Eastman Kodak

    D. Panasonic

    E. IBM

(　　) 8. Due to the technical limitations, sight and sound are the only two senses that can be duplicated almost _____ today.

    A. flaw

    B. flawless

    C. flawlessly

    D. flawlessily

(   ) 9. Duplicating a full sensory environment beyond the basic tactile, sight, sound, and smell feedback is _____ to be a goal in industry.

      A. likewise

      B. unliked

      C. unlike

      D. unlikely

(   ) 10. The machine is _____.

      A. costly

      B. cost

      C. costs

      D. costing

Applications of Nanotechnology in Bio-Engineering

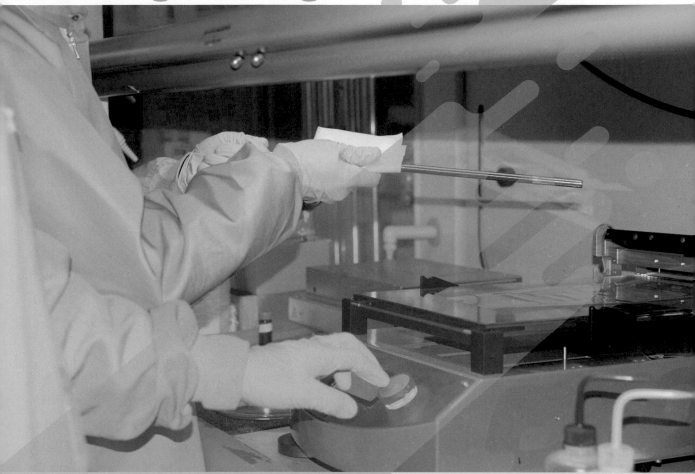

Questions & Discussions

1. What is biomimicry?
2. In tissue engineering, how can nanotechnology be used to promote the acceptance of an implant?

Vocabulary

1. nanotechnology [ˌnænotɛkˈnɑlədʒɪ]
   奈米科技 (n)；1 nanometer = 10^{-9} m

2. tissue [ˈtɪʃʊ]
   身體內之組織 (n)

3. organ [ɔrgən]
   器官 (n)

4. mineral [ˈmɪnərəl]
   礦物質 (n)

5. biomimicry [baɪəˈmɪmɪkrɪ]
   生物仿造物、生化模擬 (n)

6. vest [vɛst]
   背心 (n)

7. polymer [ˈpɑlɪmə]
   聚合體 (n)

8. infection [ɪnˈfɛkʃən]
   感染 (n)

9. graft [græft]
   移植 (n)

10. adult [əˈdʌlt]
    成熟的 (adj)

11. stem [stɛm]
    主幹 (n)

12. heal [hil]
    治療 (v)

Nanotechnology is a rapidly growing area that will affect people in their lives. Research is now under way investigating areas in which [1]nanotechnology can improve the quality of life through the engineering of bone, [2]tissue, and [3]organs.

Nanotechnology is being used in teeth and bone substitutions duplicating the manner nature itself lays down [4]minerals. This process is called [5]biomimicry. Biomimicry is already the basis of new tough and light materials for bullet proof [6]vests and other defense applications.

The use of nano-patterned [7]polymers may reduce the long recovery times, scarring and [8]infection associated with bone [9]grafts. Scientists are trying to use this technique to breed [10]adult [11]stem cells that will turn into bone. As soon as the process of growing tissue on patterned scaffolding is perfected nano-structured devices can be fixed to further improve bone growth rates and reduce [12]healing time. The devices have electrodes producing an electric current which has been shown to stimulate bone growth.

Nanotechnology enables the development of artificial skin, re-constructured tissue and wound treatments. Nanotechnology will support the regeneration of tissues and even the entire organs. The [13]regenerated organs will [14]substitute organs that have failed due to disease or aging. [15]Impregnating substances into regenerating tissues to stimulate healing and counteract infection is also possible by applying nanotechnology.

Tissue engineering at the nano-scale level is leading to the development of viable substitutes which can reestablish, sustain or enhance the function of human tissues. Regenerating tissue can be achieved by using biomaterials to transmit signals to neighboring tissues to recruit cells that promote [16]inherent regeneration. Using cells and a biomaterial scaffold to act as a framework for developing tissues is also one alternative to regenerate tissues.

The acceptance of an [17]implant by surrounding tissues is a critical medical problem. Especially designed outside layer using nano-scale techniques and nano-[18]textured surfaces to create a cell friendly environment assists the implant to join the surrounding tissues. The implant will, consequently, function well and survive longer.

Source:

The A to Z of Nanotechnology, AZoM.com, the Institute of Nanotechnology, 2004.

Vocabulary

13. regenerate [rɪˈdʒɛnəret]
    再生 (v)

14. substitute [ˈsʌbstəˌtjut]
    取代 (v)；替代物 (n)

15. impregnate [ɪmˈprɛgnet]
    注入、填充 (v)

16. inherent [ɪnˈhɪrənt]
    固有的、天生的 (adj)

17. implant [ɪmˈplænt]
    移植 (v)；植入物 (n)

18. texture [ˈtɛkstʃə]
    紋理 (n)

1. establish (v) 建立

   reestablish (v) 重建

   establishment (n) 建立

   Establishment of a friendly environment for the implants is important.

   為植入物建構一個友善的環境很重要。

2. generate (v) 產生

   regenerate (v) 再生

   generable (adj) 可生產的

   generation (n) 世代

   Depending on the app, a VR device may generate various virtual images for both entertainment and business purposes.

   視應用軟體而定，一個VR裝置可在娛樂與商業用途上產生多樣的虛擬影像。

3. implant (v) 植入

   implanted (adj) 被植入的

   implant (n) 植入物

   implantation (n) 植入

   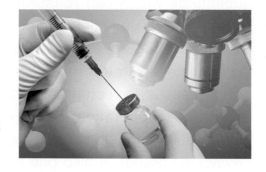

   (1) The implanted organs must be monitored at all times to assure they are function well.

   植入的器官必須隨時監測以確保其功能正常。

   (2) The implants must be monitored at all times to assure they are function well.

   植入物必須隨時監測以確保其功能正常。

   (3) Implantations of IC chip in household animals are required by the law.

   法律規定家有動物必須植入IC晶片。

4. neighbor (n) 鄰居

   neighborless (adj) 沒有鄰居的、孤獨的

   neighborly (adj) 像鄰居似的、親切的

   neighboring (adj) 鄰近的

   neighborhood (n) 鄰近地區

   The acceptance of an implant by neighboring tissues is a critical medical problem.

   植入物被鄰近組織接受是一個關鍵的醫學問題。

5. organ (n)器官

organic (adj) 器官的、有機的
organically (adv) 器官的、有機的
organism (n) 有機體
Organ implant techniques have been developed for medical purposes.
醫學目的之器官置入技術已被開發出來。

6. cover (v) 遮蓋、掩護   ⟷   uncover (v) 打開
covered (adj) 被蓋著的   ⟷   discover (v) 發現（cover的反義字）
cover (n) 蓋子、遮蓋
recover (v) 復原
recoverable (adj) 可復原的
recovery (n) 復原

(1) The patient has been recovered very quick.
病人很快的復原了。

(2) Scientists have discovered a critical biotech phenomenon.
科學家們發現了一個重要的生技現象。

7. substitute (v) 取代

substitutive (adj) 替代的
substitution (n) 替代
substitutional (adj) 代理的
substitute (n) 替代物

(1) Mark will substitute George as the manager in accounting.
Mark將會取代George成為會計經理。

(2) His appointment is substitutional.
他的任命是代理性質。

Researchers at Northwestern University have managed to recreate the micro-scopic structure of bone by using "designer" molecules that can be encouraged to assemble themselves into so-called "_____（奈米結構）" that mimic the appearance of collagen fibers. If the _____（奈米結構）can be incorporated into a gel, it is possible that they could be placed into the gaps between fractures to facilitate the natural _____（治療）process of _____（骨骼）, therefore the molecules could be highly beneficial to people with serious fractures, joint replacement patients, and those with _____（骨骼）cancer. Researchers believe that it may also be possible to develop _____（奈米結構）that attract different types of cells, for example nerve or cartilage cells, thus enabling sci-entists to _____（再生）other types of damaged _____（組織）. This is good example of the application of _____（奈米科技）in bio-engineering.

1. rapidly（很快的）可用 quickly, fast, promptly 取代。

   Nanotechnology is a rapidly growing area that will affect people in their lives.

   奈米科技是一門快速成長並會影響到人們生活的領域。

   ⇒ Nanotechnology is a q_____ growing area that will affect people in their lives.

   ⇒ Nanotechnology is a f_____ growing area that will affect people in their lives.

   ⇒ Nanotechnology is a p_____ growing area that will affect people in their lives.

2. breed（繁殖、培育）可用 propagate, produce 取代。

   Scientists are trying to use this technique to breed adult stem cells that will turn into bone.

   科學家正嘗試使用這項技術，來培育會轉換成骨質的成熟幹細胞。

   ⇒ Scientists are trying to use this technique to p_____ adult stem cells that will turn into bone.

   ⇒ Scientists are trying to use this technique to p_____ adult stem cells that will turn into bone.

3. substitute 可用 replace 取代；同理 substitution 可用 replacement 取代。

   (1) The regenerated organs will substitute organs that have failed due to disease or aging.

   再生器官將會取代因為疾病或老化而衰竭的器官。

   ⇒ The regenerated organs will r_____ organs that have failed due to disease or aging.

   (2) Nanotechnology is being used in teeth and bone substitutions duplicating the manner nature itself lays down minerals.

   奈米科技被應用於牙齒和骨骼之替代品，就像大自然本身沉積礦物質的方式一樣。

   ⇒ Nanotechnology is being used in teeth and bone r_____ duplicating the manner nature itself lays down minerals.

4. alternative（選項）可用 option, choice 取代。

Using cells and a biomaterial scaffold to act as a framework for developing tissues is also one alternative to regenerate tissues.

使用細胞與生物材料支架，來扮演一個架構以發展組織，也是組織再生的一個選項。

⇒ Using cells and a biomaterial scaffold to act as a framework for developing tissues is also one o_____ to regenerate tissues.

⇒ Using cells and a biomaterial scaffold to act as a framework for developing tissues is also one c_____ to regenerate tissues.

5. surrounding（周圍的、鄰近的）可用 neighboring, adjacent, nearby 取代。

The acceptance of an implant by surrounding tissues is a critical medical problem.

周邊組織對於移植體的接受是一個關鍵的醫學問題。

⇒ The acceptance of an implant by n_____ tissues is a critical medical problem.

⇒ The acceptance of an implant by a_____ tissues is a critical medical problem.

⇒ The acceptance of an implant by n_____ tissues is a critical medical problem.

6. assist（幫助、促進）可用 help, facilitate, enhance 取代。

Especially designed outside layer using nano-scale techniques to create a cell friendly environment assists the implant to join the surrounding tissues.

使用奈米技術進行特殊設計的外層，以建立一個對細胞友善的環境，能幫助植入物與周邊組織結合。

⇒ Especially designed outside layer using nano-scale techniques to create a cell friendly environment h_____ the implant to join the surrounding tissues.

⇒ Especially designed outside layer using nano-scale techniques to create a cell friendly environment f_____ the implant to join the surrounding tissues.

⇒ Especially designed outside layer using nano-scale techniques to create a cell friendly environment e_____ the implant to join the surrounding tissues.

Choose the most appropriate one in the following questions

(   ) 1. The process of using nano-technology in teeth and bone substitutions is called _____.

    A. biomimicry

    B. bioengineering

    C. biotechnology

    D. tissue regeneration

(   ) 2. Which technology has been used in developing new tough and light materials for bullet proof vests?

    A. biomimicry

    B. bioengineering

    C. biotechnology

    D. tissue regeneration

(   ) 3. Which one in the followings can not be solved by nanotechnology?

    A. developing new bone substitutions

    B. developing artificial skin

    C. support the regeneration of tissues

    D. reduce the long recovery times associated with bone grafts

    E. breeding red blood cell

(   ) 4. Regenerating tissue can not be achieved by _____.

    A. using biomaterials to transmit signals to neighboring tissues

    B. using biomimicry process

    C. developing viable substitutes

    D. impregnating substances into regenerating tissues

    E. using a biomaterial scaffold to act as a framework

(   ) 5. How can nanotechnology be applied in solving the acceptance of an implant by surrounding tissues problem?

    A. creating a cell friendly environment for the implant

    B. developing artificial skin

    C. providing new tough material

    D. breeding adult stem cells

    E. eliminating bacteria

(   ) 6. Scientists are trying to use this technique to _____ adult stem cells that will turn into bone.

A. briefing

B. breed

C. breeding

D. brooding

(   ) 7. Nanotechnology is being used in teeth and bone _____.

A. substitutions

B. substitute

C. substituting

D. substituted

(   ) 8. The _____ of an implant by surrounding tissue is a critical medical issue.

A. accept

B. accepted

C. acceptance

D. acceptable

(   ) 9. The implant will _____ well and survive longer.

A. functions

B. functioned

C. functioning

D. function

(   ) 10. Using cells and a biomaterial scaffold to act as a framework for developing tissue is also one _____ to regenerate tissues.

A. alteration

B. alterating

C. alternative

D. alter

Research in Stem Cells

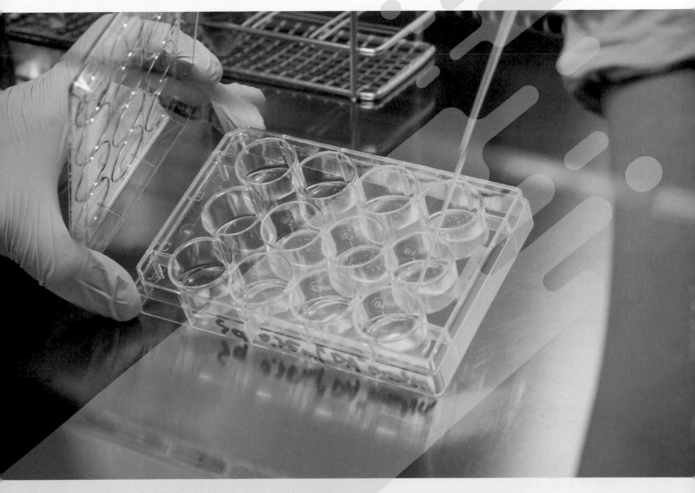

Questions & Discussions

1. There are two kinds of stem cells from animals and humans. What are they?
2. What are the major roles of adult stem cells in a living organism?

1. therapy [ˈθɛrəpɪ]
   治療；療法 (n)

2. regenerative [rɪˈdʒɛnə,retɪv]
   再生的 (adj)

3. reparative [ˈrɛpərətɪv]
   修補的 (adj)

4. appealing [əˈpilɪŋ]
   誘人的 (adj)

Terminology

a. adult organism
   成熟的有機體（組織）

Research in stem cells is enhancing knowledge about how an organism develops from a single cell and how healthy cells substitute injured cells in [a]adult organisms. Stem cells have remarkable potential to develop into many different cell types in the body. Serving as a sort of repair system for the body, they can divide without limit to restock other cells as long as the person or animal is still alive. When a stem cell divides, each new cell is possible to either remain a stem cell or become another type of cell with a more specialized function, such as a brain cell or a red blood cell. This promising area of science is directing scientists to investigate the possibility of cell-based [1]therapies to treat disease, which is referred to as [2]regenerative or [3]reparative medicine.

Stem cells are one of the most [4]appealing areas of biology today. But like many expanding fields of science, research on stem cells brings up scientific questions as rapidly as it introduces new discoveries. Stem cells have two important characteristics that discriminate them from other types of cells. First, they are unspecialized cells that renew themselves through cell division. The second is that under certain physiologic or experimental conditions, they can be induced to become cells with specific functions such as the [5]insulin-producing cells of the [6]pancreas or beating cells of the heart muscle.

There are two kinds of stem cells from animals and humans: [7]embryonic stem cells and adult stem cells. Embryonic stem cells are derived from [8]embryos. Specifically, embryonic stem cells are derived from embryos that develop from eggs that have been [9]fertilized [b]in vitro, in an in vitro fertilization clinic, and then [10]donated for research purposes with the [c]informed consent of the [11]donors. They are not derived from eggs fertilized [d]in vivo, or from a woman's body.

Scientists had found methods to obtain stem cells from mouse embryos more than 20 years ago. Many years of thorough study of the biology of mouse stem cells led to the discovery of how to isolate stem cells from human embryos and grow the cells in the laboratory. These are called human embryonic stem cells. The embryos used in these studies were produced for [12]infertility purposes through in vitro fertilization procedures and when they were no longer needed for that

Vocabulary

5. insulin [ˈɪnsəlɪn]
   胰島素 (n)

6. pancreas [ˈpæŋkrɪəs]
   胰臟 (n)

7. embryonic [ˌɛmbrɪˈɑnɪk]
   胚胎的 (adj)

8. embryo [ˈɛmbrɪˌo]
   胚胎 (n)

9. fertilize [ˈfɝtḷˌaɪz]
   使受精 (v)

10. donate [ˈdonet]
    捐贈 (v)

11. donor [ˈdonɚ]
    捐贈人 (n)

12. infertility [ˌɪnfɚˈtɪlətɪ]
    不孕 (n)

Terminology

b. in vitro
   玻璃皿內的

c. informed consent
   書面同意

d. in vivo
   生物體內的

13. lung [lʌŋ]
肺 (n)

14. marrow [ˈmæro]
髓 (n)

15. differentiated [ˌdɪfəˈrɛnʃˌetɪd]
已區分爲特定者 (adj)

16. renew [rɪˈnju]
更新、恢復 (v)

17. inhabit [ɪnˈhæbɪt]
棲息、存活於 (v)

Terminology

e. adult tissue
成熟的組織

f. blood-forming adult stem cell
造血成熟幹細胞

purpose, they were donated for research with the informed consent of the donor.

Stem cells are important for living organisms for many reasons. In the 3 to 5-day-old embryo, stem cells in developing tissues give rise to the multiple specialized cell types that make up the heart, [13]lung, skin, and other tissues. In some [e]adult tissues, such as bone [14]marrow, muscle, and brain, discrete populations of adult stem cells generate substitutes for cells that are lost through normal wear and tear, injury, or disease.

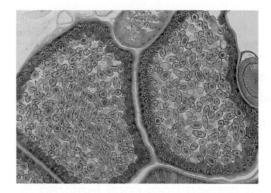

Adult stem cells are undifferentiated cells found among [15]differentiated cells in a tissue or organ. They can [16]renew themselves and can differentiate to generate the major specialized cell types of the tissue or organ. The major roles of adult stem cells in a living organism are to maintain and repair the tissue in which they reside. Unlike embryonic stem cells, the origin of adult stem cells in mature tissues is not known. Adult stem cells normally generate the cell types of the tissue in which they [17]inhabit. For example, a [f]blood-forming adult stem cell in the bone marrow typically produces types of blood cells such as red blood cells, white blood cells and [18]platelets. Until recently, it was believed that a blood-forming cell in the bone marrow could not produce cells of a very different tissue, such as cells in the [19]liver. However, many studies over the last several years have raised the possibility that stem cells from one tissue may yield cell types of a completely different tissue. This phenomenon is known as [20]plasticity. Examples of such plasticity include liver cells made to produce insulin and blood cells becoming [21]neurons. Therefore, investigating the possibility of using adult stem cells for cell-based therapies has become a very attractive and active area in scientific research.

Source:
Stem Cell Information, National Institute of Health, USA.

Vocabulary

18. platelet ['pletlɪt]
    血小板 (n)
19. liver ['lɪvɚ]
    肝臟 (n)
20. plasticity [plæs'tɪsətɪ]
    可塑性 (n)
21. neuron ['njʊrɑn]
    神經元；神經細胞 (n)

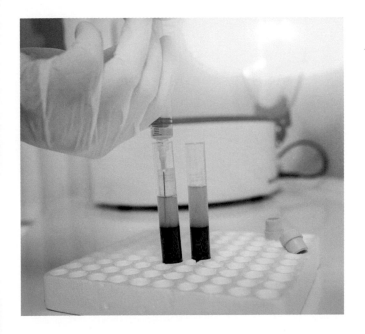

Some _____ cells（幹細胞）have the potential to turn into different cells, leading scientists to believe that they may be useful in treating medical disorders such as _____（糖尿病）. In an online discussion group, Christ's mother, Mrs. Howard, read about the possibility that _____ cell（幹細胞）injections could cure _____（糖尿病）. Even though she was worrying about the risk of such injections to Christ and was concerned about the cost that health insurance doesn't cover, she eventually decided to try it. Dozens of foreigners per month, many of them are children like Christ, have been flying to hospitals in China, seeking _____ cell（幹細胞）injections for a variety of conditions. There is no widely accepted scientific evidence that the injections work or are even safe. These injections are not _____（核准）by the governments in the U.S. and many other countries. Nonetheless, desperate patients are spending thousands of dollars, hoping to find _____s（療法）for _____（糖尿病）, cerebral palsy and other disorders with uncertain origins and a range of symptoms, from the failure to develop language skills to the inability to sense the feeling of others.

1. injuried（受傷的）可用 damaged 或 impaired 取代。

Research on stem cells is enhancing knowledge about how an organism develops from a single cell and how healthy cells substitute injured cells in adult organisms.

幹細胞的研究增進了我們對於一個細胞如何發展成組織，及成熟組織中健康細胞如何取代受傷細胞方面的知識。

⇒ Research on stem cells is enhancing knowledge about how an organism develops from a single cell and how healthy cells substitute d_____ cells in adult organisms.

⇒ Research on stem cells is enhancing knowledge about how an organism develops from a single cell and how healthy cells substitute i_____ cells in adult organisms.

2. restock（補充）可用 replenish 或 refill 取代。

Serving as a sort of repair system for the body, they can divide without limit to restock other cells as long as the person or animal is still alive.

在身體修補系統的扮演上，只要人或動物仍然活著，它們可以無限制的分裂來重新補充其他細胞。

⇒ Serving as a sort of repair system for the body, they can divide without limit to r_____ other cells as long as the person or animal is still alive.

⇒ Serving as a sort of repair system for the body, they can divide without limit to r_____ other cells as long as the person or animal is still alive.

3. inhabit（存在於; 棲息）可用 reside 取代。

Adult stem cells normally generate the cell types of the tissue in which they inhabit.

成熟的幹細胞通常會產生它們所棲息組織處的細胞種類。

⇒ Adult stem cells normally generate the cell types of the tissue in which they r_____.

4. normally（通常的）可用 typically（典型的; 通常的）取代。

In the 3 to 5-day-old embryo, stem cells in developing tissues normally give rise to the multiple specialized cell types that make up the heart, lung, skin, and other tissues.

在年齡三到五天的胚胎中，發育組織內之幹細胞可產生多種特定類型之細胞，這些細胞可組成心臟、肺、皮膚及其他組織。

⇒ In the 3 to 5-day-old embryo, stem cells in developing tissues t_____ give rise to the multiple specialized cell types that make up the heart, lung, skin, and other tissues.

5. produce（產生）可用 give rise to 或 yield 取代。

A blood-forming adult stem cell in the bone marrow normally produces many types of blood cells such as red blood cells and white blood cells.

一個造血的成熟幹細胞在骨髓內通常可產生多種血液細胞，如紅血球與白血球。

⇒ A blood-forming adult stem cell in the bone marrow normally g_____ produces many types of blood cells such as red blood cells and white blood cells.

⇒ A blood-forming adult stem cell in the bone marrow normally y_____ many types of blood cells such as red blood cells and white blood cells.

6. discriminate（區分）可用 distinguish 取代。

Stem cells have two important characteristics that discriminate them from other types of cells.

幹細胞有兩種區分，它們與其他細胞有不同的特性。

⇒ Stem cells have two important characteristics that d_____ them from other types of cells.

Adult stem cell
(multipotent)

New skin cell

7. heal（治療）可用 treat 或 cure 取代。

Scientists believe that stem cells may become the basis for healing diseases such as Parkinson's disease and diabetes in the future.

科學家相信在未來，幹細胞可能成為治療諸如巴金森疾病與糖尿病等疾病的基礎。

⇒ Scientists believe that stem cells may become the basis for t_____ diseases such as Parkinson's disease and diabetes in the future.

⇒ Scientists believe that stem cells may become the basis for c_____ diseases such as Parkinson's disease and diabetes in the future.

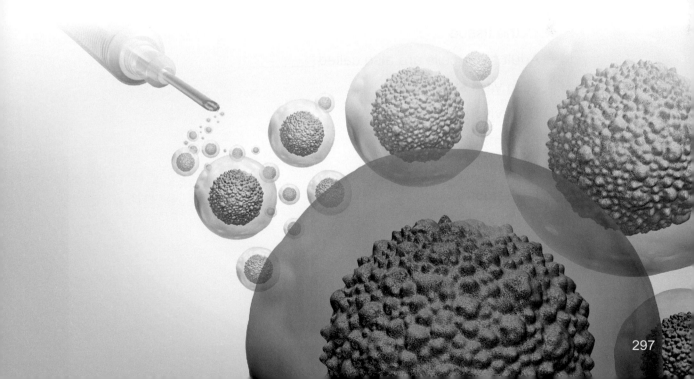

(   ) 1. From which kind of creatures had scientists found methods to obtain stem cells from embryos?

A. rabbit

B. mouse

C. dog

D. ram

E. chick

(   ) 2. The phenomenon that stem cells from one tissue may yield cell types of a completely different tissue is known as _____.

A. plasticity

B. duplicability

C. reproducibility

D. reparativity

E. regenerativity

(   ) 3. Which one in the followings is referred to as regenerative medicine?

A. utilizing the division of stem cells to discover how to isolate stem cells from human embryos and grow the cells in the laboratory

B. utilizing the division of stem cells in in vitro fertilization of eggs

C. utilizing the division of stem cells in in vivo fertilization

D. utilizing the division of stem cells to replenish the damaged cells in the tissue

(   ) 4. Adult stem cells are also called _____.

A. in vitro stem cells

B. in vivo stem cell

C. somatic stem cell

D. somatic embryo

E. mature stem cell

(　　) 5. How are the human embryonic stem cells used in scientific research generated?

A. They are isolated from the stem cells of mouse.

B. They are generated from adult stem cells.

C. They are produced through in vitro fertilization procedures and then donated with the informed consent of the donor.

D. They are produced through in vivo fertilization procedure and then donated with the informed consent of the donor.

(　　) 6. What are the major roles of adult stem cells in a living organism?

A. They are to maintain and repair the tissue in which they reside.

B. They are to maintain and repair the tissue in another creature.

C. They are to maintain and repair the tissue in the surrounding organs.

D. They are to generate embryos stem cells in which they reside.

(　　) 7. Which one in the followings is not believed as one of the benefits which may be resulted from stem cell research?

A. leading to cell-based therapies

B. help in solving infertility problems

C. help in studying new drugs

D. help in understanding birth defects

E. help in healing diseases such as Parkinson's disease and diabetes

(　　) 8. Stem cells are one of the most _____ areas of biology today.

A. appealing

B. appeal

C. appeared

D. appearance

(　　) 9. When a stem cell divides, each new cell is possible to either remain a stem cell or become another type of cell with a more _____ function.

A. special

B. specialized

C. specialization

D. specially

(   ) 10. Stem cells are important for living _____ for many reasons.
        A. organized
        B. organizations
        C. organ
        D. organisms

中譯與解答

單元 1　2019 冠狀病毒大流行 （課本第 2 頁）

COVID-19 是由一種名為 SARS-CoV-2 的新型冠狀病毒，所引起的疾病。在中國武漢一批「病毒性肺炎」病例被報導後，這種新病毒於 2019 年 12 月 31 日為公眾所知。COVID-19 最常見症狀，包括發燒、乾咳和疲勞，另外還有少數人會出現的症狀，包括：

- 味覺或嗅覺喪失
- 鼻塞
- 結膜炎（也稱為紅眼）
- 咽喉痛
- 頭痛
- 肌肉或關節疼痛
- 腹瀉
- 不同類型的皮疹
- 發冷或頭暈
- 噁心或嘔吐

嚴重 COVID-19 染疫症狀包括呼吸急促、食慾不振、意識模糊、胸部持續疼痛或壓力、高燒。其他不太常見症狀包括易怒、意識模糊、意識不清、焦慮、抑鬱、睡眠障礙。更嚴重和罕見的神經系統併發症包括中風、腦部炎症、精神錯亂和神經損傷。

所有年齡的人如果有發燒或咳嗽症狀，並伴有呼吸困難或呼吸急促、胸痛或胸悶、無法言語或行動，都應立即就醫。在出現症狀的人中，約 80% 的人無需住院治療即可康復。大約 15% 的人病重並需要提供氧氣設備，5% 的人病危並需要重症監護。

導致死亡的併發症，可能包括呼吸衰竭、急性呼吸窘迫綜合徵 (ARDS)、敗血症、感染性休克、血栓栓塞，心臟、肝臟或腎臟，造成的多重器官衰竭的損傷。60 歲以上的人，以及患有高血壓、心肺問題、糖尿病、肥胖症或癌症等潛在健康問題的人，嚴重疾病的風險更高。但是，任何人都可能感染 COVID-19 而患重病或死亡。染疫造成 COVID-19 染疫的人，無論是否需要住院，疫後有些人可能會繼續出現症狀，包括疲勞、呼吸系統和神經系統症狀。

病毒通過突變不斷變化，有時這些突變會導致病毒的新變種，有些變種會消失，而有些則持續存在，不斷出現新的變種。5 種 SARS-CoV-2 變種已被世界衛生組織認定為需要關注的變種：Alpha、Beta、Gamma、Delta 及 Omicron。Omicron 變種是 2021 年底宣布的最新變種，儘管世界衛生組織在 2022 年初聲稱「目前尚不清楚 Omicron 與 Delta 等其他變種相比，是否更具傳染性，感染 Omicron 是否會導致更嚴重的疾病。」

世衛組織正在與世界各地的研究人員和患者合作，設計和展開針對超出初始急性病程的患者研究，以了解具有長期影響的患者比例、持續時間以及發生原因。這些研究將用於為患者護理制定進一步指導。

新冠疫情，可採取一些簡單的預防措施保持安全，例如：保持身體距離、戴口罩，尤其是在無法保持距離的情況下，保持房間通風良好，避免和人群密切接觸，勤清潔雙手，咳嗽時曲肘或以紙巾遮擋，並依居住和工作所在地的防疫建議防疫。

在大多數情況下，分子測試可用於檢測 SARS-CoV-2 並確認感染，聚合酶鏈反應 (PCR) 是最常用的分子測試，醫務人員可用拭子從鼻子或喉嚨收集樣本，進行分子測試，通過將病毒遺傳物質放大到可檢測水平，檢測樣本中的病毒，確認活動性感染。取樣時間通常在接觸病毒後幾天內，和症狀開始的前後時間。

快速抗原檢測（有時稱為快速診斷檢測或 RDT）是篩查 COVID-19 感染者的替代方法，檢測病毒蛋白（稱為抗原）時，使用拭子從鼻子或喉嚨收集樣本。RDT 比 PCR 便宜，並且更快地提供結果，儘管 RDT 檢測較不可靠，但當社區感染擴大，以及個體傳染性最強的時期，採用快速抗原檢測的效果最佳。

隔離和檢疫都是為了防止 COVID-19 的傳播，任何接觸過 SARS-CoV-2 病毒感染者都需要檢疫隔離，無論感染者是否有症狀。檢疫隔離意味著須與他人保持隔離，因為接觸過病毒，可能被感染。檢疫隔離可以在指定場所或家中實施（請依政府最新公告資訊為主），針對有 COVID-19 症狀或病毒檢測呈陽性的人，採取隔離措施。隔離意味著與其他人隔離，最好是在可以接受臨床護理的醫療機構。如果無法在醫療機構進行隔離，且不屬於患嚴重疾病的高危人群，則可在家隔離。如果有染疫症狀，應該及時回報政府單位並盡快就醫。如果已感染但沒有出現症狀，同樣也需盡快就醫，並密切關注自身健康狀況。

疫苗可以保護人們免受病毒侵害，每年挽救數百萬人的生命。疫苗的作用是訓練和預備身體自然防禦系統，即免疫系統，以識別和對抗目標病毒與細菌。接種疫苗後，如果接觸到目標病毒或細菌，身體內的免疫系統會立即反應，從而預防疾病。

　　有幾種安全有效的疫苗，可以防止人們因 COVID-19 患重病或死亡，這是管理 COVID-19 的一部分，此外還有以下主要預防措施：與他人保持至少 1 公尺的距離、咳嗽或打噴嚏用肘部遮住、經常洗手、戴口罩，以及避開通風不良的房間，或打開一扇窗戶。

　　截至 2021 年 11 月 15 日，世衛組織公告以下 COVID-19 疫苗已達安全性和有效性的必要標準：

- 阿斯利康／牛津疫苗
- 嬌生公司
- 莫德納
- 輝瑞／生物科技
- 國藥
- 科興
- 科瓦辛

　　即使您已經得過 COVID-19，也可以先接種任何可用的疫苗。一旦輪到您，請務必盡快接種疫苗，不要等待。儘管沒有 100% 防護力的疫苗，但經批准的 COVID-19 疫苗，可提供高度保護，以防止重症和死亡。

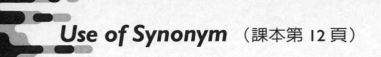

1. ⇒ Many countries are __lacking__ of goods and materials to against COVID-19 including alcohol for disinfection, facial mask, and forehead thermometer.

   ⇒ Many countries are in _deficiency_ of goods and materials to against COVID-19 including alcohol for disinfection, facial mask, and forehead thermometer.

   ⇒ Many countries are in _scarcity_ of goods and materials to against COVID-19 including alcohol for disinfection, facial mask, and forehead thermometer.

2. ⇒ Molecular tests detect virus in the sample by __augmenting__ viral genetic material to detectable levels.

   ⇒ Molecular tests detect virus in the sample by _boosting_ viral genetic material to detectable levels.

   ⇒ Molecular tests detect virus in the sample by _magnifying_ viral genetic material to detectable levels.

   ⇒ Molecular tests detect virus in the sample by _intensifying_ viral genetic material to detectable levels.

3. ⇒ Vaccines work by training the body's immune system to _identify_ and fight against the viruses they target.

   ⇒ Vaccines work by training the body's immune system to _find_ out and fight against the viruses they target.

4. ⇒ Contact your doctor if the symptoms _continue_ for more than a few days.

   ⇒ Contact your doctor if the symptoms _last_ for more than a few days.

   ⇒ Contact your doctor if the symptoms _endure_ for more than a few days.

5. ⇒ Symptoms of _acute_ COVID-19 disease include shortness of breath, loss of appetite, confusion, persistent pain in the chest, and high temperature.

   ⇒ Symptoms of _serious_ COVID-19 disease include shortness of breath, loss of appetite, confusion, persistent pain in the chest, and high temperature.

Choose the most appropriate one in the following questions （課本第 14 頁）

1.（B）2.（A）3.（B）4.（B）5.（A）6.（D）7.（A）8.（B）9.（B）10.（D）

單元 2　特斯拉 （課本第 18 頁）

特斯拉是位於加利福尼亞的美國電動汽車和清潔能源公司，產品包括電動汽車，從家庭到電網規模的電池儲能，太陽能產品以及相關產品和服務。該公司由 Martin Eberhard 和 Marc Tarpenning 於 2003 年創立，旨在紀念發明家和電氣工程師 Nikola Tesla。曾擔任董事長，現任首席執行長的 Elon Musk 表示：「特斯拉的首要目標是：幫助加速從礦山和碳氫化合物經濟向太陽能電力經濟的轉變」，它將建立各種各樣的電動汽車，包括價格合理的家用汽車。

經由 Model S，特斯拉開始在其車輛中心構建集成的計算機硬件和軟件架構，馬斯克表示特斯拉既是軟體又是硬體公司。為其汽車提供在線軟體升級，這可以免費改善已經出售的汽車之功能和性能。特斯拉是第一家直接向消費者出售汽車的汽車製造商，所有其他汽車製造商都經由獨立的經銷商來賣車，馬斯克認為現有的經銷商存在利益衝突，不會推廣特斯拉或任何製造商的電動車，因為與銷售汽車相比，他們的維修服務賺錢更多，而電動汽車的維修成本很低。因此，特斯拉在網路銷售汽車，而不是通過傳統的經銷商網絡，服務策略是通過主動監控、遠程診斷和維修、移動技術人員以及特斯拉擁有的服務中心為其車輛提供服務，目標是不在維修服務上獲利。

特斯拉的製造策略是不斷改進其汽車的硬體，而不是等待新的車型誕生。生產戰略包括高度的垂直整合，其中包括生產汽車零件以及建立客戶可以為特斯拉汽車充電的專有站。垂直整合在汽車行業很少見，在汽車業，公司通常將 80% 的組件外包給供應商，並專注於引擎製造和整車組裝。

2014 年，特斯拉謹慎地啟動了其充電網絡，為酒店、飯店、購物中心和其他全方位服務站提供充電站，從而以比普通家用充電站大兩倍的功率，為車輛提供現場充電。特斯拉認證的承包商免費安裝目的地充電站，這些場所必須免費為客戶供電，所有已安裝的充電站均顯示在車載導航系統中，與其他汽車製造商不同，特斯拉不使用單個大型電池，而是使用數千個小型圓柱形鋰離子商品電池，如消費類電子產品中使用的電池。特斯拉使用這些電池的一種版本，該版本設計為通過消除一些安全功能，比標準電池更便宜、更輕。特斯拉表示，那些安全功能是多餘的，因為先進的熱管理系統和電池中的膨脹化學物質可防止火災。松下是電池供應商。特斯拉汽車的電池放置在車底下方，這樣可以節省內部空間和行李箱空間，但會增加碎屑或撞擊損壞電池的風險，S 型具有 6.4 毫米鋁合金防護板。2020 年，特斯拉宣布了其未來電池的新設計，這種設計將擴大特斯拉汽車的哩程，這也將使未來的電動汽車價格能夠與汽油車的價格競爭。目前，特斯拉從松下採購電池，但是隨著新電池的設計，馬斯克宣布了內部生產電池的計劃，預計新電池將在 2023 年量產，它們的價格將降低 56％，並使汽車行駛的里程增加 54％。

除清潔能源外，自動駕駛也是特斯拉汽車的重要功能。自動駕駛旨在協助駕駛處理比較累人的部分，以使特斯拉汽車隨著駕駛時間延長變得更安全、功能更強大。特斯拉指出當前的自動駕駛功能需要駕駛員的監督，並且不會使車輛完全自動駕駛。從 2014 年開始，所有特斯拉汽車均搭配感應器和軟體以支持自駕功能，特斯拉在 2016 年對其感應器和軟體進行了升級，以支持全自動駕駛，該系統包括八個攝影鏡頭，十二個超音波感應器和前向雷達，馬斯克預測駕駛員在開車時將能夠入睡。2019 年 4 月，特斯拉宣布其所有汽車都將包括自動駕駛儀軟體發展的標準功能，完整的自動駕駛軟件是一個額外的成本選擇。2020 年 4 月 24 日，特斯拉宣布所有汽車軟體升級至全自駕功能，經此升級，汽車可以識別並減速，並自動在停車標誌處停車，直至駕駛確認可以安全的通過交通號誌。特斯拉承認這個軟體仍在測試的第二個階段，離完成還早。

With the Model S, Tesla started to build an integrated computer hardware and software architecture at the center of its vehicles. Musk indicated that Tesla is a software company as much as it is a hardware company. Tesla provides online software upgrade to its cars. This allows improvement of the functionality and performance of the cars already-sold for free. Tesla is the first _automaker_ that sells cars directly to consumers. All others use independently owned _dealerships_. Musk believes existing _dealerships_ have a _conflict_ of _interest_ and will not promote _electric_ cars from Tesla or any manufacturer, because they make more money servicing than selling cars, and _electric_ cars have lower servicing costs. For this reason, Tesla's sell its vehicles online rather than through a conventional _dealer_ network. The service strategy of Tesla is to service its vehicles through proactive monitoring, remote _diagnosis_ and repair, mobile technicians, and Tesla-owned service centers. Tesla's goal is not to make a profit on service.

Use of Synonym （課本第 26 頁）

1. ⇒ Musk give an order to _accelerate_ the research and development of the next generation automobile energy.

   ⇒ Musk give an order to _speed_ up the research and development of the next generation automobile energy.

2. (1) ⇒ Touch screen operation is one of the major <u>characteristics</u> of a tablet computer.

  (2) ⇒ Asus' Transformer followed, continuing the common trends towards multitouch and other natural user interface <u>characteristics</u>.

  (3) ⇒ A tablet computer is <u>characteristics</u> by touch screen operation.

  (4) ⇒ Autopilot is one of the major _characteristics_ of Tesla cars.

    ⇒ Autopilot is one of the major _attributes_ of Tesla cars.

3. (1) ⇒ Tesla _prudently_ launched its charging network by providing on-site chargers for vehicle charging at twice the power of a typical home charging station.

    ⇒ Tesla _carefully_ launched its charging network by providing on-site chargers for vehicle charging at twice the power of a typical home charging station.

  (2) ⇒ This company has shut down ten of its branches _imprudently_ .

    ⇒ This company has shut down ten of its branches _carelessly_ .

4. (1) ⇒ Automobile companies typically _subcontract_ 80% of components to suppliers, and focus on engine manufacturing and final assembly.

  (2) ⇒ Personal computer manufacturers normally _subcontract_ the printed circuit boards and batteries to their local suppliers.

Choose the most appropriate one in the following questions （課本第 28 頁）

1.（D） 2.（C） 3.（A） 4.（B） 5.（D） 6.（B） 7.（D） 8.（A） 9.（D） 10.（C）
11.（C） 12.（B） 13.（B） 14.（D） 15.（C）

單元 3　平板電腦 （課本第 32 頁）

　　平板電腦，或簡稱平板，是一個主要以觸控螢幕操作的單件移動式電腦。使用平板時，使用者的手指發揮像是滑鼠或游標一樣的功能，這樣去除了傳統桌上型或膝上型電腦之傳統輸入裝置的需求；平板的螢幕上可隱藏式的虛擬鍵盤被整合到顯示器上作為輸入之目的。有許多不同平板的設計：可轉換筆電有可用轉動接頭或滑動接頭隱藏的鍵盤，這樣只露出螢幕作為觸控操作。混合型平板有一個可分開的鍵盤，這樣一來觸控螢幕可單獨作為平板使用；手冊型平板包括兩個觸控螢幕，並用其中一個螢幕顯示虛擬鍵盤，當作筆電使用。平板電腦有許多尺寸，即使最小的觸控也比智慧型手機或個人數位助理大得多。

　　平板電腦與個人電腦在許多地方都有相當的差異，包括使用者介面、操作系統、處理器與應用，另一個主要不同，就是平板主要是被用來當作不昂貴的媒體使用裝置，這樣一來，原始處理能力與內容分配平臺比較起來，就沒有那麼重要了。在許多方面，平板與智慧型手機的架構很像，許多是源於後者之架構。平板在市場上比智慧型手機對個人電腦有較高的破壞性衝擊，智慧型手機與個人電腦是互補的，但平板的互補性少了許多，平板電腦顯著的改變了個人電腦使用者的行為，在侵蝕個人電腦銷售上沒那麼多，但較多部分，在導致個人電腦使用者，轉移電腦的使用到平板，而不是取代個人電腦。

　　平板電腦與相關的特殊作業軟體，是筆計算技術的一個例子，因此平板的發展有其深遠的歷史根源，在平面資訊顯示上以電子裝置進行數據之輸入與輸出，早在 1888 年就以電報傳真機的例子存在。上個世紀，一些科幻小說的作品裡，就出現一些和當代平板類似的東西。1951 年，Isaac Asimov 寫的小說 Foundation 裡，描述的計算器平板就是一個例子；1972 年 Alan Kay 發表一篇文章，「各種年齡兒童使用的個人電腦」裡，就提出用觸控螢幕當作可能的輸入裝置，並且命名這個裝置為 Dynabook；美國有名的電視影集 Star Trek，也在表演中凸顯平板電腦，並稱為「padds」。

　　1999 年，Intel 公司發布一款觸控平板電腦，並命名為 WebPAD，這款平板後來被重新定為 Intel Web Tablet 品牌。在 2000 年間，微軟公司嘗試定義，平板電腦概念為商業戶外使用的移動電腦，然而，他們的東西因為價格與使用性問題，使其不適合在有限預期目的之外使用，而未能被廣泛使用。2010 年蘋果公司發表 iPad：一個強調使用媒體的平板，這個設計目的的改變，同時結合增加的可用性、電池壽命、簡潔、低的重量與價格，及和之前平板相較的整體品質，被視為定義了一個新的消費裝置等級。這款平板在隔年塑造的平板電腦的商業市場。

最成功的平板電腦是使用 iOS 作業系統的 iPad，它在 2010 第一次出現，就讓平板風行成為主流，華碩的變形金剛與其他產品隨後問世，他們延續了平板朝向多點觸控、自然使用者介面特質共同趨勢、及快閃記憶固態儲存驅動的共同趨勢。此外，標準外接 USB 與藍芽鍵盤也可被使用，某些平板還有 3G 電話功能。

直到 2012 年 3 月，美國 31% 的網際網路使用者被報導已有平板電腦，而其主要被用來瀏覽出版的內容，包括影片與新聞。在 2012 年市場上的平板電腦中，銷售最好的是 iPad，從上市到 2012 年 10 月中，已賣出一千萬臺，其次是 Amazon 的 Kindle Fire，共賣了 7 百萬臺，再來是 Barnes & Noble 的 Nook，共賣了 5 百萬臺。

Fill in the blanks （課本第 38 頁）
using the words you have just learned in this lesson

When using a _tablet_, the user's finger essentially functions as the mouse and _cursor_, removing the need for traditional input devices necessary for a desktop or _laptop computer_. Available in a variety of sizes, even the smallest's touchscreens are much larger than those of a _smart phone_ or _personal digital assistant_. _Tablets_ differ considerably from PCs in many ways, including user interface, operating system, and applications. Another crucial difference is that _tablets_ are used primarily as _____inexpensive_____ media consumption devices, so raw processing power is not as important as the content distribution platform. _Tablets_ have dramatically changed user behaviors for PCs, not so much by _cannibalizing_ PC sales. In 2010, Apple Inc. released the iPad, a _tablet_ with an emphasis on media consumption. The shift in purpose, together with increased usability, _simplicity_, lower weight and cost, and overall quality with respect to previous _tablet_ s, was perceived as defining a new class of consumer device.

1. (1) ⇒ Touch screen operation is one of the major __characteristics__ of a tablet computer.

   (2) ⇒ Asus' Transformer followed, continuing the common trends towards multi-touch and other natural user interface _characteristics_.

   (3) ⇒ A tablet computer is _chactered_ by touch screen operation.

2. ⇒ Hybrids have a __separable__ keyboard so that the touchscreen can be used as a stand-alone tablet.

   ⇒ Hybrids have a __removable__ keyboard so that the touchscreen can be used as a stand-alone tablet.

3. ⇒ Hybrids have a detachable keyboard so that the touchscreen can be used as an __independent__ tablet.

   ⇒ Hybrids have a detachable keyboard so that the touchscreen can be used as an __indivisual__ tablet.

4. ⇒ A __vital__ difference between a tablet and a laptop is that the former does not have a keyboard.

   ⇒ An __important__ difference between a tablet and a laptop is that the former does not have a keyboard.

   ⇒ A __essential__ difference between a tablet and a laptop is that the former does not have a keyboard.

5. ⇒ Its __first__ __appearance__ in 2010 popularized tablets into mainstream.

   ⇒ Its __coming__ __out__ in 2010 popularized tablets into mainstream.

6. (1) ⇒ The ASUS has _announced_ the Transformer Book as both a laptop and a tablet.

⇒ The ASUS has _introduced_ the Transformer Book as both a laptop and a tablet.

(2) ⇒ Ten million iPads have been sold since this tablet was _announced_ in 2010.

⇒ Ten million iPads have been sold since this tablet was _introduced_ in 2010.

(3) ⇒ The _announcement_ of iPad has defined a new personal mobile device in the market.

⇒ The _introduction_ of iPad has defined a new personal mobile device in the market.

7. ⇒ This tablet has _sculpted_ the commercial market for tablets in the following year.

⇒ This tablet has _molded_ the commercial market for tablets in the following year.

⇒ This tablet has _modeled_ the commercial market for tablets in the following year.

Choose the most appropriate one in the following questions （課本第 42 頁）

1.（E）2.（A）3.（D）4.（B）5.（A）6.（C）7.（B）8.（D）9.（C）10.（B）

單元 4 觸控螢幕 （課本第 46 頁）

　　觸控螢幕常用於像是遊戲操控臺、合為一體電腦、平板電腦、及智慧型手機等裝置，它們也在像個人數位助理、衛星導航裝置等數位用品上扮演突出的角色。觸控螢幕是讓使用者以單一或多手指，以簡單或多點觸控手勢來輸入之視覺顯示裝置。有些觸控螢幕也可偵測像是針筆，普通或特殊表層手套之物體，使用者可以用觸控來對螢幕顯示的東西來反應，並且控制其如何呈現，例如放大字體的尺寸。

　　智慧型手機、平板電腦及許多資訊用品的風行，驅動了觸控螢幕作為可攜式與功能性裝置的需求與可接受性，觸控螢幕在醫療與重工業都很受歡迎，還有像博物館或室內自動化之資訊臺，在那些工業與地點，鍵盤與滑鼠通常無法允許適當、直覺、快速、準確的使用者與顯示內容之間的互動。

　　歷史上，觸控螢幕感應器與它們隨附的控制器，為基礎的韌體已被許多的系統整合者提供，而不是由顯示器、晶片、或主機板製造商提供。世界各地的顯示器與晶片製造商，已經了解接受觸控螢幕當作高度令人嚮往的互動介面元件的趨勢，並且已開始整合觸控螢幕到他們產品的基礎設計中。

　　電阻與電容式觸控，是兩種主要的觸控技術，電阻式觸控板包括兩片薄並且透明有電阻的層次，這兩層被一細微空間分開，兩層互相靠近但中間有間隙；上層螢幕，或者被觸摸的，在其下表面有一塗層，而在其下方是在基板上之類似電阻層，電壓加到一層時會被另外一層感應到；當一個物體，例如指尖或針筆尖下壓到外表面時，兩層接觸並在那一點相連；面板即扮演一對電壓的分配器，一次一個軸向，經由在各層間快速變換，螢幕上壓力點的位置可以被讀取。

　　由於其對於液體與其他污染物的高抗拒性，電阻式觸控被使用在像飯店、工廠、醫院等公共區域，這個技術的一個主要好處就是其成本低廉。另外，只要有足夠的壓力就可被感應，它們可穿戴手套或以其他硬的手指／針筆替代物都可使用。這個技術的壞處包括需要下壓與被尖銳物體損壞的風險，由於有從螢幕上多層物質額外之反射問題，電阻式觸控螢幕的對比較差。

　　電容式觸控螢幕板包括一個像玻璃的絕緣體，塗了一層透明的導體，由於人體是帶電的導體，人體碰觸螢幕會導致螢幕靜電場的變形，這可由可量得的電容變化感應，不像是電阻式的電容，我們不能經由像手套似的大部分絕緣材料來使用電容式電阻，這個壞處影響消費性電子產品的可用性，例如觸控平板與電容式智慧型手機在寒冷的天候中，然而，這個可用特殊電容式針筆或特殊應用手套，手套上用針織繡上一層有導電性的線，來連結並接觸使用者的指尖來克服。

Use of Synonym （課本第 52 頁）

1. ⇒ The popularity of information appliances has __compelled__ the demand of touchscreens.

   ⇒ The popularity of information appliances has __pushed__ the demand of touchscreens.

   ⇒ The popularity of information appliances has __propelled__ the demand of touchscreens.

2. ⇒ The two layers face each other with a thin _break_ between.

   ⇒ The two layers face each other with a thin _crack_ between.

   ⇒ The two layers face each other with a thin _split_ between.

3. ⇒ The top screen, or the one that is touched, has a _covering_ on the underside surface.

   ⇒ The top screen, or the one that is touched, has a _spreading_ on the underside surface.

4. ⇒ The panel then _acts_ as a pair of voltage dividers, one axis at a time.

   ⇒ The panel then _performs_ as a pair of voltage dividers, one axis at a time.

   ⇒ The panel then _works_ as a pair of voltage dividers, one axis at a time.

5. ⇒ As human body is an electrical conductor, touching the surface of the screen results in a _contortion_ of the screen's electrostatic field, measurable as a change in capacitance.

   ⇒ As human body is an electrical conductor, touching the surface of the screen results in a _deformation_ of the screen's electrostatic field, measurable as a change in capacitance.

6. ⇒ An interactive kiosk _accommodates_ a computer terminal that often employs custom kiosk software designed for special functions.

   ⇒ An interactive kiosk _contains_ a computer terminal that often employs custom kiosk software designed for special functions.

   ⇒ An interactive kiosk _lodges_ a computer terminal that often employs custom kiosk software designed for special functions.

Choose the most appropriate one in the following questions （課本第 54 頁）

1.（E）2.（D）3.（A）4.（E）5.（A）6.（B）7.（A）8.（C）9.（C）10.（C） 315

單元 5　無人航空載具 （課本第 58 頁）

　　無人航空載具 (無人機；一般通稱的雄蜂或其他名稱) 是沒有人類飛行員在上面的飛機。無人航空載具被定義為具有動力而不載操作人員、使用氣體動力學提供載具上升、可自主或遙控導航飛行、為消耗性或可回收的、並且可裝載致命或非致命的運載量。因此，飛彈不被視為無人航空載具，因為飛彈雖然也是無載人，並可遙控引導飛行，但其本身是不可重複使用的武器。

　　無人航空載具在相同的概念下，有許多名稱，公眾常用的雄蜂是用來將外表難看又具有大而規律馬達聲的老式軍用無人機，比擬為雄蜂一般，這個稱呼的使用卻被民航專業人士與政府監管機構強烈反對。美國國防部、民航局、及歐洲民航當局採用無人機系統 (UAS) 這個名詞，凸顯飛機以外單元的重要性，包含單元如：地面控制站、數據鏈與其他支援裝備；類似的名稱還包括無人機載具系統 (UAVS)、遙控導航飛行載具 (RPAV)、遙控導航飛機系統等 (RPAS)。

　　嘗試開發動力無人航空載具最早是在 1916 年，一次世界大戰中，與戰後無人航空載具一直有持續發展。在 1980 與 1990 年代，由於相關應用技術的成熟化與小型化，對於無人航空載具的興趣延伸至美國軍事高層。在 1990 年代，美國國防部提供一項合約給 AAI 公司與以色列的 Malat 公司，美國海軍採購了由 AAI 與 Malat 聯合開發的 AAI 先驅者無人機，這批無人機大多都有參與 1991 年的波斯灣戰爭；無人機展現了便宜、多戰鬥機器的能力、無人員傷亡風險的可部屬性之可能性。早期世代的無人機主要是當作監控飛機，但有些會攜帶武器，例如 General Atomics 公司的 MQ-1 掠奪者機型可發射 AGM-114 地獄火空對地飛彈。

　　無人航空載具通常優先用於對人類來說單調枯燥、骯髒或具危險性的任務，雖然無人航空載具的用途已擴展到商業、科學、娛樂與其它應用，例如偵察與監控、空中攝影、農業與無人機競賽，它們初期大部分的應用都在軍事領域。無人航空載具飛行操控具有不同程度的自主性：由人類操縱者遙控、或全部或間斷式的油機上的電腦自主控制。

　　無人航空載具一般有六種功能性的類別：

- 標靶與誘捕器—擔任模擬敵人飛機或飛彈，提供地面或空中火炮射擊標靶
- 偵察—提供戰場情報
- 作戰—在高風險任務提供攻擊能力

- 運籌學—送貨
- 研究與發展—改善無人航空載具技術
- 民航與商用—農業、航空攝影、數據收集

　　美國軍事無人航空載具分級系統，是軍事規劃者在整個使用計畫中用來指明不同個別飛機單元，載具可以依航程與飛行高度來分級，以下是被採用的分級：

- 手持式 2000 英呎 (600 公尺) 高，大約 2 公里航程
- 接近 5,000 英呎 (1,500 公尺) 高，達 10 公里航程
- 北大西洋公約型 1 萬英呎 (3,000 公尺) 高，航程達 50 公里
- 戰術型 18,000 英呎 (5,500 公尺) 高，約 160 公里航程
- MALE (中高度，長航程) 達 3 萬英呎 (9,000 公尺) 高，航程超過 200 公里
- 高高度，長航程 (HALE) 超過 3 萬英呎 (9,100 公尺) 高，航程無限遠
- 超音速 (1–5 馬赫) 或超高音速 (5 馬赫以上) 5 萬英呎 (15,200 公尺) 高或次地球軌道高，航程超過 200 公里
- 低地球軌道 (25 馬赫以上)
- 地球 – 月球軌道轉換

　　其他分類：

- 業餘玩家無人機 – 可再分為

　 ＊準備飛行 (RTF) ／下架即飛 (COTS)

　 ＊組裝即飛 (BNF) – 需要最基本的知識來飛這個平台

　 ＊幾乎準備飛行 (ARF) ／自行組裝 (DIY) – 需要相當的知識才能飛行

- 中型軍用與商用無人機
- 大型軍用 – 特殊無人機
- 秘密行動作戰無人機

　　依據飛機重量的分類非常簡單：

- 微空中載具 (MAV) – 最小的無人航空載具重量少於 1 公克
- 小型無人航空載具 – 重量在 25 kg 以下
- 重型無人航空載具 – 重量超過 25 kg

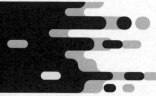

Use of Synonym （課本第 66 頁）

1. (1) ⇒ This experiment is simply a _preliminary_ study of the project.

   (3) ⇒ We need a _navigator_ to pilot the ship into the harbor.

2. ⇒ Initially, UAVs are primarily used in _investigation_ missions in the battlefield.

   ⇒ Initially, UAVs are primarily used in _inspection_ missions in the battlefield.

   ⇒ Initially, UAVs are primarily used in _survey_ missions in the battlefield.

3. ⇒ UAVs are often preferred for missions that are too _boring_, dirty or dangerous for humans.

   ⇒ UAVs are often preferred for missions that are too _monotonous_, dirty or dangerous for humans.

   ⇒ UAVs are often preferred for missions that are too _tedious_, dirty or dangerous for humans.

Choose the most appropriate one in the following questions （課本第 67 頁）

1.（A）2.（B）3.（B）4.（D）5.（A）6.（B）7.（D）8.（D）9.（B）10.（C）

單元 6　加速度計與陀螺儀（課本第 70 頁）

　　加速度計與陀螺儀是廣泛被用在當代移動電子器材，如：智慧型手機與平板電腦上的元件。加速度計是量測物體加速度的器材，加速度的單位是每秒一米，或常以重力為單位表示，高度敏感的加速度計是飛行器與飛彈的慣性導航系統的零組件，單軸與多軸模式的加速度計，可用來偵測加速度的大小與方向，也可用來感應方位、座標加速度、震動與衝擊；電子裝置使用加速度計來依裝置被握持方向來調整螢幕，例如直式與橫式間的轉換；微加工的加速度計越來越多被用在影像遊戲控制器，來偵測裝置位置或提供遊戲輸入。

　　一個自由墜落感應器，是一種用來偵測一個系統是否被掉落與下墜的加速度計，它提供了諸如硬碟讀寫頭停駐，以避免撞擊時讀寫頭損毀，而造成資料損失這方面的安全度量，這個元件被用在許多一般的電腦與消費性電子產品上，它也被用在一些數據紀錄儀上來監測貨櫃的處理操作，自由墜落的時間，常被用來計算下墜的高度與估計對於包裹的衝擊。

　　陀螺儀是包含一個轉子與兩個或多個平衡環的機械裝置，轉子被安裝來對一個轉軸來旋轉，這個轉軸則是被安裝在一個內平衡環上，內平衡環則是對著一個被裝在外平衡環或陀螺儀架上的另一個轉軸旋轉，外平衡環或陀螺儀架則是被安裝來對其自身平面轉軸來旋轉，此平面是由支撐來決定。轉子對一軸旋轉，並且能同時對另外兩個軸擺盪；因此，它可針對任一固定點在任何方向轉動。

　　在 1860 年代，電動馬達的出現讓開發陀螺儀羅盤變為可能，第一個功能性的陀螺儀羅盤在 1904 年取得專利。二十世紀初期，發明家嘗試使用陀螺儀作為早期導航系統的基礎，類似原則後來被用來開發彈道飛彈的慣性導引系統。二次世界大戰期間，陀螺儀變成了飛行器的主要構件，戰後，陀螺儀在導引飛彈與武器導航系統上，微型化的競爭導致了微型陀螺儀的開發與製造。

　　除了被用在羅盤，陀螺儀也被應用在消費性電子產品上，因為陀螺儀允許方位與轉動的計算，設計師便把它們整合到現代技術裡，陀螺儀整合允許比以往單獨使用加速度計，更精確地識別 3D 空間動作，消費性電子產品裡的陀螺儀常與加速度計合併使用，來產生更強健的方向與動作感應。使用陀螺儀的智慧型手機例子包括 HTC® One 系列、Samsung® Galaxy 系列，及 iPhone 系列產品，Nintendo® 也整合陀螺儀到 Wii 的遙控器上，3DS 也使用陀螺儀來偵測遊戲者轉動時的動作。

1. (1) ⇒ This theory has great __influence__ on the developing of contemporary biochemistry.

   (2) ⇒ How does the _crash_ of an automobile on a barricade affect the safety of the driver is an important research issue.

   ⇒ How does the _collision_ of an automobile on a barricade affect the safety of the driver is an important research issue.

   (3) ⇒ It provides safety measures such as parking the head of a hard disk to prevent a head crash and resulting data loss upon _collision_.

2. (1) ⇒ The outer gimbal is mounted so as to _spin_ about an axis in its own plane.

   (2) ⇒ It is free to _spin_ in any direction about the fixed point.

3. ⇒ Inventors _tried_ to use gyroscopes as the basis for early navigational systems.

4. ⇒ The race to _make_ gyroscopes _smaller_ for guided missiles and weapons navigation systems resulted in the development and manufacturing of midget gyroscopes.

Choose the most appropriate one in the following questions （課本第 77 頁）

1. （A） 2. （C） 3. （E） 4. （B） 5. （C） 6. （A） 7. （B） 8. （B） 9. （B） 10. （D）

單元 7　知識管理 （課本第 80 頁）

　　知識經濟的產生，顯示企業的技術知識已經變得比傳統經濟資源更重要。再者，知識現在已被視為最具策略性的重要資源，而學習則是企業部門最具策略性的重要能力，因此知識資產必須以細心、系統化及專業管理以確保公司的生存。

　　知識管理定義為：持續管理能滿足現存與未來各種需求的知識，並確認能夠利用現有與新取得的知識資產來開發新機會，它也可以定義為確認、最佳化及積極的智慧資產管理以創造價值、提高生產力並取得和維護競爭優勢。知識管理涉及知識的分享與一些操作，Tiwana 在 2002 年指出這些操作包括對知識的搜尋、創新、包裝與組合、應用、重複使用與再驗證。

　　知識可分為兩種，內隱知識與外顯知識；內隱知識是非常個人化的，是由經驗的累積而來，而且不容易訴諸於文字說明；它因此不容易傳播與分享。另一方面，外顯知識則是較正式而有系統化，大部分的外顯知識可以文字說明，所有書籍、手冊、網頁上的知識都是外顯知識，這種知識很容易傳播與分享。傳統的教育訓練課程都專注於傳達現有的外顯知識或者引介「我們知道我們所知道」；在另一方面，內隱知識或「我們不知道我們所知道」的分享與管理，則是非常不足。

　　許多大企業已在公司內建立了知識管理的責任劃分，並提供預算、人員、資訊基礎結構等相關資源，這些資源是否足夠並不容易評估，不同的公司會有不同的需求與優先順序，因此，攏總地提出知識管理的全部經費是不切實際的，一家企業應該發展出同時涵蓋短期與長期需求的實施計畫。

1. ⇒ Knowledge management is defined as the process of <u>continuously</u> managing knowledge of all kinds to meet existing and emerging needs.

   ⇒ Knowledge management is defined as the process of <u>constantly</u> managing knowledge of all kinds to meet existing and emerging needs.

   ⇒ Knowledge management is defined as the process of <u>uninterruptedly</u> managing knowledge of all kinds to meet existing and emerging needs.

2. ⇒ Knowledge management is defined as the process of persistently managing knowledge of all kinds to <u>find out</u> and utilize existing and acquired knowledge assets.

   ⇒ Knowledge management is defined as the process of persistently managing knowledge of all kinds to <u>discover</u> and utilize existing and acquired knowledge assets.

3. ⇒ The <u>conventional</u> education and training program has been focused on the communication of the existing explicit knowledge.

4. ⇒ The traditional education and training program has been <u>concentrated</u> on the communication of the existing explicit knowledge.

   ⇒ The traditional education and training program has been <u>centered</u> on the communication of the existing explicit knowledge.

5. ⇒ Knowledge is <u>considered</u> the most strategically important resource and learning the most strategically important competence for business sectors.

   ⇒ Knowledge is <u>esteemed</u> the most strategically important resource and learning the most strategically important competence for business sectors.

6. ⇒ Many large companies have made resources _available_ in terms of budget, staff, and IT infra-structure.

  ⇒ Many large companies have made resources _obtainable_ in terms of budget, staff, and IT infra-structure.

  ⇒ Many large companies have made resources _reachable_ in terms of budget, staff, and IT infra-structure.

7. ⇒ Whether those resources are _enough_ or not is difficult to evaluate.

  ⇒ Whether those resources are _sufficient_ or not is difficult to evaluate.

Choose the most appropriate one in the following questions （課本第 88 頁）

1.（E） 2.（E） 3.（C） 4.（A） 5.（E） 6.（B） 7.（C） 8.（A） 9.（E） 10.（B）

單元 8 什麼是商標？ （課本第 92 頁）

　　商品標章是在商品交易時，用來指明貨物來源，以便和其他貨品有所區分的文字、名稱、符號或圖案，服務標章除了指服務而非貨品的來源與區分外，其他皆與商品標章相同，「標章」常用來稱呼商品標章及服務標章兩者。

　　商標權可用來防止他人使用會造成混淆的類似標章，但卻不能防止他人使用明顯不同標章，來生產或銷售同類的貨物或提供服務，使用於跨州或國外貿易的商品標章可以在「美國專利暨商標局」（USPTO）申請註冊。

　　任何時候，人們宣稱擁有某個標章的權利時，可以使用「TM」（商品標章）或「SM」（服務標章）的字樣來提醒社會大眾，不論他們是否已經向「美國專利暨商標局」申請註冊。然而，只有在向「美國專利暨商標局」註冊某個標章之後，而非在送件申請期間，才能使用聯邦註冊符號「®」。同時，註冊符號只能使用於聯邦商標註冊中所列舉商品或服務有關的事物上。

　　擁有聯邦標章註冊有如下所列好處：

· 註冊者對公眾宣告，其擁有該項標章的所有權。

· 在合法推定註冊者擁有該項標章所有權後，註冊者就有獨占權使用該項標章於註冊登錄的相關商品或服務上。

· 在聯邦法庭上，可對該項標章行使法律行動。

· 可依據美國專利權來申請外國的專利權註冊。

· 向美國海關提出專利權聲明，防止侵權的國外商品之輸入。

　　「美國專利暨商標局」審核該項商標的聯邦註冊申請，並決定申請案件是否符合聯邦註冊要求，「美國專利暨商標局」並不判定某個人是否有權利使用某個標章，即使未經註冊，人們仍可使用任何標章來標示其貨物或服務的來源，一旦商標註冊核准後，標章的擁有者可自行決定，是否依聯邦註冊擁有權，來強制執行其標章權利。

Use of Synonym （課本第 96 頁）

1. ⇒ A trademark is a word, name, symbol or device which is used to indicate the _origin_ of the goods and to distinguish them from the goods of others.

   ⇒ A trademark is a word, name, symbol or device which is used to indicate the _manufacturer_ of the goods and to distinguish them from the goods of others.

   ⇒ A trademark is a word, name, symbol or device which is used to indicate the _supplier_ of the goods and to distinguish them from the goods of others.

2. ⇒ A trademark is a word, name, symbol or device which is used to indicate the source of the goods and to _characterize_ them from the goods of others.

   ⇒ A trademark is a word, name, symbol or device which is used to indicate the source of the goods and to _discriminate_ them from the goods of others.

   ⇒ A trademark is a word, name, symbol or device which is used to indicate the source of the goods and to _differentiate_ them from the goods of others.

3. ⇒ They may use the registration symbol with the mark only on or in connection with the ___commodities___ and/or services listed in the federal trademark registration.

   ⇒ They may use the registration symbol with the mark only on or in connection with the ___merchandises___ and/or services listed in the federal trademark registration.

4. ⇒ Owning a federal mark registration provides a number of _benefits_ .

Choose the most appropriate one in the following questions （課本第 98 頁）

1.（A） 2.（A） 3.（E） 4.（E） 5.（B） 6.（C） 7.（C） 8.（A） 9.（E） 10.（A）

單元 9   什麼是著作權？（課本第 102 頁）

　　著作權是提供給原創性工作者的一種保護，對象包括文學、戲劇、音樂、藝術與特定之智慧作品，不論是已出版或是未出版。美國於 1976 年的著作權法案，提供著作權擁有人獨占之權利重製受著作權保護的作品、製作衍生作品、銷售其複製品或唱片、公開表演或陳列。在美國，著作權可向國會圖書館著作權辦公室申請，並且可以用「Copyright © 年份」的字樣來宣告。

　　著作權保障的是表現方式，而非作品本身。例如，一部機器的說明，可以受著作權的保障，這樣可防止他人複製該項說明，但是卻不能防止其他人，以自己的方式來撰寫這樣說明，也不能阻止他人生產或使用這部機器；資料只有出版方式可以受保障，資料本身不能受著作權的保障，例如，如果將他人文字中資料轉換成表格的方式呈現，則不需要使用許可（但仍需要說明出處），諸如改變表格中行的順序之小幅度修改，在法律上對避免使用許可之必要是不夠的。（註：課文並無此段文字。）包括特定資料表格是可以被著作權所保障，但卻不能阻止他人以圖形來描述那些資料。

　　如果某人想要依據他人作品來撰寫東西，則他有責任要取得所有受到著作權保護的作品使用許可，使用許可必須取得原始著作權擁有者允許，通常是出版商，有些出版商會要求他禮貌性的取得原始作者使用同意，如果使用許可無法取得，則作者有三個選擇：(1) 將作品內容大幅地改變或重畫，這樣就不需要使用許可；(2) 找其他適當的替代內容；(3) 由著作中刪除那些內容。

　　一旦取得使用許可之後，作者應依著作權所有人要求，在稿件中以加上底線方式註明資料來源，加上底線方式註明資料來源，應插入適當位置；在表格下方或圖標題後面等等，沒有註明出處的圖與表格，會被認為是原創作品，它們必須證明是原創的。

　　使用受著作權保障的內容需要獲得許可，包括：

- 任何表演、詩或歌曲的一個段落
- 引用任何期刊 50 字以上的內容
- 引用任何書籍 400 字以上的內容
- 任何表格、圖、圖示和圖解說明

　　許多政府出版品是屬於公共領域，也就是說它們是不受著作權保護。然而，許多政府贊助的機構即使獲得政府贊助，仍會對其出版品申請取得著作權保護，當使用他們的作品內容時，必須要取得著作權使用許可。

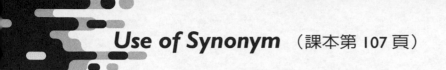

1. ⇒ The US 1976 Copyright Act generally gives the owner the exclusive right to display the copyrighted work _in_ _public_ .
   ⇒ The US 1976 Copyright Act generally gives the owner the exclusive right to display the copyrighted work _openly_ .

2. ⇒ The copyright protects the form of expression rather than the _topic_ matter of the writing.

3. ⇒ It would not prevent others from writing a ___depiction___ of their own or from making and using the machine.

4. ⇒ Some publishers may require that he/she obtains the original author's permission as a _politeness_ .
   ⇒ Some publishers may require that he/she obtains the original author's permission as a _civility_ .

5. ⇒ Copyright is a _kind_ of protection provided to the author of original works.
   ⇒ Copyright is a _type_ of protection provided to the author of original works.

6. ⇒ A copyright does not _preclude_ others from writing a description of their own.
   ⇒ A copyright does not _prohibit_ others from writing a description of their own.

Choose the most appropriate one in the following questions （課本第 109 頁）

1. （E） 2. （B） 3. （A） 4. （C） 5. （C） 6. （D） 7. （B） 8. （E） 9. （B） 10. （C）

單元 10　美國的專利（課本第112頁）

　　專利是一種智慧財產權，它提供專利所有人，有權在一段有限時間內，排除他人生產、使用、銷售或輸入美國該項專利保護範圍內物品的權利。新的專利在支付專利年費情況下，保障該項專利從申請日起20年在美國的專利權，或由較早的相關申請日起算，美國專利只有在美國領土與領地內有效。

　　「美國專利暨商標局」（USPTO）是負責審核專利申請與核發專利的政府機構，USPTO決定某個特定案件是否應核發專利，但是如果USPTO認可專利權，專利所有人必須自行去執行他的權利。

　　專利有不同種類，包括實用、設計與植物專利，實用與植物專利也有二種不同專利申請——臨時性與非臨時性。每年USPTO收到大約30萬件專利申請，大部分都是非臨時性的實用專利。

　　實用專利可以核發給任何發明，或發現任何新與有用的程序、機器、製品或物品的組成成分，或任何新興而有用的改良。設計專利可以核頒給任何發明製品新的、原創與式樣設計的人，實用專利保護商品的使用方式，而設計專利保護商品的外觀，如果一項發明同時牽涉到實用與式樣外觀，則該項發明可以同時取得設計專利與實用專利。雖然實用與設計專利有法律上個別保障，但是物品實用與式樣卻是不易分開的，製品可以同時擁有功能性與式樣上的特徵，植物專利可以核發給任何發明，或發現以無性繁殖任何個別與新的植物品種之人。

　　臨時性的專利申請不需要提出正式專利聲明、宣誓、申報或任何揭露資訊的聲明，臨時性專利申請從臨時申請提出日起，算為期12個月的未定期，此12個月未定期不能展延。因此，提出臨時性申請的申請人，在臨時申請的12個月未定期間內，必須提出相關的專利非臨時性申請，才能接續上較早的臨時性申請。

　　法律上規定，臨時申請從其臨時申請日起，12個月期滿後會自動廢止。單獨發明者應該完全了解，臨時申請在申請人未進一步提交申請下，不會自動獲得專利核准。某些發明專利代辦公司誤用臨時申請程序，讓發明者無法取得專利。

　　專利申請書是一件複雜的法律文件，最好由受過訓練的人來準備。因此，任何希望提出專利申請的人，可能需要向註冊的專利律師或代理人諮詢。

Use of Synonym （課本第 118 頁）

1. ⇒ It gives the patent holder the right to ___prohibit___ others from making, using, offering to sell, or selling the subject matter that is within the scope of protection granted by the patent.

   ⇒ It gives the patent holder the right to ___eliminate___ others from making, using, offering to sell, or selling the subject matter that is within the scope of protection granted by the patent.

2. ⇒ It gives the patent holder the right to exclude others from making, using, offering to sell, or selling the subject matter that is within the scope of protection _approved_ by the patent.

   ⇒ It gives the patent holder the right to exclude others from making, using, offering to sell, or selling the subject matter that is within the scope of protection _permitted_ by the patent.

3. ⇒ The United States Patent and Trademark Office is the government _organization_ responsible for examining patent applications and issuing patents.

4. ⇒ A provisional application for patent allows filing without an _official_ patent claim.

5. ⇒ Independent inventors should ___completely___ understand that a provisional application will not mature into a granted patent without further submissions by the inventor.

   ⇒ Independent inventors should ___thoroughly___ understand that a provisional application will not mature into a granted patent without further submissions by the inventor.

6. ⇒ Anyone who wishes to file a patent application may need to _discuss_ with a registered patent attorney or agent.

   ⇒ Anyone who wishes to file a patent application may need to _deliberate_ with a registered patent attorney or agent.

   ⇒ Anyone who wishes to file a patent application may need to ___talk___ to a registered patent attorney or agent.

Choose the most appropriate one in the following questions （課本第 120 頁）

1.（A）2.（E）3.（A）4.（D）5.（C）6.（B）7.（E）8.（C）9.（A）10.（E）
11.（D）12.（B）13.（C）

單元 11　設計專利的申請 （課本第126頁）

　　設計包含了製品本身具有，或者應用到製品上的式樣特性，既然設計是以外觀來顯示，因此設計專利申請的主要內容與下列事項有關：物品的構造或形狀、應用到物品的表面式樣或是構造與表面式樣的組合。表面式樣無法與牽涉到的物品分開，因此不能單獨存在，它必須是應用到製品表面的明確式樣，一項式樣設計可能牽涉到整個物品或是物品的一部分，或是應用到物品的裝飾，如果一項設計只是表面式樣，它必須繪圖顯示如何應用在物體上，該物體並非設計的一部分，必須以虛線表示。

　　每一件設計專利只能單獨申請，獨立而明顯不同的設計無法一次處理，而必須分開申請，兩件以上物品之間若是沒有明顯關係，就算個別獨立案件。例如，一付眼鏡與一個門把手是個別不同物品，它們必須分開申請專利，即使是相關連物品，如果有不同形狀與外觀，也被視為個別設計；例如，兩個有不同表面式樣的花瓶，因為明顯不同外觀，必須分開申請；但是，僅有微小形態差異的花瓶，可視為單一設計概念，兩者的式樣可包含於同一申請中。

　　專利聲明規定申請人希望獲得物品本身具有或應用上的專利，專利聲明必須以正式的用詞「（本身具有或應用物品）的式樣設計，如圖所示」表達，聲明中物品的描述應該與發明標題所用術語一致。

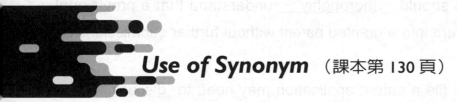

Use of Synonym （課本第 130 頁）

1. ⇒ A design for surface ornamentation is _indivisible_ from the article to which it is applied and cannot exist alone.

   ⇒ A design for surface ornamentation is _undividable_ from the article to which it is applied and cannot exist alone.

2. ⇒ It must be an _explicit_ pattern of surface ornamentation, applied to an article of manufacture.

   ⇒ It must be an _uambiguous_ pattern of surface ornamentation, applied to an article of manufacture.

3. ⇒ If a design is just surface ornamentation, it must be shown applied to an article in the <u>sketch</u>.

⇒ If a design is just surface ornamentation, it must be shown applied to an article in the <u>draft</u>.

⇒ If a design is just surface ornamentation, it must be shown applied to an article in the <u>diagram</u>.

4. ⇒ Designs are independent if there is no <u>obvious</u> relationship between two or more articles.

⇒ Designs are independent if there is no <u>evident</u> relationship between two or more articles.

5. ⇒ Designs are considered <u>individual</u> if they have different shape and appearances even though they are related articles.

6. ⇒ Two vases having different surface <u>decoration</u> creating distinct appearances must be claimed in separate applications.

7. ⇒ Vases with only minimal configuration differences may be considered a single design concept and both embodiments may be <u>incorporated</u> in a single application.

Choose the most appropriate one in the following questions （課本第 132 頁）

1.（D）2.（B）3.（A）4.（D）5.（A）6.（C）7.（E）8.（C）9.（D）10.（A）

單元 12 非臨時性實用專利申請

（課本第 136 頁）

　　非臨時性實用專利申請，必須包括一份設計說明書、一份或數份聲明書、必要圖樣、一份宣誓書或申報書，以及規定的申請費用。

　　設計說明書是有關發明和相關製造，及使用方法和程序的書面描述。設計說明書必須要完整、清楚、簡明及正確的詞彙，以使任何具技術或科學知識的人，能夠依樣式製造或使用。

　　聲明書必須特別指出或明確聲明，你認為是發明的主體事物。聲明書定義了專利保護的範圍，一項專利是否會被核准，絕大部分程度取決於聲明書中所用詞彙。非臨時性實用專利申請，必須至少包含一份聲明書，聲明書章節必須由新的一頁開始，如果這部分有許多頁，則必須以阿拉伯數字依序編頁碼，並以最少限制聲明作為第一頁。

　　如果需要以圖樣才能說明，想要申請專利的主要內容，則專利申請文件必須包括該圖樣，圖樣必須顯示在聲明書中，所指示發明的每個特徵，若未附上圖樣可能會導致申請被視為不完整。

　　宣誓或申報必須由實際的發明人簽署，宣誓可由在美國境內任何一人監誓，或經由美國授權他國外交或領事官員監誓，申報則不需要人員監誓與證明其簽署。因此，申報是申請人比較願意採行的方式。

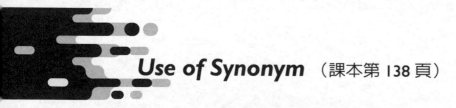

Use of Synonym （課本第 138 頁）

1. ⇒ The specification is a written <u>depiction</u> of the invention and of the manner and process of making and using the same.

   ⇒ The specification is a written <u>explanation</u> of the invention and of the manner and process of making and using the same.

   ⇒ The specification is a written <u>illustration</u> of the invention and of the manner and process of making and using the same.

2. ⇒ They should be numbered __continuously__ in Arabic numerals, with the least restrictive claim presented as claim number 1.

⇒ They should be numbered _uninterruptedly_ in Arabic numerals, with the least restrictive claim presented as claim number 1.

3. ⇒ The drawings must show every _characteristics_ of the invention as specified in the claims.

4. ⇒ A non-provisional application for a utility patent must _comprise_ of at least one claim.

⇒ A non-provisional application for a utility patent must _consist_ of at least one claim.

⇒ A non-provisional application for a utility patent must _include_ at least one claim.

5. ⇒ _____Negligence_____ of drawings may cause an application to be considered incomplete.

⇒ _Oversight_ of drawings may cause an application to be considered incomplete.

6. ⇒ A declaration does not require any witness or person to administer or _confirm_ its signing.

⇒ A declaration does not require any witness or person to administer or _prove_ its signing.

⇒ A declaration does not require any witness or person to administer or _substantiate_ its signing.

Choose the most appropriate one in the following questions （課本第 140 頁）

1.（E）2.（B）3.（A）4.（D）5.（A）6.（B）7.（B）8.（D）

單元 13　彈性製造在美國 （課本第 144 頁）

　　美國工業在製造方面，現在正站在一個新世代入口——這是以完善的自動化生產方式，開啟這個世代的序幕。美國製造業者由於面臨日益增加的國外競爭威脅，明顯地以彈性製造方法，來提高美國廠商在製造方面競爭力，自動化技術在工業界最需要時，從實驗室移轉到業界使用。

　　為了減少製造產品所需工時所採用轉換生產線的方式，現在被更具有彈性的系統所取代，彈性製造提供了更好的生產力，並降低產品價格，同時也保持強化品質優點。彈性製造不僅提供更高的生產效率，也讓使用者能更快適應產品改變。再者，彈性製造彌補了美國製造業者在製造方面專業人力的不足。

　　彈性製造特別適用於有複雜製程，與小批量需求的企業，航太工業是很好的例子。像是汽車與家電業等大量製造業，當批量很小時，就必須檢討資本投資，經過適當設計、自動化彈性製造系統，不僅可以支援小批量經濟生產，也能加速從一條生產線轉換到另一條生產線。

Use of Synonym （課本第 148 頁）

1. ⇒ Flexible manufacturing is becoming a <u>remarkable</u> part in the American approach to achieve competitiveness in manufacturing.

   ⇒ Flexible manufacturing is becoming a <u>noteworthy</u> part in the American approach to achieve competitiveness in manufacturing.

   ⇒ Flexible manufacturing is becoming an <u>important</u> part in the American approach to achieve competitiveness in manufacturing.

2. ⇒ Flexible manufacturing provides better productivity and product affordability, yet it <u>keeps</u> the advantage of enhanced quality.

   ⇒ Flexible manufacturing provides better productivity and product affordability, yet it <u>maintains</u> the advantage of enhanced quality.

   ⇒ Flexible manufacturing provides better productivity and product affordability, yet it <u>preserves</u> the advantage of enhanced quality.

3. ⇒ Flexible manufacturing <u>offsets</u> for a decrease in the manufacturing professionals available in the US manufacturers.

   ⇒ Flexible manufacturing <u>counterbalances</u> for a decrease in the manu-facturing professionals available in the US manufacturers.

4. ⇒ Flexible manufacturing not only <u>provides</u> greater production efficiency but also enables users to adapt to changes in product promptly.

   ⇒ Flexible manufacturing not only <u>supplies</u> greater production efficiency but also enables users to adapt to changes in product promptly.

   ⇒ Flexible manufacturing not only <u>supports</u> greater production efficiency but also enables users to adapt to changes in product promptly.

5. ⇒ Flexible manufacturing provides better productivity and product affordability, yet it retains the advantage of <u>improved</u> quality.

   ⇒ Flexible manufacturing provides better productivity and product affordability, yet it retains the advantage of <u>better</u> quality.

6. ⇒ A properly designed manufacturing system not only supports economical production of small lot sizes but also facilitates the __changeover__ from one production line to another.

⇒ A properly designed manufacturing system not only supports economical production of small lot sizes but also facilitates the _shifting_ from one production line to another.

⇒ A properly designed manufacturing system not only supports economical production of small lot sizes but also facilitates the _switching_ from one production line to another.

Choose the most appropriate one in the following questions （課本第 151 頁）

1.（E）2.（E）3.（A）4.（D）5.（D）6.（E）7.（C）8.（A）9.（B）10.（B）

單元 14　田口對於品質的想法 （課本第 154 頁）

　　產品都有可用以描述與消費者需求或期望有關功能方面的特性，產品品質即依據這些特性來決定，品質與產品在其生命週期中，所造成的公共損失有關；一個高品質的產品將會在其生命週期中造成最小損失；公共損失是由消費者與製造者所遭受損失合併而成的；消費者損失可以有許多方式，但通常是產品功能喪失產生或財產損失。如果一個產品無法依照預期操作，消費者就會經歷一些損失；製造者的損失則是無謂使用昂貴材料、零件或製程。田口建立了一個損失函數，來確認消費者對於產品貨真價實的要求，與製造者要求生產低成本產品的希望。

　　田口把一個產品或製程設計分成三階段計畫；系統設計、參數設計以及公差設計。系統設計階段發生於當使用新觀念、構想、方法來創造或提供新產品或改良產品給消費者時；參數設計是用於不以控制或消除變異原因來改善品質，以使產品更堅固耐用來對抗損害原因；參數設計階段對於改善產品的均一性是不可或缺的，並可在不需要費用，甚至可節省費用情況下完成，這意謂可設定產品或製程的某些參數，讓效能較不受變異原因所影響。

　　當使用參數設計仍無法適當減少變異時，才採用公差設計。公差設計是以最小成本來改善品質，緊縮產品或製程公差來減少其功能變異，以改善品質，這只有在使用過參數設計之後才能使用。在產品開發時遇到問題，一般設計者可以直接進入公差設計：當公差緊縮後，變異將會減少，而品質也就改善了。然而，緊縮公差可能會很昂貴，甚至在先使用參數設計的情況下，可能完全不需要。設計者可能犯下一個嚴重錯誤，就是對產品在可採用參數設計的方法下，可使用低成本項目時，卻採用昂貴材料、零件或製程。

Use of Synonym （課本第158頁）

1. ⇒ Taguchi <u>treated</u> the design of a product or process as a three-stage project.

   ⇒ Taguchi <u>regarded</u> the design of a product or process as a three-stage project.

2. ⇒ Tolerance design is <u>adopted</u> when the efforts of parameter design have not proved adequate in reducing variation.

   ⇒ Tolerance design is <u>used</u> when the efforts of parameter design have not proved adequate in reducing variation.

3. ⇒ System design is the <u>phase</u> when new concepts or methods are created to provide new products to customers.

4. ⇒ Taguchi considers the design of a product or process as a three-stage <u>assignment</u>.

   ⇒ Taguchi considers the design of a product or process as a three-stage <u>program</u>.

5. ⇒ The parameter design stage is essential to improving the <u>consistency</u> of a product.

   ⇒ The parameter design stage is essential to improving the <u>homogeneity</u> of a product.

Choose the most appropriate one in the following questions （課本第160頁）

1.（E) 2.（B) 3.（E) 4.（A) 5.（C) 6.（A) 7.（E) 8.（B) 9.（A) 10.（D)

單元 15　CAD/CAM/CAE（課本第164頁）

　　因為電腦效能顯著進步，以及有更多設計與生產軟體工具可供使用情況下，工程師們現在已可以使用 CAD/CAM/CAE 系統於日常工作上，而非僅在展示時使用。

　　電腦輔助設計（CAD）是使用電腦來支援設計的建構、修改、分析和最佳化的技術。任何電腦程式包含電腦繪圖功能，以及在設計過程中，能夠幫助工程設計的應用程式，都可被歸類為 CAD 軟體。易言之，CAD 工具可以是處理形狀的幾何工具，也可以是進行分析與最佳化自行編寫的應用程式，在這兩者之間，現有標準工具包括可進行公差分析、建立有限元素模型，與分析結果的視覺化顯示等操作。因為幾何設計在產品開發階段中，對所有後續操作都很重要，CAD 所扮演最基本的角色就是定義和描述機械零件、建築結構、電子電路、建築物配置等幾何設計。

　　電腦輔助製造（CAM）是經由和所有生產資源以介面連結的電腦，來計畫、管理、監測與控制整個製造過程，應用 CAM 最成熟的領域就是電腦數值控制，或者稱為 CNC，CNC 是使用程式化指令來控制工具機進行研磨、切割、鑽孔、沖製、折彎或將原材料製成零件成品的技術。另一個值得注意的 CAM 功能，就是機器人程式設計，機器人可以執行工廠裡像銲接、組裝、搬運等個別作業，它們也可以在一個工作站配置中，為 CNC 機器安排工具，與加工件的選取與放置作業。

　　電腦輔助工程（CAE）是使用電腦系統，來分析 CAD 幾何技術，設計者因此可以模擬與研究不同設計的表現，這樣可以進行產品設計的改良與最佳化工作，用在許多分析上的 CAE 工具均可取得；動力學程式可用來決定一個結構中連桿的移動路徑與速度即是一個例子，大尺度位移動態分析程式已被用於像汽車這種複雜機構，決定其中的負載與位移；模擬複雜電子電路操作的邏輯計時軟體，也是 CAE 工具的一個例子。

1. ⇒ Geometric design is _important_ to all the subsequent activities in the product developing stages.

   ⇒ Geometric design is _essential_ to all the subsequent activities in the product developing stages.

   ⇒ Geometric design is _crucial_ to all the subsequent activities in the product developing stages.

2. ⇒ Geometric design is vital to all the ____following____ activities in the product developing stages.

   ⇒ Geometric design is vital to all the ____succeeding____ activities in the product developing stages.

3. ⇒ Computer-aided-design (CAD) is the technology ____related____ to the use of computers to support the construction, alteration, analysis, and optimization of a design.

   ⇒ Computer-aided-design (CAD) is the technology _involves_ using computers to support the construction, alteration, analysis, and optimization of a design.

4. ⇒ CAE tools are _accessible_ for many analyses.

   ⇒ CAE tools are _obtainable_ for many analyses.

5. ⇒ This enables _enhancement_ and optimization of the design of a product.

   ⇒ This enables _improvement_ and optimization of the design of a product.

6. ⇒ Designers are _permitted_ to simulate and study the performance of various designs.

   ⇒ Designers _may_ simulate and study the performance of various designs.

Choose the most appropriate one in the following questions （課本第 171 頁）

1.（A） 2.（A） 3.（C） 4.（B） 5.（B） 6.（E） 7.（D） 8.（D） 9.（B） 10.（E）

單元 16　製造 / 倉儲系統的模擬

（課本第 174 頁）

R.J.Reynolds 設計了一種利用許多電腦來控制產品流的製造與倉儲設施，因為此設施採用十臺電腦的階層控制系統，因此倉庫容量很有可能遇到瓶頸，對於管理影響很大，於是開發出此設施的「離散事件──連續模擬」的合併模式。

基本上，倉庫由製造部收到裝箱成品，並按照品牌貯存在擁擠的儲存區，以準備最後配送至消費者或是分銷倉庫。最初由製造樓層接收箱子，並通過一臺雷射掃瞄器來決定此產品要集中到哪一層級，然後箱子在兩臺長輸送帶上移到輸入掃瞄器，並決定箱子路線，然後箱子由一連串的光電感應器追蹤直到它抵達指定的路線上。

當一條輸送帶上收集到足夠數量的箱子後，此輸送帶即準備好自動棧板作業，一條輸出、輸送帶與確認掃瞄器，用來確認產品編號是否正確，並形成一長列包裝箱運送帶，這一長列箱子被導引至一個應急用轉向器，此轉向器可在某個棧板堆疊機故障時，將不同等級產品合併到同一棧板堆疊機上來處理。所有未經輸出掃瞄器適當的確認箱子，都被送到人工棧板堆疊區，而經過確認的箱子，則被送到依品牌自動棧板堆疊機處理。位在應急用轉向器與棧板堆疊機之間的可控制邏輯選擇與皮帶式輸送臺，可確保在很重視箱子數目的包裝區域，能夠維持箱子之間的間隔，以便清點正確數目。它們也確保在應急處理模式操作下，各種包裝箱列能夠適當合併。

這個模擬的一個有趣地方，就是所建立模型涉及到兩種常用輸送帶，因為箱子間隔不太重要，所以滾筒式輸送帶只有偶爾開啟與關閉。如此一來，箱子的載入與卸下可以用離散事件模式來處理。然而，皮帶式輸送帶因為下游後續狀況需要經常開動或關閉，因此箱子的輸送時間無法控制，這些輸送帶就被利用狀態變數來建立操作模式，輸送帶的位置被視為一個狀態變數，而輸送帶上的箱子則使用指標來定位。

本研究結果指出，由於利用輸送帶操作，棧板堆疊機的最大使用效率可達87％，由於特定設備故障會造成預期使用率降低，我們也估計在內，經由增加「淨空」光電感測器，並改變另外一具感測光電器的位置，就可提升最大效率。本研究結果經過實作，在發生設備故障的應急情況下，也達到預期系統效能的改善。這個模擬模型曾被擴充並被用來有關評估在控制情況下，突然增加的輸入量、以區域畫分的輸送量以及負載水準（量）的不同演算法，使用本模擬模型在系統營運上有令人印象深刻的改善成果。

Use of Synonym （課本第 179 頁）

1. ⇒ The boxes are first received from the manufacturing floor and pass a laser scanner to determine on which tier the product is to be _accumulated_ .

2. ⇒ The roller conveyors are _infrequently_ turned on and off.
   ⇒ The roller conveyors are _rarely_ turned on and off.
   ⇒ The roller conveyors are turned on and off _once in a while_ .

3. ⇒ The box train is routed to a contingency diverter where trains from both tiers can be _jointed_ to a single palletizer in the event of a palletizer failure.
   ⇒ The box train is routed to a contingency diverter where trains from both tiers can be _merged_ to a single palletizer in the event of a palletizer failure.

4. ⇒ When a _sufficient_ number of boxes have been accumulated in a lane, the boxes are loaded on a pallet automatically.
   ⇒ When an _enough_ number of boxes have been accumulated in a lane, the boxes are loaded on a pallet automatically.

5. ⇒ An output belt and a _confirmation_ scanner are used to _confirm_ correct product codes and to build box trains.
   ⇒ An output belt and a verification scanner are used to _ensure_ correct product codes and to build box trains.

6. ⇒ The simulation model has been _extended_ and has been used to assess various algorithms.

7. ⇒ _Spectacular_ improvements in system operations have been recorded by employing the simulation model.
   ⇒ _Remarkable_ improvements in system operations have been recorded by employing the simulation model.

Choose the most appropriate one in the following questions （課本第 181 頁）

1.（C）2.（A）3.（B）4.（D）5.（C）6.（D）7.（A）8.（A）9.（D）10.（A）

單元 17　電子商務在製造營運上的發展

（課本第 184 頁）

　　諸如全球資訊網（WWW）、寬頻與無線傳輸的新技術，在近年來已為全球商業帶來驚人經濟與策略改變，它們擴展了商務範圍，不同電子商務技術在製造營運上，所一直扮演的角色更為吃重。

　　製造營運若是沒有其龐大的商業群體與相關企業經理人，則其功能將無法發揮，諸如物料需求規劃（MRP）、企業資源規劃（ERP）、產品與製程設計系統、產品文件說明與資料管理等系統是製造業常常使用的，這些專注於內部製造系統的擴充與整合，是因為電子商務技術已有顯著進步，對一家公司來說，現在已經不再是在這些領域中取得競爭優勢的問題，而是關乎企業生存的大事。

　　電子商務在製造上的持續發展與成熟，已在工業界顯現出來，但學術界在研究與協助工業界來提升關鍵性技術的理解與知識累積上卻很緩慢。虛擬觀念與反應靈敏的企業，已讓不同電子商務工具在管理上更為重要。但是，理解與進一步發展這些工具的研究，卻沒有隨之蓬勃發展。

　　以網際網路為基礎的電子化市場，已在國際競爭與經濟上變得愈來愈普遍，電子商務可以發生於企業之間（B2B），或是企業與消費者之間（B2C），但網際網路也在虛擬市場上含蓋廣大、多樣的潛在商業活動、資訊交流與商機，在交易伙伴當中，有三種組織之間的關係，包括交易、資訊分享及合作關係，這些關係主張以交易為導向的市場較於合作導向的市場，在程度上較不仰賴供應鍊管理（SCM）的原則。

　　在 2000 年，企業對企業之電子商務基礎建設之總投資已超過 2000 億元，即使出現某些技術泡沫化現象，這些科技仍然持續地成長，電子商務技術已深深植入組織機能、政策及實務中。在供應鍊當中，B2B 市場槓桿操作的力量取決於賣方與買方的競爭力，網際網路協助解決買、賣方間取捨，並讓供應鍊中各伙伴間進行必要整合，以網頁為基礎的技術，現在是供應鍊預測、規劃、排程與執行上不可或缺的，顧客與供應商之間整合的資訊交流愈大，在整個網路上供需平衡就變得愈容易。

Fill in the blanks（課本第 189 頁）
using the words you have just learned in this lesson

Internet-based electronic marketplaces are becoming more common in international _competition_ and economy. E-commerce can take place among businesses (B2B) or between businesses and _consumers_ (B2C), but the internet also covers a greater variety of potential commercial activities and information exchanges and chances in a virtual market. Three broad aspects of _organizational_ relationships between trading associates have been identified including _transactional_, information-sharing, and _collaborative_ relationships. These relationships suggest that _transactional_-oriented markets are to a lesser degree relying on supply chain management (SCM) principles than _collaborative_-oriented markets.

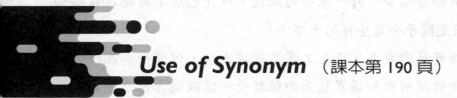

Use of Synonym（課本第 190 頁）

1. ⇒ New technologies such as World Wide Web (WWW), broadband, and wireless have brought _remarkable_ changes in global business in recent years.
   ⇒ New technologies such as World Wide Web (WWW), broadband, and wireless have brought _exceptional_ changes in global business in recent years.

2. ⇒ The _expansion_ and integration of such internally focused manufacturing systems has stepped forward significantly because of e-commerce technologies.

3. ⇒ Three broad aspects of organizational relationships between trading _partners_ have been identified
   ⇒ Three broad aspects of organizational relationships between trading _colleagues_ have been identified
   ⇒ Three broad aspects of organizational relationships between trading _confederates_ have been identified

4. ⇒ Even with the _emergence_ of the technology bubble, there is still continued growth in these technologies.

⇒ Even with the appearance of the technology bubble, there is still continued growth in these technologies.

5. ⇒ Web-based technologies are now requisite for supply chain forecasting, planning, scheduling and implementation.

⇒ Web-based technologies are now required for supply chain forecasting, planning, scheduling and implementation.

6. ⇒ In 2000, the total investment in business-to-business (B2B) infrastructure surpassed $200 billion.

⇒ In 2000, the total investment in business-to-business (B2B) infrastructure was more than $200 billion.

Choose the most appropriate one in the following questions （課本第 192 頁）

1.（A）2.（D）3.（A）4.（B）5.（C）6.（D）7.（A）8.（D）9.（C）10.（B）

單元 18　遠距通訊的數位化 （課本第196頁）

　　數位化是在遠距通訊與數位音響系統（光碟）、機器的數位控制等領域的技術趨勢，數位方法比類比系統有較高的系統準確性與穩定性，驅使數位化的原動力是來自於超大型積體電路與電腦，它們讓數位化系統所使用的電路變為可能。

　　在遠距通訊領域中，交換式電話網路數據與數位語音傳輸、數位微波通訊與數位光纖通訊都已有創新技術。與這些系統相比，移動式無線通訊數位化發展已經落後了。不過，近來在數位移動通訊研發的爆發性，似乎已彌補了數位化進程的延遲，這方面提升又進一步被個人通訊服務、筆記型電腦、移動多媒體等數位移動通訊新的應用，更往前推進。

　　某些數位技術能夠應用到任何領域，而其他的技術則因特定技術領域需求的差異而無法直接應用。對於移動通訊而言，強韌以對抗訊號快速衰退、頻譜的有效運用、功率效能、小巧和低價的設備，都很重要。數位的調變／解調變是滿足這些移動通訊需求的關鍵技術。

Fill in the blanks （課本第198頁）
using the words you have just learned in this lesson

In telecommunication fields, technological innovations have been made on data and _digital_ speech transmission on switched telephone networks, _digital_ microwave communications, and _digital_ _optic_ communications. _Digitization_ in mobile radio communications has lagged behind as compared to those developments. However, explosive activity in recent research and development of _digital_ _mobile_ communications seems to recover the delay in the _digital_ progress. This enhancement is further spurred by novel applications of _digital_ _mobile_ communications such as personal communication services, _digital_ computing, and _digital_ multimedia.

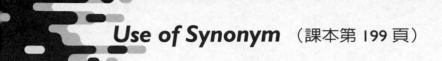

Use of Synonym （課本第 199 頁）

1. ⇒ <u>Pushing</u> forces for digitization are VLSI (very large-scale integrated) circuits and computers.

2. ⇒ Many <u>innovative</u> applications of digital mobile communications have been reported recently.

   ⇒ Many <u>new</u> applications of digital mobile communications have been reported recently.

   ⇒ Many <u>original</u> applications of digital mobile communications have been reported recently.

3. ⇒ This enhancement is further <u>advanced</u> by novel applications of digital mobile communications.

   ⇒ This enhancement is further <u>impelled</u> by novel applications of digital mobile communications.

   ⇒ This enhancement is further <u>propelled</u> by novel applications of digital mobile communications.

   ⇒ This enhancement is further <u>stimulated</u> by novel applications of digital mobile communications.

4. ⇒ Some digital technologies can be applied in common to any <u>area</u>.

   ⇒ Some digital technologies can be applied in common to any <u>domain</u>.

   ⇒ Some digital technologies can be applied in common to any <u>province</u>.

5. ⇒ Robustness against fast <u>weakening</u> is essential for mobile communications.

6. ⇒ Digital modulation/demodulation is the critical technology to <u>achieve</u> these requirements for mobile communications.

   ⇒ Digital modulation/demodulation is the critical technology to <u>realize</u> these requirements for mobile communications.

Choose the most appropriate one in the following questions （課本第 201 頁）

1.（A) 2.（C) 3.（F) 4.（E) 5.（A) 6.（D) 7.（D) 8.（A) 9.（A) 10.（B)

單元 19　積體電路的起源 （課本第 204 頁）

固態技術一直被用來製作電晶體、二極體、電阻器及電容器。真空管是 1900 年代早期最主要的電子元件，電晶體是其改良品，電晶體有兩種主要功能：開關與放大；二極體在電路中做為開關的元件，電阻器是限制電流的元件，電容器則在電路中儲存電荷。

在 1947 年，第一顆固態電晶體的推出，開啟了固態電子的紀元與微電子工業，微電子工業由半導體工業與電子工業組成，電子工業設計和生產許多半導體元件組成的產品；從消費性電子產品到電腦。許多消費性電子產品中的印刷電路板（PCB）是許多電子公司的主要產品。

半導體工業又可以區分為兩個部分，一部分是使用一種稱為晶圓製作的製程，來生產半導體固態元件與電路公司，晶圓製作也稱為晶片製作或微晶片製作。另一部分則是開發與供應晶圓製作所需特殊設備、原材料與服務公司，半導體服務業的功能包括晶片設計、測試與封裝。

在 1950 年代初期，半導體工業供應電晶體收音機及電腦所需元件正活躍進行。那時候，半導體工業生產單顆的電晶體、二極體、電阻器及電容器，因為每個晶片只包含一個元件，因此也稱為離散元件，離散元件並非尖端產品，但它們大部分是精密電路中不可或缺的，且占所有半導體元件銷售額的 20% 至 30%。

離散元件在固態電路中占有支配地位的情況在 1959 年就結束了，當時 Jack Kilby 在一片鍺半導材料上面設計了一個完整電路，他的發明結合了多個電晶體、二極體、電容器，並使用鍺晶面原來就有的電阻當電路中的電阻器。這是第一次在同一個半導體材料上，完成完整電路的成功整合，被稱為積體電路（IC）。

由簡單的 Kilby 積體電路（IC）開始，積體電路的技術進展從未停止。每年單一電路上的元件數目不斷增加。1964 年 Gordon Moore 預測積體電路的密度每年將會倍增，這項預測就是我們所知的 Moore 定律，已被證明非常正確。

Fill in the blanks （課本第 207 頁）
using the words you have just learned in this lesson

Solid _devices_ are manufactured in four stages. They are material preparation, crystal growth and _wafer_ preparation, _wafer_ _fabrication_, and _packaging_. _Devices_ or _integrated circuits_ are actually formed in the _wafer_ in stage three, or the _wafer_ _fabrication_ stage. Up to several thousand identical circuits are formed on each _wafer_, although 200 to 300 are common. Each area on a _wafer_ occupied by a discrete or _integrated circuit_ is called a _chip_. The _wafer_ _fabrication_ process is also called *fab*, or *microchip fabrication*.

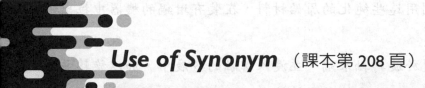

Use of Synonym （課本第 208 頁）

1. ⇒ In 1947, the _declaration_ of the first solid-state transistor initiated the solid-state electronic era.

   ⇒ In 1947, the _introduction_ of the first solid-state transistor initiated the solid-state electronic era.

2. ⇒ Discrete devices are not leading _edge_ products.

   ⇒ Discrete devices are not leading _rim_ products.

3. (1) ⇒ The semiconductor industry is divided into two _segments_.

   ⇒ The semiconductor industry is divided into two _areas_.

   (2) ⇒ There are 2,000 operators in the chip fabrication _division_ of this company.

   ⇒ There are 2,000 operators in the chip fabrication _department_ of this company.

   ⇒ There are 2,000 operators in the chip fabrication _sector_ of this company.

4. ⇒ His invention _combined_ several transistors, diodes, and capacitors in one chip.

   ⇒ His invention _united_ several transistors, diodes, and capacitors in one chip.

5. ⇒ The _supremacy_ of discrete devices in solid-state circuits was terminated in 1959.

   ⇒ The _ascendancy_ of discrete devices in solid-state circuits was terminated in 1959.

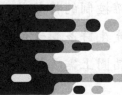

Choose the most appropriate one
in the following questions （課本第 210 頁）

1.（B）2.（A）3.（C）4.（E）5.（A）6.（C）7.（D）8.（A）9.（D）10.（A）

單元 20 積體電路的製作 （課本第 214 頁）

IC 的製作涉及許多複雜步驟，這些步驟可以歸納為四類製程：(1) 原始材料，(2) 成像，(3) 沈積與成長，以及 (4) 蝕刻與光罩作業，這些製程可將原始的矽土轉換成許多內含高達數百萬個電路的個別 IC。

生產矽晶圓的第一步驟，是把從海砂或是瑪瑙狀岩石沈積物中提煉的矽土，加以純化，原始的矽土可在高溫爐中加熱，將不純物分離與移除，而留下經化學純化的多晶矽材料，單晶矽晶錠可以利用這些純化的原始材料，在裝有坩鍋的機器中拉出形成結晶。

晶錠成長是將單晶種子置於旋轉軸末端，並浸入熔融的矽液中，加以旋轉並逐漸拉離來完成。在單晶種子與熔融矽液的接面上，熔融的矽會完全按照種子結晶結構凝固結晶。高度自動化的電腦控制拉晶長晶機可用來生產高品質晶錠。

由拉晶長晶機產生的晶錠，經由鑽石切片鋸切成晶圓，然後切片的晶圓再經過研磨去除因切割造成的損壞與不規則形狀。機械研磨是由研磨機來進行的，產生高品質成像表面的最後步驟，就是矽的化學蝕刻，這步驟可藉研磨移除雜質，並將矽晶表面磨平，形成像光學的「鏡子」一般。

旋轉塗料是在晶圓塗上光阻劑的一種技術，晶圓在表面滴上光阻劑後，塗料機快速旋轉整個晶圓，在晶圓上形成一層均勻薄膜，塗料是在高度控制的無塵環境中進行。晶圓塗層是在預先設定塗層參數的自動匣式載入系統進行，塗層的目的是要提供一層均勻、無瑕疵並且對光或電子敏感的光罩材料。

濕式與乾式蝕刻技術常用於成像製程中，蝕刻依需求移除不要的半導體層，蝕刻控制參數包括時間、均勻度、溫度與蝕刻藥品（液體或氣體）濃度。

矽的氧化過程是沈積與成長製程中最關鍵部分，矽的氧化過程會形成一種高度穩定和有用的材料——二氧化矽（SiO_2），二氧化矽是用來當作成像作業表面，是在氧氣或者小蒸氣的氣壓環境下所形成，這樣的氣壓環境是由一具氧化管（又稱擴散管或氧化爐）提供。

離子植入也是一個重要製程，它在半導體不同深度層次中，以精確控制的摻雜離子濃度植入摻雜物或離子。離子植入機功能是提供由電子與原子碰撞產生許多離子的離子源，摻雜所需的離子是由磁鐵選取並送至加速管，最後直接送到晶圓上需要摻雜的區域。

光罩製造是 IC 製程中必需的，光罩蝕刻可多樣化運用於不同蝕刻材料及蝕刻方法，硬表面的光罩主要是在玻璃基板上，塗布上某些金屬或氧化物形成的光罩，鉻是主要的硬表面光罩塗層材料，它提供了高解析度、耐久性與容易製作的優點。正光阻劑用在鉻金屬層的蝕刻成像與光罩上，鉻金屬層可形成光亮、黑色或是抗反射表面，鉻光罩蝕刻可產生非常高品質的光罩，可使用於高階超大型積體電路與傳統積體電路的製作。

Fill in the blanks （課本第 224 頁）
using the words you have just learned in this lesson

The oxidation of silicon is the most critical process in the deposition and growth stage. The oxidation of silicon results in the formation of a highly stable and useful material, carbon   dioxide (SiO_2). Carbon   dioxide is used as the surface for imaging operations. It is formed in either an oxygen or steam atmosphere. This atmosphere is provided by an oxidation tube. Ion   implantation is also an important process which places impurity, or doping, ions in semiconductor layers at various depths and with accurate control of dopant ion concentration. The ion   implanter functions by providing an ion source in which collisions of ions and atoms result in many ions . The ions required for doping are selected out by a magnet and routed to an acceleration tube that goes directly onto the area on the wafer where the doping is desired.

1. ⇒ The _division_ and removal of impurities of the raw silica is performed in a high-temperature furnace.
   ⇒ The _partition_ and removal of impurities of the raw silica is performed in a high-temperature furnace.

2. ⇒ This produces a surface of optical quality by removing debris from the lapping operation and leveling the silicon surface _at the same time_.
   ⇒ This produces a surface of optical quality by removing debris from the lapping operation and leveling the silicon surface _concurrently_.

3. ⇒ By removing _wreckage_ from the lapping operation and leveling the silicon surface simultaneously, the process produces a shiny surface on the wafer.
   ⇒ By removing _fragment_ from the lapping operation and leveling the silicon surface simultaneously, the process produces a shiny surface on the wafer.
   ⇒ By removing _remains_ from the lapping operation and leveling the silicon surface simultaneously, the process produces a shiny surface on the wafer.

4. ⇒ Chromium mask etching results in very high quality masks for advanced VLSI and _traditional_ IC fabrication.
   ⇒ Chromium mask etching results in very high quality masks for advanced VLSI and _typical_ IC fabrication.
   ⇒ Chromium mask etching results in very high quality masks for advanced VLSI and _customary_ IC fabrication.

5. ⇒ The _purpose_ of coating is to provide a uniform and defect-free layer of a photo or electron-sensitive masking material.
   ⇒ The _aim_ of coating is to provide a uniform and defect-free layer of a photo or electron-sensitive masking material.

6. ⇒ Chromium is the _principal_ hard-surface photomask coating material.
   ⇒ Chromium is the _superior_ hard-surface photomask coating material.

Choose the most appropriate one in the following questions （課本第 227 頁）

1.（A） 2.（B） 3.（C） 4.（E） 5.（B） 6.（C） 7.（D） 8.（D） 9.（D） 10.（B）

單元 21 　半導體的殺手 （課本第 230 頁）

　　半導體元件容易受到包括微粒、金屬離子、化學物質及細菌等多種汙染而損壞，這種敏感性主要由於晶圓上元件的微小尺寸與細薄的沉積層所致，晶圓上元件的尺寸在數個微米之間（μm），一微米等於 10^{-6}m。你也可以想像微米尺寸就是人類頭髮直徑大約 100 微米，元件實體的微小尺寸，讓它們容易被來自工人身上或由設備產生空氣中的微粒損壞。

　　當元件大小與薄膜尺寸變得更小，空氣中能夠容許的粒子尺寸也要控制得更小。一個簡單判斷原則，就是粒子尺寸必須小於最小元件設計尺寸的十分之一，一個 0.3 微米元件很容易受到直徑 0.03 微米粒子的損壞，在晶片上關鍵區域的粒子會損毀其功能，並造成所謂的嚴重瑕疵。在任何晶圓上都有微粒存在，有些掉落在較不敏感區域的粒子是無害的，目前一般製程，都尋求控制在一片 200 毫米晶圓上的微粒數目不超過十個 0.3 微米微粒。

　　因為我們有能力在晶圓上建立兩種導電類型，透過摻雜技術控制晶圓上電路的電阻值，以及在元件上建立陰極－陽極接面，因此我們可以製造出半導體元件，這三種特性是在晶體中摻入特定的摻雜質來達成，不幸的是很小量特定具導電性的汙染物，就可能會損壞晶圓上元件的導電特性、功能及可靠性，造成這類問題的汙染物就是一般所謂的離子污染物（MICs）。

　　游離性離子汙染物就是在半導體材料中，以離子型式存在的金屬原子，這些離子在半導體材料中有高度移動性這種游離性讓金屬離子能夠在元件內移動，並造成元件損壞；即使元件在通過測試與封裝後也會發生。不幸的是，在矽晶元件中造成這類問題的金屬，存在於多數化學藥品中。在一片晶圓上，每一平方厘米的 MIC 污染必須控制在 1010 個原子以下，鈉是在大多數未處理過的化學藥品中，最常見的游離性離子汙染物。因此，在矽製程中，鈉的控制是一件主要工作。

　　半導體製程中，第三種主要汙染物就是不想要的化學物質，製程中使用到的化學物品和水，都可能會被不想要的微量化學物質汙染而干擾製程，它們可能會造成不需要的表面蝕刻、產生無法由元件上移除的化合物，或造成非均一化的製程。氯即是製程化學藥品中需嚴格控制的這類汙染物之一。

　　半導體也可能會被細菌汙染，細菌是在供水系統中生長之有機物，並且存在於未經常清理的物體表面上，元件上之細菌就像微粒汙染，可能在晶片表面上造成不想要的金屬離子。

Fill in the blanks （課本第 235 頁）
using the words you have just learned in this lesson

Semiconductor devices are very <u>vulnerable</u> to many kinds of <u>contamination</u>, including <u>particles</u>, metallic <u>ions</u>, chemicals, and <u>bacteria</u>. The sensitivity is mainly due to the small sizes of the devices and the thinness of deposited layers on the <u>wafer</u>. The dimensions of the devices are in the range of <u>micron</u> (μm). One <u>micron</u> is equal to 10^{-6} meter. Another way to image the size of a <u>micron</u> is that the diameter of a human hair is about 100 μm. The small physical dimension of the devices makes them very <u>vulnerable</u> to <u>particles</u> in the air, coming from the workers, or generated by the equipment. As the device size and films become smaller, the allowable <u>particle</u> size in the air must be controlled to a much smaller dimension.

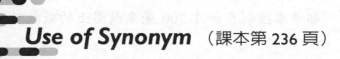

Use of Synonym （課本第 236 頁）

1. ⇒ Semiconductor devices are fabricated through our ability to create Negative-Positive <u>joint</u> in the devices.
   ⇒ Semiconductor devices are fabricated through our ability to create Negative-Positive <u>connection</u> in the devices.
   ⇒ Semiconductor devices are fabricated through our ability to create Negative-Positive <u>intersection</u> in the devices.

2. ⇒ The <u>scale</u> of the devices are in the range of micron (micrometer or μm).

3. ⇒ Control of sodium is, therefore, a <u>major</u> task in silicon processing.
   ⇒ Control of sodium is, therefore, a <u>main</u> task in silicon processing.

4. ⇒ These three properties are achieved by <u>doping</u> specific dopants into the crystal.

5. ⇒ They may <u>generate</u> compounds that cannot be removed from the devices.
   ⇒ They may <u>produce</u> compounds that cannot be removed from the devices.

Choose the most appropriate one in the following questions （課本第 238 頁）

1. （C） 2. （B） 3. （B） 4. （A） 5. （C） 6. （C） 7. （A） 8. （B） 9. （B） 10. （D）

單元 22　TFT-LCD 顯示器（課本第 242 頁）

　　液晶最早是在 19 世紀由一位奧地利植物學家 Friedrich Reinitzer 所發現。「液晶」這個名稱則是在後來由一位德國物理學家 Otto Lehnann 所創造。

　　液晶是一種幾乎透明的物質，同時顯現出固體與液體性質，當光線通過液晶時，會依其組成分子的排列穿過，這是固體物質性質。在 1960 年代，科學家發現在液晶通上電流會改變其分子排列，並改變光由其間通過路逕。

　　自從 1971 年液晶顯示器（LCD）被引進作為顯示媒介以來，它已用在許多消費性電子產品上，包括迷你電視、數位照像機與終端機。今日，LCD 被認為是最有可能取代 CRT 顯示器的產品，LCD 技術目前已有快速進展，現在產品已經不再像古早那樣笨拙，而且又是單色顯示器。許多公司已採用薄膜電晶體（TFT）技術來改善彩色畫面，在一個 TFT 螢幕裡，一個電晶體矩陣連接到 LCD 面板，每個電晶體都對應到一個光點的一種顏色，這些電晶體驅動光點並消除一直困擾 non-TFT-LCD 的鬼影及反應速度慢問題，結果讓螢幕達到 25ms 反應時間，對比在 200：1 到 400：1 之間，以及亮度值介於 200 到 250 平方米燭光。

　　每個光點上液晶元件在沒有施加電壓的狀態下，穿過被動式過濾器的光線會被極化以便通過整個螢幕，當電壓施加到液晶元件時，它們會依電壓比例來改變極化角度，最多可達 90 度，並進而阻斷光的通路。電晶體控制了液晶元件極化角度的變動，並進一步影響形成顯示器影像光點的紅、綠、藍成分強度。

　　TFT 螢幕可做得比 non-TFT 螢幕要薄得多，使其更輕一些。每個 TFT 螢幕需要大量電晶體，一個解析度 1024×768 的螢幕需要 2,359,296（1024×768×3）個電晶體，每個電晶體都必須是好的，全部電晶體矩陣是放在單一矽晶圓上，如果在晶圓上發現超過一定數量雜質，則該晶圓就必須拋棄，雜質會造成有問題的電晶體並導致顯示器上出現瑕疵光點。

　　LCD 上的瑕疵光點可能是「亮」點或「暗」點，亮點是在黑色背景上的任何位置出現的紅、藍或綠的光點；「暗」點或「消失」點則是在白色背景上出現的黑點。亮點較常見，它是因為電晶體的功能異常而導致光點永遠導通。很不幸，這樣的電晶體在組裝為成品後是不可能修復的，一個有問題的電晶體可以雷射光來使其失效，但是，這樣就會在白色或彩色的螢幕背景上產生一個黑點。

永久開啟的光點在 LCD 製造上是很常見，依據使用者回饋消息與製造成本資料，LCD 製造商已設定一塊面板上可接受瑕疵光點數目之限度，設定這些限制目的是為了維持合理的產品價格，又能降低使用者因為瑕疵光點造成的不滿意。例如，一個 1024×768 解析度的面板上共有 2,359,296 個光點，其上若有 10 個瑕疵光點就產生光點故障比例 (10/2,359,296)×100% = 0.0004%。

Fill in the blanks （課本第 247 頁）
using the words you have just learned in this lesson

LCD displays use ___liquid crystals___, an almost ___transparent___ substance, to control the passage of light. The basic structure of a TFT-LCD panel may be thought of as two glass substrates sandwiching a layer of ___liquid crystals___. The front glass substrate is fitted with a color filter, while the back glass substrate has transistors fabricated on it. When ___voltage___ is applied to the transistors, the ___liquid crystals___ elements twist to change their ___polarization___, allowing light to pass through to form a pixel. A light source is located at the back of the panel and is called a backlight unit. There is a ___passive___ filter in the front glass substrate to control the color on each pixel. Combinations of pixels in different colors form the image on the panel.

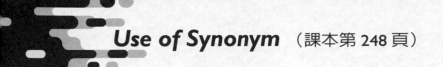

1. ⇒ The LCD technology has been advanced remarkably since its _inception_.
   ⇒ The LCD technology has been advanced remarkably since its _beginning_.

2. ⇒ These transistors drive the pixels, eliminating the problems of ghosting and slow response speed that _bother_ non-TFT LCDs.
   ⇒ These transistors drive the pixels, eliminating the problems of ghosting and slow response speed that _trouble_ non-TFT LCDs.

3. ⇒ The computer monitors used in 1970s were _awkward_.

4. ⇒ The whole wafer must be ___thrown away___ if more than a certain number of impurities are found on it.
   ⇒ The whole wafer must be ___abandoned___ if more than a certain number of impurities are found on it.

5. ⇒ Permanently turned on pixels are _quite_ common in LCD manufacturing.
   ⇒ Permanently turned on pixels are _very_ common in LCD manufacturing.

6. ⇒ LCD manufacturers have _set up_ limits for acceptable number of defective pixels on a given panel.

Choose the most appropriate one in the following questions （課本第 250 頁）

1. （A) 2. （C) 3. （D) 4. （A) 5. （C) 6. （C) 7. （D) 8. （A) 9. （A) 10. （D)

單元 23　LED 與 OLED 顯示器

（課本第 254 頁）

　　發光二極體（LEDs）常用在消費性電子產品的指示燈與數字顯示器，基本的 LED 包含了通上電流就會發光化合物的固態元件，它含有一個架在導線支架上反射杯的半導體二極體晶片，並由電線接出，然後封裝在一個環氧樹脂的聚焦鏡片內，當二極體上的能量位準改變時，LED 就會發光，光的顏色由能量位準與 LED 晶片上使用的半導體材料種類決定。

　　當第一顆 LED 在 1960 年代開始銷售時，其半導體是由鎵、砷及磷化物三種成分組合而成，它們會發出紅光。其他材料也被研究過，一種會產生綠光的材料組合在 1970 年代中期已被發現；在 1980 年代晚期，一種可產生藍光的化合物被發表出來，但其 LED 產品不是很亮；後來，LED 製造商使用了一種被稱為「磊晶」的技術，此技術可讓不同半導體材料的結晶層在其他材料上成長，晶體的磊晶製程使用了新化合物，而發展出亮光的藍色 LED。

　　LED 非常有效率，因為大部分它們放射的光都在可見光的頻譜範圍內。然而，直到最近，產生亮度不夠與缺乏顏色選擇，使其用途受到很大限制。LED 有非常快的轉換時間，在亮光藍色 LED 公布之後，製造大尺寸顯示器所需的由紅、綠、藍矩陣形成的 LED 叢簇變為可行。

　　用在 LED 的發光材料有二種：無機與有機材料。傳統的 LED 使用無機材料，使用有機材料的 LED 被稱為 OLED，基本的 OLED 單元結構，包括夾在透明陽極與金屬陰極之間的薄有機層，當施加電壓於此單元時，射出的正電荷與負電荷在發光層重新結合並產生光線，有機層之結構與陽極與陰極之選擇都經過設計，以使 OLED 輸出之光線達到最亮。

　　OLED 顯示器可由被動陣列或是主動陣列來驅動，要驅動被動陣列的 OLED，可由附屬的驅動器在所選擇的行和列上施加電壓，就能在對應的光點通上電流而發光，一個外部控制器電路，提供了所需的輸入電源及影像數據信號。

　　相對於被動陣列 OLED 顯示器，主動陣列 OLED 有一個基板，上面對每個光點至少有兩個電晶體，這些電晶體連結到互相垂直的陽極線與陰極線，它們可以將任何活動光點「維持」在 ON 狀態（發光狀態）直到下一個掃瞄期。因為需要較多零件，主動陣列顯示器製造上較為複雜，不過它們相較於較低成本的被動陣列顯示器能夠提供較亮的影像。

全世界有許多的研究團隊參與了 OLED 研究，他們大部分的努力都放在解決 OLED 效率不佳及短壽命期兩個主要問題。然而，這些問題預期都可以被克服，並且在 2010 年左右，全彩以 OLED 為基礎的顯示器將會取代 TFT-LCD 成為市場之主流顯示技術。

依據發光材料分子大小，OLED 可以區分為發光聚合體（LEP）及小分子有機發光二極體（SMOLED），前者使用較大分子而後者使用較小分子，當電流通過薄膜區時，兩者都會發光，研究結果顯示，還需要很大努力來改善 SMOLED 效能。反之，很高效率的 LEP 不需要太多努力就可以做得出來。

Fill in the blanks （課本第 258 頁）
using the words you have just learned in this lesson

There are two types driving methods used in OLED displays: passive-matrix (PM) and active-matrix (AM) driving. AMOLEDs use TFT with a capacitor to store data signals in order to control the brightness level. The manufacturing procedure for PMOLEDs is relatively simple and is less costly. However, PMOLEDs have the limitations of size (not more than 5 in) and low resolution. Large scale OLED displays with higher resolution can only be manufactured using active-matrix driving. Active-matrix driving pixels can maintain their brightness after data line scanning. Pixels using passive-matrix driving, on the other hand, emit light only when they are scanned. Therefore,   active-matrix   driving results in longer lifetime, higher efficiency and higher resolution. Essentially, TFT-OLED with active-matrix driving is suitable for display application of high resolution.

Use of Synonym （課本第 259 頁）

1. ⇒ The solid-state device contains a chemical compound that <u>emits</u> light when an electric current passes through it.
   ⇒ The solid-state device contains a chemical compound that <u>gives off</u> light when an electric current passes through it.
   ⇒ The solid-state device contains a chemical compound that <u>generates</u> light when an electric current passes through it.

2. ⇒ Low light output and a lack of color options have severely <u>restricted</u> their use.
   ⇒ Low light output and a lack of color options have severely <u>confined</u> their use.

3. ⇒ With the <u>declaration</u> of bright blue LEDs, it became possible to produce large scale LED displays.
   ⇒ With the <u>proclamation</u> of bright blue LEDs, it became possible to produce large scale LED displays.

4. ⇒ An <u>exterior</u> controller circuit provides the necessary input power and video data signal.

5. ⇒ It is expected that these problems will be <u>vanquished</u> in the near future.

6. ⇒ OLEDs are <u>categorized</u> as Light-Emitting Polymers and Small Molecule Organic Light Emitting Diodes.

Choose the most appropriate one in the following questions （課本第 261 頁）

1. （A） 2. （C） 3. （B） 4. （D） 5. （E） 6. （A） 7. （E） 8. （A） 9. （C） 10. （A）

單元 24　　虛擬實境 （課本第 264 頁）

　　虛擬實境是一種允許使用者與由電腦產生環境發生互動的科學方法，大部分虛擬實境環境是視覺上的經驗，他們是經由電腦螢幕或特殊立體顯像方式呈現，某些模擬會增加諸如由音箱，或是耳機呈現額外聲音訊息，比較先進的系統現在已可以提供觸覺上互動，此即一般我們所知常用於醫學與遊戲上的力量回饋，使用者可以經由標準輸入裝置如滑鼠，或是多模式裝置，如線控手套，與全方位跑步機，與一虛擬環境或虛擬物體產生互動。系統產生的虛擬環境可以與真實世界相似，如模擬飛行或是作戰訓練，也可以與真實世界有顯著不同，例如遊戲裡的場景，由於技術限制，目前還很難建構一個虛擬高傳真環境。然而，未來當處理器、影像及數據通訊技術功能變得強大又省錢後，這些限制終將被解除。

　　虛擬實境這個名稱來源並不清楚，有人將其歸功於 1982 年 Damien Broderick 寫的一本小說 The Judas Mandala，然而其故事背景和前面定義有些不同，Myron Krueger 提出的名詞「人工實境」在 1970 年代即開始使用。虛擬實境概念的流行，是經由電視網路在大眾媒體上傳播，虛擬實境最早在電視上的例子，可能是胡博士影集，這個故事描述一個電腦產生如夢似的虛擬環境，使用虛擬實境想法最有名的影集，大概是星際爭霸戰，這部片是以一個全甲板為特色，在戰艦上有一虛擬實境之設施，以允許隊員可以重建或經歷任何他們想要的環境。虛擬實境研究在 1990 年代澎渤發展，部分是歸功於 Howard Rheingold 所寫的虛擬實境一書，這本書嘗試將在此之前此領域利基處的神祕面紗除去，以讓較低技術層次研究人員與熱衷者能夠接觸到它。

　　虛擬實境未來發展會到甚麼地步並不清楚。短期內，影像經由頭戴式顯示器呈現，將可以很快達到逼近真實的效果，音效方面將進一步逼近到新的三度空間音響，這涉及到操作者上方及下方將有外加的聲音管道，虛擬實境在這種未來技術之應用，大概將經由頭戴耳機來呈現。

　　由恐懼症到較新的退伍軍人後壓力創傷症候群的治療，虛擬實境在醫療角色上之應用，是其在不同暴露治療上之應用，作為一個介於基本暴露，如使用幻影與真實暴露間步驟，一個包括簡單視覺及聲音設計之基本虛擬實境模擬，已被顯示在治療恐懼症上很有價值。美國海軍最近執行了一項研究計畫，使用較複雜的模擬，將有後創傷症候群的退伍軍人，置身於一虛擬的都市作戰場景，這可能聽起來與我們的直覺相反，暴露治療應對於有後創傷症候群的人效益有限，一個合理的解釋，這是由特別周邊系統改變或是壓力反應之改變,所造成心理改變的結果,與治療恐懼症很像的是,把有創傷或恐懼的受測者暴露於虛擬實境中,有除去敏感性及顯著減輕症狀的效果。

由於技術限制,現在影像及聲音是僅有二種可以幾乎完美複製的感覺。然而,有許多努力已投注於複製氣味。例如,多項致力於後創傷症候群的研究計畫已被啟動,這些計畫將退伍軍人暴露於具有不同氣味的虛擬作戰場景,前面討論說明未來虛擬實境發展將與醫療、訓練、與工程需求有關論點。因此,超越基本觸覺、影像、聲音與嗅覺回饋之完整感覺環境之複製,不大可能成為工業界目標。值得一提的是,縱然氣味可以複製很真實,製造每一種氣味需要龐大研發費用。截至目前,諸如燃燒橡膠、火藥、及汽油等基本而強烈的氣味已被製造出來了。

若要產生其他如觸覺與味覺的感覺,大腦必須能夠被直接觸及,這會將虛擬實境推進至如夢的逼真境地,雖然這樣的技術目前尚未被開發出來,新力公司已經跨出第一步,在 2005 年,新力宣布他們已經申請並獲得一項構想專利,這個構想是以非侵入式方式,將不同頻率與型式的超音波,直接射入大腦以建構所有五種感覺,雖然其他研究者已顯示這種可能性存在,新力卻宣稱這只是一種構想而已,他們尚未進行任何這類測試。

Fill in the blanks (課本第 272 頁)
using the words you have just learned in this lesson

A ____wired____ glove is a glove-like input device for ____virtual reality____ environments. Various sensor technologies are used to capture physical data such as flexion of fingers. Often a motion tracker, such as a magnetic device or inertial tracking device, is attached to capture the global position/rotation data of the glove. These movements are then interpreted by the software that accompanies the glove, so any one movement can mean any number of things. Expensive high-end _wired_ gloves can also provide _tactile or haptic_ feedback, which is a _simulation_ of the sense of touch. This allows a _wired_ glove to also be used as an output device. An alternative to _wired_ gloves is to use a camera and computer vision to track the 3D pose and trajectory of the hand, at the cost of _tactile or haptic_ feedback.

Use of Synonym （課本第 273 頁）

1. ⇒ More sophisticated virtual reality systems now provide _haptic_ feedback.

2. ⇒ "Artificial reality," a related term _coined_ by Myron Krueger, has been in use since the 1970s.

   ⇒ "Artificial reality," a related term _named_ by Myron Krueger, has been in use since the 1970s.

3. ⇒ The virtual reality application of this future technology will probably be _displayed_ over headphones.

4. ⇒ The previous discussions _explain_ the point that the future of VR is very much linked to therapeutic, training, and engineering demands.

   ⇒ The previous discussions _demonstrate_ the point that the future of VR is very much linked to therapeutic, training, and engineering demands.

5. ⇒ For this reason, _copying_ a full sensory environment beyond the basic tactile feedback, sight, sound, and smell is unlikely.

   ⇒ For this reason, _replicating_ a full sensory environment beyond the basic tactile feedback, sight, sound, and smell is unlikely.

   ⇒ For this reason, _reproducing_ a full sensory environment beyond the basic tactile feedback, sight, sound, and smell is unlikely.

6. ⇒ Sony has not _performed_ any such tests and claims that it is only an idea.

   ⇒ Sony has not _carried out_ any such tests and claims that it is only an idea.

7. ⇒ It's worth mention that simulating smells requires _expensive_ research and design to make each odor.

8. ⇒ Immersive VR can provide users with experiences of _multiple_ sensory that replicate reality or create scenarios that are impossible or dangerous in the physical world.

   ⇒ This headset is a _multiple_ purpose one.

   ⇒ We provide cakes with _multiple_ layer.

Choose the most appropriate one in the following questions （課本第 276 頁）

1. （A） 2. （D） 3. （A） 4. （D） 5. （C） 6. （B） 7. （A） 8. （C） 9. （D） 10. （A）

單元 25　奈米科技在生物工程之應用

（課本第 280 頁）

　　奈米科技是一門快速成長並會影響到人們生活的領域，奈米科技透過骨骼、組織及器官重建工程，來改善生活品質方面的研究，目前已在進行中。

　　奈米科技在模擬自然界累積礦物質的方法，轉而運用在牙齒與骨骼替代物的開發上，這種過程被稱為「生化模擬」，「生物模擬」已經製造出新的輕又韌之防彈背心材料，與其他防衛方面應用。

　　奈米成型聚合體運用在骨質移植上，能夠縮短長時間的恢復期、傷病與感染。科學家們現在正嘗試使用這項技術，培育將會轉換成骨骼的成熟幹細胞，一旦讓組織在成形支架上成長的技術完成之後，奈米架構的裝置就能夠調整，以進一步提升骨骼成長速度與縮短復原時間，具有電極的裝置能夠產生電流，證明能夠刺激骨骼生長。

　　奈米科技能促進人造皮膚、重建組織及傷口處理方面發展，奈米科技將能支援組織，甚至於整個器官的再生，再生器官將會取代因疾病或衰老而失效的器官，應用奈米科技也能把物質注入再生組織，以刺激復原和對抗感染。

　　在奈米尺度的組織工程，能帶領可存活物質發展，這些物質能重建、維持或提升人體組織之功能，組織再生能夠經由使用生物材料傳輸訊號給鄰近組織，以恢復細胞原有再生能力，使用細胞與生物材料支架，來當作組織發展架構，也是組織再生另一種方式。

　　周邊組織對一個植入物的接受度，是一個關鍵的醫療問題，使用奈米尺度技術與奈米特徵表面特殊設計，來建立一個對細胞友善的環境，以幫助植入物與周邊組織結合。如此，植入物才能正常發揮功能並存活較久。

Researchers at Northwestern University have managed to recreate the microscopic structure of bone by using "designer" molecules that can be encouraged to assemble themselves into so-called " nanostructures " that mimic the appearance of collagen fibers. If the _nanostructures_ can be incorporated into a gel, it is possible that they could be placed into the gaps between fractures to facilitate the natural _healing_ process of _bone_ , therefore the molecules could be highly beneficial to people with serious fractures, joint replacement patients, and those with _bone_ cancer. Researchers believe that it may also be possible to develop _nanostructures_ that attract different types of cells, for example nerve or cartilage cells, thus enabling scientists to _regenerate_ other types of damaged _tissues_. This is good example of the application of _nanotechnology_ in bio-engineering.

SOURCE/REFERENCE: Reported by www.bbc.co.uk on the 25th November 2001

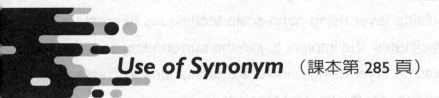

Use of Synonym （課本第 285 頁）

1. ⇒ Nanotechnology is a _quickly_ growing area that will affect people in their lives.

   ⇒ Nanotechnology is a _fast_ growing area that will affect people in their lives.

   ⇒ Nanotechnology is a _promptly_ growing area that will affect people in their lives.

2. ⇒ Scientists are trying to use this technique to _propagate_ adult stem cells that will turn into bone.

   ⇒ Scientists are trying to use this technique to _produce_ adult stem cells that will turn into bone.

3. (1) ⇒ The regenerated organs will _replace_ organs that have failed due to disease or aging.

   (2) ⇒ Nanotechnology is being used in teeth and bone _replacements_ duplicating the manner nature itself lays down minerals.

4. ⇒ Using cells and a biomaterial scaffold to act as a framework for developing tissues is also one _option_ to regenerate tissues.

⇒ Using cells and a biomaterial scaffold to act as a framework for developing tissues is also one _choice_ to regenerate tissues.

5. ⇒ The acceptance of an implant by _neighboring_ tissues is a critical medical problem.

⇒ The acceptance of an implant by _adjacent_ tissues is a critical medical problem.

⇒ The acceptance of an implant by _nearby_ tissues is a critical medical problem.

6. ⇒ Especially designed outside layer using nano-scale techniques to create a cell friendly environment _helps_ the implant to join the surrounding tissues.

⇒ Especially designed outside layer using nano-scale techniques to create a cell friendly environment _facilitates_ the implant to join the surrounding tissues.

⇒ Especially designed outside layer using nano-scale techniques to create a cell friendly environment _enhances_ the implant to join the surrounding tissues.

Choose the most appropriate one in the following questions （課本第 287 頁）

1.（A） 2.（A） 3.（E） 4.（B） 5.（A） 6.（B） 7.（A） 8.（C） 9.（D） 10.（C）

單元 26　幹細胞的研究 （課本第 290 頁）

　　幹細胞研究增進我們對於一個細胞如何發展成組織，及成熟組織中健康細胞如何取代受傷細胞方面的知識，幹細胞在身體內，發展成許多不同類型細胞方面具有非凡潛能；以其在身體內擔任一種修復系統的角色而言，只要人或動物仍然活著，幹細胞可以無限制分裂以補充其他細胞，幹細胞分裂時，每一個新細胞可以維持為幹細胞，或是變成一具有某種特定功能之細胞，如腦細胞或是紅血球細胞。這一個前途看好的領域，正引導著科學家去調查細胞基礎治療法，在醫療上的可能性，此一領域稱為再生或修補醫學。

　　今日，幹細胞是生物學中最引人注意的領域之一。但是，正如其他快速擴充的科學領域，幹細胞研究帶來新問題的速度，跟其產生新問題的速度一樣快。和其他細胞相比，幹細胞有兩種重要特性，第一，他們是可藉由細胞分裂來自我更新的非特定細胞；第二，在某些生理或實驗狀況下，他們可以被誘導變成具有特定功能細胞，例如胰臟內可分泌胰島素的細胞，或是心臟肌肉的心跳細胞。

　　在動物或人體中有兩種幹細胞：胚胎幹細胞與成熟幹細菌。胚胎幹細胞來自於胚胎。具體而言，胚胎幹細胞是由捐贈者以書面同意方式，捐贈其卵子進行科學研究，並在人工受精診所內，以玻璃皿中進行人工受精所得之胚胎，他們不是來自於生物體或婦女體內受精所得的胚胎。

　　至少在二十年以前，科學家們發現了由老鼠胚胎取得幹細胞的方法。多年來，老鼠幹細胞生物學上深入的研究，引領了如何由人類胚胎分離出幹細胞，並在實驗室中培養技術的發現，這些細胞稱為人類胚胎幹細胞，這些研究用胚胎，是由捐贈者以書面同意方式，捐贈其因不孕而進行人工受精剩餘不用的胚胎。

　　因為許多原因，幹細胞對於存活的有機組織很重要。在一個年齡三到五天的胚胎中，發育組織內之幹細胞可產生多種特定類型之細胞，這些細胞可組成心臟、肺、皮膚及其他組織。在某些成熟組織中，諸如骨髓、肌肉及大腦，離散分布的幹細胞群體可產生因正常損耗、破壞或因疾病而失去細菌之替代細胞。

　　成熟幹細胞是組織或器官中，在特定細胞間發現之非特定細胞，他們可自我更新並特定化，以產生組織或器官內之主要特定類型細胞。在成熟有機體中，成熟幹細胞之主要角色，是維持並修補其棲身之組織。某些科學家稱幹細胞為體幹細胞，與胚胎幹細胞不同的是，成熟幹細胞的來源並不清楚，成熟幹細胞通常會產生他們棲息組織中之特定類型細胞，例如骨髓內形成血液的幹細胞通常會產生諸如紅血球、白血球、血小板等類型細胞。一直到最近，科學家們相信骨髓內形成血液的細胞不能產生不同組織之細胞，例如肝臟內之細胞；然而過去幾年裡的多項研究，提出了一個組織中幹細胞產生另外一完全不同組織之細胞類型之可能性，這種現象稱為可塑性，可塑性的例子諸如把肝臟細胞轉變成會分泌胰島素的細胞，及將血液細胞轉變成神經細胞。因此，使用成熟幹細胞進行細胞基礎治療可能性研究，成了一個非常吸引人並很活躍的科學研究領域。

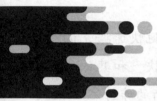

Fill in the blanks （課本第 294 頁）
using the words you have just learned in this lesson

Some _stem_ cells have the potential to turn into different cells, leading scientists to believe that they may be useful in treating medical disorders such as _diabetes_. In an online discussion group, Christ's mother, Mrs. Howard, read about the possibility that _stem_ cell injections could cure _diabetes_. Even though she was worrying about the risk of such injections to Christ and was concerned about the cost that health insurance doesn't cover, she eventually decided to try it. Dozens of foreigners per month, many of them are children like Christ, have been flying to hospitals in China, seeking _stem_ cell injections for a variety of conditions. There is no widely accepted scientific evidence that the injections work or are even safe. These injections are not _approved_ by the governments in the U.S. and many other countries. Nonetheless, desperate patients are spending thousands of dollars, hoping to find _therapies_ for _diabetes_, cerebral palsy and other disorders with uncertain origins and a range of symptoms, from the failure to develop language skills to the inability to sense the feeling of others.

Use of Synonym （課本第 295 頁）

1. ⇒ Research on stem cells is enhancing knowledge about how an organism develops from a single cell and how healthy cells substitute damaged cells in adult organisms.

   ⇒ Research on stem cells is enhancing knowledge about how an organism develops from a single cell and how healthy cells substitute impaired cells in adult organisms.

2. ⇒ Serving as a sort of repair system for the body, they can divide without limit to replenish other cells as long as the person or animal is still alive.

   ⇒ Serving as a sort of repair system for the body, they can divide without limit to refill other cells as long as the person or animal is still alive.

3. ⇒ Adult stem cells normally generate the cell types of the tissue in which they reside .

4. ⇒ In the 3- to 5-day-old embryo, stem cells in developing tissues typically give rise to the multiple specialized cell types that make up the heart, lung, skin, and other tissues.

5. ⇒ A blood-forming adult stem cell in the bone marrow normally gives rise to produces many types of blood cells such as red blood cells and white blood cells.

   ⇒ A blood-forming adult stem cell in the bone marrow normally yield many types of blood cells such as red blood cells and white blood cells.

6. ⇒ Stem cells have two important characteristics that distinguish themselves from other types of cells.

7. ⇒ Scientists believe that stem cells may become the basis for treating diseases such as Parkinson's disease and diabetes in the future.

   ⇒ Scientists believe that stem cells may become the basis for curing diseases such as Parkinson's disease and diabetes in the future.

Choose the most appropriate one in the following questions （課本第 298 頁）

1.（B） 2.（A） 3.（D） 4.（C） 5.（C） 6.（A） 7.（B） 8.（A） 9.（B） 10.（D）

Vocabulary Index

國家圖書館出版品預行編目(CIP)資料

科技英文選讀 = Selective readings in technology and
management / 李冠慧編著. -- 六版. -- 新北市 :
全華圖書股份有限公司, 2022.04
　面 ; 公分
ISBN 978-626-328-116-5(平裝)

1.CST: 英語 2.CST: 工作職場 3.CST: 讀本

805.18　　　　　　　　　　　　　111003754

科技英文選讀

作 者 / 李冠慧
發 行 人 / 陳本源
執行編輯 / 蔡佳玲
封面設計 / 盧怡瑄
出 版 者 / 全華圖書股份有限公司
郵政帳號 / 0100836-1號
印 刷 者 / 宏懋打字印刷股份有限公司
圖書編號 / 0904905
六版二刷 / 2024年10月
定 價 / 新台幣 500元
ISBN / 978-626-328-410-5

全華圖書 / www.chwa.com.tw
全華網路書店 Open Tech / www.opentech.com.tw
若您對書籍內容有任何問題，歡迎來信指導 book@chwa.com.tw

臺北總公司(北區營業處)
地址：23671新北市土城區忠義路21號
電話：(02) 2262-5666
傳真：(02) 6637-3695、6637-3696

中區營業處
地址：40256臺中市南區樹義一巷26號
電話：(04) 2261-8485
傳真：(04) 3600-9806(高中職)
(04) 3601-8600(大專)

南區營業處
地址：80769高雄市三民區應安街12號
電話：(07) 381-1377
傳真：(07) 862-5562

國家圖書館出版品預行編目(CIP)資料

科技英文導讀 = Selective readings in technology and management / 李開偉編著. -- 六版. -- 新北市：

全華圖書股份有限公司, 2022.04

　面；　公分

ISBN 978-626-328-116-5(平裝)

1.CST：英語 2.CST：科學技術 3.CST：讀本

805.18　　　　　　　　　　　　　111003754

科技英文導讀

作　　者／李開偉

發 行 人／陳本源

執行編輯／黃艾家

封面設計／盧怡瑄

出 版 者／全華圖書股份有限公司

郵政帳號／0100836-1號

印 刷 者／宏懋打字印刷股份有限公司

圖書編號／0904905

六版二刷／2023年10月

定　　價／530元

I S B N／978-626-328-116-5

全華圖書 www.chwa.com.tw

全華網路書店 Open Tech / www.opentech.com.tw

若您對本書有任何問題，歡迎來信指導book@chwa.com.tw

臺北總公司（北區營業處）

地址：23671新北市土城區忠義路21號

電話：(02) 2262-5666

傳真：(02) 6637-3695、6637-3696

中區營業處

地址：40256臺中市南區樹義一巷26號

電話：(04) 2261-8485

傳真：(04) 3600-9806（高中職）

　　　(04) 3601-8600（大專）

南區營業處

地址：80769高雄市三民區應安街12號

電話：(07) 381-1377

傳真：(07) 862-5562